A GAME OF FAE

BOOK 3 OF THE PURPLE DOOR DISTRICT

Titles by Erin Casey

The Purple Door District Series

The Purple Door District

Wolf Pit

A Game of Fae

Fates and Furies Series

Coming Soon

A GAME OF FAE

BOOK 3 OF THE PURPLE DOOR DISTRICT

ERIN CASEY

ISBN: 979-8-218-00491-0

Dedicated to anyone who needs a community to call their
own. You're not alone. Welcome to the District.

Dedicated to my mom who never stopped believing in my
literary dreams.
Miss you and love you always.

Acknowledgments

Dozens of people were involved in the making of *The Purple Door District* series. Most notably is AE Kellar, my fellow author-in-crime, who keeps editing out my explosions. That's 2, Kellar.

Much love goes out to my editors, Ellen Rozek and Leona Bushman, and my proofreaders, Shakyra Dunn and AE Kellar. Artist Brooke Lydick of Creating Meraki Studios brought my fae Vesp to life and created the Crystal Corvid Apothecary logo. Oni Algarra and Gabriella Bujdoso also created beautiful portraits. Sara Cunningham and Amanda Bouma helped develop marketing materials. "Les" made the incredible cover for all three books. Humbled thanks goes to Brian K. Morris who helped me adopt the "rising tide" theory and has become an incredible mentor.

A very special thanks goes to my sensitivity readers. Leslie Kung and Jessica Larson-Wang helped me come up with Shen Yanlei's name and reviewed my cultural references. Leslie also helped me revise a scene with Yanlei's family in *A Game of Fae*. Shakyra Dunn checked my character accuracy with Nick and several others. I'm thankful, and humbled, that they took the time to teach me and guide me so I could properly represent these characters.

Thank you to everyone who supported me through my Kickstarter. Without you, this published book would not have been possible.

This series is about community, and that's what you see here. Thank you, everyone. I couldn't have done it without them, or you, the reader! To those who have taken the time to review my book and talk to me about how it touched them, I can't tell you how much I appreciate your words and encouragement.

Forward

About the Delay of *A Game of Fae*

A Game of Fae was supposed to come out in December 2020 to follow the time line of the first two books. Unfortunately, during production, Covid-19 struck, and I lost both my mom and my aunt. Between grief and isolation, I had to step back and take time to heal. Losing my mom generated a lot of mixed feelings between myself and my craft. I couldn't even think about writing a word in the series knowing she'd never read it. I also knew some scenes in the book would be extremely difficult for me to write while my grief was raw.

So I took my time. I attended therapy, participated in a grief journaling course, and worked to recreate a healthy relationship between myself and my writing. I was diagnosed with ADHD and CPTSD, which meant restructuring some of my therapy. I say all this not to garner sympathy, but to be transparent and open. I've always said I'm an advocate for mental health. These are the steps I had to take so I could go back to creating and bring this book to you.

There's no shame in seeking help for your mental health.

To all who have lost loved ones (especially during Covid-19), my thoughts and heart go out to you.

Thank you to my readers who have waited patiently for the third book in the trilogy. I hope it lives up to your expectations.

About *The Purple Door District Series* and Content Warnings

The world of *The Purple Door District* started out as the stubborn brainchild of AE Kellar and myself. We have spent years writing together, researching, brainstorming, and developing characters and rules governing our parahumans and worlds. Our main series, *Fates and Furies*, is still in production but occurs in the same urban fantasy setting.

When we started to design the District, I latched onto it and suddenly had ideas blossoming in my head about creating one in Chicago. Plus, as a birdmom of six feathered kids, it gave me the chance to professionally write about a werebird, even if I still get the side eye. With AE's blessing, I wrote *The Purple Door District* series to introduce you to our world and insanity.

We jokingly say that AE is the brain and I'm the heart, but I think it's very true. While AE fills our books with well-researched facts and logic, I add feeling, creativity, and literary flair. I couldn't have done it without my walking encyclopedia. All you see here exists because of our love for storytelling and our incessant need to get fewer than 8 hours of sleep a night.

Keep an eye out. *Fates and Furies* is on the horizon.

CW: Violence, SA implications, death, suicide, mind control

About AE Kellar

AE Kellar works as a professional wingman by day, while by night pretends to write by hiding behind a laptop and listening to a well-crafted, shuffled playlist. With a penchant for dark humor and plenty of snark, AE writes urban fantasy with a smattering of sci-fi and Paranormal thrown in for spice.

Serving as the creative consultant on Erin Casey's *The Purple Door District*, AE is also co-creator and co-author of *Fates and Furies*, an as-yet unpublished fantastical urban fantasy series upon which *The Purple Door District* is based.

In addition to the world of *Fates and Furies*, AE has written a sci-fi short story called *Remember Nevada*, with hopes to publish before Mars is colonized.

Chapter 1
New Destinations

Nick

Nick grunted as he hefted a bundle of metal poles onto his shoulder. The task would have been so much easier if his wrists weren't shackled, but the Hunters weren't willing to risk another escape attempt from the parahumans as they set up the next pit. Their new destination had taken hours to reach; at least, it had felt like hours. They couldn't be too far away from Chicago, maybe another state or two over. But for all he knew, they'd driven in circles before landing in a spot near the old hideout.

He walked with his head bowed, though his eyes darted around to take in the other captive parahumans forced to carry the Hunters' materials. He traversed through an underground tunnel, the slap of his bare feet against stone echoing around him. He rolled his shoulders a bit to help the metal settle more comfortably.

Shen Yanlei reached his side partway through the tunnel, boxes propped atop both of her shoulders, and pressed against her short brown and reddish-orange hair. She glanced sideways at him and spoke in a low voice only he could hear. "Anything smell familiar to you?"

"No, just dirt, water, bleach, and sweaty, bloody bodies. You?"

"Same. I had hoped we were still somehow near the old subway."

"Yeah…me too." Nick glanced around, searching for the rest of his group, but Brighton was still too wounded to do much, and if Augustine wasn't caged, she was likely tethered between the Hunters.

Nick slumped wearily. They'd been so close to rescue, so close. He could feel it in his bones. His pack had found him once, but would they locate him again? He wanted to be hopeful, but after watching the Hunters mercilessly kill innocent parahumans to leave behind as "examples," his positivity was fleeting.

Yanlei nudged his arm. "Keep your chin up. Don't let them know you're defeated."

Nick gave a wry smile. "Wouldn't it be better for the Hunters to think they've beaten me down?"

"Not them. The others." She nodded toward a few werewolves who walked past them, noted his posture, and dropped their heads as well. He hadn't noticed the eyes on him before.

"I don't get it," Nick murmured.

"They look at you as a strong leader. And if a leader is going to give up, what hope do they have?"

Nick grunted. Leader. Yeah, right. Like he had any right to guide a single soul.

At least he could find comfort in Yanlei being alive and well. When he'd thought the Hunters had murdered her and Kat, he'd nearly lost his mind and gone on a suicidal mission to avenge them. They were his pack, even if Yanlei wasn't officially a member. So long as she was with him, she was under his protection. Not that she needed much of it.

Okay, maybe he did understand the leader bit. Paytah had always said he demonstrated some Alpha traits.

The tunnel opened up into blinding light, causing him to wince in pain. He lifted one arm to protect his eyes then blinked through the glow.

The pit before him was nearly three times the size of the one in Chicago. Two giant rings bordered by bleachers sat in the center of the room with smaller sparring rings set up off to the side. The scaffolding and pathways surrounding the ring were far more heavily occupied by Hunters, like they had more to defend and protect at this pit.

A blazing flash of magic told him why.

A fire magus fought in the primary ring against a werewolf transformed into his bipedal form. Flames snarled around the wolf who quickly dodged them, barely missing the fire arching for his tail. He raced toward the magus with deadly speed and raised his claws. The magus thrust her hand forward, sending a fireball into his chest. But the magic looked weak, and the werewolf pounced on the magus, who went down with a terrified scream.

Nick looked away, his stomach twisting. A magus? They had magic users here? So, it wasn't just werewolves and vampires. They were pitting even more parahumans against each other. "How?" he asked Yanlei. "How are they able to hold magi here? Wouldn't they use their magic to attack the Hunters?"

"Maybe they can't," Yanlei replied. She crouched and set the boxes down where a Hunter indicated. "They keep us laced with mild doses of wolfsbane so we're not at our strongest. The same could be happening to the magi. Not to mention these." She tapped her metal collar.

Nick lowered the poles nearby. He rubbed his shoulder and rotated it slowly before he started to make his way back to the trucks for another load. He watched the shackled parahumans around him trudge along and grimaced at how feeble they looked.

Just how long would he and his friends survive here?

***

By the time the trucks were unloaded, Nick was spent. He lumbered along beside Yanlei as they were guided through the halls toward a caged area. Instead of individual rooms with cages inside, bars lined the walls, keeping parahumans locked in large cells. At least they'd have room to stand. Small mercies.

The Hunter guarding them opened the door to an empty cell and shoved Nick then Yanlei inside. Nick growled at the Hunter before walking over to a clean patch of stone. He sat down, leaned back, and rubbed his face. "I can't believe how close we were to rescue."

"The more you think about it, the more it'll eat at you. We have to start planning for our next chance to escape."

Nick arched an eyebrow. "How can you be so optimistic after everything that's happened?"

She shrugged. "Simple answer would be that I'm stubborn. But I also don't give up hope easily. We were almost rescued once. The next time it may happen."

"Or we could all be killed," Nick said, and Yanlei frowned at him. "Or we could be rescued," he amended. "I'm afraid of losing anyone. When I thought you and Kat were dead, I…" He shook his head, his heart clenching with grief all over again. He prayed Trish had told him the truth about Kat surviving.

To his surprise, Yanlei swatted him lightly on the head.

"Hey! What was that for?"

"Don't talk like that," Yanlei said and crouched in front of him. "Even if Kat and I were to die, that doesn't mean you should forfeit your life too."

"But—"

"If something happens to me, you have to promise you won't do anything stupid. Your life is important, and you have far too many people who need you here to help see them back home."

Nick clutched her hand. He raised his other and ran it along her cheek. "Don't talk like that. The idea of losing you or another packmate . . . I can't." He shuddered. "I'm not strong enough."

"Yes, you are," Yanlei insisted. She cracked a little smile. "But I'm too stubborn to just give up, so I don't think you'll have to worry about me." She leaned closer, growing somber again. "Please, promise me."

Nick sighed and rested his head against hers. "I'll try," he murmured.

"You had better, or I'll come back to haunt you."

Despite the seriousness of their conversation, Nick couldn't hold back a tiny chuckle.

They were left alone for another hour before Brighton and Augustine were brought to the cage. Brighton looked like he'd been hit by a bus. He walked slowly, his head bowed as the Hunters opened the cage and pushed him inside. Augustine was in human form again, but the crazed look in her eyes betrayed she was more wolf than woman. Her wrists were shackled behind her. Poles hooked to her collar guided her into the cage. The poles were only removed when Augustine was positioned as far away from the door as possible.

After the Hunters departed, Nick looked over Augustine. She growled low under her breath, her eyes burning with rage. He swallowed, wanting to reach out to her but not knowing what would calm her.

"Augustine," Brighton called. "August." It took him two more tries, but Augustine finally looked in his direction. He met her eyes, his gaze taking on a wolfish glint. They stared at each other for a long time before Augustine blinked and then sat down against the wall with a bone-weary sigh.

"Thanks," she said.

"You're welcome." Brighton sank to the ground and rubbed his chest. He glanced around and smirked. "Well, at least we're not shoved in tiny cages this time."

"Yippie," Augustine growled under her breath.

Nick folded his hands between his knees. "Did you see the magi?"

Brighton lifted his head slightly. "What? No. Though I thought I smelled charred fur and flesh."

"You saw the size of this place," Nick said. "I don't think this is a regular wolf pit. If anything, it's meant for all parahumans."

"But how can they keep the magi in check?" Brighton asked, then frowned. "You...didn't see Tess at all, did you?"

Nick shook his head. "No, not here. I'm sure she escaped." She had to have escaped. They'd need her help to get free. "There's something else here. Something...I don't know how to describe it, but it's making my fur stand on end."

"I feel it too," Yanlei added. "This place is much darker than the last pit. And there's an aura here, like tainted magic, surrounding us."

"Well, there's nothing we can do about it right now," Brighton said and settled down against the stone wall. "Maybe Trish will have more to tell us if she gets the chance to visit."

Nick frowned.

If anyone had ever told him he'd one day have to depend on *Trish* to stay alive, he would have laughed in their face. He just hoped she didn't decide to stab them in the back like she'd done to almost everyone else.

Chapter 2
Little Bat

Trish

"What's wrong, little bat?"

Trish opened her eyes, Gavin's ghostly voice fading with the rest of her dreams. She stared into the darkness, a lump rising in her throat. He'd been gone for almost two years now, and yet she missed him as much as the day he'd died. Dreaming about him and his voice was both a blessing and a curse. It gave her a last moment with him, but it also made it that much more painful when she woke up and remembered he was gone.

She rolled onto her back, clutching Gavin's jacket to her chest, and draped an arm over her head, her mind racing. It was strange not to wake up in her vast coven bedroom with the beautiful chandelier, the warm, comfortable bedding, and the fresh air devoid of the scents of blood, sweat, and bleach. Now? Her back ached from sleeping on a cot that offered a somewhat comfortable place to rest (better than the floor). She pushed the scratchy blanket down and ran her fingers along her neck where Gavin had bitten her years ago to help remove the forced connection between her and her sire. She caressed the tiny scars over her pale skin, comforted that in some ways he was still with her.

"What's wrong, little bat?" his ghostly voice asked again.

Trish sighed and closed her eyes. *"It's a mess, Gavin. I'm working with Hunters who are disgustingly excited about pitting parahumans against one another. Saul's betrayed our coven, and I've agreed to help him in order to save Nick and his friends. I think Nick believes I'm telling the truth, but what if he outs me? Or what if Saul figures out I'm not as loyal as he thinks I am?"*

"Sounds like quite the conundrum. You got yourself in a fine fix this time."

Trish snorted and sat up, swinging her legs over the side of the cot. *"Yeah, thanks for the support. I must be losing my mind. I'm working with Hunters and making up conversations with the dead."* She dropped her hands onto the jacket in her lap then tilted her head back and stared up at the ceiling forlornly. *"I wish you were still here so I could actually talk to you and figure out what to do."*

"You'll just have to be content with memories of me," Gavin said. *"You know what I'd say, Trish."*

"Play the part," Trish replied. She cupped the back of her neck with her hands. *"Fight when it's time to fight, and lay low the rest of the time until you need to strike. You make it sound so easy."*

"If it was easy, I'd still be alive."

Trish grimaced and looked into the darkness. She searched it, trying to make out an apparition, but of course, she saw none. The voice, Gavin, was all part of her imagination. "I miss you," she whispered.

"I miss you too, little bat."

A loud bell went off in the hall, the morning wakeup call. Trish rose and went over to the lantern on the table in her room. She turned it on, chasing away the shadows. Each Hunter had designated quarters, though sometimes they shared with others. Trish's was simple, an unimpressive stone box that left enough room for a bed, a desk, a chair, and a trunk for clothing. A thin door covered the entrance to her room, blocking the light from the hall but doing little to deaden the noises of parahumans fighting and Hunters roaming the tunnels.

She changed into a pair of black cargo pants, a matching black shirt with lace, and Gavin's leather jacket that brushed along the back of her thighs. She braided her red hair and laced up a pair of boots before stepping out of her room. Hunters were already on the prowl, heading to the mess hall for breakfast. Most who passed her kept their distance and cast a wary eye on her. It was unusual to have a parahuman on their side, and most didn't trust her yet. Trish tried to keep out of the way and not call attention to herself. She didn't want them to hunt *her* instead.

She started to follow a small group of Hunters, only to grunt as a tall man bumped into her.

"Watch it, bloodsucker," he growled, lip curled.

Trish didn't rise to the bait. The last thing she wanted was to have a fight in the hall with a dozen Hunters around to watch and make sure she couldn't escape. But her lack of response seemed to prickle him more, and he whirled and shoved her back a step.

"What? Got nothing to say? Are you too much of a coward?"

"Do we have a problem here?"

Trish turned sharply as the familiar voice came to her defense. Saul stood behind her, his presence seeming to fill the narrow hallway. He stared down at the Hunter with red eyes until the man shrank away with a scowl.

"Filth." He spit on the floor and stormed off.

Trish relaxed a little as she turned toward Saul. "Thanks, but I could have handled it. I wasn't trying to get into a fight."

"I know, but they'll try to pick one if they think they can get a rise out of you," Saul replied. He placed a gentle hand on her shoulder and squeezed it. "How are you sleeping? You look exhausted."

Trish shook her head. "Just dreaming a lot. I'm fine, Saul." Her stomach rumbled, and she made a face. "Though I could go for some food."

He chuckled and tugged on her sleeve. "Come with me. We'll take breakfast in my quarters. You'll just have the Hunters glaring at you otherwise."

Trish didn't argue. She walked at his side, grateful for his presence. She eyed the Hunters they passed and noticed they didn't glare at Saul like they did at her. Her gums itched, her fangs threatening to come out so she could bare them and scare the hateful Hunters away from her. Maybe then she'd make an impression.

They walked down two tunnels until they reached another room with a larger door. Saul pushed it open and stepped inside. Trish followed only to freeze in place.

A woman sat bound to a chair in the middle of the room, her head bowed over her chest. Shackles dug into her wrists and ankles, keeping her pinned with no hope of escape. Saul grabbed her dark hair and pulled her head back and to the side, showing off a fresh bite on her throat. "Here. Feast on her while I fetch us some food. You must be starving for blood."

Trish's fangs slipped out of her gums as she stared at the unconscious woman's neck. When was the last time she'd had blood from a living victim instead of a blood bag? She eyed her prey, noting the thick gag stuffed in the woman's mouth as if trying to stifle more than shouts and pleas. "Magus? Or Witch?" she asked.

"Witch. Less trouble," Saul said. "They've brought in some magi and witches for the ring, but the Hunters are letting me pick from the spent witches so I don't eat *them* instead. Go on. She's not going anywhere." He let the woman's head drop again as he headed for the door. "If she wakes up, charm her to go back to sleep." He slipped out, leaving Trish and the witch alone.

Trish stared at her, every instinct urging her to feast. But she couldn't ignore the feeling of disgust either. The witch was a magic user, a parahuman like herself. Sure, they weren't exactly the same, but it felt wrong to keep her tied up and use her for food like this. Not every vampire felt that way; a human was a human, magic or not. She missed the hunts with Gavin, when they'd lure an unsuspecting victim into an alley and drink their fill. They'd always release their prey after that, except for the last time. Trish had accidentally killed a woman when she and Gavin were attacked by Hunters.

She swallowed and inched forward. She tilted the woman's head to the side, exposing her white, delicious neck, and sank her fangs into her victim's flesh. Blood flowed into her mouth, making her stomach rumble with appreciation. She drank slowly, cradling the woman's head in her hand like a lover. Trish was mindful to not kill her so Saul wouldn't have to get another packaged prey for his room.

Trish pulled back after several moments and licked her lips, making sure she didn't lose one drop of blood. She ran her tongue over the witch's skin to close the fang wounds with her saliva and stepped back to stare at her. The woman had grown paler from the feast, but Trish could still hear a steady heartbeat. How long had she been in here with Saul? And when had he last fed on her?

She glanced over her shoulder, anxiously waiting for Saul to return. When she turned back around, she was met with two terrified brown eyes.

The witch released a muffled squeal and struggled in her bonds. She whipped her head back and forth, trying to dislodge the gag and free herself.

Trish swore and held out her hands. "Stop," she commanded, pushing her charm into the woman's mind.

The witch slowed and panted in terror. She flexed her fingers in her shackles and stared up at Trish, silently pleading with her for freedom.

Trish closed her eyes. Was this a test? Had Saul left her in here to see if she'd free the witch? That would be something he'd do. She shook her head and stepped forward, placing her palms on the woman's cheeks. The witch trembled in her hold and started to cry. "Look at me," Trish said and waited until the woman obeyed. "Go to sleep." She hesitated. "Go to sleep, and dream of your grove."

The witch's eyes fluttered. She lowered her head as sleep overcame her. Her pounding heart slowed to a gentle tempo. Trish touched her cheek and hoped dreaming about her fellow witches would bring her comfort.

"*Do you really think he's testing you?*" Gavin's voice asked in her mind.

Trish set her jaw and sat down on the edge of Saul's bed. She slipped her hands into her jacket pockets. "*I've switched sides enough times. I don't blame him for doubting my loyalty. But this? Couldn't he have come up with something less…disturbing?*"

Gavin chuckled. "*You've seen me do worse things to my prey, Trish. You know you can handle it.*"

"*Doesn't mean I have to like it,*" Trish growled back. She glanced at a dark corner in the room. The shadows seemed to shift and manifest into a ghostly Gavin leaning against the wall, arms crossed, his lips pulled up in a cocky smile as he watched her. "*So, is this going to become a thing between us? Am I going crazy and imagining your voice?*"

He shrugged at her and scratched the tip of his nose. "*What makes you think I'm not just a ghosty?*" he asked and wiggled his fingers, mouthing "spooky" before smirking. "You're *the one making me up in your head, aren't you? Maybe you need someone you know who isn't going to screw you over. Can't trust Saul. Can't trust Nick and his wolves. Who do you trust?*"

Trish glanced at the witch. *"You, I guess. Hell, I can't even trust myself. I don't know what I want out of this. What my goal is."*

"Yes, you do," Gavin whispered. He leaned forward and arched an eyebrow. *"You just don't want to admit it."*

The creak of the door stole Trish's attention from him. Saul walked inside, carrying a tray of food. He looked at the witch then smiled at Trish as he set the food down on a desk near his bed. Eggs, sausage, toast, and fruit filled the plate, much fancier than what she expected.

"You look better," he said, tapping his cheek. "Your complexion. When was the last time you feasted?"

Trish shook her head. "Few days? I'm not sure. Not since I got here."

Saul nodded and pushed the food toward her. He had a second plate for himself and two mugs of steaming coffee. "I added blood flakes to your coffee. I imagine you couldn't drink as much as you wanted without killing her. I'm impressed. Your control has gotten better, Trish."

Her pride from his praise felt hollow. "How long have you had her?"

"Since we arrived here. I had a wolf before." Saul sat down on another chair and sipped his coffee.

"Why a witch now?"

"Because the other parahumans have to be dosed, and it makes their blood taste sickly. The witch? Gag her, keep her hands tied, and make sure she can't use a wand, and I have nothing to fear. Besides, elderberry has a much better flavor than wolfsbane or henbane."

"Ah," was all Trish managed to say as she picked up a piece of toast. She nibbled on it, trying to ease the sick feeling in her gut. "So… this pit is a lot different than the other one. Witches and magi? They can control them here?"

"With the right amount of elderberry, yes," Saul said. "Chicago only had enough Hunters to take care of the werewolves and vampires. Here? Any parahuman is game." He smirked. "They've even gone after fae."

"Fae?" Trish said in surprise. "Have they succeeded?"

"Hm, a couple of times, but they usually have to kill the fae if they cause too much trouble."

Trish furrowed her brow. "I thought fae couldn't be killed."

"Well, their bodies can be destroyed," Saul explained. "But it's not easy. And when they die, their Ather souls go back to a magical tree in the Veil and are reborn."

Trish lifted her head in surprise. She'd never heard of that before. "Don't we have to worry about them coming back for revenge?"

Saul smirked. "Typically, no, since most fae who are reincarnated don't retain their memories. And besides, the ones who have died haven't been allowed to return to the tree."

Trish furrowed her brow. "Aren't *allowed*? How the hell do you stop them?"

"With help from another fae," Saul said. Her confusion must have been evident, because Saul chuckled in amusement. "Haven't you wondered how the pits have been so easily hidden away? Why no one found them until traitors slipped into our ranks?"

She had wondered just that. Why couldn't a magus scry and find loved ones? She'd assumed the elderberry had something to do with it, or that a magus was the one keeping everyone hidden. But if it was a fae? Her heart sank. How was the Purple Door District's council supposed to combat a fae? No one had strong enough magic to contend with a being of the Veil. "So, if Tess and her friend hadn't found us, no one would have made it to the Chicago pit?"

"Exactly. Now, the protective barrier around that pit was weaker than it is here, but that's only because the fae governing us wasn't in Chicago."

"That…fae is here?" Trish asked warily.

Saul nodded. "Yes, and she's *magnificent*."

She. So the enemy was a female fae. Who couldn't easily be killed. Damnit. What kind of help would she be if she couldn't even fight against the guardian of the pit? And why in the Nightmother's name would a fae help these people, especially when they were killing other fae? She wanted to ask, but she also feared that digging too deep might make Saul suspicious. "Have you met her?"

"Once," Saul said. "I've met many a fae in their Ways, but I've never seen anyone like her. She's…well, I hope one day you'll get the chance to see her, and then you can decide for yourself." He nudged her plate of food. "Eat. Eat. We have a busy day. And I have to assign you to your new duties."

Trish worked on the eggs, but they dissolved like ash in her mouth. "Duties? I thought I was guarding the captives."

"We rotate responsibilities here, unlike back home. Guard duty. Running the rings. And going on missions to retrieve more parahumans."

Trish tried not to blanch. *He can't seriously think I'm going to do that.* But if she was working with him now, of course he'd expect her to. It would be another test. "Have you done that?"

"Who do you think caught Nick and Brighton?"

Trish swallowed hard. Right, he was the whole reason Paytah's pack was in this mess to begin with. Acting as guard over parahumans she could do, but rushing out and kidnapping people? She wasn't sure she could stomach that. She'd had a hard enough time kidnapping Bianca to save her coven. But how was she going to make it as a spy, a traitor, if she couldn't?

Saul tilted his head. "You look unsettled."

"It's just…I understand why you wanted to take Paytah's wolves after what happened to Fraula, but going after other parahumans? Doesn't it feel…wrong? Hypocritical?"

Saul smiled. "We're only capturing the ones who are a threat, Trish. Rogues who have caused problems in local districts. Parahumans who haven't transitioned correctly and are therefore a risk to both humans and other parahumans. I know it feels uncomfortable, but we're doing a great favor to the Districts."

Trish eyed him, wondering how he believed such a lie. Nick and Brighton were both loyal members of Paytah's pack. And she doubted all of the captives were rogues or threats. There were far too many. *Is he so blinded by his grief from losing Fraula that he's lying to himself? Or is there something else going on? He's…different. Calmer. Happier. This isn't the Saul I remember.*

"Careful, little bat," Gavin warned in her ear. *"Play the game. You can't let him know you're catching on."*

Trish shook her head and forced a smile. "Well, I guess that's not so bad, then," she said. "And it'll be nice to help the District from afar. Maybe, one day, they'll understand."

"Maybe," Saul said, taking a bite of food. His red eyes darkened. "I just hope I'll be allowed to go on a mission to rid our District of their false Marshall."

"Paytah?" Trish asked before she could stop herself.

"Of course. Of all the people Gladus could have picked, it was him, a murderer. Many other parahumans are more deserving of the title. He'll bring nothing but pain and destruction to the District. No, he needs to be eradicated."

Trish decided not to comment on the fact Saul was the one causing the pain, suffering, and bloodshed he so feared Paytah would bring upon the District. "I see," she said instead. "What are my duties for now?"

"Guard and intake. You'll be responsible for guarding the parahumans and at times bringing them food. But intake will be your other task." He drained the rest of his coffee. "We have a new shipment of parahumans coming in, and I'll need your help prepping them. That means collars, shackles, and doses of whatever keeps them sedated."

Trish drank her coffee to hide the urge to vomit. *I can't do this. This goes way beyond what I can fake.*

"*Yes, you can,*" Gavin's warm, disembodied voice whispered. "*Play the game, love, and you can save the ones you bring into captivity. You just have to wait.*"

Wait? Wait and let more parahumans suffer under the Hunters' thumbs? How could she call herself a vampire and let that happen?

"Trish?" Saul pressed.

She shook her head. "Sorry, this'll be an adjustment for me. I've never done anything like this."

Saul nodded gravely. "I'll teach you, don't worry. You're under my protection." He reached across the table and squeezed her hand. "I won't let anything happen to you. You're my coven, my family."

Trish wanted to feel comforted, but his words stung. If only he knew the deception that burned through her like wildfire.

She finished her breakfast in silence as Saul spoke more about the pit and where she could find the mess hall, bathroom, armory, control room, and more. He spoke with such animation and excitement that it almost felt like she wasn't talking to the Saul she knew and loved. Or maybe he was so lively because he finally had another vampire from his coven to work with. She had always looked up to him like a mentor, a father. And at one time, she'd hoped he saw her as a daughter.

No longer.

They gathered up their plates and tray and left the room, leaving the unconscious witch behind. Trish carried the plates to a drop-off area near the mess hall, Saul on her heels to keep the Hunters off her, or so he said. She still felt his eyes follow her every step, waiting for her to bolt.

Once they'd passed off their dishes, Trish followed Saul down the main tunnel toward the intake area where parahumans were brought in trucks. As they approached, someone wheeled out a cart of shackles and collars, while another carried a medical case filled with doses of henbane, mistletoe, wolfsbane, and elderberry. Her stomach twisted.

She inspected the Hunters surrounding the truck and recognized both Gale and Hendrickson, as well as the mysterious and aloof Slater. They opened the back of a truck and started to pull people out of it, taking little care how they grabbed them. Some of the parahumans fell to the ground, wounded from being kidnapped. Trish folded her arms and watched them, her nose taking in the mixed scents of wolf, cat, avian, and vampire. They were different races and cultures, though she could tell by the way some of the parahumans clung together that they were from the same packs or covens.

"Come on!" Hendrickson shouted into the truck, and when no one came out, he started to climb in.

"Wait," Gale said and pushed him back. "I'll get them." She disappeared inside and returned a few moments later pulling along two Indian parahumans who couldn't have been more than teens. The boy, his kurta ripped from the scuffle, kept in front of the girl as much as he could. The girl pressed her head into the back of his shoulder, crying in fear. Her dark hair had come loose from her tight braid. She trembled, causing the vibrant colors of her blue sari to ripple like water. Hendrickson waited impatiently, but Gale didn't let him come near as she brought both teens down the ramp.

Saul nudged her. "Time to get to work."

Trish's heart pounded in her chest. This was wrong, so very wrong. The way the parahumans clung to each other and cried or swore at the Hunters…they were terrified. None of them looked like the vicious rogues who plagued Districts and harassed unsuspecting victims. How could Saul not see that?

To her horror, she found herself burdened with a load of shackles and collars and pushed toward the teens. The boy glared at her and shoved, presumably, his sister behind him. "Stay back, Pavati."

"Ayaan, don't," Pavati whimpered.

Trish shut her eyes. The faster she got this done, the better. "What are they?" she asked Gale. She didn't smell anything parahuman about them. She eyed the pair. "The sooner you let me chain you, the better. I don't want a fight."

Before Gale could answer, Ayaan glared and thrust out his hand with a wand. But all that appeared was a little spark of green.

Witch.

He stared at his fingers in fright and tried again. Trish took advantage of his distraction and looped a shackle around his wrist, then jerked him away from his sister so she could shackle the other one. He struggled, but a fledgling witch couldn't stand up against a vampire. In three swift moves, Trish had the collar on his throat, and Gale had dosed him in the shoulder with the elderberry. Ayaan swayed and fell to his knees, dazed.

"No!" Pavati screamed. She reached for her brother and looked him over, searching into his eyes for whatever ailed him.

Had these teens never been under the influence of elderberry before? She grimaced and reached for the girl. Pavati turned and swung out her hand, producing her own wand, and Trish expected nothing to happen.

Icy water filled with shards struck her in the face, cutting her cheeks and splitting her lip. Trish staggered back in surprise and touched her mouth. Blood oozed out of the wounds.

Pavati looked just as shocked. She stared from her wand to Trish then lifted her arm to do it again.

"Little witch!" Hendrickson snarled and snatched her wrist. He jerked it behind her back, causing her to cry out in pain and drop the wand.

"Oy!" Trish shouted at him. She grabbed the girl back and shoved him away from her with more force than she meant to. "You're the idiot who left their wands with them!"

Hendrickson glowered at her. "We got the brats from a tiny school that trains newbie witches and magi. Not like they can do much damage."

"My face begs to differ," Trish snarled back. Her cheek was already starting to heal, but she tasted blood from her lip. "Why don't you do something about those wands instead before I let her blast ice in your face next?"

Hendrickson stalked closer to her. "Just because you're that vampire's little pet doesn't mean you get to touch me or order me around, you filth."

Trish bared her fangs. "Come closer and say that again, *human*."

They glared at one another, Hendrickson reaching for the gun at his hip. A glare from Gale made him think twice, and he dropped his hand. "You're not worth it," he spat at Trish and stalked off, though not before grabbing the wands.

Trish didn't realize how savage and scary she looked with her fangs out until she saw her face reflected in Pavati's horrified gaze. The vampire grimaced and shook her head. She didn't want to scare the teen to death.

She took a shackle and tethered the girl's hands. Pavati struggled a little, but it seemed Trish's rage had cowed her enough that she didn't fight back. So it was with even more reluctance that Trish stuck a second syringe in Pavati's shoulder and sent the dazed girl to the floor beside her brother. He cradled her in his lap and glared at Trish.

"You're a vampire. Why are you doing this to us? We're just like you."

"No, you're not," Trish murmured. *You're better than me.*

With the teens drugged and chained, Trish pulled them to their feet and searched for Saul for guidance. He had a werewolf, a vampire, and a werecat under his control, the cat bearing a bruised eye that was likely from her efforts to fight back. "Where do they go?" Trish asked.

"Follow me," Saul said.

Trish sighed and pulled the two teens along. Ayaan stayed quiet, but Pavati sobbed behind her. She could almost taste the salt of the girl's tears as they rolled down her cheeks and stained her dress. Trish doubted the teen would stay in such a lovely thing for very long before it was torn to pieces during fights. Newbie witches…what on Earth could the pit want with *them*? And why steal them from a school? It didn't make sense.

They walked down another set of halls to a caged area. She searched behind the bars, trying to find Nick or one of the other wolves, but she was met by glares, growls, and flipped middle fingers when she stared too long. Eventually, they arrived at an empty room. Trish pushed the two teens inside.

Movement to the right caught her eye, and she almost sighed in relief.

Nick stared back at her between the bars, his gaze going to the teens then back to her. She said nothing aloud but spoke into his head. *"I'm stuck on intake. Saul's letting things slip. If I can bring dinner to you later, I'll fill you in."*

In response, Nick rose and struck the bars. "Traitor," he growled. "Stealing children now?"

"Would you rather I brought you Paytah?" Trish bit back at him then turned and headed down the tunnel with Saul. Even as she walked, Pavati's quiet sobs haunted her.

Chapter 3
Hospitals and Hauntings

Rozene

Thunder crackled and rain pelted the windows of Crystal Corvid Apothecary. Rozene leaned back in her seat, waiting for a lull in the storm so she wouldn't get drenched running inside.

"I could go in for you or take you straight to the hospital," Jackson said beside her.

Rozene glanced at the beta of her pack, his dark brow creased in concern while his eyes held the weight of many sleepless nights. How many evenings had he spent watching over Paytah or the rest of the pack, waiting for another Hunter to come and steal their brethren? It was a thing of nightmares for them all.

She reached for his hand and squeezed it. "I'm fine, Jackson. There's no danger at the apothecary, and the things I need might help." She leaned forward and kissed his temple affectionately. "Thank you for your concern."

Lightning split the sky, but the rain ebbed for a moment. Rozene pulled her hand away and slid out of the car, shutting the door behind her. She ran the short distance to the store and stepped inside just before the clouds opened up again.

"Good Fates, the skies are angry tonight," a cheerful voice greeted her at the counter.

Rozene looked up at the heavy-set woman, her white-streaked

blonde hair held up with a small ring of white flowers. "Good morning, Olive. It's good to see you."

Olive smiled, her bluish-gray eyes crinkling at the corners. The earth magus and her husband had owned the shop for decades, and it had been in Olive's family for even longer. If someone ever needed an herb, talisman, wand, or a friendly smile, Olive was there to provide them all.

Olive grabbed a blanket and marched herself over to Rozene's side, her tie-dyed skirt flowing around her thick legs. "You too, dear. Look at you, you're drenched!" She flung the blue blanket around Rozene's shoulders. "How is your pack?"

Rozene sighed. "Healing, both physically and mentally. Some are still in the hospital, and the rest are trying to keep themselves strong at home before we make our next move."

"Paytah?"

"Stubborn as ever," Rozene said with a half-smile. "Wanting to give orders while he's still doubled up in pain. My mate doesn't quite understand that he's no longer the young pup he used to be and doesn't bounce back as quickly."

Olive chuckled and rubbed Rozene's arms. "He's always been that way. Now, what can I get for you?"

Rozene pulled a list from her woven bag. "Some of your ointments for Paytah's joints; he's stiffer than usual. Pedro and Quince said their daughters are having nightmares after all that's happened. They're afraid a monster is going to snatch them up in the middle of the night."

"Poor dears," Olive said and guided Rozene over to a wall of herbs, oils, lotions, and other medicinal potions. "I was afraid that might happen. What of Kat and her nightmares?"

"They're back, but different. Being in the hospital isn't helping."

"Hmm." Olive nodded and snapped her fingers. "I think I have something to help with that." She picked up a bag and filled it with a mixture of herbs. Rozene recognized the scents of chamomile and lavender. "I have dream pillows for the little girls. Fill them with these herbs and tuck them under their heads at night. That'll help. You can select the patterns of the pillows here."

Rozene looked along a wall of pillows that ranged from Celtic knots and starry nights to the latest My Little Pony character and Black Panther. She chuckled to herself and picked a full moon for Eliza and a wolf with a Celtic knot for Phoebe. By the time she'd chosen, Olive had filled a bag with ointments for Paytah.

"Come this way," Olive said and brought her into the next room. A beautiful metal tree stood in the middle holding a plethora of glass witch balls painted in every color Rozene could imagine. The soft sound of rain washed over them from the open window.

Rozene walked around the tree and touched the balls with delicate fingers. Inside, colors swirled to resemble a tree, lightning, or flowing waves. "What would you suggest?"

Olive smiled. She reached up for a purple ball and pulled it down. "This one. Purple will remind Kat she's safe. And this is one of my husband's favorite creations. He'll be happy to hear it went to her."

"Thank you." Rozene cradled it in her hands and motioned to one more item on the list. "I need this as well."

Olive eyed it then frowned. "Is someone having trouble staying asleep, too?"

"More like he refuses to go to sleep."

"Ah, Jackson?"

"Jackson."

Olive shook her head. "That young man makes a wonderful beta to you and Paytah, but he pushes himself too hard for both the pack and the community. I'll see what I have. A small dose of valerian root perhaps."

Rozene waited while Olive slipped out of the room. She looked over the tree then walked to the window to listen to the rain. Rozene shut her eyes. The wind flowed softly through the room and stirred her braided hair. She ran her finger along the starburst piece that matched Paytah's and kept her hair in place. She breathed in the fresh scent of the grass and flowers out in the little private garden. Her shoulders sank with exhaustion. Jackson wasn't the only one struggling with sleep, but they all had their demons to contend with.

Rozene opened her eyes.

Ray's ghostly visage appeared before her, his face twisted in a painful death mask.

Rozene yelped and jumped backwards as the lightning flashed again. She blinked a few times, but the image of her dead packmate's face had vanished. She grasped her pounding chest and took a few shaky breaths.

"Rozene? Are you all right?" Olive asked as she hurried back into the room.

Rozene stared at the open window. "Yes…no. I…saw something."

"Outside?" When Rozene nodded, Olive placed a gentle hand on her back. "The witch balls ward off bad dreams, spells, and omens. But they have to have somewhere to go. Sometimes they linger in the garden, but in the garden they'll stay. It's unfortunate that the bad dreams keep going there. They've been much worse lately, though I suppose that shouldn't be a surprise what with all the people who have gone missing or gotten hurt. That's sure to cause nightmares. Kat had a similar problem when she saw me a few months ago. I think I need to bless the garden with sage again. That's the third time this month." She tilted her head. "Do you want a witch ball too?"

Rozene shook her head. "No, no, that's all right. I'll be fine." She took a calming breath and smiled at the magus. "Thank you for all your help, Olive."

The woman nodded and motioned to the cash register. "Let me check you out."

***

The hospital was becoming an all-too familiar place.

Carmen. Ray. Her beloved Paytah. And now Kat. Who would be next? And more importantly, would any of them show up in the morgue to join Ray?

With each visit, Rozene wore a calm, soothing mask, while the natural werewolf side of her, a murderous thing when pushed, snarled for revenge. Her mate and pups had been injured and taken from her unjustly, and this mother wolf wouldn't stand for it.

She tightened her hold on a crystalline vase of white and yellow roses, the water sloshing inside. Her woven bag swung against her hip, filled with her items from the apothecary and fresh pumpkin chocolate chip bread, one of Kat's favorites. She brought each person something different. Sweet treats and fizzy non-alcoholic fae drinks for Carmen. Fresh-brewed coffee and jerky for Paytah. Home baked goods for Kat.

Ray didn't need mortal possessions anymore, though Rozene

longed to sit at his side and clasp his hand, cold and stiff as it was. Vic had used a magic spell to keep Ray's body suspended in the local funeral home, preventing him from decaying until they found the rest of their packmates and could have a proper funeral. She'd never expressed how it bothered her that he had yet to be laid to rest. But his wife should be there to see him put into the ground or cremated. Augustine would want that.

If she survived.

Come now, Rozene, don't let your thoughts sour your visit with Kat. It may be the last time you see her for a while. She glanced at the time on her phone and took a shaky breath. She couldn't linger if she wanted to make it back home in time for her trip. Especially if she wanted to bid a proper farewell to Paytah.

She followed the elevator to the District-friendly hospital floor and found Kat's room. Her ears perked up at the familiar voices coming from inside, drawing a smile to her lips.

Bianca sat at Kat's bedside, a small stuffed bird that looked very much like Bianca's inner caracara sitting on Kat's stomach. The Latina avian perched with her black and red-tipped hair pulled back behind her, her shoulders wrapped in a warm purple cardigan. She held Kat's hand between hers and rubbed the werewolf's fingers.

Bruises decorated Kat's pale white face. Her once-long golden hair had been brutally hacked short and shaved on one side of her head, which bore bandages. Lacerations blotched her body in a morbid display that acted as a warning to anyone who tried to come after the Hunters again.

Carmen sat in a wheelchair beside Kat's bed. The young woman looked better than the last time Rozene had seen her, her white cheeks fuller and with more color. She was recovering well after the coma, but she still needed help learning how to properly walk again. The werewolf smiled at Rozene and held out an arm.

Rozene went to her first after setting down the flowers and gave her a tight hug. "How are you?"

"Better than Kat, I think. Though I'm still digging the new haircut," Carmen said and offered Kat a smile. She brushed her own long yellow hair out of her eyes. "I don't know, I might have to get mine cut, too."

"Shut up," Kat growled playfully. "Only one of us gets a new hairstyle."

Rozene heard the humor in her voice, but fear echoed in it, too. She sat down at the foot of Kat's bed and reached out to rub her leg affectionately. "Have the doctors been by to check on you?"

Kat nodded and motioned to Bianca.

Bianca pulled out a folder. "They told us more about her wounds and aftercare. They want her to stay another couple of days, but then she can come home and rest. Since she'll be staying with me and the cloister, I have her instructions."

Rozene took them and flipped through the files, reading the recommendations, some of which matched Paytah's. Since both he and Kat worked around humans, they had to be careful about showing how quickly their wounds were healing. It didn't make sense for two mugging victims—because that was the easiest explanation for their wounds—to be limping around one day, then walking easier the next. "They prescribed you painmakers," she said dryly. Painmakers did just what their name implied; they caused pain to the already wounded areas, though there was no further damage. Cruel medicine, in Rozene's opinion, but if it kept Kat and Paytah safer so that they weren't discovered, then so be it.

Kat didn't look happy about it either. "I think I have to worry less than Paytah since I work around other parahumans."

"I'd rather keep you home until you're healed," Bianca grumbled as if she'd already had this discussion with Kat.

Rozene handed the folder back to Bianca. "I have something to fix that frown." She retrieved the chocolate chip pumpkin bread and held it out to her. One sniff, and Kat's eyes went wide in delight. As Kat ripped open the wrapping, Rozene held her bag out to Carmen so she could see the sweets and fizzy drinks.

"Oh my god, yesssss!" Carmen dove into the bag and plucked out a bag of homemade candy. She tossed one into her mouth and sighed happily. "So much better than hospital food."

Rozene chuckled, though her smile didn't quite reach her eyes. She hated leaving her pups behind. They were in good hands, and wings in Bianca's case, but the urge to stay and protect them was strong. Paytah could do that while he healed; she had to remind herself.

"Rozene?" Kat asked. She lowered a half-eaten slice of bread.

Rozene patted her leg. "Fretting over you lot, the usual." She glanced at all three, growing more somber. "I'm leaving for Wisconsin today. Vic got in touch with the wind magus there who may be able to help us find the others."

All three women exchanged looks. Carmen leaned forward, whispering, "You really think she can help?"

"Vic is confident in Evelyn's abilities. But...." She hesitated. Should she tell them the news and make them worry? Oh, they'd worry either way. "We learned her school was attacked, and two of her students were kidnapped during the fight. So, she has even more of a personal reason to be invested."

Bianca grimaced. "That's not good. I mean, I'm glad she can help, but if she can't even find her own students, how is she supposed to help us find our people?"

"I'm not just meeting with her," Rozene said with a small smile. "We'll be talking with her fae wife. And with the local pack as well."

Kat perked up. "Wait, does that mean Alpha Wapasha?"

Rozene beamed. "He's agreed to help since the kidnapping occurred near his territory."

"Give him a hug from me," Kat said.

"And me!" Carmen replied.

Bianca frowned in confusion. "You know him?" she asked the two younger wolves.

Rozene chuckled. "Of course they do. He's my son." The look of surprise on Bianca's face was priceless.

"I thought family packs usually stayed together," the avian said.

Rozene shrugged. "Some do. Wapasha was always Alpha material. He and his father often butted heads over pack politics when he was younger. So Wapasha went away for school, which happened to be in Wisconsin. And there he found a new pack. Many years and a mate and two pups later, Wapasha is now Alpha of that very same pack. Paytah and I are very proud of him."

Kat reached for Bianca's hand and squeezed it. "He comes here sometimes. I met him when I first arrived; he was home visiting. He helped get me situated and was warm and welcoming. Even threatened to go after Christopher if I thought that would help me heal."

Bianca grinned. "Okay, I like him already."

Rozene chuckled. "I'm glad to hear he has your approval." She looked at her three pups. (Even if Bianca was a bird, choosing Kat made her part of the family.) The urge to stay lingered, but Jackson was also waiting for her in the car. She needed to get on the road. The longer they wasted time, the longer their packmates suffered. She took a breath and leaned forward to kiss Kat on the head. She did the same to Carmen and Bianca. "Stay close together. Keep each other safe. I'll be back as soon as I can, and hopefully with our people."

Kat grabbed her hand. "Rozene, please be careful." Tears stung her eyes. "We can't afford to lose anyone else."

"You know me," Rozene said. "My pack comes first, but I promise to do my best to stay safe." She squeezed Kat's hand and rose, taking the bag back after Carmen retrieved her drink. With a final nod, she headed out the door. She checked the time again.

"Rozene?"

She lifted her eyes as a young, fellow Native American man walked toward her with a tablet in her arms. "Quince," she greeted him. "I was just about to look for you."

Her packmate offered a tired smile. "Carmen and Kat are healing well. I check in on them often, and Tamara has stopped by to act as a guard. She headed out to get some non-hospital food for the girls."

Rozene nodded in gratitude. The remaining members of her pack, the ones who weren't injured or MIA, were taking turns watching over Kat and Carmen. While she doubted anyone would try to take Carmen, she feared for Kat's safety. She had been left for dead as a message. Kat didn't think the Hunters had expected her to survive the brutal attack, which meant their secrets weren't secrets anymore. But so far Kat could remember only so much of her time in the pit. They were relying on getting more information from either Legion, or Tess and her…Hunter companion.

Rozene still couldn't reconcile how Tess could be working with a Hunter after all this, but at least the man had tried to help them instead of kill them.

She opened her phone and checked the timetable of when her different packmates were scheduled to stop by the hospital. Tamara, Jackson's mate and another beta, had most of the day, and then Mikayla was set to come in that evening after her classes. Good. The girls would have plenty of protection.

Rozene put her phone away and held the bag out to Quince. "I visited Olive. She gave me herbs and pillows for your daughters to help them with their nightmares."

Relief cascaded across Quince's face, washing away some of his weariness. "Thank you. We had another long night with them. Phoebe was up until almost four AM crying because she thought she heard a Hunter outside. It was just the tree branches knocking against her window and our roof." He shook his head. "I think we're going to look into putting the girls in therapy with everything that's happened. I don't want them to be scarred for life after this."

"No," Rozene agreed. "But some healthy fear is important too so they know not to trust the wrong people."

"You mean like Tess trusts *that* Hunter?"

"Quince...." His eyes dropped, and she reached out to cup his cheek. "I feel the same, but Arjun did help us get information about the wolf pit."

"Right before they all pulled out and vanished." Quince held the tablet to his chest with his right hand and ran the left through his dark hair. "Be honest with me, Alpha. Do you really think we'll get them back?"

"Yes," Rozene said without an ounce of hesitation. She chose not to mention that she wasn't sure if they'd get their family back alive. Her mind drifted to Ray, and she shuddered. "We'll find them, Quince."

He eyed her then enveloped her in a warm hug. Rozene stiffened for a moment, wanting to be strong in front of him. But Quince had always had a warm, loving heart. She sank into his embrace and sighed. "Thank you."

"Be safe. And give Wapasha my best regards."

"I will." She touched his cheek and kissed his brow. Then she bid him goodbye and strode through the hospital, her mind returning to her duties. She had one more stop to make before she and Jackson went on their way.

***

The last time Rozene had visited Gladus's home was well before the Violet Marshall's death. She stood at the foot of the stairs, staring up at the tell-tale purple flower pot hanging in front of the door, signifying a safe spot for parahumans. She closed her eyes, remembering the water magus's smile, the bright colored cloths always wrapped in her hair, and the scent of herbs and tea that wafted off of her body. Gladus had governed the Purple Door District for decades before her murder. Even after almost two years, her death left a weight in Rozene's heart.

She walked up the stairs and fished a key out of her pocket. She unlocked the door and stepped inside, greeted by murmured voices in the parlor. Paytah had planned to use the house as a safe zone for new people who visited the Purple Door District. But after the attack on their pack, he'd turned it into the new neutral council headquarters instead of designating one of their homes. It was safer than drawing Hunters to their personal abodes.

Rozene walked down the hall, the creaking floor announcing her presence. Conversation halted for a moment as a beautiful Black woman stuck her head out from around the corner. Her long, golden nails gripped the wall like claws briefly until she sent a smile—it always resembled a smirk—in Rozene's direction.

"It's Rozene," Mia said. The pride Queen slipped back into the room.

Rozene walked into the parlor and held up her hand when the others started to rise in greeting. "Please, I just came to speak to my husband and fetch Vic."

Carlos, an older Latino man with a distinguished graying mustache, smiled at her. "It's good to see you, Rozene. How are your pups?"

"Healing," Rozene said. "Quince is watching over them." She looked at another council member. "How's Joseph?"

Selene, a gorgeous Greek goddess of a vampire, nodded. She had taken Joseph's place as Duchess on the council while he dealt with his own mental health. Saul's invasive charm had left him an emotional mess, but how could it not? Saul had been his second, his closest friend, and he'd performed the ultimate act of betrayal by invading Joseph's mind. Who wouldn't have PTSD after that? "He's making improvements. But he still needs time."

"Of course. I'm glad you can be here to act as his voice," Rozene said. She looked at Akeno, a young Chinese man and the grove Priest, and nodded her head politely before settling her gaze on her mate. Paytah sat tall and proud as he always did, but she recognized the faint beads of sweat on his brow and the way he shifted to the left in his chair. He was still in pain from the assassination attempt.

Akeno set his tablet down. "Why don't we take a break?" He rose and passed by Rozene, brushing his hand comfortingly against her shoulder.

Mia, Selene, and Carlos likewise stood and headed out of the room, leaving Rozene with her mate and Vic.

Vic, a thin, pale-faced man with blonde hair, hefted a bag over his shoulder. His tired eyes bore dark bags as well. "I can go wait outside in the car with Jackson."

Rozene nodded her thanks and waited until he'd left before she sat next to Paytah. She pulled a tissue from her purse and swept away his brow sweat. "You're pushing yourself too hard," she reprimanded him.

Paytah smiled and caught her wrist. He brought it to his mouth and kissed her hand affectionately, one of his long, black braids caressing her skin. "Would you expect me any other way, my love?" He gave a tired sigh. "We're almost done with the meeting. I plan to head home after this. Don't worry, Carlos is driving me."

"Good." Of all the members of the council, she trusted Carlos the most. He and Paytah had been friends since they first met. And as the adopted father to Bianca, Carlos had an especially vested interest in keeping Paytah and the pack safe.

She pulled him into a hug and pressed their heads together. "I don't like leaving you behind."

"I know. But Wapasha will listen to you better than anyone else. Besides, you'll get to see our grandpups."

"Jealous?" Rozene teased.

Paytah nipped at her nose and growled huskily under his breath. "Very. I expect pictures and a full report when you get back." He kissed her cheek then pressed his mouth to her ear, his warm breath tickling the sensitive hairs within. "Rozene…please come back to me."

She ran her hand along his cheek and kissed him on the lips. "If you promise to still be here when I return."

They smiled at each other and sat in peaceful silence for a moment, basking in each other's presence. The trip to Wisconsin, under normal circumstances, wouldn't be dangerous. But with Hunters on the prowl and possibly watching every move they made, they couldn't be sure.

The Hunters had already taken out three of their wolves by causing a truck accident. What was to stop them from following Rozene's path and attacking her on the road? Jackson and Rozene's departure also left the pack even more defenseless. They wouldn't be gone long, but Rozene still didn't like it.

They squeezed each other's hands and exchanged a deep kiss before Rozene stood up. She lingered at his side a moment longer, staring into his warm eyes and memorizing every feature on his face. "I love you."

"I love you too," Paytah said.

Rozene knew if she didn't leave then, she might never get to the car. Steeling herself, she headed for the door, her eyes stinging with tears of worry and also rage toward the people who had attacked her family. She grabbed the door handle, sharp claws pushing through her fingers.

"Rozene," Mia called behind her. When Rozene glanced over, the normally cocky Queen inclined her head respectfully. "We'll watch over him and your pack. You have my word."

Rozene was surprised by the declaration, but it warmed her heart nonetheless. "Thank you, Mia." She slipped out the door, the claws retreating under her flesh by the time she shut it behind her. She hurried down the steps, trying not to imagine Gladus's lifeless body lying at the bottom in a pile of snow and puddle of blood. She rolled her shoulders and got into the passenger's seat.

Jackson glanced at her. "Ready?"

"Let's get this over with."

Chapter 4
Training

Tess

Tess ducked the fist flying toward her face and twisted around her opponent, her hand slapping his arm away before he socked her in the stomach. Sweat stung her eyes, and her heart pounded like a drum against her chest. She shifted to the balls of her feet and launched herself at the man, aiming for his cheek. In one swift move, he caught her wrist in his hand and twisted it and her arm behind her back. Tess yelped as she was jerked toward him and bent forward. Cool metal touched her throat.

"You're dead," Arjun said. He squeezed her wrist then pulled the knife away and released her.

Tess stumbled forward, rubbing her throat. He hadn't cut her, but the lingering feeling was not comfortable. "Ugh, I don't get it. Paytah taught me how to fight." She reached for a towel hanging over a chair and wiped her drenched face.

"He taught you how to fight like a wolf. You're a human, so you have to use that to your advantage and also recognize your disadvantages."

Tess grabbed her water bottle bad-temperedly and swallowed a few gulps. She flexed her fingers and called fire to the tips. Flames licked the air, sparking with Ether magic. "Why can't I just blast you?" she asked and flicked her hand, sending a few sparks in his direction.

He didn't even flinch as they danced around his head.

"Because you won't always have your magic, or did you forget about elderberry?"

Right…yeah, she definitely hadn't forgotten what elderberry could do to her. She'd been dosed with enough of it in the past month to last her a lifetime, some by his hand. She folded her arms and scuffed her foot against the wooden floor.

They stood in a room below Arjun's flat where he usually worked out or trained other new Hunters like Tess. They'd been going at it for days now, and while she appreciated the lessons, she hated *waiting* instead of doing something to help her friends.

"We should be looking for Nick," she murmured, not for the first time.

Arjun picked up his water bottle. He sprinkled water in his hair and then squeezed a stream into his mouth. "I have someone on that. Better to wait for word. Besides, I'm not taking a half-trained Hunter out there with me."

"Didn't stop you before."

Arjun sipped the water. "You weren't carrying the honorable name of 'Hunter' then." With a sigh, he set the bottle down and pulled his shirt off over his head, showing off his bronze, muscular chest. His curly black hair fell to his shoulders and skimmed past the facial hair growing around his lips. Without his shirt, his black Hunter mark stood out on his arm in the form of an arrow with an arrowhead shaped like a heart. A single drop of blood dripped from the tip. Other ebony designs angled around the shaft, forming the feathers.

She blushed as he stretched his arms above his head. "You're an ass," she grumbled and took another drink.

Arjun chuckled. "Yes, I've been told I have quite the nice ass."

Tess sputtered.

Arjun smiled at her in amusement. He set his shirt down and motioned with his hand. "Come again."

Tess set her drink off to the side and walked toward him. This time, she produced a hair tie and bound her dark tresses behind her head so they would keep out of her eyes. She shook out her hands and rolled her head around her neck before taking a stance. "Ready."

Arjun threw himself at her without much preamble. His fist aimed for her face and she crossed her arms, blocking it. But that left room for his other fist to move and catch her in the side. It would have hit her full in the stomach if she hadn't anticipated his move and shifted slightly out of the way. The blow still winded her. She staggered back with a grunt and kicked off the ground, charging him and trying to body him backwards. She hit his broad chest, the musky scent of his skin filling her nose and swarming her senses. Her cheeks flushed from being so close to him, and she lost her footing for a second.

Arjun moved out of the way, letting her stumble forward. He hit her in the small of her back with his fist, sending her toppling to the ground with a cry of pain. She rolled onto her back as he came after her. She bunched her legs against her chest and kicked. The blow knocked him backwards onto his ass.

"Yes!" Tess crowed and scrambled to her feet. She leapt forward as he started to get up and wrapped her arms and legs around him, taking him back to the ground. Arjun grunted as she pinned him. Finally! It had taken her long enough to win! "Got you," she growled playfully.

"Do you?" Arjun asked.

Before Tess could prepare herself, he flipped them over, sending her onto her back. Air whooshed out of her lungs as her body met the wooden floor. Stunned, there was nothing she could do as Arjun straddled her and pinned her wrists on either side of her face. Tess gasped for breath and glared up at him. She squirmed, trying to get free, but his grip was far too strong. She almost considered blasting him with fire, but he was right. If she wanted to be a Hunter, she had to fight without always relying on magic. "That was dirty."

Arjun chuckled and squeezed her wrists affectionately. "Don't crow about defeating your opponent until you're sure he's down for the count. Surely Paytah taught you that."

"He might have," Tess muttered. She set her head on the ground with a sigh and looked up at Arjun. Her heart pounded, and it had nothing to do with the fight. He was so close, his face mere inches from hers. His strong legs held her body in place, preventing her from moving. And the hands on her wrists, the force in his hold sent pleasant chills through her. She swallowed hard and licked her lips. Arjun's expression shifted from admonishment to amusement then adoration.

Tess leaned forward and caught his lips with hers. She kissed him deeply, her hands fisting as he kept her restrained. His warm lips moved against hers, drinking her in and stirring her heart and stomach. She swept her tongue into his mouth. Slowly, he moved one hand from her wrist and cradled her head, pulling her even deeper into the kiss.

Tess used her free hand to grasp his hair. She tangled her fingers through his curly tresses and kissed him deeper, wanting to feel every inch of him against her, taste the flavors swirling in his mouth. He lowered his body and released her other hand to slip his fingers underneath her shirt. Tess shivered against his touch and broke the kiss. She tilted her head back as he worshiped her neck and sucked on the tender flesh. Her eyes rolled back, and she gasped in delight as he took hold of her breast in his strong hand. His legs loosened on her body as he shifted to get more comfortable.

With a smirk, Tess yanked his hair and slammed her fist into his warm chest, knocking him off of her. She rolled with him until he was on his back. Before he could move, she ripped the knife from his hip and pressed it to his throat. Her other hand hovered near his cheek, flames dancing in her palm. They glistened in his eyes. "Dead," she purred.

Arjun stared back at her with disappointment and a hint of pride. "And you say I'm an ass."

Tess chuckled and waved the flames away. The knife clattered to the floor. She kissed him again and sat on his chest, keeping him down. "Hey, you said I had to use my weakness to my advantage, right?"

"And here I thought you really wanted a little taste of what else I can offer."

Tess's eyes flashed, and she leaned down to capture his mouth again. She pressed their foreheads together, panting softly. "Maybe I'd like that, too."

He smiled and wrapped his strong arms around her, pulling her down to his chest and taking her mouth once more.

"Am I interrupting something?"

Tess and Arjun looked up sharply at a woman leaning against the doorframe. She stood a few inches taller than Arjun due to her thick-heeled boots. Her skin was darker than Tess's but lighter than Arjun's. She wore her hair buzzed on one side and long on the other, the natural chestnut brown strands tipped with blue. What Tess could only describe as steampunk goggles rested on top of her head. A red corset covered her chest, stopping just above the black shorts and fishnet leggings she had on. She crossed her toned arms, her black leather jacket squeaking a little with the move, the fabric sweeping down to the back of her legs. A belt held two guns that Tess could see and a few knives. She smirked at them with blue-painted lips.

Tess tensed, but Arjun sighed dramatically and rolled his eyes. "Hello, Skye."

Skye? This was the woman Arjun had been telling her about, his fellow Hunter? She slid off of him and yanked her shirt back into place. Arjun glanced at the Huntress as he sat up.

"Haven't I told you to knock before coming in?"

Skye shrugged. "I heard fighting, so I thought I'd take a peek. Didn't want to disturb you. Though apparently, I interrupted something else," she added with a playful smirk.

Arjun grunted as he looked her up and down. "The corset is new. I like it, but how can you breathe in that thing?"

"Heh, I can breathe better in this than I could in the skinny jeans I wore back when I still had a beard," Skye replied casually and planted her hands on her hips, giving them a little playful wiggle.

Tess lifted an eyebrow. Beard-wearing days? Was Skye trans? She tilted her head at the woman then shrugged her shoulders.

Skye dropped her arms to her sides and walked toward them, appraising Tess with her fierce eyes. "So, is this the little fire magus you told me about?" she asked.

Tess fidgeted and held out a hand. "Tess Montgomery."

Skye nodded but didn't return the gesture. "Skye. Careful who you give your last name to. You never know who's a friend and who's happy to stab you in the back." She leaned forward and winked. "So long as you don't screw with my dear, sweet Arjun, we can be friends. Although," she added, tapping her chin, "I guess there are other ways you can *screw* him."

"*Skye…*" Arjun moaned.

Tess blushed crimson. Just how much had Skye seen when she walked in? She shook her head and stuck her hands into her pockets. "Arjun said you were looking into where my pack got taken?"

Skye grinned. "You get right to the point, don't you? I like that." She glanced over at Arjun. "You want to get your shirt on and we'll go have a talk upstairs?"

"Yes, yes, we'll be there in a moment."

"Good. Oh, I brought you a few groceries. Clara was very disappointed not to get a smiley face on her omelet last time."

Tess blinked and looked at Arjun as Skye headed out of the room. "Wait? She's the smiley face person?"

Arjun grinned. "Her daughter Clara is, but Skye also gets put off if I don't add it to her breakfast too." He reached for his shirt and pulled it on. "That woman can slit a man's throat without a second thought, but God forbid I forget to put an avocado smile on her meal. She acts like the world's going to end."

Tess chuckled to herself and grabbed her water bottle. "I think I'm going to like her."

They walked upstairs together and entered Arjun's flat. Though all the windows were blacked out, his home felt warm and welcoming. A heat lamp warmed the little herb garden in his kitchen, which he used generously in his meals. Lightbulbs and lamps filled the flat, and richly colored curtains hung from the walls even if he didn't need them.

Skye had her nose in the fridge and came back out with part of a protein shake Arjun had made for them that morning. She sipped it and sat down at the table. She crossed one leg over the other and waited for Tess and Arjun to join her. "So, I scouted out the area where Legion's been cleaning up the wolf pit. They took everything out of it, but yours truly managed to slip in and get a few things downloaded before they dismantled the security cameras. The Hunters left a lot behind, so my guess is that Legion could have missed one or two things. I got the information downloaded from the SD card but left the card behind to help them in their search."

Tess lifted her head. "Did you see anything of interest?"

Skye nodded. "A bit, but I'm still going through the files. Some of them got damaged in their escape. My plan is to head down there again and scope the area out, see if there's anything Legion left behind that might be useful. Figured you two would want to help."

Tess nodded in earnest. "Yes, if there's anything I can do to help Nick and the others, I want to be there."

"Good," Skye said and took a drink of the shake. "I'm headed down that way at about 8:00 tonight. You two can meet me at the chained-door entrance. They still haven't managed to close up the hidden door that leads into the area, at least not the last time I checked.

Think they're having some *magical* issues." She wiggled her fingers.

Arjun rubbed his bearded chin, thinking. "Tess, didn't you say you felt Ather signatures there?"

"Yeah. I felt something magical, and it wasn't just Ether. I'm thinking somehow Ather is involved, but that doesn't make sense. Why would anyone with Ather help them?"

Skye shrugged. "Maybe they don't have a choice. Or maybe the Hunters found someone who has a similar objective."

The latter was way more troubling in Tess's mind. Who in their right mind would help Hunters and risk killing hundreds of parahumans? It felt wrong. Evil. Not even warlocks were so cold. "Why do we have to wait until tonight to go? Why can't we go now?"

Skye smirked and glanced at Arjun. "Eager, isn't she? Well, hon, I have a kiddo to pick up for one thing. And for another, the later we go, the less chance there is we'll be detected. I'm sure you two can keep each other busy until then." She wiggled her eyebrows, causing Arjun to roll his eyes. "Anyway, I wanted to check in and make sure the little firebug here hadn't sent you up in flames."

Tess looked indignantly at Arjun. "You told her about my nickname?"

He held up his hands. "No, no, of course not."

"Ohhh, is this a nickname you don't like?" Skye asked with a Cheshire smile. "Lovely. I'll remember that." She chuckled and finished off the protein shake before standing up. "I'll see you little lovebirds tonight, then."

Tess folded her arms and eyed Skye as the woman left. She wrinkled her nose, trying to decide if she found the Huntress interesting or irritating. Maybe a mixture of both. She huffed out a breath through her nose and tilted her head toward Arjun. "Well, I guess we have time to kill. I don't think I'm up for another round of fighting. My muscles are sore enough as it is. Sooo, I think it's my turn to train *you*."

Arjun leaned back in his chair. "Is that so? And where do we start, oh wise mentor?"

"The apothecary." At Arjun's anxious look, Tess laughed. "What? Are you afraid of an apothecary?"

"Not exactly. My sort usually doesn't go there. Bad rap and all. And let's just say I don't feel like getting attacked by a parahuman who might have a vendetta against me."

"Well, here's some advice," Tess said and kicked his leg lightly under the table. "How about you stop dressing in all black and giving people the 'I'm a vicious Hunter, rawr,' glare. You look much better with one of your natural smiles anyway."

Arjun laughed under his breath. "Fine. I'm sure I can find something other than black. But the same goes for you."

"Hey, I brought plenty of clothes with me to look normal. Besides, I know the owners of the Crystal Corvid. They won't bat an eye with me there." Tess got up and pulled her hair down. "I'm going to take a shower first, though. Oh, we should also stop at this little shop called the Lavender Lyre. Kat works over there, and they've got the most amazing scones and chai lattes."

Arjun draped an arm around the back of his chair and grinned at her as she shook out her hair. "Is this our first official date then? Magic and scones?"

Tess faltered and bit her lip. It was, wasn't it? What a normal thing to do, visit an apothecary and a coffee shop. Heh, a date. She'd never even thought about that. "I guess it is," she said. She couldn't hide the blush. "I'm uh…yeah, gonna go now."

"You want help?" Arjun teased as she headed for the shower.

"Only if you want to see who really has the best ass in town." Tess shook her butt meaningfully and stepped into the bathroom. As she pulled off her shirt and turned on the water, she heard Arjun shut the door behind them.

Chapter 5
The Wand

Tess

"I feel ridiculous," Arjun complained as they walked through the Chicago streets to Crystal Corvid Apothecary. He tugged on his deep green turtleneck and stuck one hand into his jeans pocket.

Tess snorted. "You feel ridiculous wearing regular clothes?" She wore black jeans with a red v-neck top and a black jacket. Belatedly, she realized her colors matched what Skye had been wearing. Jealous? No, of course not.

"It's just odd to go out normally in public and not be on a mission," he said. "I've been doing my job for far too long, I suppose."

Tess wove her arm through his and pulled him closer as she rested her head on his shoulder. "Well, let me introduce you to the world of normal people. Who, you know, go on walks and dates together."

Arjun blew out a breath and kissed her temple. "You're adorable when you're taking charge, you know that?"

Tess wrinkled her nose. "Yeah, a few people have mentioned it. I hate it."

Arjun barked out a laugh.

They stopped in front of the apothecary and Tess looked inside the window, searching for anyone she recognized. But the shop seemed pretty quiet. Olive set a new display of crystals in the front window and looked up. When she saw Tess, she grinned and waved at them. Tess waved back and tugged on Arjun's arm. "That's Olive. She's amazing, like another mom."

Arjun followed her inside. Fragrant incense washed over them and helped push away some of Tess's anxiety. She felt Arjun relax beside her.

"Tess! It's been so long," Olive said and pulled Tess into a warm embrace. She looked Arjun up and down. "And who's this strapping young gentleman?"

Arjun blustered a little and bowed his head politely. "Arjun, ma'am. Tess has spoken very highly of your shop."

"Oh," Olive waved her hand. "Don't ma'am me. You can just call me Olive." She clapped her hands together. "I saw Rozene recently. How are things? Or is that something we should talk about later?"

Tess smiled a little. Olive was usually very careful about the type of information she gave away unless she knew who Tess came with. "Later, I think. But thank you. We're actually here to help Arjun pick out a wand."

Olive's eyes lit up, and she bounced with excitement. "A wand? I see. A young witch in training?"

"You might say that," Arjun replied.

Tess patted his arm. "He wants me to teach him how to use magic. I'm not sure if I'm the best mentor, but I can give it a shot."

Olive nodded sagely. "You might consider taking him up to see Evelyn and her wife Kafeada at their school. She works with witches and magi of all ages. She has a very good record. Oh, and you'd be doing me a favor if you went, since I could send some items with you to her."

Tess wagged a finger. "Always with the other agendas," she accused playfully.

Olive winked. "Just trying to save on shipping for both of us." She motioned for them to follow her. "Come on now. Matthias!" she called. "Keep watch over the shop. I have a special customer."

"I'll be out in a moment," Matthias grouched from behind the counter, hidden in a back room.

After all these years, Tess still had yet to meet Matthias in person. He was usually in the workshop, or in the office, or blowing glass, or busy with one thing or other somewhere else. At least she got to see the handsome items he created.

They walked through the shop and up to a purple curtain with the tree of life and Celtic knots embroidered into it. Olive flicked her fingers, and Tess felt a buzz of Ether as a spell over the cloth came undone. They stepped through, and Olive turned to put the spell up again, preventing anyone else from following them, Tess assumed.

She'd never been back in this particular corner of the shop. She turned, and her mouth dropped open in shock.

It was like walking into another world.

A fountain bubbled in the middle of the floor, filling the room with a soothing sound. Vines crawled along the violet walls and coiled around furniture, giving it a much wilder, magical feel. The lights were soft and warm. A scrying bowl sat to one side of the room beside a wicker chair. Another wall held dozens of see-through containers showing off the handles of wands. Powerful talismans, much like the red one Tess wore, dangled from hooks on the wall. Crystals surrounded some of the talismans, providing an additional protective ward. Shelves above bent beneath the burden of herbs, tonics, and poisons Olive couldn't sell out front and didn't want to fall into the wrong (or non-parahuman) hands.

Olive walked up to the wall of wands and faced Arjun. "Have you ever tested if you have sensitivity to Ether?"

"I do," Arjun said. "I've been pretty good about telling if there's a magus near me."

"Oh? How do you know?"

Arjun considered that for a moment. "A tingling in my skin. It's faint, but I've grown to recognize it over the years as magic."

Olive smiled. "Well, we may have a natural witch here. How wonderful." She tapped her chin and searched the wands. "And what kind of magic are you most interested in?"

Tess glanced at Arjun. She had been wondering what he would choose. It'd be easier for her to show him fire, but he didn't seem like the pyro type.

Arjun looked down at his hand and rubbed his fingers together. "Earth," he said and nodded. "I'm good with plants, and I feel a connection to the earth."

"Good choice," Olive said. "Now, commanding the earth comes in different forms. Are you thinking you want to learn the ability to use soil? Roots? Plants? Healing magic?"

"I…guess I never considered," Arjun said hesitantly. "I think plants, and healing? Yes, those would be most beneficial."

Tess grinned. "We can always use more healers."

"Agreed," Olive replied. She stared at the wands a little longer then gestured for Arjun to join her. "It's better if you feel the wands. They're made of different types of wood, stone, and crystals, and some have crystals attached while some don't. A wand helps you connect with the Ether, the way the eighth chakra does for me and for Tess. So you want to feel a bond with the wand. Each of the cases has an opening at the end. Flip it up and pull the wand out if it feels like the right one to you."

Arjun glanced at her. "How will I know?"

"Oh, you'll know." Olive took Tess's hand and pulled her back, leaving Arjun to inspect the wands.

He moved his fingers over the cases. He flipped the clear ends open and touched several wands before closing the lids and going to others. This went on for a while before he started looking at the upper row.

Tess whispered to Olive. "Is it possible there isn't a wand here that works for him?"

"Yes," Olive said, "but unlikely. Any wand he chooses can help him bond with the earth, but there's usually one that will stick out to him. It might have the right crystal or be cut from the correct wood. He may even need to make his own. You never know. As much as we practice magic and study it, there's still much we have yet to learn about it."

Tess nodded in understanding. She was glad she didn't have to use a wand, though she relied on her talisman from time to time. She couldn't imagine having an object that, with a snap, would ruin her chance of using magic. At least witches weren't forced to use only one wand. It wasn't a one-and-done deal. But they also couldn't just go down to the local Wal-Mart and pick up their replacement.

Arjun suddenly froze with his hand over a lid. He pulled his fingers back, the tips curling into his palm. With a deep breath, he flipped the case open and slid the wand out. It was around nine inches and made of ebony wood. It appeared mundane until Tess got a better look and noticed the faint vine design etched into the surface. The handle was a bit thicker than the tip and carved to look like a tree stump.

Arjun held it in his hand for a long moment then turned to Olive and showed her. "This one."

"What do you feel when you hold it?" Olive asked.

"The same kind of tingling I feel from Tess, but stronger. Almost a vibration."

Olive grinned widely and nodded in satisfaction. "Then that's the one for you. Good, good. Now, there are a few things you can add to it to enhance its connection with the earth." She looked at the wall beside her and pulled down a thin-chain necklace with a gold leaf at the end. It embraced a green stone Tess sensed was filled with Ether magic. "If you wear this while also using your wand, it will help you connect better with the Ether in the beginning. You'll recognize what it should feel like. Think of it as witch training wheels."

She let him take it then looked around and picked up a small offering dish. "And this. When you practice growing plants, start with an actual plant and place it in this dish. I've heard it helps witches focus better and build a stronger bond with the items they put in the dish. Creating an altar is also beneficial. It's a place to meditate, cleanse your mind and soul, and focus solely on your magic. Fill it with items of meaning to you and powered crystals, herbs, etc. I have books that can guide you. Oh, and you'll want a grimoire to store spells, especially if you join a grove and learn other spells from them."

Arjun took the items into his arms and looked between Tess and Olive. "How long does it take to become a witch?"

"It all depends on the person," Olive said. "Some spend years studying it and barely scratch the surface. Others are naturals and can call the Ether with the help of their wand from the start. And yet, there are still those who practice every day but never develop the ability to use magic. I think you'll have a better chance because you can already sense Ether. But be patient with yourself."

Arjun nodded, his eyes alight with nervous excitement. "Never in my life did I think I'd ask to be a witch."

"For what it's worth," Tess said, "I think you'll do well. And listen to what Olive says. If using that talisman helps, then definitely use it." She glanced at Olive. "He can get it charged here, right?"

"Yes. When the stone turns clear, the Ether magic has been spent. You can bring it to any apothecary, tell them what sort of magic you use, and they'll fill it for you, for a fee of course."

"Of course," Arjun said. "I'm a little scared to see how much this sets me back."

Olive tapped her nose. "That's why we have payment plans, heh."

They walked out to the front, Arjun cradling the wand, dish, and talisman like precious treasures. Tess touched his back, looking over the items. The necklace seemed very fitting for him. She pulled out hers, red magic snarling inside of the jar. "Hey, we'll both have magical necklaces to wear now."

"But you can use the Ether without a wand," Arjun said. "Why do you need a talisman?"

"Well, there's a big difference between how magi and witches use magic, but I can explain that during our first lessons."

"Thanks." Arjun set the items on the front counter. Olive placed a book on top called "Witch in Training" and then a beautiful grimoire wrapped in green leather and covered with vine designs. To Tess's surprise, Arjun didn't even bat an eye at the price when Olive rang him up. He handed over a credit card and looked through the glass top of the counter to several decks of tarot and oracle cards. "Do those actually work?"

Olive flashed a smile. "You can buy a deck and find out."

Arjun gave her a challenging grin and pointed to a deck with a woman wielding fire on the cover. "That one."

Olive's eyes drifted to Tess then back down to the deck. "Good choice," she said and set the deck next to the rest of his items. Arjun paid and waited patiently as Olive placed everything in a cloth sack with the Crystal Corvid Apothecary logo emblazoned on the front. A three-eyed raven wearing a sugilite stone around his neck stood on a perch with his wings tucked against his body. He held a wand proudly in his mouth. Crystals, a potion bottle, and dried lavender hung from his little branch while the Crystal Corvid Apothecary text surrounded him like a full moon. "May good fortune follow you. I added a card in there with the information of Evelyn and her school, in case you need another teacher." Her soft eyes went to Tess again. "And that's no offense to you, dear. It's hard for magi to teach witches."

Tess waved her hand in understanding. "No offense taken. Ready, Arjun?"

Arjun stood there a moment, holding the bag close to his chest. A torn expression crossed his face before he held out his hand to Olive.

"It was very nice to meet you."

Olive stared in surprise, but she clasped his hand and shook it tightly. "And you."

Tess bid her goodbye and walked out with Arjun, noting the way his shoulders had stiffened and his eyes had grown distant. Once they were outside, she hurried in front of him and placed a hand on his. "Hey…what's wrong? I thought you'd be excited about this."

"I am," Arjun said. He glanced down at their hands instead of meeting her eyes. "It just hit me what I'm about to do. And how far I've come."

"What do you mean?"

Arjun sighed deeply and looked up at the sky. "I don't know if it's something you would want to hear. I follow the old code of Hunters, but when I started, I wasn't as forceful in my beliefs as I am now. I did things I'm not proud of, Tess. And I've spent years trying to atone for my sins."

A knot formed in the pit of Tess's stomach. Arjun had told her a bit about his past, but he hadn't gone very much into his history with Hunters. He made it a point to only hunt parahumans who caused harm, and he was willing to go against Hunters he believed broke the code. She trusted him not to hurt her or any of the people she loved and cared about, but the way he talked about the past…something *bad* had happened. "Tell me," she said and squeezed his arm. "Arjun, if we're going to work as a team, I should know, shouldn't I?"

He touched her hand and looked through the window at Olive. "I told you my mother died when I was sixteen, and my father almost killed himself shortly after. I never told you *how* she died, and I feel like the reason is a bit of a prerequisite for a lot of Hunters."

Tess tensed. "Was she…did a magus—?"

"No, it wasn't a magus," Arjun said. He tugged on her arm and started to walk down the street, keeping his voice low. Whenever they passed someone, he grew quiet. "My mother and I went into town to get groceries. It was late, but since I was tall for my age, my father didn't think anyone would cause us trouble. While we were walking home, two people ambushed us and dragged us into the alley. My mother started screaming for help, but the woman who'd grabbed her said something, and my mother went silent. But I remember the fear in her eyes. A man held me, and I stood there and watched the woman dig her fangs into my mother's throat and feed on her. I don't think their intention was to kill us, just feast. But when I saw what was happening to my mother, I panicked. I had a knife with me, and I sliced the man. He threw me against the wall and said he had to make an example of sheep who didn't obey. The woman tried to persuade him to stop, but instead he grabbed my mother. I fought him until he looked in my eyes and charmed me to stay still and silent. There wasn't anything I could do. He made me watch as he drained my mother to the brink of death." He swallowed. "He snapped her neck in front of me."

Tess stopped when Arjun did, watching in concern as he pressed a hand to his face. Her stomach twisted with grief. She knew how violent vampires could be, but they weren't all like that. Just like not all werewolves and werebirds and magi were violent. Rogues were another story, but now wasn't the time to say that. Instead, she rested her head against his shoulder. "Arjun, I'm so sorry."

He sighed. "It was a long time ago. My father initially blamed me for not protecting my mother. But when he realized it was a vampire who'd killed her and could have killed me, that's when he turned the blame on himself and . . . well, like I said, he almost ended his life." Arjun flexed his hand. "I was angry. I wanted to kill the ones who'd taken my mother. So I started going out at night with a knife, garlic, because I didn't know any better at the time, and my father's gun. Night after night I went searching for the vampires, and one evening, I got lucky. I found them in the same area where they'd killed my mother. They had another woman pinned and were feasting on her. I drew my gun, and I fired. My father had taught me how to use one properly so I wouldn't end up hurting myself. His lessons paid off, because I got the male vampire through the temple. Killed him instantly." He closed his eyes. "I remember his mate's scream; I still hear it some nights. In outrage, she came after me, and I kept shooting at her, but without that point blank shot to the head, her healing ability prevented her from dying. She had me up against the wall by my throat when a woman stepped in and killed her." He glanced at Tess. "A Huntress. She'd been tracking the same vampires, and she was impressed I'd killed one. Therefore, she offered to train me.

"She taught me the ancient code of the Hunters. How we're supposed to protect the innocent from parahumans. But what she never elaborated on was how we were also supposed to protect parahumans from other parahumans. She was more like the Hunters you know. We worked together, me as her apprentice. The first target I was assigned to? An earth magus."

Tess's breath caught in her throat as she thought of Olive. Anyone who even entertained the idea of taking out the woman was heartless. She gripped his arm a little harder, but when he stopped talking, she looked at him. "Go on," she said softly.

"I didn't know much about her, other than that she'd come into the area recently and was hexing people, or some other nonsense story that I, in my ignorance, believed. I found out where she lived, and one night while she was alone, I went in and…took her life. I was proud of myself. I'd handled the threat. But my mentor said that wasn't the end of it. She had an adult daughter, too, who had magic. So I was sent back out on the hunt. Something about knowing that I'd just killed a woman with a child didn't sit well, but they were both magi. Who was I to question my mentor? But instead of just killing her, I decided to follow her. I figured I could protect anyone she tried to hex or hurt. But I didn't see any of that. She lived a normal life. Went to work at a local pharmacy, attended dance lessons on Wednesdays, visited her father and brought him meals while he mourned for his wife. Laid flowers on her mother's grave. The only time I saw her use magic was to fill a sack with vegetables for someone or heal a young boy who'd scraped his knee. There was nothing *evil* about her.

"I told my mentor this, and she reminded me that anyone with magic, anyone who wasn't *human* was evil. When I tried to point out the discrepancies in the Hunters' texts from her lessons, she called me a blind fool." He squared his jaw. "She said I was the reason my mother had died. If I'd been strong enough, been able to act, maybe she'd still be alive."

"Arjun…"

"I know I didn't kill her," Arjun said quietly. "But at the time, the guilt ate at me, and I thought if I killed the magus, I'd prove how strong I was. I wouldn't let feelings get in the way. I followed her to her mother's grave with the intention of killing her and…I couldn't. I listened to her cry over her mother like I'd cried over mine. I threw down my blade. I warned her someone was after her. If she didn't leave the city, she'd be killed. I think my mentor expected me to defect, so she'd followed me. She screamed at me for being weak, and when she tried to kill the magus herself, I took up my blade against her." He grew quiet and looked ahead, his hand shaking on top of hers.

Tess tightened her hold. "You don't have to tell me what happened."

"You need to hear it, and I need to remember my oath." He took a steadying breath and went on. "The magus and I fought my mentor. She tried everything in her power to kill us, but between my speed and the magus's powers, my mentor didn't stand a chance. The magus landed the final blow. Despite being lied to and manipulated, I cried over her body. She was the person who'd trained me for three years, and now she was dead. I tried to apologize to the magus, but she wanted nothing to do with me. She told me to live with the guilt so that if I tried to raise my blade to an innocent person again, I'd remember the pain. And I did. I found a new mentor, someone who followed a more proper code. And that's how I met Skye." He smiled faintly. "We trained together in our twenties and went on missions as partners. And then I watched her fall in love and have a daughter, and I was happy for her. And…that's me," he added with a little, broken laugh. "So, if you're wondering why I'm a little shocked and anxious about learning earth magic, that's why. It almost feels…not wrong, but—"

"It's a balance," Tess said. "You learned from your mistakes, and since earth magic was taken from this world, now you're giving it back. Restoring what you took."

Arjun licked his lips. "Yes, I like the sound of that. It's why I asked you to teach me magic. I wanted to understand it better, in honor of her."

Tess hugged his arm and stopped so they could face each other. She touched his cheek. "I'm sorry you went through that, Arjun. But you're not that same person anymore. You *help* parahumans. You learned that there are both good and bad parahumans as well as good and bad Hunters. You changed, and I like the person you've become."

He lifted his hand and wrapped it around hers. He held her palm to his cheek then turned his head and kissed it, his beard tickling her skin. "Thank you, Tess. For giving me a chance to explain. And for believing me when I told you I'm different from other Hunters."

"Well, having you save my ass and offering to rescue my pack kind of helped." Tess chuckled. She stepped forward and kissed him tenderly on the lips. "I don't want secrets. I want you to trust me, okay? We're in this together."

He pulled her closer and nodded. "Together."

They stood for a time, Tess digesting everything he'd told her. It was a sad, painful story, but she meant what she said. He'd changed, and she would not hold him accountable for the wrongdoings of his past. He wasn't the same person.

She took a breath and bumped his chin with her nose. "Come on. Let's cheer you up with a scone and latte."

Arjun nodded and let her tug him down the road to the Lavender Lyre.

Chapter 6
Alpha Wapasha

Rozene

Rozene swiped through her phone while she listened to the GPS give Jackson directions to Evelyn's home. She'd already received several texts from her packmates checking in to ensure her safety. Even Paytah had messaged her, which made her smile and roll her eyes. She would have done the same if she was in his position, but he needed rest. She checked the Purple Door District's private network for any articles that might contain a link between the Chicago wolf pit and Wisconsin. Nothing.

Her phone beeped, and she lifted an eyebrow when she saw a text from Tess. She tapped it open.

"Arjun and I are headed back to the pit to check things out with another Hunter tonight. Let you know what we find when I can."

Rozene chewed on the tip of her nail, thinking. Rozene and Paytah still had some misgivings about their little pup leaving the pack to become a Hunter. Granted, Arjun had saved their lives, and Rozene was aware of real good Hunters—rare breed though they were—but Tess's decisions twisted her gut. Tess was rash sometimes, and Rozene wasn't certain if she'd joined the ranks because she honestly believed in what Arjun was doing, or because he had a pretty face. Rozene very much hoped it was the former.

The fact Tess continued to share information with them made her feel better about the situation though. Tess was still looking out for the safety of the pack.

She sighed and texted back. *"Be careful. They might have watchers. We're almost to our location. Have you called your mom at all?"*

She thought of Iris. With her husband, Brighton, missing and Tess with the Hunters, Iris was lonely. Paytah and Rozene always opened their house up to pack members, and Iris had started staying with them soon after Tess left. Rozene didn't expect the magus to leave anytime soon, which was fine by her. But she still worried. Iris's history of depression didn't help her nerves.

Her phone beeped again.

"Yes. I told her Arjun and I would make dinner for her Saturday. YOU be safe."

Rozene chuckled at Tess's emphatic message. She flipped her phone over and looked outside as darkness settled in, making it much harder to see the Wisconsin landscape.

"Almost there," Jackson said.

"Hm, can you tell I'm anxious?" Rozene asked with a half-smile.

"Considering your foot has been tapping for the last hour?"

Rozene paused her foot, and the muscles in her calf pulsed. Heh, she hadn't even noticed.

Vic settled his hand on her shoulder from the backseat and squeezed. "Don't worry. Evelyn will be able to help."

"You said she was having problems of her own."

"She is, but if she herself can't aid us, I think her wife can."

Rozene pressed her lips together. Kafeada…the fae. She had no problems with fae, but it wasn't unusual for trouble to follow them around. Their Ather magic was something to behold, and while most didn't flaunt it so they could keep a low profile, the ones who did often gave parahumans a bad name.

They turned down suburban street and pulled into the driveway of a beautiful two-story house. Rozene lifted her eyes, taking in the pebble-like stone walls, the arched windows, and the gothic-style entryway covered in high, dark points. Warm lights flowed through the windows, washing across a little pond with fish and the rich green shrubbery surrounding it. A large stone wall hid the backyard from view.

Jackson whistled and got out of the car. "If they wanted to keep a low profile, this definitely isn't the way to do it. It's a beautiful place, but damn. Look at that wall."

"It keeps her students hidden," Vic explained as he shut the door behind him. "It's much bigger and more impressive inside of the magical barrier." He gestured at them and carried his bag up to the door. They'd be staying with the magus for the night at least, and possibly a few more days depending on what sort of help she could offer.

Rozene glanced at the driveway, searching for her son. But either he hadn't arrived or someone had dropped him off to help avoid detection. It wouldn't have been a bad idea for them either, but she wanted both Jackson and Vic present for their meeting.

Vic picked up the knocker, the metal woven into elegant Celtic knots, and struck the door three times. They waited together under the porchlight. Rozene looked over her shoulder, listening with her strong werewolf hearing for any sounds of trouble, but all she heard were a few frogs by the pond and a distant cheer from someone's open window as they watched a game.

The door swung open, revealing a tall, beautiful Black woman wearing green lipstick, jeans, and a long-sleeved emerald shirt that fell off her shoulders. She brushed a ringed hand through her braided green hair, flicking it behind her. "Well, look what the wolf dragged in."

Vic smiled at her. "Nice to see you, Kafeada. This is Beta Jackson and—"

"Alpha Rozene," Kafeada said with a wink to the magus. "I study my pack history." She motioned for them to come in. "Evelyn, Wapasha, and his wolves are waiting."

Ah, so they did get dropped off, Rozene mused. Smart. She smiled in pride and walked into the house. Her nose itched momentarily as if she'd just been doused with magic. She rubbed her face and looked around before turning back to Kafeada, who was no longer a human woman.

Instead, a fae stood in front of her, her skin an even deeper, richer brown. Intricate, glowing green designs flowed along her arms, matching the hoops dangling from her pointed ears. Her braided hair, now tipped purple, was piled high on her head and held there by black roses. A single vine wrapped around her throat like a choker with vicious thorns protruding on one side. The jeans and green shirt remained, but leaf-like wings poked through holes in the back of the shirt. She walked barefoot, toenails painted bright purple. Kafeada grinned when she noticed Rozene watching. "Barrier on the house helps me keep my glamor in place so I don't have to keep shifting back and forth. Also helps in case I go to the door in fae form by accident."

"Which she's done before," a voice said fondly from behind her.

A heavy-set white woman with plush curves and long, flowing white hair walked up to the fae's side and gave her a quick kiss. She wore jeans and a multi-layered blue shirt that rippled over her body like water. A white cardigan rested on her shoulders like a cloud. She tipped her head, her blue eyes taking in the group. "I'm Evelyn."

"Evie," Vic said affectionately and went to sweep her into a hug.

Evelyn held up her hand. "Gently," she said. "I'm still healing."

Vic frowned and hugged her carefully before looking her over. "They did a number on you, didn't they?"

Evelyn rubbed her side. "It could have been worse, but yes. Come this way." She took Kafeada's hand and walked into the dining room.

Rozene lingered near Jackson as they followed her. She didn't really see the dining room when they walked in, her eyes immediately going to the young man sitting at the table with a drink in his hand. He looked up at her, and for a moment she saw a very young Paytah in front of her. Except Wapasha wasn't quite as built as his father, and instead of two long braids, Wapasha wore a single thinner braid with a starburst piece that matched hers and Paytah's. His warm brown eyes crinkled as he smiled at his mother.

"Ma," he said and went to her side, sweeping her into a hug. Rozene held him close and breathed in his scent, tears of joy stinging her eyes. It'd been far too long since they'd last seen each other. "Have you been eating? You feel thin."

Rozene snorted and nipped at his nose playfully. "Shouldn't I be the one mothering you?" She patted his belly, but only felt muscle. "You're keeping fit."

"Marion makes sure of that." Wapasha chuckled.

"You bet I do," Marion said and rose from the table as well. She smiled at Rozene, her dark eyes filled with the soul of a powerful wolf. She wore her black hair up in a loose ponytail, but Rozene could still spot the sunburst in the band. Rozene and Paytah had given Wapasha matching sunbursts in hopes he'd give one to his wife. And, to their delight, he'd found her in the very pack he now governed. Marion was part of the Oneida Nation of Wisconsin, and while she still followed her Nation's customs, she'd adapted to Wapasha's as well.

Rozene smiled and pulled the woman into a tight hug. "How are those grandpups of mine?"

"Loud," Marion said with a laugh. "And opinionated, but they are *our* children, so I wouldn't expect anything else." She stepped back, and Wapasha wrapped an arm around her shoulders.

"I hope you'll stay long enough to see them," he said.

Rozene sighed. "We'll see. I would love to. And I wish Paytah were here as well."

Wapasha frowned, and his eyes burned with a deep anger. "Is he getting better?"

"Slowly but surely," Rozene replied. "He could have traveled if he wanted to, but it's better for him to stay with the rest of the pack. He and the council were meeting before I left."

Marion shook her head. "Your father can never sit still." She patted Wapasha's chest. "Just like his son."

Wapasha kissed her then nudged her toward the chairs. "We should talk," he said and settled down on one side of the table with his wife.

It was only then that Rozene noticed another woman with them. Rozene wasn't as familiar with all of Wapasha's pack members, so it wasn't a surprise to find one she didn't recognize. Still, something about this woman caught her attention. Scars marred her white face, especially along her neck above her black turtleneck shirt. She sat with her arms crossed, her short black hair pulled back in a ponytail. The top of her right ear was missing skin, like someone had cut into it. The woman eyed Rozene, her irises starting to shine as her wolf came through, almost in an attempt to intimidate her.

Rozene lifted her head and let her eyes shift as well in warning. This girl might be from her son's pack, but she was not going to challenge another alpha. They stared long and hard at each other until Wapasha snapped his fingers at the woman.

"Not here," he said.

The woman rolled her head, cracking her neck before turning her attention back to the table. "Sorry," she said.

Jackson growled in warning beside Rozene. She tapped his arm. "It's fine," she whispered. "She's not going to do anything." Instead, she offered a smile to the unknown werewolf. "We haven't had the pleasure of meeting one another," she said. "I'm Rozene."

The woman glanced at Wapasha then back to Rozene. "Daniella. Wapasha talks fondly of you."

"I would hope," Rozene said with a chuckle. Daniella didn't smile, but she did seem to relax a little now that introductions were over.

Rozene and Jackson took a seat across from her son and daughter-in-law, noticing a nice spread of cheese, meat, and crackers had been laid out for a snack. Rozene got comfortable and stared at the unfamiliar wolf for a long moment. Something was different about her. Daniella didn't quite give off the "rogue" vibe, but there was something Rozene couldn't quite put her finger on. Was she still adjusting to pack life? Maybe she was recently turned? That could explain why her eyes had shifted so quickly. But why bring an untrained, undisciplined wolf to a meeting?

Vic settled down on her left side, Jackson to her right. Evelyn took her seat at the head of the table while Kafeada crossed her legs and floated next to her wife in her own magical chair. Evelyn settled her hands on top of her stomach and looked around. "Vic called and told me what happened to your pack, Rozene. I'm sorry for your loss, both of the ones who were taken, and the one who was killed."

Rozene nodded her head in thanks. "Vic mentioned you've had trouble here as well that might be Hunter related?"

Kafeada's wings flared with magic as Evelyn's hands clenched. "Yes. Our home was attacked and two of our students, Ayaan and Pavati, were kidnapped. Siblings. Their family came from out of town for me to train them the past few months."

Rozene frowned. "How did they get in? I thought your wall was protected by magic."

"It is," Kafeada grumbled. "But somehow they broke both my spell and Evie's. They blew a hole through it. We're lucky no one was killed, though Evie took a bad hit."

The wind magus waved her hand. "I'm more concerned about the children than myself right now. The Hunters were organized when they came in. Shot me full of elderberry and attacked the children with darts. I don't think they were expecting Kafeada, though."

The fae shook her head. "They would have brought cold iron. But still, *how* did they break through a magical barrier, especially one fueled with Ather?"

Rozene pulled out her tablet which contained notes from Tess, Arjun, Paytah, Kat, and the many other people she'd spoken to. "When my packmate infiltrated the wolf pit set up in Chicago, she said she felt magic at the entrance, and it was magic that kept the pit hidden from wandering eyes. They have *someone* with Ether or Ather helping them."

"Ather is more likely," Kafeada said. "An Ether user wouldn't have been able to break through like that. And whoever it is, they're *strong*."

Vic grimaced. "How bad was the attack?"

Evelyn grunted as she rose. "Let me show you." She motioned to them and headed through a pair of glass doors that led out to a dark garden covered in debris. "Kafeada will use her magic to play the scene for you."

The fae reached for the handle and waved her hand, sending sparkles of Ather spiraling through the air.

The moment the doors opened, Rozene's breath caught in her throat in wonder.

The debris vanished, and the garden reshaped itself into something beautiful. Sunrays filled the area with light and warmth. Vic was right; it was far bigger than she'd expected from the outside.

Rozene looked across the rows of young witches and magi scattered throughout the garden, some sitting at small tables covered with candles, stones, herbs, and other magical items. A wide stone wall decorated with ivy and purple fae roses surrounded the training area.

The ground where they worked was covered in gray cobblestone, but the garden was also sectioned off for different elements: fire pits filled with crackling wood, fountains bubbling with water, rich soil and seeds, wind chimes and bamboo pipes, lightning rods and more.

Another version of Evelyn stood beside a vast tree filled with witch orbs. A second Kafeada floated beside her, the two in quiet discussion while the students worked together. A young Indian witch waved her wand over a bowl, causing water to slowly spiral out of it into the air. The teenage boy beside her grinned and tapped the water. He held a lotus flower in one hand and ran his wand around it, bringing more pale purple petals to life.

The wall to Rozene's left exploded with a roar, sending her stumbling back into Jackson. He steadied her as Kafeada's voice spoke in their heads.

"Be calm. Nothing will harm you; these are memories of the past." Her tone echoed with sadness and rage.

Past Evelyn was thrown across the garden, inches from smashing her head against another stone wall. Only a gust of her wind magic slowed her enough that she merely bumped into it and fell to her knees. Blood dripped from cuts on her face, arms, and side where she'd been struck with flying debris. She struggled to stand, gasping in pain as something dug sharply into her thick side.

The students coughed, huddling together and away from the massive hole in the stone barrier. Through the haze, Past Kafeada flew toward the students and wove a protective shield around them.

Black-clad Hunters holding weapons in their hands appeared through the dust and smoke. At the front, a tall Black man stared down his nose at the students. He was flanked by two younger white Hunters, a woman with black-cropped hair who carried knives, and a man with a vicious smile that sent chills down Rozene's spine.

Nearby, Daniella growled, but Rozene couldn't see the other werewolf through the spell unfolding before them.

"Go," the lead man grunted, and the Hunters poured into the garden. Darts flew through the air, aiming for the children.

Past Evelyn sent wind to intercept them, but that meant she didn't protect herself from the two darts that lodged into her shoulder and chest. Her magic appeared to weaken, and she used what little she had left to hurl a Hunter back out the opening. Another she flipped overhead and slammed down on the lightning rod. He died on impact, the metal piercing his spine and gut.

But her magic ebbed far too quickly, and as two Hunters moved to subdue her, others went after Kafeada and the children.

Past Kafeada flared her wings and thrust a second shield forward, sending the Hunters staggering backwards and away from her. She reached for her collar of small thorns. She plucked them free and hurled them after the Hunters. Those who were scraped with the thorns staggered, limbs falling asleep. But those who had the thorns embedded fell to the ground, grasping at their throats for breath.

Another explosion went off, but this one came with a blinding light and a concussion of air that knocked everyone off their feet again, disrupting Kafeada's shield. As the shimmering barrier fell, students and Hunters both yelled, and Rozene watched the male Hunter who had chilled her to the core swoop down and snatch the two Indian witches up into his arms. Seconds later, the rest of the children vanished from sight in a renewed wave of Kafeada's magic, all except Ayaan and Pavati who had been dragged out of the garden, hands clamped over their mouths. A third explosion sent the Hunters fleeing out through the broken wall.

The spell dissolved in front of Rozene's eyes, unveiling the aftermath. A massive hole appeared in the stone barrier. They hadn't seen it when they'd walked in, but it was likely hidden by magic. Debris lay scattered about, and tables and chairs were stacked up nearby. The hole gaped like an open wound. Evelyn walked toward it while Kafeada flicked her hand, causing fae lights to come to life all around them. Rozene got close and stared at the hole. She could see her car out in the driveway. She touched one of the broken walls and grimaced.

Kafeada fluttered to her side. "I blipped the students to a safe place, but I was too late to save Ayaan and Pavati. The explosions and attacks distracted me."

"You were right when you said you're lucky no one was killed," she whispered. She stepped back and took a picture to file it with the rest of her information.

"More than lucky," Daniella snarled. As their eyes all turned to her, Daniella bared her teeth at the wall in disgust. "It's her. I'd recognize her and that lilac scent anywhere."

"Who?" Rozene asked. She sniffed, catching a whiff of lilacs, though she didn't see any of the flowers in the area.

"One of the Hunters," Wapasha replied. He nodded toward the woman. "She knows the Hunter personally, and she usually smells like lilacs."

Rozene frowned then blinked in surprise. "Wait," she said and went into her tablet again. She scrolled through rapidly, searching until she found Kat's notes. "Lilacs. She said one of the Hunters always smelled that way. That could be the same one."

Kafeada snorted. "So your Hunters fled from Chicago and decided to come up here? And here I thought the Bears were the only bad thing that came from Chicago."

"Kafi, be nice," Evelyn scolded and bumped her fae wife with her hip. Kafeada smirked and stroked her hair.

"I told you that you married a sports lover."

Wapasha cleared his throat to get their attention. "What else can you tell us about the Hunters?"

Rozene went to speak then paused and eyed Daniella. Something about the way she'd reacted to the Hunters rubbed her the wrong way. She slowly lowered the tablet and looked between her son and his packmate. "First, I think there's something you're not telling me about your wolf here, Wapasha. *How* does she know these Hunters?"

Daniella set her jaw then folded her arms.

Wapasha touched the woman's shoulder comfortingly. "It's all right. You can tell her. My mother is someone you can trust."

Daniella stared long and hard at Rozene. It wasn't until Marion patted her other arm that the wolf sighed and glanced at the hole. "The Hunter, the woman with the knives? My sister Gale. And the white man with her is our brother, Hendrickson."

Rozene sucked in a sharp breath. Jackson moved closer to her side, his hand spreading and starting to grow claws, but Rozene grasped his wrist and shook her head. "Explain. How did you come to be with my son's pack? And are you only with him to track the Hunters?" She looked at Wapasha. "Can *she* be trusted?"

Daniella narrowed her eyes, but before she could speak, Wapasha stepped in front of her. "Yes. When I was still earning my rank in the pack, one of our wolves fell in love with Daniella while she was human. She agreed to be changed, and he bit her." He glanced at Daniella who looked away. "The transformation didn't go well."

"I lost my mind," Daniella said bluntly. "Begged my family for help, but they couldn't do anything." She curled her lip. "Well, except kill me. They were all Hunters. Funny that a Hunter would fall for a parahuman, right?" She looked down at her hands. "I didn't know my strength. I was angry, and I attacked my parents, and when I smelled their blood I . . ." she sighed. "Everything just kind of went dark. The next thing I remember, Gale and Hendrickson had me in chains, bloody, broken. They planned to sell me to a fighting ring. I guess they didn't want to get their hands dirty by killing me."

"But they killed our wolf," Wapasha said. "He'd come back to us to tell us what had happened to her. We promised we would get her out of the fighting ring. He said he'd do it himself; he didn't want anyone else to get hurt. He didn't get the chance though. The Hunters found him first. Killed him."

Rozene eyed Daniella. "And how did you get away?"

"My sister," Daniella said. "Gale told Hendrickson she would take me to the ring. I thought she was planning to kill me herself. But when we were far enough away, with me stuck in a cage, she dropped me off in the middle of the woods right after a snowstorm. She didn't say a word, just left." She rubbed her arm and nodded to Wapasha. "Wapasha and Marion were the ones who found me. I was still half mad. The pack wanted to do away with me. Wapasha wanted to give me a chance."

Marion touched her chest. "It's not her fault the transition didn't go well. We worked with her. Helped her hunt to get adjusted to her wolf." She waved her hand. "We've kept her safe and hidden; we didn't need her siblings finding her."

"Not before I find them myself," Daniella said with a growl. "Hendrickson would have sold me or killed me himself. Gale?" The snarl faded a little. "Well, I can at least track her scent better than anyone else. And that," she waved toward the ghostly scent surrounding the wall, "was Gale."

Rozene studied the wolf. A Hunter turned parahuman. It wasn't like it had never happened before, but she was a bit put off that Wapasha had never mentioned it. Then again, he'd done exactly what Rozene and Paytah often did these days: take in strays. Wasn't their pack full of former lone wolves? Nick. Kat. Wolves who had lost family or come to them abused and broken.

Rozene relaxed her shoulders. "I'm glad you had them," she told Daniella. "And we'd appreciate any help you have to offer. You were a Hunter. Do you know about any of the bases in Chicago or Wisconsin?"

"If I did, I would have told you all by now. Gale, Hendrickson, and I were trained as Hunters, but our parents were the ones who always made the drops if we kept parahumans for the ring. Most times we killed them. Less work and fewer resources than keeping them alive." Daniella pressed her lips together and cleared her throat after Wapasha gave her a look. "Sorry, old habit. My guess is that Gale and

Hendrickson might have found a path to the pits in our parents' things. Otherwise, why would Gale say she was taking me there?"

Evelyn shifted, calling Rozene's attention back to her. "Your sister let you go. Do you think we could reach her? Would she change sides to help us save our students?"

Daniella shook her head. "I don't know. She was as dedicated to killing parahumans as my brother. More so in the beginning. She never would have let one go. And yet…when I told her about the werewolf, she listened. Asked questions." She touched her chin. "Maybe? I think she spared me because I'm blood. But then again…."

Evelyn sighed. "I was afraid you'd say that. It's bad enough they steal adults, but to take teenagers? Ayaan and Pavati don't deserve this. Why take witches and magi anyway? They can't fight well in the rings without their powers."

Rozene glanced at her tablet again. "There weren't any in the Chicago wolf pit, but if the Hunters have someone magical helping them now, especially someone with Ather, it would be easier to keep magic users under control. Could their helper be draining them for their power?"

Evelyn and Kafeada exchanged looks. The fae touched the wall and fluttered her wings. "It's possible, but the bodies that have turned up have been broken and bloody. They were obviously forced to fight. And an Ather user would get more out of draining another Ather user. Ether magic is more like junk food for us."

Evelyn rubbed her chin. "It wouldn't be a succubus or incubus either, since they can't use Ather magic like this. And warlocks, well, there would be signs of both Ether and Ather married together."

Rozene made some notes. "Then a fae's probably helping them. But *why*, that's the question. I don't know as much about the Veil, outside of visiting Fae Ways."

Kafeada chuckled. "And Fae Ways would be more like a tame amusement park compared to what you would find in the Veil. No, this one, whoever it is, isn't a regular fae causing problems, I don't think. We keep to ourselves most of the time, but if we stay on Earth too long, we can get what's called Ether sickness. Our bodies don't always adjust well to the magic here. It's why I go back to the Veil periodically. But if someone *is* Ether sick and doesn't realize it, they could be doing these things because they're not in their right mind."

Daniella clenched her fist. "I'd rather not give them the benefit of the doubt if they're stealing children."

Kafeada chuckled darkly. "Interesting, coming from a former Hunter. How many babes did you snatch while you were on the hunt?"

Daniella snarled, her eyes turning more wolfish as fur started to poke through her skin. Wapasha grabbed her arm and muttered something deep into her ear. It took a moment, but Daniella blinked the wolf away and sighed.

Wapasha shot Kafeada a glare. "That was a long time ago. We shouldn't be condemned for our past mistakes if we're trying to take the right steps forward."

Kafeada held up her hands. "I'm just saying. A sick fae may not realize what she's doing. The Hunters could be using her."

Daniella barked out a low laugh. "Because you're completely unbiased."

The fae and werewolf glared until Evelyn got between them. "Kafi, enough," she said and took Kafeada's hand. "This isn't going to get Ayaan and Pavati back."

A tense quiet fell over them all as they reined in their tempers. Vic finally stepped forward and touched Evelyn's shoulder. "Evelyn, you're the best scryer I know. We had hoped you'd be able to find our people, and yours. Have you had any luck?"

Evelyn shook her head. "I'm still healing, but I have tried, and there's a block between me and my students that wasn't there before. I can't pinpoint their location. Maybe with more magic, I can do it. Kafi and I were going to try together with her powers fueling mine."

"But?" Vic pressed.

Kafeada tilted her head toward him. "It's not that simple. I give her too much magic, I could fry her from the inside. Ather trumps Ether, dear. You should know that. That's why warlocks are so scary."

"Kafi," Evelyn murmured. "They're just trying to help."

"They're acting like we haven't even considered these things," Kafeada retorted. "And now we have a former Hunter in our midst who doesn't have anything helpful to add, as well as an alpha who is sharing things we already know." She folded her wings down her back and flipped her hand. "Forgive me if I think this little get together was a mistake, especially when you should be resting."

Rozene made a note on her tablet and took a breath to control her temper. This meeting was *not* a waste of time. She was the one who usually calmed Paytah; she needed to do it for herself now. Especially with Jackson growling beside her. She leaned closer to him, brushing his arm with hers comfortingly.

"She shouldn't be so rude," he rumbled deep in his throat.

"Infighting won't help," Rozene said. "Perhaps we're refreshing what you already know, but at least we have more minds to come up with plans." She looked at Kafeada and did her best to keep her tone respectful. "Say this is a sick fae under the influence of Hunters. Can we trace the magical line from here back to them?"

"Again, I tried," Kafeada drawled, only to grunt when Evelyn nudged her in the gut with her elbow. She rolled her eyes. "I tried, but the Hunters must have blipped somewhere else, so the trail died." She pursed her lips and glanced at the hole. "Although…" She walked toward it and ran her hand over it thoughtfully. Rozene didn't see anything, but Kafeada's hand started to glow. "Magic leaves a signature behind. Fae signatures are unique because of the Ather. If I can memorize this signature and look for ones in Wisconsin that match it, that might give us some clues."

Rozene nodded. "That's a start. My…." She hesitated. Tess wasn't exactly her packdaughter anymore, was she? She fisted her hand. No, it didn't matter where Tess went. She would always be a daughter to the pack. "My packdaughter will be in touch with us soon with more information regarding what she and her companions find in the Chicago pit."

"We can hope," Wapasha said.

Evelyn pressed her hands together. "For now, maybe it's best we eat and rest. It's gotten late, and we'll do better with full bellies and a good night's sleep. You are all welcome to stay here as guests in our home."

Daniella grumbled and looked at Wapasha.

"It'll be fine," he said then shot a glare at Kafeada. "Right?"

The fae smiled charmingly, her eyes glinting with magic. "I promise to play nice."

Wapasha and Kafeada stared each other down until Evelyn rubbed the fae's arm. "I'll make sure she does."

Rozene was satisfied with that. She had Jackson and Vic with her, who she trusted, and she knew Wapasha and Marion would keep Daniella under control. It still felt odd to be staying at the magus's house and not with her beloved Paytah, but they had work to do. She just hoped Tess didn't put herself in more danger by getting the information they needed.

As they headed inside, she checked her phone. No blinking light alerting her of a message waited for her. "Please, be safe," she whispered.

Chapter 7
Hunter Territory

Tess

After sharing delicious chai tea lattes and scones at the Lavender Lyre, Tess checked the time on her cellphone. It was starting to get late, closer to the bewitching hour when they were supposed to meet Skye. She grabbed her jacket off the back of her chair and dangled it over her shoulder by two fingers as she and Arjun slipped out into the night after leaving a nice tip on the table.

They were quiet as they walked together to the parking garage where Arjun had stashed his car. They were still a good distance away from the former pit, and neither was interested in taking the subway in case any Hunters who might recognize Tess and Arjun were still lurking about.

The cool night air brushed over Tess's skin. By the time they were halfway there, she slipped her jacket back on and stuck her hands into the pockets. She glanced sideways at Arjun, but he kept his gaze forward, when he wasn't looking at every alley or nook and cranny they passed. She smiled slightly to herself. Always on the watch. She needed to get better about that.

Suddenly, he moved down an alley to the right. Tess followed, furrowing her brow. She hadn't spotted anyone that would cause him to make such a sharp turn, but she knew better than to question him. Tess kept to his side, Ether moving through her veins and toward her hands.

They traversed a few alleys before Arjun spoke. "I'm making sure we're not being followed. I'm sure most of the Hunters cleared out, but some will be left behind to tie up loose ends or to see who's trying to scope out the old place." He wrinkled his nose. "I'd rather not have a run in with Legion either."

"Why?"

"Too many questions," Arjun said.

For a moment Tess thought he meant her, and she pouted. He looked at her, frowning.

"I don't mean you," he apologized. "*Legion* asks too many questions. And I've done a few things that have put me on their radar. I'd rather not have a confrontation with them." He fingered his keys and looked at the garage ahead of them.

They paid a small fortune for their parking ticket and drove out into the night. The crescent moon peeked through the smog and light pollution surrounding the Chicago skyline. Tess rolled down her window and breathed in the air. Not the best smelling, but the freshness was nice.

She curled her fingers underneath her chin and watched the dark waves off of Lakeshore Drive flow by. "Do you think anything vital is left in the pit? I mean, Skye said she found some things, but Legion's pretty thorough."

"So are Hunters," Arjun replied. "They left in a hurry. Something could have gotten lost in the dirt, in the corner of the cave, between the cracks in the walls. You just don't know."

"Legion will have guards, won't they?" Tess said.

"Likely," Arjun replied matter-of-factly. "Skye will take care of it."

Tess narrowed her eyes. "What do you mean *take care of it?*"

But Arjun didn't elaborate. Just how deadly was Skye? And was she someone they could trust? Arjun believed in her. That didn't mean Tess had to.

She sat back and crossed her right leg over the left and rested her magic, just in case.

They parked three blocks away from the abandoned subway. Arjun gestured to the car as they got out, and Tess cast a spell on it, hiding it from sight.

"Hm, that's helpful," he said.

Tess beamed with pride.

The entrance to the subway didn't look any different than the last time, but why would it? Legion would want to keep everything under wraps, and police tape screamed, "Come and look!"

Tess followed Arjun down the staircase. Each step made her stomach twist, and she swallowed a lump in her throat as they came to the chained gate at the bottom. Arjun fished around in his pocket and took out his tools to pick the locks.

"What's wrong?" he asked as he worked.

"Nothing."

"*Tess.*"

"The last time we were here, so were my friends. I should have tried to get them out, but instead I let them get taken again."

The lock popped. Arjun put his tools aside and unhooked the lock. Instead of opening the gate, he looked at her. "If you'd revealed yourself to save them, we *both* would have been killed. We're lucky Trish was willing to stay behind."

Tess grimaced, causing Arjun to sigh.

"I'm not helping, am I?" he asked.

"No, but thanks for trying." Tess reached past him and pulled the door open. Once they were through, she touched his shoulder and made them both turn invisible. Arjun hung the lock back on the gate and made it look locked without snapping it shut. They walked down the dark, eerie tunnel together. The hair on the back of Tess's neck stood up like it had that night when she'd felt the magical entrance.

She stopped in front of the wall entrance and pressed her lips together. Squeezing Arjun's hand, they stepped through.

No chime rang this time. Instead, they were met with partial darkness. Spotlights shined on the ramp and the entrance, but she found no Legion agents awaiting them. Tess glanced around and stepped quietly across the metal bridge. "*Do you know where she is?*" she asked Arjun mentally.

He shook his head and moved down the stairs with Tess. A painful silence hung over the pit, though Tess could still hear the ghostly cries of her friends, family, and fellow parahumans forced to fight against one another. She looked to where she'd last seen her father fighting for his life. Then the other cage where Kat had fought against Shen Yanlei.

And then her mind went to Trish and how she'd sacrificed herself to save them. It was also possible Trish had sold them out to save herself, but in that moment, when Trish had taken Saul down, Tess thought she'd seen the vampire for who she really was. A very flawed woman who was just doing her best in a world she'd never meant to be part of. Trish had had her humanity unwillingly stripped from her and lived with a coven that cared little for her. Well, a coven and a District. Could she really be faulted for all the things she'd done?

Arjun jerked her hand, pulling her from her thoughts. She frowned as he pointed toward a pair of Legion agents crumpled on the ground. Tess gasped and rushed toward them, breaking free of Arjun and dropping her shield. She knelt down, checking their pulses.

"Relax," a voice said from the shadows. "I didn't kill them."

Tess still checked their necks and sighed in relief at the steady beat beneath her fingers. She eyed the shadows until Skye stepped out, her body swathed in black except for the bit of her red corset peeking through. The woman smirked and tilted her head. "Come this way. Might have found something."

Tess stood up and stepped over the Legion agents. "Aren't they going to know someone was here?"

"Yep, but we'll be long gone," Skye said.

"What about cameras?"

"Taken care of, sweetie." The Huntress tilted her head back to look at Tess. "Any other questions?" When Tess didn't say anything, she grinned and looked ahead. "Hey, that cloaking spell of yours was pretty nifty. Wouldn't have even known you were here if you hadn't dropped it like an idiot and rushed to the agents. That's a good way to get caught."

Tess sputtered. "I thought you'd killed them!" She looked at Arjun, but he shrugged.

"She has a point, Tess. You went out in the open, exposed us both, and made yourself a target."

"Considered pouncing her to teach her a lesson," Skye said. "But I didn't feel like getting my hands dirty."

Tess scowled. "I would have blasted you with magic."

"Not if I'd gotten elderberry in you first." Skye pulled a tube from a pouch on her belt and twirled it between her fingers. "You didn't even know I was there. One puff, and you'd have had an elderberry dart in your throat."

Tess ground her teeth in frustration.

They stepped into a gaping cave with bars. It took Tess a moment to recognize it as the same cell her father and friends had been kept in.

Tess shuddered, her chest tightening as a panic attack threatened to strike. Now was not the time. Yes, her pack was gone now, but she would find them and save them. She had to.

Skye plopped down on a ledge and held up something small between her fingers. "*Someone* was being sneaky," she said and held the object out to Arjun.

Arjun took it and flipped it over in his palm for Tess to see.

"An SD card?" Tess asked.

"Yep," Skye said, delighted. "Stuck in the cracks beneath where a camera was mounted. Either someone dropped it by mistake. Or," she added, tapping her nose, "someone wanted it to be found, but not by Legion."

Tess stared at the card and swallowed. "What's on it?"

"Don't know yet, sweetie, but once we get it back to my office, I'll crack into it. The other files I got should be done encrypting by now too."

Arjun tensed and glanced at Skye. "Why not just bring the information back to my place? We all know it."

"Do you want to waste more time?" Skye asked and hopped off of the ledge. She walked toward them and reached out, snagging the card from his hand. "We go straight there, we can check the files I already have, *and* get this baby loaded. Win-win, right?"

Tess glanced between Skye and Arjun, unsure why he seemed so uptight about going to Skye's office. It was just an office, wasn't it? She touched Arjun's arm. "Arjun, she's right. The less time we waste, the better."

Arjun sighed deeply and stepped away from Tess, leaving her hand to grope the air. She frowned in concern and made to follow, but Skye got in front of her instead. Tess blinked, surprised.

"Oh, if you're afraid I'm going to spill the secret of where your office is, you don't have to worry," Tess assured her.

"I know," Skye said.

Something sharp stabbed into Tess's stomach. She gasped and looked down, staring at the barrel of a small gun in Skye's hand. The gun blurred and split into two. Tess had a second to reach for Arjun's back before she collapsed to the ground.

Chapter 8
Pit Life

Nick

Nick skidded backward, clutching his gut in pain. He fell to one knee and glared across the battle arena at the werewolf facing off against him. Scars lined the white man's toned body from years of fighting and abuse. His brown hair hung long and shaggy around his shoulders, though he'd roughly cut away the strands in front of his eyes to prevent them from blocking his view. He curled a lip at Nick and snarled as he darted forward.

Nick stayed in a kneeling position as the werewolf came upon him. He counted, waiting until the man was just the right distance away. Suddenly he pitched forward, dropped low, and swept his leg out, catching the wolf's ankle. The man staggered and fell, landing in a heap a few feet away. Nick jumped up and wiped blood off his lip as he bounced from foot to foot, waiting for the man to rise.

Hendrickson clicked his tongue. "How boring," he complained to his sister. "They should fight as wolves. It's no fun in human form."

Nick glanced briefly over his shoulder at Hendrickson then Gale while she cleaned one of her knives. She arched an eyebrow at her brother. "You're the one giving the orders," she said simply. "Why not ask *her* if she'll agree to wolf vs wolf." She nodded across the arena to a Huntress standing near the cage door.

If Gale looked threatening, this woman was the polar opposite, which actually terrified Nick more. She wore her bright blonde hair up in pigtails behind her head, the ends brushing her neck. Though dressed in black slacks, boots, and gloves, her shirt was a vibrant pink. A matching scarf with sparkles hung around her shoulders. She even wore makeup and an expression that screamed "cheerleader" more than vicious Hunter.

Hendrickson tapped his chin. "Hey, Samantha! Wanna do wolf?"

Samantha flashed bright white teeth. "Totally, hon." She pulled a crop from her belt and hit the cage lightly. "Time to shift now, pet."

The other man looked back at her with reverence then faced Nick again and glared. Fur sprouted across his body, a deep brown coat replacing his flesh.

Nick didn't hesitate. He flexed his shoulders and started his change, forcing it to go faster than usual. After spending so much time in the ring, he'd learned how to speed up his transformation so he didn't become a victim to someone who changed faster. His size grew, his hands and feet doubling and bearing vicious claws. He shook his head as his face shifted into an elongated muzzle filled with razor-sharp teeth. His vision had just turned from human to werewolf when the other bipedal werewolf, who had shifted much faster than Nick expected, launched himself at Nick.

Nick tried to get out of the way, but too late. He crashed to the ground with a yelp as the other werewolf brought him down. Claws dug into his sides and back without compassion, spilling blood across the dirt. Nick howled in pain and whipped his head around. He snapped his fangs down on the werewolf's arm, digging his teeth into the parahuman's flesh. Blood exploded in his mouth, a taste that momentarily disgusted him then urged him to bite harder. He shook his head, tearing flesh and listening to the werewolf yelp.

Another kick to his gut sent Nick skidding. He hit the cage close to Gale and Hendrickson. The crackle of an electric rod had him instantly rolling away. It was a *wonderful* tool Hendrickson had added to his arsenal to keep his wolves motivated.

Bastard, Nick growled to himself and darted after the other wolf on all fours. They met head on, smashing their bodies against one another and trying to drive each other back with brute force. His opponent was older and larger than Nick, but Nick was stubborn. He dug his claws into the dirt and pushed, teeth gnashing near the wolf's ear. The werewolf snarled back and raked his claws across Nick's stomach. Nick gasped in pain and contemplated striking back, but then another thought came to mind. He pushed against the wolf harder, egging him on to do the same.

With a grunt, Nick jerked to the side, sending the parahuman flying forward and into the dirt. Nick whirled on his back foot and pounced, landing hard on the werewolf's back and dragging claws down his spine for good measure. As his opponent yowled in pain, Nick closed his teeth around the wolf's neck and bit down just enough to apply pressure and threaten his life if he moved. The wolf froze, panting, blood dripping down his neck and back.

Samantha sighed loudly and nodded to the bell ringer. He struck the golden bell, calling an end to the fight. "Enough, enough. Get off before you ruin him," she called to Nick.

Nick sighed in relief and pulled his jaw back. He worked his sore mouth loose and stood up, offering a paw to help the werewolf up. He didn't blame the man for attacking him. The Hunters had forced them, and if they didn't try hard enough, they were always punished.

The other man slapped Nick's paw away and rose, standing several inches over Nick. He growled in Nick's face and shifted back. Nick did the same.

"Dude, come on," Nick said once he had his mouth back. "You know I had to—"

The man slammed his fist into Nick's face, knocking him off his feet. Stars burst around Nick's head as it bounced on the ground. He lay there, stunned, mouth hanging open as blood flowed from his nose onto his lips. Though he heard shouting, all he could pay attention to was the man standing over him, fists clenched.

"You embarrassed me in front of my mistress," he snarled at Nick. "I won't forget that the next time we meet."

He kicked Nick in the side for good measure before crying out as his collar lit up. He fell to the ground, grasping his neck. Nick wiped blood from his mouth as Samantha stepped into the ring. Her heels dug into the dirt as she walked toward her werewolf, hips swaying. She clicked her tongue reproachfully and nudged the man onto his back before she retracted her thumb from the collar controller. "Now, Pet, what did you go and ruin his pretty face for?" She crouched and lifted his chin with the tip of the crop. "You know I only have eyes for you."

The wolf moaned and rolled onto his stomach. To Nick's horror, he kissed her boots. "Forgive me, Mistress."

She ruffled his hair and straightened up, looming over him. "Let's get you clean."

"Eh hem," Hendrickson interrupted. He stalked past Nick and held out his hand. "The payment? And I expect extra to pay for an elixir to heal his face."

Samantha sighed dramatically and dropped a card into his hand. "Fine, fine. Ugh, you're so needy, Hendi. Maybe you should find your own pet to enjoy."

Hendrickson spat on the ground near her feet, causing her werewolf to snarl in warning. "I don't sleep with animals. And you shouldn't either."

Samantha smirked. Her crop shot out, catching Hendrickson beneath the chin and pulling him closer. "Then how about you either find a woman or learn to rub one out so you're not such a raging asshole all the time, hm?"

Hendrickson flushed and smacked the crop away before storming toward the gate amidst laughter from the other Hunters. "Get up, boy," he growled at Nick.

Nick sighed and slowly pushed himself up. His head spun from the blow, but he managed to drag himself over to the gate where Gale waited for him. She looked him up and down and handed him a towel. "You did well. Low blow from him, though."

"You think?" Nick grumbled and used the towel to dry his head and neck and try to get the blood off his face. He touched his nose tenderly and grimaced.

"Broken?"

"Dislocated, I think," Nick said.

Gale reached out, grabbed his nose, and jerked it back into place. He yelled, swatting her hands away. "What the hell!"

"You have a double fight in less than an hour. I don't need your nose distracting you."

Nick spit blood onto the floor and pressed the towel to his nose. "Thanks for the concern," he sneered and followed her with his head tipped back to stop the bleeding. He stared up at the lights and listened as more Hunters cheered or booed beside the surrounding smaller rings.

By the great alpha, he was getting tired of this. He'd lost track of the number of fights he'd done between the old pit and the new. Usually, he was alone, but they did paired fights here. Brighton had yet to join him, but both Yanlei and Augustine had fought at his side. When he was with Yanlei, they balanced each other's fighting skills. It helped that they went over battle tactics while they were held captive in their cage.

But Augustine? Nick could sit back and let her take down both opponents if he wanted. The longer they were kept prisoners, the more savage Augustine became. She fought without restraint, crippled some opponents, and killed the ones who proved too troublesome. Even when she sat in human form, she seemed less human. Her eyes held a werewolf glow and she didn't talk to them as much, as if she were plotting her own escape or slowly falling into a world of madness.

Ray's death had destroyed her. He'd thought they'd talked some sense into her, but each time she fought, she only grew more vicious. Gale and Hendrickson used her more often, giving the others a reprieve.

Maybe that was the point. Augustine was doing the dirty work so the rest of them could rest and get stronger.

Because thinking she was letting a more feral side take over was too terrifying and heartbreaking to consider.

They reached the cage and Gale opened the door, letting him in. Nick sat down on the ground near Augustine, who was sharpening her claws with a stone. She looked up at Gale with hateful eyes. The Hunter stared back a moment then glanced at Nick. "You and that one will be next," she said, gesturing to Yanlei.

"And me?" Augustine challenged.

Gale lifted her chin. "We have a bigger fight for you tonight. To the death. Don't disappoint."

Augustine snorted at her and resumed sharpening her claws. "Have I yet? When's the food? You want me to fight, I need meat."

"It'll be here shortly," Gale said and turned to leave.

Yanlei leaned forward from where she sat perched on a ledge. "The next battle. Is it for money or for new recruits?"

"Recruits, though I'm going to try to change it to money. I'm not really interested in their kind." Before they could ask further, Gale left.

Nick frowned. "Their kind?" he murmured.

Yanlei slipped down from the ledge and went to his side. She took the towel and dabbed it along his wounds, staunching the flow of blood. With a low dose of wolfsbane in their systems, their quick healing took longer. They could still shift, with effort, but not fast enough that a Hunter couldn't just shock them into submission. "Must be another kind of parahuman. Gale and Hendrickson only seem interested in wolves."

Nick reached up and took Yanlei's hand in his before giving it a soft kiss. "You're probably right," he said, letting her go back to her work. Her hair brushed against his skin as she started to massage his muscles. He moaned in appreciation, up until she jerked her thumb in a way that unraveled a knot. "Damn, warn a brother next time," he complained until she found the right spots again. They were lucky she'd gone to school for orthopedics or they'd all be in worse shape.

"Gripe, gripe, gripe," Yanlei teased and kissed the back of his neck.

Augustine rolled her eyes and moved away from them.

Nick grimaced. They really needed to stop showing affection in front of Augustine, especially after what she'd lost, but he couldn't help it.

He glanced over at a ledge where Brighton rested on his back, arm draped over his stomach. "How are you feeling after this morning's match?"

"Sore," the cop said and rolled his head a bit to work out the knots in his neck. "But pleased I was able to take the other wolf down. I'm getting my strength back."

"Good," Nick said. They'd almost lost Brighton after a few fights went wrong. The man looked better, but Nick knew he was slower than usual. That alone could cost him his life.

Nick rested with Yanlei, letting her finish working on his muscles before he nestled in beside her. They'd been given scratchy blankets and some makeshift pillows, more so they wouldn't freeze or get sick than out of any kindness of the Hunters' hearts. He draped a blanket around them both and pulled her close.

Sometime later, Nick heard the tell-tale squeak of the food cart. He glanced up to see who was on duty this time and fought to hide a smirk.

Trish stopped in front of their door and pulled out a key.

"Oh goodie," Augustine growled. "The traitor gets to feed us." She leaned back and crossed her arms as Trish stepped into the room and brought a few metal bowls with her.

The food here was a little more humane than at the other wolf pit. There, Nick had been forced to eat raw meat in his wolf form. Here? They provided cooked or packaged protein, water, and other bland food for sensitive stomachs. They were even allowed to shower in a communal area, so at least this pit was more hygienic.

Trish showed off one of the remotes that controlled their collars in warning. Nick growled at her and moved aside as she set the bowls on one of the ledges. Even if they tried to escape, Hunters roamed the halls. And if Nick used Trish as a hostage, the Hunters were more likely to shoot them both. What loss was it to them if their vampire got killed?

Augustine watched Trish with narrowed eyes as the vampire turned to grab bowls for water. "So they have you on cooking duty? My, how high you've climbed since joining the ranks of Hunters," she spat.

Trish curled her lip, showing off a fang. "Better than wasting away in a pit and being treated like an animal."

Augustine took a threatening step forward, but Trish lifted the remote. "Do it," Augustine snarled at her. "See what happens to you."

The two women glared at one another before Trish scoffed and grabbed a jug of water. "You're not worth my time." She filled the dishes near Nick. He growled as well but opened his mind to her, just in case she had information.

"She does realize I'm trying to help, and I'm not really on their side, doesn't she?" the vampire said to him mentally.

Nick flicked his nose with his thumb and gave a subtle nod while still glaring. He couldn't respond to her mentally in his human form.

"I spoke with Saul. The person leading this place is a fae. That's why no one can find it. I guess she's too powerful."

Nick's eyes widened in surprise. A fae? Why on Earth would a fae want to help Hunters? His stomach twisted with despair. There were fae in The Purple Door District, but would any of them actually help his friends locate him? Fae generally kept to themselves and didn't like to get involved in the affairs of other parahumans. So why would one *lead* a Hunter ring?

Trish must have seen the confused expression on his face. *"I don't have any new intel for you other than that. They're keeping me assigned to menial tasks like feeding the captives or taking them in. Saul is willing to divulge information to me, but he's also not acting like himself, so I don't know how much I can trust what he tells me. Anyway, you and Yanlei are set to fight a couple of magic users tonight. Not sure if they're witches or magi, but it's getting the Hunters hot and bothered. They want to see what you both can do since the pair will be able to use their powers."*

Nick lifted an eyebrow and murmured low so only she could hear him. "How?"

"The cage will be electrified. The magi or witches try to escape...well, they can't. Not even with their magic. So try not to get thrown into a wall this time."

Nick rolled his eyes. It wasn't like he meant for it to happen. At least now he and Yanlei could prepare themselves for the fight. He glanced at Yanlei worriedly, and she lifted an eyebrow. Nick suddenly realized Trish was only speaking to him. Maybe she didn't want to risk broadcasting her thoughts to too many people.

"Good luck," the vampire said and slipped out of the cell. Augustine jerked forward, like she was going to attempt to escape. Trish held the controller toward her face and slammed the door shut.

The wolf grinned ferociously. "Coward," she called.

Trish narrowed her eyes and ventured to the cage next to them. Nick watched her as she opened the door and prepared the food. The newcomers had arrived a couple days ago, and so far, most of them seemed to be rogues who tried to take what they needed for themselves. He watched with a frown as a feline, a vampire, and a wolf quickly snatched the food and water away for themselves, the latter two emptying the bowls of the two witches sitting off to one side of the room. Trish didn't stop them. She locked the door and moved on.

Brighton scooted off of his ledge and picked up the bowls. He passed them out. "Eat, keep your strength," he said.

Nick took his food and glanced at it. Slices of cooked and jerky-type meat and a potato. It would help restore his energy before the fight.

Brighton took some of his jerky and plopped it in Nick's and Yanlei's bowls.

"Brighton," Nick protested.

The man held up his hand. "You and Yanlei need it more for the fight tonight. I'm fine, I promise." He passed another set of bowls to Augustine, who was watching the other cage as the trio feasted and left the two teenagers huddled together.

Augustine ground her teeth then picked up the sliced meat. She knocked her fingers against the bars, startling the teens. "Here," she said and passed the food through the bars.

They stared at it in surprise before the young man took it from her. "Thank you."

The vampire snorted and walked toward the teen. "Why waste the food on them? Not like they'll be doing much fighting. You should give it to us."

Augustine bared her teeth. "Back off. I won't tell you twice."

The vampire laughed. "What are you going to do, eh? Can't come in here and get us." He looked at the teens and reached out to snatch their food away.

Augustine was faster. Her arm flew through the bars and snatched the vampire's wrist and jerked him to her. She smashed his face against the bars, and he cried out as she brought his arm toward her canines. She pressed them against his skin, causing him to panic.

"Wait! No! NO!"

Augustine growled deeply in her throat and held his arm tight. "You threaten them or take their food one more time, and I won't hold back here or in the ring. We'll see how long you last with werewolf venom coursing through your veins." She shoved hard, sending him flying backward into the two lycans, who quickly scattered. Augustine glared at him until he went to a corner as far away from her as possible. Satisfied, she crouched down next to the teens. "Hey, just keep to this side. We'll protect you." She motioned to Nick, Yanlei, Brighton, and herself.

The boy swallowed hard. "Thank you. But why help us?"

Augustine scoffed. "You think I'm going to let another parahuman or a Hunter abuse you? We're all in this together, kid. So let us help you if we can." She held out her hand to him. "I'm Augustine."

The teen stared then took her hand. "Namaste. I'm Ayaan. This is my sister, Pavati."

Pavati gave a tiny wave. Her pretty long hair had come loose from its tie and was tangled around her face.

Nick moved closer to Augustine and smiled warmly at them. "I'm Nick. And like she said, we'll help you. Do you know who your Hunter handlers are?"

The teens exchanged looks and shook their heads. "No," Ayaan said. "They haven't bothered with us, really. They take them," he said, gesturing to the werewolf, werecat, and vampire. "But they've left us alone. I don't know why they want us. My sister and I can't fight."

"Shh, shh," Yanlei said softly, coming over. "Don't let them hear you say that. If you are put into a pit, you have to fight. What magic do you use?"

Pavati bit her lip and wrapped her arms around her legs. "Water."

"Earth for me," Ayaan said. He chewed on a piece of meat and passed a chunk to his sister. "But they took our wands. We were stolen from a school that teaches magic."

"What are they going to do with us?" Pavati whispered, fat tears stinging her eyes.

Nick reached through the bars and touched her shoulder gently. "Stay low and try not to draw attention to yourselves. They may leave you alone." Doubtful, but he hoped that would be the case. Why steal children, especially ones who were still learning how to use their magic? Unless…. "Who are your teachers?"

Ayaan spoke in a hushed voice. "A wind magus named Evelyn, and a fae named Kafeada."

Nick drew back in surprise. A fae. The fae here was attacking one of her own kind? "Were your mentors taken as well?"

Ayaan shook his head. "I don't think so. They snatched us and went after our mentors, but Evelyn and Kafeada are strong. They chased the Hunters away."

Yanlei touched Nick's shoulder, and he looked back at her. "Bait," she whispered. "They could be used as bait to draw their mentors out."

Which was exactly what Nick was thinking. The real targets had been the teachers, not the students. Poor kids. That wasn't fair at all. He frowned at the sudden fear in Ayaan's eyes as he pieced it together as well.

Augustine spoke before Nick had the chance. "Just stay close to us," she said. "We'll do whatever we can to protect you."

They nodded and Pavati leaned against the bars, Ayaan's body blocking her from their cage mates.

Augustine grabbed her blanket and passed it through the bars to them. "Keep yourselves warm and fed. If they try to steal your food again, we'll deal with them."

Nick nodded. They could all spare some of their portions for the teens.

"Thank you," Pavati whispered. She sniffled and brushed tears out of her eyes. "I'm scared."

The hardness on Augustine's face broke as she stared at the girl. She glanced at her meal and, as she set it on the floor near the bars, fur rippled across her body.

"Augustine," Nick said in surprise. She shouldn't be wasting her energy like that! Especially not if she was going to be forced to fight soon!

But Augustine ignored him and shifted into her four-footed werewolf form. She shook out her mottled fur and settled down next to the bars, pressing herself close so Pavati could feel her fur and heat. Pavati hesitantly reached out and pet Augustine. The werewolf turned her head and licked the girl's hand in comfort then munched on her meal.

Nick settled back down on the floor with Yanlei to eat while Augustine comforted the teens. He smiled. It was the first time he'd seen the Augustine he knew. And for kids no less. She wasn't a mother, but she was one of the strongest protectors of their pack. Of course she'd want to make sure they stayed safe.

Nick ate slowly and waited until they'd all finished their food before he gestured for Brighton to come closer. The man crossed his legs beside Nick. They were near enough to Augustine that he was sure she would listen.

"I have some news," he said. "Apparently the pit is run by a fae."

"A fae?" Brighton said in surprise. Augustine looked over at them and frowned as only her wolf face could.

Nick nodded. "And the ones Yanlei and I are fighting are magi or witches." He touched Yanlei's hand. "Electric fence. Don't get thrown into them."

Brighton grimaced. "They're letting magi or witches use their powers?"

"I guess they're confident enough that this fae can stop them if they try to escape." He rubbed his legs with both hands, working out a few sore muscles from the last fight. "It's more information than we had to work with."

Brighton's shoulders fell. "But if there's a fae guarding this place, how the hell are we supposed to get out? Or be found?"

Nick shook his head. "I don't know, but I think the best chance we have is to make friends rather than enemies." He glanced at Augustine who shot a glare at the trio in the other cage. "I'm serious," he insisted. "There are more parahumans here than at the other pit. And if they're letting magi and witches use their powers? We could stand a chance."

"To do what?" Augustine asked mentally. *"Create a rebellion?"*

"Why not?" Nick said. "We have to face facts. The others might not find us anytime soon because of the magical shield around this place. So we try to fight from the inside out."

Brighton looked doubtful, but Yanlei took Nick's hand and squeezed it. "It's the best chance we have," she agreed.

Nick looked at Augustine who reluctantly bobbed her head in agreement. He nodded in return. "Then we have work to do. Talk with your opponents. Get whatever information you can, and if you feel they'd be willing to join the cause, tell them what we have planned."

And hopefully they wouldn't be the only ones with that idea.

Chapter 9
Duo Duel

Nick

Nick rested against Yanlei as they waited for Gale and Hendrickson to retrieve them for their next battle. He kept an eye on the teens while Augustine slept next to them (or pretended to sleep, he couldn't quite tell). His gaze drifted out of his prison to the other captives, studying the cage structures and the people trapped inside. Some of the parahumans slumped with exhaustion and defeat. Others prowled like trapped animals. And some lounged on ledges, as if resigned to their fate and content with it. It made him think of the man he'd fought that morning.

He hoped he died before he became that submissive.

Hunters came and went, checking on the parahumans and bringing some to battle or to the showers. Nick didn't pay attention to much of it until one of the cages near the end of the hall was opened. A short man with a scruffy beard and long hair was yanked out. Nick hadn't noticed him before, and he hardly looked like someone who was fit to fight. In fact, based on the way his eyes jolted around the room, he appeared half mad. He whimpered as a leash was attached to his collar.

"No, no, please," he begged. "Not again. Not again!" He reached for the cell and grabbed a bar, trying to break free. But the Hunter jerked the leash hard, causing the man to choke and lose his grip. He grasped his head, sobbing. "Don't, not again. I don't want her to do it again. You told me that was the last time!" He clawed at his face with his fingers. "Kill me. Kill me!" he pleaded and tugged back on the leash.

The Hunter looked at him with boredom. "It's your turn. I don't make the rules."

The parahuman panted and looked around frantically for help, but of course, none came. He touched the collar with his hand then closed his eyes.

Nick tensed.

Fur sprouted across the man's hands and cat claws sliced through his flesh. The werecat brought the claws to his neck, just above the collar.

"Shit," Nick swore and looked sharply at the teens who were watching the struggle. Augustine scrambled to her feet, blocking their view.

Nick glanced back at the same time the werecat fell to the ground, blood pouring out of his throat. The Hunter shouted and knelt down, reaching to staunch the flow. But it was too late. The werecat's arm flopped to the side, his eyes staring vacantly up to the ceiling.

Nick grimaced and held Yanlei tighter. What horror awaited him that had made him take his own life? Had he battled too many times in the pit? Who was the "her" he'd mentioned? Nick swallowed a lump in his throat as more Hunters moved in to clean up the body and blood without an ounce of remorse. The other parahumans had fallen silent, watching as the werecat's body was dragged away.

The same Hunter returned after a few moments and ventured into the werecat's cage. This time, he pulled out a younger man who looked just as haunted. The Hunter shackled his wrists together and attached them to a chain at his waist before guiding him through the hall. The young man looked at the stain on the ground where the older cat had died. Tears ran down his cheeks, and he bowed his head, following the Hunter through the hall.

Augustine folded her legs beneath her and flopped to the floor. *"What the hell just happened?"* she asked.

Nick shook his head. A desperate man had been driven to suicide. How long had he been here?

How long before the rest of them went mad?

His nose twitched, and he glanced at the door as Gale appeared, the lilac fragrance following her. He squeezed Yanlei's shoulder and got to his feet as the Hunter opened the door. Gale motioned to them both and he and Yanlei headed out, leaving Brighton and Augustine to rest.

Nick searched for Hendrickson, but there was no sign of the Hunter. "Where's your brother?"

"Busy," Gale said and guided them away from their cell. He was thankful not to be dragged around with a pole any longer. Gale and Hendrickson had made it painfully clear what would happen if they tried to escape. His neck sometimes still ached from the shocks he'd received upon arriving at the pit. "You're fighting against a water magus and a fire witch who will have a wand available."

Nick lifted an eyebrow. "How do you make sure they don't try to kill all of you?" Best to play dumb so she didn't realize Trish was talking to him.

"They're collared like the rest of you. And we have our ways to stay safe."

Nick didn't like the way she said that. He frowned at her then stretched his arms over his head. "Are we going wolf, human, what?"

"Whatever you think will help you defeat them," she said. "No killing. Their handler doesn't enjoy fights to the death. We managed to make it a fight for money."

Nick rolled his eyes. Of course it was. Well, at least he and Yanlei only had to focus on putting the magic users down. The witch would probably be easier to take out. Get the wand away and knock him or her out. He glanced at Yanlei. He was better in his bipedal form than human, but Yanlei? Her speed in her four-footed form could almost rival an avian's. She smiled at him and brushed her hand against his, offering him silent encouragement. He touched her hand back then grimaced as they walked into the brightly lit main room.

The roar of fighting assailed his ears and made him touch them both to drown out the sound. The bright lights stung his eyes. He glanced at the cages, noting that most of them were full and Hunters were crowded around, cheering and booing. He spotted Slater in the mix, the tall, dark-skinned Hunter—and former owner of Yanlei—watching his warrior closely.

Nick was still grateful Yanlei had chosen to let him beat her so she didn't have to stay with Slater. If he thought Hendrickson was cruel,

Slater gave evil a new name.

They walked up the ramp to the main fighting ring. It was bigger than the rest and meant for duo battles like these. He eyed the fence, but it didn't look electrified yet. He and Yanlei stepped into the pit and stretched as they waited for their opponents. Yanlei bent down and touched her toes, popping a couple of muscles in her back that made Nick wince. "Are you going bipedal or four-footed?" he asked.

"I'll change into my dhole form," Yanlei said and stood up next to him, ignoring the jeers from a few of the male Hunters. "I'm faster, and I can talk to them in private while we fight. I'll try to drive them toward you."

"Watch the fire," Nick warned. "I don't want either of us to get burnt." At least they could roll in the dirt to put it out. He rotated his shoulders as a male Hunter approached the arena with two captives. Gags covered their mouths and they had their hands chained to their sides. That would disable the witch more than the magus. Funny that the Hunters were more worried about magic users rather than werewolves tearing the Hunters' throats out.

One opponent appeared male, the other female. The man stood taller than Nick and had very pale skin and reddish hair. Thick freckles dotted his nose. Nick assumed he was the fire witch because, seriously, his hair looked like it could burst into flames. The woman was shorter but looked a few years older. Someone must have taken a knife to her brown hair, because it fell in odd angles around her white cheeks. She met Nick's eyes and bit down on the gag savagely. He frowned. Great, were they Hunters' pets too?

Once inside the pit, the Hunter undid his captives' bonds and gags. He pulled a wand out of his back pocket and handed it to the woman, surprising Nick. So she was the fire witch.

Nick stepped back and glanced over his shoulder as he heard a crackle. The cage came to life, electricity racing and humming through the bars. The Hunter closed the door behind him and stood to one side while Gale hovered near Nick and Yanlei.

"Don't do anything stupid," Gale told them. "And don't underestimate the witch."

"Noted," Nick said and nodded to Yanlei. Together, they shifted into their chosen forms. He watched Yanlei's body twist and reshape beautifully, the mixed colors of the dhole's coat rushing over her body and wrapping around her legs. She was a small wolf in comparison to his bipedal form and both gorgeous and powerful. He towered over her and looked at the magus and witch. The woman glared back at him and held her wand to the side, the tip flickering with magic.

"Well, this is going to be fun. I think they're very determined to kick our asses," he said to Yanlei.

"I get that impression, too. If you're able, snag the wand from the witch."

Nick nodded and waited.

The bell rang. Yanlei flew across the pit toward the two magic users. The man moved first, swinging out his hand and sending water rushing at Yanlei. She jerked to the side and dove beneath the flowing waves. Before she could strike the man though, he flicked his hand and caused water tendrils to spring to life. He grabbed Yanlei, wrapped her up, and hurled her at the electric wall. Yanlei twisted gracefully in the air and landed inches away from it.

Nick winced. Nope, these guys were not messing around.

He glanced at the witch, but while the magus was busy fending off Yanlei, the witch had yet to move. Was she powering herself up? Or was she afraid to face him? He didn't know. He glanced at Yanlei as she dodged more water and circled around the pair to drive them closer to Nick. He loped forward, snarling and baring his teeth.

The magus sent a wave of water crashing into Nick. He dropped down to all fours and dug his claws into the dirt, letting his weight hold him steady as the water streamed across his body. He grunted and pushed through the waves, getting closer as the magus fought to keep both him and Yanlei at bay.

The water broke, and Nick charged.

A line of fire fell upon him, wrapping around his arms and torso and burning both fur and flesh. He yowled in agony and threw himself to the ground to try to break free of it, but it was like he was bound in a flaming whip. It would not let him go! The scent of burnt fur and flesh filled his nose, and he kicked and yelped.

Yanlei leapt at the water magus. He gasped and created a shield over his head, which she used to springboard off of and throw herself into the fire witch. The other woman jerked her attention away from Nick, breaking the hold she had on him. He gasped in relief and gripped his burnt arm as she sent fireballs shooting at Yanlei. Yanlei dodged most, but one caught her paw and lit it on fire. She jumped to the ground with a yelp, running it through the dirt to put it out.

Yanlei backed away, snarling. *"They're strong. That witch…she's far more of a threat than the magus."*

"I noticed. At least he's just using waves and tendrils and not like icicles or something."

As if he'd read Nick's mind, the magus lifted his hands and sent water above the ring. It split and spiraled into sharp icicles that glittered like diamonds beneath the spotlight.

Yanlei shot Nick a glare, and he grimaced. *"Me and my big mouth."*

They braced themselves as the magus swirled the crystals through the air then sent them screaming toward Yanlei and Nick. Nick dove to the side and ducked low, avoiding several, but two cut across his leg and arm. Yanlei yelped in pain, but he didn't have time to check and see how badly she'd been hurt because the witch sent another barrage of fireballs down on them.

Nick was grateful his fur was already wet, because when one of the balls caught him in the side, it singed his fur, but didn't reach his flesh or set the rest of his coat on fire. He raced toward her, trusting Yanlei to take care of the water magus. The witch glared and pointed at the dirt.

Nick jumped the moment he felt heat rise. Fire danced around his paws as he tried to keep out of range of her magic. He dug his claws into the dirt and listened as she chanted the spell to keep the fire burning. With a growl, he grasped a paw-full of dirt and hurled it at her face.

A watery hand slapped the dirt out of the air, causing it to fall in a muddy pile in front of the witch. Then a tendril smacked across Nick's chest and sent him skidding toward the fence. He dug his claws into the dirt to stop from crashing into it. He lay on the ground for a moment, panting, listening as Yanlei attacked the two magic users.

They were strong, way too strong. If he and Yanlei weren't partially drugged with wolfsbane, they'd probably have stood a better chance, but they couldn't even get in close! The fire and water blocked them.

Nick lifted his head as Yanlei jumped back and forth between the pair, snapping and driving them toward the fence and away from him, likely to give him a chance to recover. But that meant she was taking more blows from both water and fire. The witch glowered and ducked another attack before swinging her arm out. A fire-like cord cut across Yanlei's face, causing her to yowl in agony. Nick snarled in protest and struggled up, but too late. Water caught Yanlei and hurled her back at Nick. She hit the ground and rolled. He launched forward, grabbing her before she struck the fence.

She panted in his arms while the witch and magus advanced. "*I can't break through those shields,*" she rasped and blinked through the pain. A deep burn covered part of her beautiful face. Nick held her steady and helped her back to her paws as he got up as well.

"*I have an idea. We charge them again, but switch targets when they attack. I'm going to shout in their heads, see if I can startle them enough to give us an edge.*"

Yanlei nodded.

Nick sucked in a breath and waited, facing the water magus while Yanlei took the fire witch. As one, they attacked. Nick watched the man lift his arm and the woman raise her wand.

"*Now!*" Yanlei shouted.

They switched places swiftly, and Nick blasted a thought into the fire witch's head. "*We don't want to hurt you!*"

The shout did the trick and caused her to falter. Nick grinned and leapt, tackling the woman to the ground. She cried out and swung her wand, but a sharp blow from his paw knocked it from her grasp. He pinned her and pressed his fangs to her throat. She froze and then trembled in fear beneath him.

"*We don't want to hurt you,*" he repeated in her head. "*We're all on the same side. Stay down, and no one else has to get injured.*"

The witch continued to shake, but she responded back in a whisper. "We can't forfeit the match. They'll do worse to us."

Nick frowned. "*What do you—*"

Yanlei shrieked in pain. Nick looked to the left, watching in horror as the water magus twisted water around Yanlei's body, squeezing, suffocating the life out of her. He raised her up and looked at Nick. Blood dripped down his face where Yanlei must have gotten him with her claws.

"Let her go!" he shouted. "Or I swear I'll break her neck."

Nick growled darkly and lifted his mouth from the woman's neck but kept his paws on her. Without her wand, she was helpless. *"Let her go. I don't want to hurt either of you."*

The magus snorted. *"Yeah, well, we don't have a choice."* He swung his arms, and Yanlei was hurled hard at Nick to knock him off the witch. He caught Yanlei, but the water kept pushing them back… right into the fence.

Bolts of electricity raced through Nick's spine. He howled in agony, his body twitching as the electric barrier met fur and flesh. He dropped Yanlei to save her the same pain and tried to get away from the wall, but the magus kept the magic pressed against his body, trapping him. Every nerve felt like it was on fire. Blood pounded in his ears as he kept screaming. The world swirled in his eyes, light sparking and flashing in his vision.

And then the water fell away.

Nick toppled to the ground, gasping for breath. Smoke rose from his charred fur and filled the air with a putrid scent.

"No!" the witch screamed.

Nick lolled his head to the side, staring through blurred vision.

Yanlei stepped back, her face covered in blood. The water magus lay on the ground, his shoulder spewing crimson. He gasped for breath, his eyes staring up at the sky. The witch scrambled to his side and pressed her hands over the wound, shouting at him to hold on.

Nick blinked a few times as Yanlei limped toward him, and then the world faded.

The last thing he heard was the witch's mournful shriek.

Chapter 10
The Guest

Tess

Tess woke to the beeps and whirs of machines. Her head pounded something fierce, her blood throbbing in her ears. Something tasted bad in her mouth, and she felt the steady burn of elderberry in her veins.

What the hell?

She lifted her hand to her head. She expected to hear the rattle of chains or feel the coarse fibers of rope, but there was nothing except a cool compress on her brow. Tess grimaced and opened her eyes. Her vision went in and out of focus for a few moments before she realized she was lying in darkness on a soft couch. She rolled her head to the side and saw Skye standing in front of a desk covered in several computer screens.

Skye…she'd shot Tess with elderberry.

Tess reached down to her stomach and grimaced, feeling a tender spot where she'd been struck. Not a bullet then. Thank god for that. But why? Why knock her out but leave her unbound?

"Tess?"

Tess rolled her head back toward Arjun's voice. He wavered and multiplied in front of her a couple of times before becoming whole. He stared down at her worriedly and reached to touch the compress. "Let me swap that for a cool one."

"What…the hell?" Tess croaked.

"Ah, our student is awake," Skye said cheerfully. She turned around and leaned against the desk, her hands bracing her from behind. "How do you feel?"

"You shot me," Tess said point blank.

"Obviously. Sorry, hon, but I couldn't have you seeing where my office was located or leaving a magical breadcrumb trail behind so you could find it later. Hence the elderberry."

"You shot me," Tess repeated.

Skye tilted her head. "Yes, I thought we had gotten past that part." She looked at Arjun. "Are you sure she's as bright as you say she is?"

Arjun returned to the couch and sat down near Tess's head. He cradled her head in his lap while placing another cloth on her brow. The merciful coolness eased some of the ache, and Tess sighed in relief. "I'm sorry about this, Tess. If it makes you feel any better, Skye did the same thing to me when she first introduced me to her office."

Tess reached up and touched the cloth. "You couldn't have just explained to her that I don't plan on giving away our secrets?"

"Your phone says otherwise," Skye said and wiggled the phone in the air.

Tess tensed and tried to sit up, but a wave of dizziness sent her back down to Arjun's lap. She reached out. "Give that back."

"Nope. Not until you're back home, girl. I checked your messages." She looked at Arjun. "Did you know she told her alpha about us scoping out the pit? You sure you can trust this one?"

Tess glared. "She needs to know to help us save the pack."

"Yeah, and what if someone intercepted your phone or stole it? They could have gotten information about you, your pack, Arjun...even me. That puts us all at risk." She set the phone on the desk and stared down her nose at Tess. "You need to learn how to sever connections with other people and change your means of communication if you want to stay safe and unobserved by Legion and other Hunters. You haven't done that yet, so of course I took precautions bringing you here. And I'll take precautions sending you home, too."

Tess closed her eyes. "Meaning you're going to shoot me again."

"I might be nice and give you a tea that puts you to sleep instead. Less of a hangover then."

"I should be so lucky," Tess grumbled. She breathed slowly and rested on Arjun as her head continued to pound. "I think I'm going to fall asleep again."

Arjun brushed her hair. "Rest. We're still going through the files."

Tess nodded and drifted off, her hand falling away from the cloth. Her mind was quiet while she slept, thankfully. She didn't know how long she was out, but when she woke, Skye was tapping away at the keyboard. Her head felt better. She held up her hand and tried to call on her magic, but her fire fizzled before it even got to her fingers. Sighing, she snuggled in Arjun's lap a little more and stared at the Huntress.

"How are you feeling?" Arjun asked. He ran his hand along her cheek and massaged her neck, bringing some comfort. She closed her eyes.

"Better."

"Good, because I found something that's going to interest you both." Skye turned around in her chair, a stick hanging out of her mouth. She pulled it out, showing off a bright green sucker. "I got the first files unencrypted, and there's some fascinating film in them. The second set? Well, it focuses on just one group of people. Come have a seat and look."

Tess rolled off the couch. She wobbled a bit, but Arjun's hand on her shoulder steadied her. She ambled over to the screens and winced at the bright light. There were a dozen monitors, all displaying different bits of data, though one screen also had a YouTube channel playing videos of birds and other raptors. Skye saw her looking and minimized the screen. "Don't judge. Even Hunter hackers need a break."

Tess held up her hands and sat down. Arjun offered her a warm mug. "It's not drugged," he promised. "It should help clear your head."

"Without giving you your magic back," Skye added. "So please don't try to use it and then vomit on the floor because the elderberry made you sick."

Tess gave the woman a deadpan look. "Such kindness. Such love."

Skye grinned and pointed to one of the screens. "Watch this." She tapped a button and sat back.

Tess watched the security camera come to life near a hallway. Two Hunters stood guard at a door. They were armed to the teeth and likely had more weapons hidden in their clothing. "What are we watching?" Tess asked.

"Wait for it."

Two more Hunters appeared, dragging a short man down the hall. He struggled against them, his long hair tangled around his face and spittle flying across his beard. But the Hunters kept hold. The two guards opened the door, and the man was thrown to the ground. He hit the floor hard and started to shift.

Black tendrils shot through the door and wrapped around him, stopping his transformation. He was yanked out of the hall with a cry, and the door slammed shut behind him.

Tess set the mug down hard. "What the hell was that!"

"Right?" Skye said, excited. "I haven't seen something like that in a long time. It looked like incubus tendrils."

Arjun frowned. "They could have been, but those were thicker than what I've seen before or felt."

Tess glanced at him with an arched eyebrow.

"What?" he asked. "I've been to the Fae Ways before. Ubi provide more pleasures than just sex."

"Uh huh," Tess murmured.

"Shush, look," Skye interrupted and pointed to another screen. "This was taken like an hour after the dude was dragged in."

The door opened once more, and the man's body was shoved out of the room and dropped unceremoniously next to the Hunters. He held himself, trembling, but he didn't appear injured. No, his eyes bore a haunted look and were bloodshot from crying. The Hunters picked him up and dragged him away, leaving the entrance empty for a moment. A delicate, feminine arm reached through the door. It curled a finger with a razor-sharp nail, and a Hunter walked toward it. He nodded and then quickly retreated.

Skye sped the video up, and this time a younger parahuman was brought to the room, a woman. She walked beside the Hunters, looking confused. When the door opened, the tendrils didn't snatch her up but rather slithered out and wrapped around her waist and pulled her into the room. The parahuman gasped and grabbed for the door, but it was no use. She was yanked in. A few moments later, courtesy of a feed skip, the girl staggered back out into the hall, eyes wide and cheeks white like she'd seen a ghost. The Hunters snatched her up and carried her away.

Tess crossed her arms. "So something's feeding on them? Is that why the pit exists in the first place?"

"Hardly," Skye said and motioned to another video of parahumans fighting in a ring. "I've watched plenty of feeds of the battles going on. Parahumans die quite a lot or are traded back and forth. It's common. Pits don't normally have any sort of magical involvement, especially not from something like an ubi or a fae." She swiped a screen. "Now, this is what was captured when you and Arjun made your spectacular entrance. They tried to scramble and delete the data. Heh, they weren't expecting to come up against me."

Tess swallowed and watched the screen change to the night she and Arjun had tried to rescue their friends. Once again, she had to watch her father fight against another werewolf in the ring. She grimaced and looked away, unable to bear seeing him hurt. Arjun squeezed her shoulder, and she glanced up. Another ring showed Kat and the other woman, Yanlei, battling together. She searched the sides of the screen for signs of her and Arjun and found him guiding her and Trish through the pit with Slater in the lead. She and Trish really had looked beaten down, which made her feel better about the ruse. But then the feed shifted to Hunters running and tearing down their base. Parahumans helped them. If they protested, they were shocked to the ground. Many were shot and left to bleed out on the floor.

Tess turned away. "Stop, I can't watch."

"You're going to miss it. Look, girl. If you can't handle this, then you can't be a Hunter. Death is part of life. And sometimes the good guys die. That's just the way of things. You have to watch it all so you don't miss any clues."

Tess swallowed the bile in her throat and looked back. But she didn't see the main room anymore. Instead, the door opened. A dark figure swept out of the room, gigantic wings folded down its back. It moved so fast, Tess questioned if she'd seen anything at all. Even when Skye slowed it down to frame by frame, they couldn't see much except for a dark blur.

Tess narrowed her eyes. "Are those feathered wings?"

"Yep," Skye said with a grin. "Weird, right? I mean, fae have a mix of wings, but tendrils and feathered wings? And look at that speed. It didn't want to be caught on camera. The fae probably could have just destroyed it, but if they were in a rush, it might have gone to help with break down. Unfortunately, the feed from the main room was too corrupted for me to repair." She rubbed her chin and leaned her head toward Tess. "Now, the card we found in the prison room? That one's even more interesting."

She played the feed and pointed to another screen closer to Arjun and Tess.

Tess's mouth dropped as she saw her friends and father sitting in a cave together, chained and held captive. Nick rested with Yanlei. Her father lay on his back, holding his side while blood dripped from his nose. Augustine was forced into a cage and clawed at the bars, yelling obscenities at nothing.

Tess licked her lips. "How much of this is there?"

"Quite a few different segments. I was speeding through them to see if I noticed anything worth examining, but mostly it's just of them. My guess is they were being watched by some master computer. It looked like there were cameras in all of the rooms. But here is where it gets curious." She sped up and stopped as Arjun and Tess faced off against Trish, Saul, and Gale.

Tess swallowed as she watched herself protect Arjun after he was shot and Trish threatened to shoot her, but then turned on both Gale and Saul. Arjun and Tess bolted out of the room, leaving Trish standing over Saul. She cradled his head and slowly roused him. The audio was out, but Tess could see the flash of charm in Trish's eyes as she spoke to Saul. Then she woke Gale and flashed the same charm in her eyes.

Another Hunter, Hendrickson, ran into the room. He pointed his gun at Trish until Saul held out his hand, protecting Trish from being shot. It all seemed pretty normal, but then the video shifted as Nick, Yanlei, Augustine, and her father were dragged into the room and tossed to the ground. Yanlei looked injured and Nick supported her, glaring up at the Hunters. Hendrickson stalked toward Saul and started yelling in his face while Gale hovered behind them, arms crossed.

Tess glanced at Skye. "Do you have any idea what's going on?"

"Oh, this is about the time that they figured out Legion was coming." She tapped at the time. "Now watch that female Hunter."

And Tess did. Gale seemed fidgety on her feet and kept glancing at Nick and Yanlei. Saul towered over Hendrickson while he shouted. All of a sudden, Saul grabbed Hendrickson's gun and pointed it at Nick's head. Tess froze, her stomach lurching.

But then Gale was there, grabbing Saul's arm and jerking it back, causing his shot to hit the stone beside Nick's head. She pushed him away and shouted at the vampire, planting herself between Saul and Nick.

"She's insisting the parahumans belong to her," Skye said. "That he has no right to kill them. They're her's and her brother's." She glanced at Tess's confused expression. "I can read lips pretty well," she said proudly.

"Okay, so she protected Nick. So what? Hunters would want to protect their property."

"Keep watching."

Saul faced off against Gale. A dark figure stopped near the cave, and a black tendril slithered across the floor and coiled around Saul's leg. He froze then slowly relaxed and looked over his shoulder. He didn't say anything. He just stared at the hidden figure and dropped the gun to the floor. He walked out of the cave, leaving Hendrickson to snatch up his weapon and Gale to sigh. Hendrickson pointed up at the camera then departed the room. Gale stood still for a long moment then went up to the camera. She fiddled with it then stared into the lens and pressed her lips together in determination. The feed died.

Tess was quiet for a long moment as she considered what she'd seen. "So, the fae or ubi, or whatever, is involved with Saul?"

"Seems that way," Skye said. "The rest were left screaming, but the vampire? He went to it willingly, and he seemed to calm down within its presence. But I'm more fascinated by what Gale was doing."

Tess frowned at her. "What? She just shut off the camera."

"Right, but then how did the SD card get in the dirt?" Skye leaned back in her chair and revolved toward them. "She could have just unmounted the camera. There was no reason for her to hide the card there, unless she wanted it to be found. My guess? Your little vampire friend, Trish, I think you said her name was, may have created a second mole in their midst. Gale protected your friend from getting shot. She left the SD card behind." She tapped the desk with a long nail. "Which means both she and Trish might be the key to finding them. Gale will know how to use the computer. She can get close. Maybe even send us a message."

Tess frowned at her. "But how would we respond back?"

"Sweetie, what do you think this is all for?" Skye said, spreading her arms. "This isn't my first time hacking into a Hunter base. I'm going to create an open line…try to connect with either Gale or Trish."

"It could be a trap," Arjun suggested. "Maybe Gale wanted you to think she was helping, so that she could trap whoever reached out and use them to bring more victims in."

"True," Skye said. "But I'd like to see them try to break past my firewall." She typed down notes on another screen. "So we think our baddy is a fae, which sucks considering we don't know its' abilities. The weird thing is that the schematics of where that door is do not make sense based on the layout of the pit."

"What do you mean?"

"Exactly what I said," Skye replied. "That door? That hall? They don't exist. I'm thinking the feed we see there—" she tapped on the screen where they'd watched the fae drag in the helpless parahumans, "—I think that was showing where the main base is. And then when it came out to touch Saul? I think that was it coming to help break down the pit in Chicago and get everybody out before Legion showed up. The fae's the ringleader."

Tess picked up the mug and held it between her cold palms as dread filled her. "But...how do we fight a fae?"

"Oh, we got ways," Skye said and grinned at Arjun. "Don't we?"

Arjun nodded. "I'll show you," he said to Tess. "But back at my place. You need rest, and we can't do anything else here while Skye checks the other videos."

Skye sighed. "Yes, and—" she glanced at the time, "—I need to spend time with my family. Ah, a Huntress's work is never done." She turned in her chair to Tess. "Your friends have got themselves mixed up with something big. And I mean BIG. That fae? Yeah, it's screwing with too many parahumans and humans alike. But I'm not surprised. Fae like to play games. Arjun and I gotta go in."

Arjun nodded in agreement, and Tess tensed. "I'll get in touch with our other contacts. See if we can get a few more Hunters to help."

"Wait, wait, wait, you're going to try to go up against these Hunters too?" Tess said. "I thought you were helping so I could send the pack in."

Skye barked out a laugh. "Honey, your fellow parahumans are getting plucked off the street. They haven't been able to stop this. What do you think a single pack can do?"

Tess frowned. It wouldn't just be a single pack, or so she hoped. That was the point of Rozene going up to Wisconsin, to recruit help from a magus and another pack. But she didn't think she wanted to tell Skye that, not after the woman had drugged her. "So, what, you and Arjun are going to go in as a wrecking ball team and try to take them down yourselves? What makes you think you can survive against a fae like that?"

Skye smiled. "We have practice. And besides, you're going to teach Arjun to use some magic. That'll come in handy."

Tess laughed this time. "It takes years to learn magic. If a magus can't fight that, neither can Arjun. I …what if you just scare them off again? Then we'll be on another wild goose chase."

Skye drummed her fingers on the desk. "Like I said, honey, I have connections. Trust me."

"Trust you, right. Trust the person who drugged me to keep her secrets safe."

Skye stretched out her fingers and admired her nails. "Better than someone airing out all her dirty laundry for the world to see."

Tess stood up sharply, hands fisted at her side. But Skye was immediately in her face, their noses almost touching.

"Sit down, princess, before you get yourself hurt," Skye said. "Face it. You screwed up going in there the first time. You didn't bring in help, and they escaped because of you."

"Skye," Arjun tried to interrupt, but Skye cut him off.

"Nah, nah, she needs to hear it, Arjun." She poked Tess in the chest, knocking her back a few steps. "You went in unprepared. You tipped them off. You left one of your own to fend for herself so you and Arjun could escape. Yeah, you alerted Legion, but too late. And you know what? They didn't go in right away, because that pit wasn't the big one. The one governed by that thing?" She pointed at the screen with the fae's hall. "That's the big one. That's the one we need to invade, the one we gotta take down, otherwise this will keep happening. And more people are gonna die. So you are gonna need to learn to sit down, shut up, and take orders before you get anyone else killed."

Tess shrank under Skye's accusatory gaze. She sank into her chair and stared at her hands. Memories of Ray's dead face flashed in front of her eyes. Trish's voice, urging her to escape and save herself, echoed in her ears. Legion's video feed when they found the dead parahumans and Kat lying in a bloody, broken mess buzzed in her mind.

Skye was right. She'd done this. Her failure to gather intel and wait had led to their deaths. And now she was planning to run in with Rozene and the other packs, like they'd be able to stop this thing at all. They couldn't, not without help.

She looked up at Skye, the woman still towering over her. "Then tell me how to help. Tell me what to do to make sure I don't get people killed again."

Skye nodded. "Asking that is the first step. You wait. You go and focus on training Arjun, and he'll get you into shape to be a better fighter. When the time comes, when I've made the connection, then we go in." She looked between Tess and Arjun. "All of us. Including your packs. Including whatever Legion folks we can pull together. We do it as a team and don't go in all half-assed."

Tess swallowed and nodded in agreement. She could do that. Waiting…it was so hard, but Skye was right. If she tried to play the hero again, how many others would lose their lives?

Skye reached for Tess's mug and handed it to her. "Here, have a drink and calm down. You look like you're going to throw up."

Tess took the mug and drank down the lukewarm liquid. She barely made it a few sips before her vision blurred. She blinked at Skye and saw the woman holding a tiny capsule in her hand. Skye smiled and wiggled her fingers.

"Night, night."

"Damnit," Tess managed to get out before she slumped forward into darkness.

Chapter 11
Magic's Price

Rozene

Rozene tapped her fingers on her cellphone, staring at her empty text screen. It had been days since Tess last checked in. Rozene had messaged her multiple times, and while Tess would give a vague response, she never fully answered Rozene's questions. Perhaps she was busy. Or maybe something terrible had happened to her. It did nothing to calm Rozene's nerves, and the longer she waited, the more agitated she grew.

It didn't help that she wasn't making any headway with her son's pack, Evelyn, or Kafeada. When Evelyn wasn't checking on her students to ensure their safety and rebuilding the wall outside with Kafeada's help, she was tucked away in her private sanctuary scrying for Ayaan and Pavati. Sometimes she'd scry from sunup to sundown, and by the time Kafeada went in to retrieve her, Evelyn's skin was pale as snow, the life drained from her eyes.

Magic came with a price, something Rozene knew all too well thanks to Vic and Gladus. She wished Gladus was here now. Rozene didn't doubt Evelyn's skill or determination. She just felt the Violet Marshall, rest her soul, would have either had more connections with people or somehow found a way to break through by now. That had been Gladus's way. When someone was in trouble, she'd never rested until they were safe. Unfortunately, that had led to her death.

Rozene pinched her eyes and set up her tablet on the reading nook in her guest bedroom. She turned on Zoom and waited for Paytah to log in.

Someone knocked on the door.

Rozene kept her head down as she read through her notes. "Come in." Her nose twitched as the door opened and Jackson stepped in, carrying a fresh mug of chai tea. He walked to her side and set the mug down along with a plate of eggs, fruit, and a scone.

"I thought you might be hungry. I didn't want you to miss breakfast while talking to Paytah."

Rozene smiled and patted Jackson's arm affectionately. "Thank you. I was distracted this morning." She sipped the hot tea and leaned back in her chair. "I'm getting inpatient."

Jackson sank down onto the edge of her bed. The frame creaked under his broad frame. "I am, too. Vic is antsy to get back home. It feels like we're at a standstill so long as we don't hear from Tess." He frowned. "Has she—?"

"Nothing," Rozene said with a grumble. "A brief call or an emoji in her texts but nothing else. No additional information. I swear, if that Hunter has harmed a hair on her head, he will never be able to escape my fangs."

"Or Paytah's," Jackson agreed. He squeezed her shoulder. "Maybe she's still digging for clues and doesn't want to disappoint you."

Rozene gave him a look. "Have you ever known that girl to keep anything from me?"

"Fair point. What if she's afraid her phone is being tracked? Or she's being watched?"

Rozene bit her thumbnail. "I hadn't thought of that." That opened up a new jar of worries, but she could find solace in the fact that Trish was still texting her, vague as her messages might be.

Jackson nudged her arm and pointed at the screen. "Looks like Paytah's on. Can you tell him to send Tamara my love?"

"Of course." Rozene leaned over cand gave Jackson a kiss on the cheek. "Thank you again. Please get some rest and stop guarding my door. Vic's already put a ward up around it just in case there's trouble."

"You know I worry," Jackson said as he rose. He stifled a yawn. "But another hour of shuteye sounds good. Let me know if you, or

Paytah, need anything." He gave a tiny salute then left, shutting the door behind him.

Rozene took another sip of tea and started the video chat. The moment Paytah's face popped up on her screen, she relaxed. "My love," she greeted him. "You look so tired."

Dark circles hung like crescent moons beneath his warm eyes. He sat in his office at home, a mug of coffee close by, his hands steepled in front of him. He offered a tired smile. "I feel better now that I see you. You look tired, too."

Rozene sighed. "I've been trying to get sleep, but I feel like I should be out there doing something. I hate waiting."

Paytah chuckled deep in his throat. "Aren't you always the one telling me patience is a virtue?"

"Hang patience," Rozene said and cracked a weary smile that soon fell into a frown. "I just want our pups home."

"I know. I do, too. I do have some good news for you."

"Oh?"

"Kat and Carmen are home. They were released yesterday, though Carmen will need physical therapy for her legs."

Rozene grinned broadly. "Oh, that does my heart good to hear. Is Kat with Bianca?"

"Yes," Paytah said, then chuckled. "But I managed to convince both of them to stay at the house for a few days while Kat heals so the pack and I can also keep watch over her. They're resting together in one of the guest rooms right now, and Tamara is nearby in case they need anything."

"Hmm, good," Rozene said. "Jackson misses Tamara and sends his love."

"You can send it right back to him," Paytah replied. He wrapped his hands around his mug of coffee. "So, any news from Tess?"

Rozene shook her head. "Not since she told me she was going with Arjun to visit one of his friends. I'm worried she's gotten caught up in more than she can handle and something happened to her. Has her mother had any luck?"

"They've talked, but only briefly. They were supposed to have dinner, and Tess canceled on her. She apologized profusely but didn't give a reason why she couldn't meet with her mother. I have Iris staying here as well so she's around family." His voice dropped a notch that told Rozene something was very wrong. "Rozene, I'm worried about her. She's started scrying for Brighton and Tess both. Tamara found her passed out in her room with her nose gushing blood the other day. We've had to drug her food twice to get her to sleep, because her anxiety is keeping her up. She's depressed. And if at least one of them doesn't come home soon, I don't know what she's going to do."

Rozene stiffened. "You don't…she's not suicidal, is she?"

"I don't know, Rozene," Paytah said honestly and ran his fingers through his hair. "Both she and Tess struggle with anxiety, and Iris fights depression too. She's declined since Brighton went missing, and now Tess? She's getting thinner, letting herself go. The pack is taking turns watching over her and making sure she gets to her therapy appointments, but they're not enough. If you get in touch with Tess for more than a few minutes, tell her her mother needs her."

"I will," Rozene promised. She pressed her hand beneath her chin, frowning. Iris was usually such a calm, personable woman on the outside, but they knew she struggled with her inner demons. And she wasn't the only one. Becky took medication for anxiety, and Ray had too while he was alive. She grimaced at the thought of him. Ray. Her heart ached for him all over again. Something had to go right. They knew one of the Hunters. They assumed it was a fae who was behind the pits. Why couldn't they make any more progress than that?

"Rozene?" Paytah said.

She pressed her hands to her forehead and closed her eyes. "I've never felt this helpless before. Ray's dead. Augustine, Brighton, Nick, and Tess are who knows where. And we still have no idea where the pit is located."

"I know. But we can't give up on them. Our wolves are headstrong. Nick is a natural alpha. He'll find a way to pull them together and keep them alive until we get there."

Rozene curled her hand beneath her chin and looked at her beloved mate. "Deep down I know you're right, but when I close my eyes I keep seeing Ray's face, and then I imagine it becoming Nick, or Brighton, or Augustine, or Tess." She shook her head. "We can't lose any more."

"We won't," Paytah replied, a deep determination in his voice. "Jackson is with you. The others are with me and checking in often.

I've spoken with the rest of the council members. Selene and Joseph both have their vampires out at night, checking for signs of trouble and traveling together. Mia's prides are acting as backups to the vampires, thanks to their night vision. Carlos and the cloisters are searching during the day alongside Akeno's groves. Vic's wards are setting up protection spells around the Purple Door District here." He smiled. "If any good comes out of this, it's the fact that the council has agreed to put aside its differences and work toward the common good. We're banding together, helping each other. Even the Chicago Fae Way has offered support."

Rozene blinked in surprise. "They normally keep to themselves!"

"That's what I thought, too, but Akeno reached out to them personally and one of their representatives said he'd inform us if he heard anything odd happen in the Way."

Rozene leaned back and narrowed her eyes. That seemed like such a strange offer. But then she thought about the hole in the wall, and the conclusion they'd reached about a fae being involved in this. "Paytah… have fae gone missing too?"

He opened and shut his mouth before nodding. "How did you know?"

"Just a hunch," Rozene said. "We think a fae is the one hiding the pits. I was wondering if they were helping because fae had gone missing or because they felt guilty that a fae was the one causing us all this trouble."

Paytah shook his head. "It's not guilt. If anything, it's worry. The representative said a few fae have vanished, and even after checking in the Veil to see if they'd been extinguished and reborn, he hasn't seen anything. But…there is a rumor." He looked to his left where his computer was and typed a few things in. "There's a fae at large. Details have been shared around many Ways. A fae was banished from the Veil a long time ago as punishment for . . . well, he just said an egregious crime. But that fae has been spotted snatching others away in the dead of night. They didn't bring it to our attention because they thought it was just a fae problem, but when they heard about the wolf pits, the Hunters, and all of our missing people? And the fact that we couldn't detect them?" He looked back at her. "They think it could be the same fae."

"Who is it?" Rozene asked, her throat tightening.

"Her name is Vesp, and she's a dream fae. She's able to manipulate people's dreams and cause them to be good or bad. She draws energy from and survives off of them. They said after she was banished to Earth, they rarely saw her, but then fae started claiming they were waking with nightmares. At the foots of their beds they saw a dark figure hovering over them, draining them of their Ather magic. They were too weak to call for help."

Rozene pinched the bridge of her nose. "So the Hunters could be aligned with this Vesp. Well, she'd certainly have plenty to feast on with parahumans trapped in a fighting ring. What other sorts of dreams are they supposed to have?" She rubbed her arms anxiously, a chill running up her spine. That didn't sound promising at all. While it was good to know the fae would be helping them in this endeavor, knowing there was a mad, corrupt fae out there who could make someone have nightmares or relive their worst memories left a pit in her stomach.

She frowned then sat up straight, her eyes wide. "Paytah…I need to make a call."

"Rozene?"

"Stay on the line. I'm going to call using my cell phone and put it on speaker." She grabbed her phone and checked the number for Crystal Corvid Apothecary. She dialed and tapped her foot under the desk, her stomach twisting. "Pick up," she murmured.

A moment later, Olive's bright voice chimed on the other end. "This is Crystal Corvid Apothecary, Olive speaking. What magical items do you require?"

"Olive, it's Rozene and Paytah. Do you have a moment to talk?"

"Rozene! Of course. Hang on." There was the sound of a hand going over the phone, but Rozene could still hear Olive call out. "Matthias! Watch the front of the store. I need to take this call." A few shuffling sounds later, and Olive was back on. "What can I help you with, Rozene? How are your pups?"

"Home, thankfully, or at least Kat and Carmen are. Listen, I want to talk to you about the garden outside your shop."

"The garden?" Olive said in surprise. "All right, I'll try to help."

Rozene closed her eyes, reflecting back to when she'd stood at the window and stared out into the greenery. Ray's dead face rushed back to her, and she shivered. "You told me the witch balls protect people, and your apothecary, from bad dreams and omens, right?"

"Yes."

"Kat and I both saw something there. I saw my pack mate's dead face. Do you know what Kat saw?"

Olive made a thoughtful noise in her throat. "She did mention she had been having nightmares. She didn't tell me that day, but . . . oh, oh right. When she came to get more herbs to help her sleep, she said she had been dealing with an ex-lover, and he was the one haunting her dreams. I switched up the herbs I gave her, and that seemed to help."

Rozene nodded slowly. "Have you heard anything about a dream fae on the loose, causing nightmares?"

"No…although…." Olive grew quiet for a moment. "The sale of witch balls, herbs, and items directed at fighting nightmares has skyrocketed recently. And more people have said they've seen things in the garden. Is there a fae threatening people?" She gasped. "Wait, is that why your wolves are missing?"

Rozene glanced at Paytah who wore a grave expression. "I can't be certain, but it's a possibility. Olive, make sure you put a shield around your apothecary and cleanse the garden like you mentioned to me. I don't think the fae is in Chicago any longer, not since the pit shut down, but I want you to stay safe just in case."

"Of course. Dear, please keep me up to date. I'll check with my ward members and see if they've sensed anything nefarious about. But Rozene, if there is indeed a dream fae out there causing these nightmares, I fear what sort of damage that's going to do to the minds of her victims. Fae magic is unpredictable. What another fae could handle, a parahuman may not. Ather magic can drive a person mad if it's used improperly, just like Ether can make an Ather user lose their mind. Or…merely being on Earth can corrupt a fae. Be careful. Actually, one moment." There was some tapping on the other line, and then Rozene heard her text message go off. "That's the number of an apothecary in Wisconsin, hopefully near you. And if not, they can direct you to a local apothecary. Paytah, you come here. Get yourselves crystals to protect your minds. Don't mess around with this, Rozene. You either, Paytah."

Rozene smiled appreciatively, not that Olive could see it. "Thank you, Olive. I will. Be safe."

"You too. Love to you both."

Rozene hung up and met Paytah's eyes. "It has to be the same fae.

Why would nightmares increase unless she's lurking around?" She picked up her tablet and her tea, keeping Paytah in sight. "I need to share this with the others. Once I hear anything else, I'll let you know as soon as possible."

"Good. And I'll get items from Olive for the pack to protect us. In fact, I'll pick up something for vampire charm as well since Saul is working with the Hunters. You do the same. I love you, Rozene."

"I love you too." She blew him a kiss and ended the call. Leaving the forgotten plate of food behind, she wrenched open the door and rushed down the stairs. She found Wapasha and the others in the dining room, just finishing up breakfast. Rozene approached them and set the tablet and tea down loudly. "I think we have a lead."

***

"I thought Vesp the Dream Fae was just a myth," Kafeada said as the group digested the story. She fluttered behind Evelyn, her brow furrowed in concern and confusion. "I heard fae speak of her and what she did, but it seemed strange to me she would be banished from the Veil and not eliminated for the pain and suffering she caused."

Rozene swiped open a new page of notes and typed as she listened. "Okay, so what did she do?"

Kafeada pressed her green lips together grimly. "Well, she's not a typical elemental fae like I am. My understanding is that she lived peacefully at first, feasting on the dreams of fae. Good dreams, bad dreams, it didn't matter. But she felt more powerful and fuller after bad dreams. This led her to influence nightmares, and as the energy from the nightmares bled out of fae, so did their Ather, and she drank it all in and started making them weak. It also made fae start to go mad. They'd go days without sleeping, fearing the nightmares, and bad things happened.

"It came to a head when a beloved fae, who also happened to be a dear friend to our lord, Oberon, was targeted by Vesp. Vesp started slow at first, causing minor nightmares, not enough to create much attention. But then she got greedy and pushed the nightmares until the fae woke in a blind panic. She fought with Vesp in her maddened state, and Vesp…destroyed her. Obliterated her with her magic and snuffed out her light. There was nothing left to be reborn.

"Oberon was enraged. He could have destroyed her himself, but he felt permanent death was too good for her. So instead, he banished her to Earth and sealed her off from the Veil, so she could never come back and torment the fae. The story to little fae on Earth goes: If they don't obey the rules of the Way, or they cause trouble, Vesp will come, give them nightmares, and gobble them up."

Rozene looked up from her tablet and exchanged a disturbed look with Vic and her son.

Daniella narrowed her eyes and leaned forward, arms crossed on top of the table. "Let me get this straight. This fae was so evil your lord decided to send her to Earth where . . . what? She could just have a field day destroying other fae and infecting parahumans with her dream magic? Some 'wise' lord you have," Daniella said, lifting her hands to emphasize the air quotes.

Kafeada's eyes flashed with Ather, and thorny vines sprouted from the roses tucked in her hair. "Don't you dare mock our lord."

"He's not *my* lord," Daniella said. "And it seems to me that if he'd taken care of the problem, we wouldn't be dealing with this today. I guess it's true what they say among Hunters; fae don't know how to clean up their own messes."

Before Kafeada could attack Daniella or perhaps turn her into a toad, Evelyn grabbed her wife's arm and pulled her close, shaking her head. "Don't, please," she said softly.

"I'm not going to stand by while she insults my lord! He didn't think she'd be able to cause damage on Earth because she was blocked from the Veil's Ather. And for centuries, she didn't. It's only recently that she's become a problem."

Wapasha put a hand on Daniella's shoulder when she opened her mouth. "Respectfully, Kafeada, is there a way Oberon could come and address the issue himself?"

Kafeada shook her head. "He focuses on the Veil and leaves the Earth to the Fates to govern."

"The Fates?" Daniella asked.

Kafeada opened and shut her mouth then waved her hand dismissively. "Eh, they're kind of like the Earth's version of Lord Oberon."

"So, what, like Legion?"

"Um, higher up than that, but either way, Lord Oberon washed his hands of her, so if we want her gone, we have to do it."

Jackson snorted in amusement. "She thinks the Fates are real," he murmured to Rozene.

Rozene gave him a withering look that wiped the smirk off his face. "A magus at our apothecary suggested crystals to help guard our minds and dreams. Can we get something like that around here? She sent us the name of one." She held up the text message from Olive.

Evelyn glanced at it and nodded. "I could craft some myself. Though the ones at the apothecary are stronger. I'll give you the address to that shop, and you can go there today if you'd like."

Rozene nodded in thanks and set her phone down. "In short, we may know who our enemy is. The question is how are we going to find her? Scrying isn't working, no offense to you, Evelyn. And with no lead from Tess…."

Everyone fell quiet for a moment, considering their options. A chime went off, and Kafeada glanced at the wall and sighed. "Well, while you all try to figure out our next steps, I have a body to prepare."

Jackson jerked back. "A body?" he asked, his voice rumbling with warning.

Rozene touched his arm. "Mortuary cosmetologist, remember?"

He relaxed a little then settled back in his chair with a sigh. He ran his hands wearily over his eyes; he hadn't been given the chance to take a nap because of this new information. "Sorry. We've had enough…bodies."

Kafeada frowned and floated down to land on her feet. Her body took on her human appearance, though her green lips and emerald hair were left untouched. "I heard about your friend, and I'm sorry for that. If you'd like, I'd be happy to tend to him once you're ready to prepare him for viewing. I can promise you he'll look peaceful and like his old self."

Tears stung Rozene's eyes. "Would you?"

Kafeada nodded. "Think of it as an extra thank you for helping us." She turned to Evelyn and kissed her deeply. "I'll be home soon, love. Don't overwork yourself."

"I'll try not to," Evelyn said. She touched Kafeada's arm and watched her go. With a slight shake of her head, she looked at Rozene.

"There's nothing more we can do for now. Let's get you to the apothecary so we can pick up those stones. With any luck, none of us will fall victim to that fae's nightmares and end up in a pit of our own."

Chapter 12
Growing Ranks

Nick

Everything hurt. His back, his arms, his face. Burned or bruised, he couldn't tell. Nick was even afraid to open his eyes, because at the moment they didn't ache. He swallowed hard and slowly opened them, expecting pain, but none came. He lay on his back with pillows under his body and a blanket over him. When he lifted his arm, it was human. Had he passed out and shifted back?

"Nick?" Brighton asked. He leaned over and touched Nick's shoulder. "Easy. Go slow."

Nick rolled his head toward Brighton. "What happened?"

"They brought you back unconscious, burned, and electrocuted. They gave you an elixir to stop your wounds from killing you, but you still have a long way to go."

Nick frowned. "How long have I been out?"

"Two days. We've done what we can to take care of you. The Hunters aren't happy about …what happened."

Nick tried to remember the fight. He recalled getting thrown into the electric fence, but after that everything was fuzzy. He glanced around and noticed they were the only ones in the cage. Nick tensed. "Yanlei? Where is she? Is she okay?"

Brighton grimaced. "She's better than you, but…she took a bad hit too during the fight. And….." He hesitated.

"Brighton?"

"She accidentally killed the water magus."

Nick's stomach dropped. It wasn't supposed to be a battle to-the-death. "What did they do to her?"

"They punished her. She'll be okay. She's still able to fight. They didn't want to lose a fighter like her. But Hendrickson was ranting about losing a lot of money because of her mistake."

Nick swore and dropped his head back to the floor. Right. Now he remembered. She'd bitten the magus pretty badly on his shoulder. "Was it blood loss that killed him or—?"

"Yeah. He lost too much, and they couldn't save him. The witch survived, though I don't think you'll want to face her anytime soon. I heard she tried to fry you with her magic when the magus died, which is why you're in such bad shape."

"That would explain the burning sensation." Nick sighed. "We didn't want to hurt them, Brighton. We tried to reason with them. But they just wouldn't stop. It wasn't supposed to happen like this." Poor Yanlei. They'd held back to save the magic users, and Yanlei had paid the price. All he wanted to do was take her in his arms and make sure she was safe and alive. "Augustine fighting too?"

Brighton nodded. "She's been out most of the day. Food was brought in. You should try to eat something to get your strength back."

Nick nodded and struggled to sit up. It was slow going, but he managed to right himself and lean against the wall with a pained sigh. Brighton handed him a dish of water and he sipped it, trying not to upset his stomach. His eyes drifted to the other cage, and he found Ayaan and Pavati watching him. He offered them a tired smile. "You two doing all right?"

Ayaan nodded. "The others haven't bothered us since Augustine scared them away. Are you going to be okay?"

Nick looked himself over. He had a nice network of burns on his chest from the witch's fire whip. "I'll survive." His muscles ached in protest, but he wasn't completely debilitated. He tried to stretch, but another shock of pain raced down his back. How did they expect him to fight in this condition?

He glanced at the teens again. (He had to stop thinking of them as kids since he wasn't much older). Ayaan rubbed Pavati's back while she nibbled on leftover food.

Brighton sat down beside him and draped his arms over his legs. "You suggested we talk with the other parahumans."

Nick snorted. "Didn't work out so well for me and Yanlei."

"Maybe not," Brighton said. "But Augustine and I have had some success."

Nick lifted an eyebrow in surprise. "Really?"

"We're going by cage when we can. Convincing one person who will talk to the others. They'll also talk to their opponents from other cages."

"And if we're caught?" Nick asked.

"We can deny it," Brighton said with a shrug. "Either the Hunters will hurt us or laugh in our faces, because there's no way in hell we'll be able to save each other or break free. But what else can we do, just sit here and wait? It was your idea."

"I know," Nick said and rubbed his head. "I'm starting to second guess it. But if you and Augustine have made headway, then maybe it will work. How many cages have you convinced?"

"We sent the message back to three," Brighton replied. "If each cage is like ours or theirs—" he gestured to the teens, "—then we can figure that's 12 to 15 people who might be on our side in two days. Not a bad start."

"Provided we don't keep getting pitted against the same cages," Nick murmured. But Brighton was right. It was a good start. He rubbed his head again and looked over to the cage that had held the feline who'd killed himself. "Have you seen anyone come out of that room?"

Brighton followed his gaze and grimaced. "Yeah, it's not good. I don't know what they're doing to them, but I don't want to find out, because they're barely alive when they return."

"That's what I was afraid of," Nick said. The cat had been terrified enough that he'd taken his own life. What awful fate had he been escaping?

Brighton held the water out to Nick again. "Drink."

Nick sipped it, his stomach rumbling in protest. He was ravenous, but he knew not to devour his meal without at least hydrating himself first. He picked at the meat Brighton offered and let it settle in his stomach. It was slow going, but it made him feel better.

As he was finishing off the water, there was movement outside of their cage. Two Hunters dragged a parahuman down the hall and back toward the room where the feline had been. Nick recognized the person as the one they'd pulled out after the werecat killed himself. His eyes were glazed in horror, his entire body trembling in the hands of his captors. His skin had taken on a whitish hue. He twitched and shook his head, mumbling something Nick couldn't hear as the Hunters deposited him in his cage.

"Hm, not a pretty sight," Brighton murmured to Nick. "Anyone they bring back looks like they've seen the face of Hades."

Nick shuddered.

He drifted in and out for a time, waking long enough to take a bite of food or a sip from Brighton's personal bowl of water. He was just dozing off when Brighton roused him with a nudge to his shoulder. Nick blinked blearily and looked up as the door to their cell opened. Augustine lumbered in, blood streaked across her face, hands, and shoulder. The big werewolf settled near the bars where the teens waited and they reached out to touch her, offering comfort.

Yanlei came in next, head bowed. She fell to her knees as the Hunters pushed her. Nick almost flew to his feet and snarled at the men, but he couldn't even lean forward without his burns aching. Yanlei stayed where she was until the Hunters locked the door and walked away. What made Nick anxious was that he didn't see Gale or Hendrickson. Where were they? And who had taken his friends to the fighting ring?

"Yanlei?" Nick said in a low, soothing voice.

Yanlei lifted her head, and the breath caught in Nick's throat. A scar sliced across her left eye and up her forehead where the fire whip had struck her during their fight. Her eye was closed with an ugly burn across her eyelid as well. His stomach twisted with worry. Could she even still see out of it?

"Nick," she said in relief and stepped over to his side. She sat down carefully, bruises lining the exposed parts of her body, but she looked better than Augustine. "How do you feel?"

"Like I got hit by a flaming bus, run over a few times, then chewed up by a wolf with a mouth full of fire."

"Descriptive," Augustine mumbled.

Yanlei touched his cheek and looked him over. "I was afraid when you didn't wake up by this morning. We tried to help you drink water to stave off dehydration, but I wasn't sure if we'd gotten enough in you."

"The elixir must have helped." Nick blew out a breath. "So where are Thing 1 and Thing 2? On another mission?"

Yanlei shook her head. "Gale was there during the fight. She brought me and Augustine out to the match: two on two again. Werewolf and werebird this time."

Nick winced. "What kind of werebird?"

Augustine lifted her arm, showing deep gouges in her flesh. "Bald eagle, but a younger one so not as awful as it could have been. At least it wasn't a harpy eagle."

Brighton made a strained noise in his throat. "Wait, have you seen one of them around here?"

Augustine shook her head. "Not yet, but with our luck, one would show up." She tore off a piece of her shirt and wrapped it around her arm. "Gale went to fetch the money from our fight. Said she'd bring elixirs by soon."

Nick was thankful for that. They both looked awful, and he could go for another dose himself. He touched Yanlei's face and turned it from side to side with a frown. "Your eye?"

Yanlei tried to open it, but the flesh was so burnt and swollen, she couldn't make it far. "I can't see out of it very well. I'm trying to keep it shut as long as possible to let my healing and the elixirs take care of the damage. My hope is that I don't lose it. Shifting hasn't fixed it, and my depth perception is wrecked without it."

"She's learning fast, though," Augustine said with a tone of pride. "I just cover her bad side. She took down that werebird pretty fast after the asshole hooked me with his talons."

Nick hesitated. "Take down as in—"

"He's still alive," Yanlei assured him. "I caught him in my mouth, dropped him, and knocked him out with my paw. Almost missed him; like I said, my depth perception is poor." She rested her head against the wall. Her good eye watered. "I never meant to kill the water magus. I bit down harder than I thought because I was in pain."

Nick draped an arm around her shoulders, minding both of their wounded bodies. "I know. It was an accident. Hopefully we don't come across that witch again."

Yanlei closed her other eye and rested against him. "Before the avian and werewolf went down, we managed to discuss our plans with them. They said they'll join us."

Nick brightened at the news. "So that's four cages that want in on the coup."

Yanlei nodded. "We'll keep gathering people and then figure out how to escape."

"With our mole," Nick said. Augustine had to scoot closer so she could hear better and Brighton shifted to sit in front of Nick and Yanlei so, if any Hunter walked past the cage, they wouldn't be able to read Nick's lips. "If she can disconnect the collars, we can take care of the rest. The bars won't hold us if we change and fight the doors open in our wolf forms."

Yanlei frowned. "What about the others? They won't be able to break through so easily."

"Let's hope they're housed with werewolves or magi who are able to use their magic once the collars are off," Nick said.

Augustine wrinkled her nose. "That's a lot of ifs, Nick. We have one shot at this, and if they figure out *we're* the ones leading the charge, we can kiss our asses goodbye."

Nick had to agree, which meant extra caution. It would take time, but either they'd break free, or they'd survive long enough for their friends to find them. It all depended on Trish.

Nick rubbed Yanlei's arm. "We keep reaching out and hope for the best. That's all we can do."

"And rest," Brighton said. "So you're strong enough for the next match. They might put you in pretty fast, Nick. Both Hunters were pissed they'd lost you as an opponent."

Nick snorted loudly, causing his still-healing nose to twinge. "Well, forgive me for getting my ass kicked by a fire witch and a water magus. First time I fought against them in a situation like that!"

Brighton sighed. "Doubt it'll be the last."

Nick pulled Yanlei a little closer and watched Brighton and Augustine close in as well. His poor pack. They'd been through hell.

They rested together, offering warmth and comfort. At one point, Augustine joined the teens and kept them company. Nick started to nod off yet again, but the jangle of keys stirred him awake. Gale opened the door and walked in with a container in her hands. She paused, startled, when she saw him awake, but then her face filled with relief.

Nick cracked a smile. "Aw, were you worried about me?"

"Don't want to lose a good fighter," Gale said, quickly recovering. She opened the container, revealing a few colorful vials. "Ather elixirs," she said. "They'll treat your wounds faster than the others."

Nick narrowed his eyes. "And how were you able to get those? Or afford them?"

"Never you mind," Gale, then settled her hand on her hip. "Look, do you want them or not?"

Nick held up his hands. "Yes. Yes, please."

Gale passed the elixirs around, one to each of them. Nick popped open the cork and downed the baby blue liquid. Sweetness flooded the tip of his tongue, and he thought he caught a berry flavor, but he couldn't put his finger on what kind. He licked his lips then sucked in a breath as the pain in his body eased. His flesh closed slowly around the burns, and his head stopped aching. It was such a relief that he fell back against the ledge with a stupid smile on his face.

He looked at Yanlei, watching for the transformation in her as well. The wound across her face faded, and her eye began to mend. But the scars remained, just as they would on him. Even magical healing could do only so much to fix a body. He touched her arm and lifted her chin until she opened her eyes. The right one was fine, but the left had a milky sheen to it.

"Can you see?" he asked.

Yanlei's expression faltered. "Only shadows," she said.

Nick groaned and pulled her to him in a comforting hug. The damage had been too great. He'd hoped her eye would heal, but if the elixir couldn't do it, likely nothing could. What if they got her to a doctor soon enough? Could they do surgery? He could only hope.

He looked at Augustine as her flesh healed where she'd been taloned. Brighton hadn't had as many wounds as the rest of them this time, but the elixir brought color back to his cheeks. Nick side-eyed Gale. He knew he shouldn't thank her. She was the reason he and his friends were in this mess to begin with, but still, he was grateful. "Thank you."

Gale nodded. "You have a match this evening," she told him. "Just you this time, so you can stretch your muscles. You'll be facing off against a werecat. I'll avoid magi and witches for the time being. We don't want them at all, and they cause far too much trouble."

Nick offered a thumbs up. He was totally fine with that decision. "I need to eat," he said.

"Food will be delivered before the next fight," she said and turned to leave.

Nick hesitated. Should he question her about Hendrickson? He didn't want the guy back anytime soon, but it was better to know where the enemy was than to be blind to him. "And Hendrickson? Haven't seen him for a while."

Gale paused near the door and glanced back at Nick. She frowned. "Hunting," she said and then departed.

A rock dropped in the pit of Nick's stomach. Hunting. Who was he going after? For a moment, he feared Hendrickson was attacking his pack again, but why do that? Why risk it? Unless Saul was pushing them to do it. He glanced at the teens and shook his head. No, his pack was safe. He had to believe that if he was going to survive.

Gale locked the door, and Nick settled against Yanlei again.

All they could do was wait.

Chapter 13
Pride vs Pack

Nick

Nick rested beside Yanlei, a blanket draped around them. Augustine talked quietly with the teens and showed them some basic fighting techniques. Nick smiled to himself. She was good with them, and if he weren't so tired, he would help them too. Maybe after he'd had time to heal, he could. He wished the siblings were caged with them. Augustine had scared the vampire, werewolf, and werecat off, but he could still see the vampire and werewolf lingering close by as if waiting for her to fall asleep.

Gale and Hendrickson didn't like magi or witches, but what if these witches were on *their* side? The fire witch had nailed both him and Yanlei. Their skills were beneficial.

A squeaking cart alerted them to food. Hunters spread out to deliver the dishes. To Nick's relief, Trish arrived at their door with their meals. She crouched down beside him as she arranged the food and water.

"Glad to see you're awake. You had us worried," the vampire said.

Nick scooted away from her with a growl but nodded to let her know he'd heard her.

"Still no new news for you, unfortunately. Hunters have been departing and returning with more victims, but that's not out of the

ordinary. Saul is talking about having me go on a mission. I'm hoping to stay around here so I don't have to prove my loyalty to the Hunters or something."

Nick winced at the thought. Yeah, he could imagine why she wouldn't want to take down a parahuman, though she was good at it. He glanced around, but there were no Hunters lingering nearby, so he chanced a whisper. "We're trying to put together a coup. Other parahumans have agreed to help us. But we need the collars off."

Trish lifted an eyebrow. *"You're taking a chance revealing this to me. If Saul charms me to tell him what I've heard, that'll put you at risk."* She considered. *"I'll see what I can do about the collars on my end. I don't know the controls like everyone else. But they let me walk freely, so I'll see what I can learn."*

Nick nodded his thanks and picked up his bowl of water.

Trish rose and sidestepped when Augustine snarled at her. They exchanged glares before the vampire slipped out of the cage and locked the door behind her.

Nick drank his fill and devoured his food. He didn't know how much time he had before Gale came to collect him for the fight. Yanlei ate beside him and nudged his arm.

"That was dangerous," she whispered.

"How else are we supposed to get the message to her?" He swallowed a chunk of meat and eyed the cage doors. Trish had keys. She could get in here; what about the others? "She might also be able to solve our cage problem."

Augustine prowled over to grab her food. "I still don't know if we can trust her."

"We have to trust someone," Nick said. "Otherwise, we're all on our own."

He and his pack ate together, all four recovering after their many fights. The hours ticked by, and Nick started to wonder if the fight wasn't going to be tonight. Or…this morning. He didn't know the time of day. Time lost all meaning down in the pit. The only way they knew the time was if one of the Hunters happened to mention it.

He was getting his makeshift bed ready with Yanlei when the lilac scent floated into the cage and alerted him of Gale's presence. Nick sighed. He'd hoped he could spend more time resting and be out of pain for a few hours. Gale opened the door and crooked her finger, motioning to him.

He got up and brushed his hand along his packmates' shoulders before he approached Gale. To his surprise, the cage beside him opened, and the werecat, one of Ayaan and Pavati's tormentors, stepped out.

"I'm fighting *her*?" Nick asked incredulously before he could stop himself.

The feline glanced at him and smirked as she spread her claws. "What? Are you scared?"

Nick ground his teeth. He was tempted to take her down just because she'd given the teens grief, but they could still use her help.

He stuck close to Gale as she brought them out of the cave and toward the fighting rings. The feline walked with attitude, but Nick could tell she was trying to shy away from her Hunter. Any time her captor moved too close, she flinched. It surprised Nick to see her avoiding the presence of a male. Normally, female werecats acted like males were the ones who needed protecting. But this was a Hunter, not another cat.

Nick rubbed his arms and rocked his head from side to side to work out the kinks and prepare himself for battle. There weren't as many Hunters in the fighting area as usual, which brought some comfort. He despised listening to them jeer and cheer as the parahumans ripped into each other.

They stepped up to the cage surrounding one of the smaller rings. Nick went inside without prompting, but the werecat lingered just outside, eyeing it apprehensively. Her Hunter snorted and looked at Gale. "Seems like you've got the boy whipped already. Wish I could say the same for mine." He shoved the werecat, who glowered at him, but she entered the ring.

Nick frowned. Was this her first fight? He'd been out for two days, so she could have been taken to a ring before this. But the way she looked around and stiffened like a cornered mouse suggested otherwise. Well, maybe she'd actually listen to him when they fought. He looked at Gale. "Not a death match, right?"

"No. Just money."

Nick considered the feline then leaned closer to the bars, lowering his voice. "What about a trade?"

Gale frowned. "Why would you want to do that? You wouldn't

want to risk leaving your friends."

"No," Nick agreed. "But I have a proposition. The cage the feline is in has two teenagers."

Gale snorted and folded her arms. "Witches. I'm not interested in witches."

"You saw what a witch did to me and Yanlei," Nick argued. "With some training, I bet they could be a benefit to you and Hendrickson. There's only so much my wolves and I can do against magic users. But they'd need their wands back."

Gale eyed him warily. "And why do you care about them?"

"Come off it, Gale," Nick said in a low voice. "They're kids. Maybe I just don't want to see them under a cruel Hunter's hand. I want to give them a chance. The parahumans in their cage? The asses stole food from them. Let's say I have a bit of a vendetta."

Gale considered this. She stared at Nick and the feline. "You're sure you can win?"

"To protect those kids? Oh yeah." Maybe he was biting off more than he could chew, but if he lost, he'd still be in the cage next to his friends, he'd be with the teens, and he could focus on convincing the cat and her crew to help, which was a win-win situation. Even if it did lead to a lot of pain.

Gale stared at him for a long moment then snapped her fingers to get the other Hunter's attention. She went to his side and spoke quietly, gesturing between the two of them. The Hunter lifted an eyebrow and laughed before nodding. Gale returned and shot Nick a look. "Don't let me down."

"He agreed?"

"He said I was mad to ask for the kids as a reward, but yes, he agreed. Be careful."

Nick gave a small salute with his fingers and faced the werecat. He shifted into his bipedal form and crouched low, watching. The werecat rolled her shoulders then changed.

The moment he saw the sandy-colored fur, he grimaced. Puma. *Great*. Couldn't have been some kind of house cat. No, had to be a freaking mountain lion.

At the ring of the bell, Nick launched himself forward at the same time as the feline. They met in the middle of the ring, crashing together and knocking each other away. She was strong, but he was bigger than she was. Still, he needed to keep his wits about him. Werecats were sly.

"I'm Nick. What's your name?"

His voice in her head gave her a momentary pause before she ran after him again. *"What the hell does it matter?"*

"We're both prisoners of the Hunters. Best thing we can do is work together to make it out of here alive." Hopefully he'd read her body language right. She didn't want to be near her Hunter any more than most of the parahumans.

She swiped at his face and dodged a strike. *"How do I know you're not working with your mistress over there?"*

"You don't. But believe me, I want to get back to my pack as much as I'm sure you want to return to your pride."

A flicker in her eye told him he'd hit a nerve. Yes, she missed her pride. She dodged another attack and he twisted, striking her hard with his claws. She skidded, blood streaking down her shoulder. She growled and lowered her body into a crouch, her tail lashing back and forth.

"Fine. I'm Loretta. Now what do you want?"

"The same thing you do: freedom. My pack and I have been talking to other caged parahumans to see if they'll join our coup."

Loretta jumped over his back and whirled, snapping her teeth down around his ankle. He yelped in pain and shook her off before batting her away like a toy. She grunted in his head. *"How are we supposed to run a coup when we're all collared and drugged?"*

"We have someone on the inside," Nick said. He knew it was a risk, but a pride queen or molly—upper felines beneath the queen— would do anything to get home. Unless she was a rogue, but she didn't strike him as one. Not with the way she'd reacted to his comment about her pride.

Loretta gave him a cautious look then leapt forward, her claws slicing down his back as she pounced him and jumped off. Nick snarled and swung again, hitting her in the face and sending her rolling. Her teeth left gouges in his paw, but he ignored them. She flopped to the side, and for a moment he thought he'd knocked her out, but her mind voice flowed to him.

"Okay, so can this person free us of our collars? When do we

fight?"

"We're biding our time, building our numbers. If you're willing to help us, talk to other parahumans when you get into fights like these. Get them to join us so, when the time comes and we break free, we'll know who's on our side."

Loretta grunted as she struggled to her paws. She gave herself a shake and stalked toward him, blood covering the side of her cheek. *"Deal. Now, my guess is that you made plans with your Hunter about who should win this round?"*

"If I win, we get the teens."

She gave him a surprised look. *"Why do you want them? They can't do anything without their wands."*

"Maybe not, but I can protect them from the Hunters. And I can do that better if they're with me."

Loretta lifted her chin and flicked her tail back and forth, eyeing him. *"You're a strange one, Nick. Fine, I'll take the fall. My Hunter's wanted to get rid of them anyway. At least this way they won't get killed."*

Nick went for her throat. She scratched him and bit at his muzzle, but he knocked her onto her side, hard. *"I'm surprised you care about them. You seemed pretty fine with the vampire and the werewolf stealing their food."*

"Yeah, well, the kids won't be good in a fight. But if we stay strong, I can protect them, too. And I need to survive to get home to my pride."

Nick was surprised by the answer but pleased as well. Maybe he hadn't made a mistake in trusting her. *"Good luck to you. I'll make this quick."* He pounced on her back and brought his paw down, knocking her out cold. The werecat crumbled and Nick stood over her panting, blood dripping off his wounds. She had mean claws. She'd definitely be a good fighter.

Loretta's Hunter snorted in frustration and glanced at Gale. "Guess you just earned yourself two dead weights. No skin off my back."

"You have their wands?" Gale asked. "They won't be much use to me if they can't use their magic."

The man waved his hand. "Yeah, yeah, I'll get them to you. Still don't know why you want them. No one's going to defeat that fire witch."

"Her companion didn't exactly stand a chance," Gale said coldly. She opened the gate and motioned for Nick to come to her. He limped over, only realizing then that Loretta had given him a bad bite on his ankle. He hoped he had enough elixir in his veins to heal him. He shifted back to human and limped harder, grimacing. Gale glanced at his ankle and sighed loudly. "You need to stop breaking yourself."

"I'll keep that in mind the next time I'm in a *fighting* match," Nick growled. Not like he'd meant for it to happen. He glanced over at the other Hunter as he attached a lead to Loretta's collar. To his horror, the Hunter dragged the puma by her neck out of the ring. Loretta stayed unconscious for a few minutes then started to jerk and cough, paws thrashing as she tried to get the collar off.

"Get up," the Hunter snarled at her.

She managed to roll to her feet and stagger after him, head bowed in pain.

Nick ground his teeth. Now he was very glad that he'd asked for the teens. He moved alongside Gale and tried to keep his attention away from Loretta as they were guided back to their cages. He limped into his prison and held up his hand to let Yanlei know he was fine. He settled against the wall.

Gale kept the cage ajar as the other Hunter put Loretta away. He went inside and grabbed Ayaan and Pavati by their arms. They cried out in fright. Augustine was on her feet in an instant, snarling after the Hunter.

"Augustine," Nick barked at her, drawing a surprised look. He shook his head. "Wait," he said. She glared but then perked her head up as the Hunter brought the two teens over to Gale and shoved them toward her. The Huntress caught them, preventing them from falling. With a grunt, she gently straightened them and nudged them into the cell before holding out her hand.

"Their wands."

"I'll have to grab them from my stash. I don't keep them on me," the Hunter said. He looked at the teens and snorted. "Good luck with them," he added without an ounce of sympathy in his voice.

Gale muttered something unflattering under her breath and locked the door.

Ayaan and Pavati froze once they were in the locked cell with Nick and the rest of his packmates. Augustine didn't leave them alone for long. She got up and held out her arms. "Come here. We won't hurt you."

Tears filled Pavati's eyes as she rushed toward the wolf. Augustine held her close and motioned for Ayaan to join her, but he stayed rooted and stared at Nick.

"What happened? Why did he bring us here?"

Nick rubbed some blood off his face. "I made a deal with Gale. If I won, we got you two. If I lost, I went to the other Hunter."

Ayaan frowned and looked at his sister as she sought comfort from Augustine. "You risked yourself for us."

"Yeah, well, we have to find ways to help each other, right?" Nick said and hobbled toward Ayaan. He placed a hand on the young man's shoulder and squeezed it. "Rest. We'll teach you to fight, and you'll have your wands back soon. At least then you'll have some way to defend yourselves when the time comes."

Augustine glanced at Nick. "Thanks," she told him. But then she made a face. "Would have been nice if the Huntress had brought more pillows and blankets for them."

As if on cue, Gale returned with those very items. She passed them through the bars and looked at Ayaan and Pavati. "Have you eaten?"

Ayaan nodded. "Yes, but…we're still hungry."

Gale sighed, but she didn't snap at them. Instead, she patted the bars lightly with her hand and departed. Nick watched her go and settled down on the ground next to Yanlei. She went to his foot in an instant and lifted it, checking over the damage.

Brighton walked to Ayaan's side and guided him to Augustine. "Bring those pillows to your sister, and both of you get some rest."

"Thank you." Ayaan passed Pavati a pillow and blanket, and he sat down beside Augustine. When she held out an arm, he leaned against her and sighed in quiet relief.

Brighton took a seat next to Nick while Yanlei fussed over his leg. "Did you notice how Gale seems less vicious and insane when that brother of hers isn't around?"

"Yes," Nick said. "But it also makes me wonder where Hendrickson is. Why isn't he at the fights? Just what is he getting himself into?"

Brighton shook his head and glanced at the teens. "I don't know, but hopefully it's nothing that's going to put a wrench in our plans."

Chapter 14
Conflict of Interest

Gale

Gale walked the long hallways of the pit with her head down. Watching the teens cower as they were brought to her and sending them into the cage did not sit well in her stomach. In fact, it had felt wrong grabbing them from their school in the first place. It was one thing to go after adult parahumans, but to snag children? Their entire goal had been to capture the wind magus and the fae. When that had failed, it had been Hendrickson's *brilliant* plan to attack the children. She'd been against it, but Slater had praised Hendrickson for his quick instincts. Yet no one really wanted the teens.

Well, no one except for Nick.

She couldn't figure the werewolf out. He spent so much energy protecting his pack and fighting in the ring, and he was willing to waste even more energy to take the teens under his paw. She had to wonder how close in age they were. The way Nick acted reminded her of an alpha. It didn't matter that Augustine and Brighton were older than him; they followed him. They trusted him.

And if he wasn't careful, that would get him killed. He was one of her strongest fighters, even better than Brighton. He and Yanlei worked well as a pair. And she could keep him under control. Augustine was a loose cannon. Sure, the woman was powerful and vicious, but Gale was never sure when the wolf would finally turn and rip out her throat.

She rubbed her neck and grimaced at the thought. Augustine was a demon in the ring, which both Gale and Hendrickson appreciated. It meant they could rely on her during a fight. If a Hunter wanted to put a huge sum of money on the table, Augustine was the one Gale and Hendrickson picked. She must have been one of the top warriors in her pack, someone respected and revered. But she listened to Nick. If they ever wanted to break the heart of that little group, all she had to do was remove him.

Gale shuddered at the thought. She stopped near the wall and placed a hand against it, steadying herself as her mind raced. She couldn't get their conversation from the last pit out of her head. His father had been killed by humans, leaving him an orphan at a young age, and still he didn't hate humans like she despised parahumans.

Her thoughts drifted to Daniella the night before she was poisoned by her so-called werewolf lover. Daniella had been nervous and excited to join him. She'd seen pack life for herself, learned about it from him, and she'd fallen in love with both.

Gale should have known from the beginning theirs was a doomed romance.

***

"But it's against our oath," Gale said, wringing her hands while her sister gathered items into a bag. She sat on the edge of her bed, feet planted on the wooden floor and fingers digging into the firm mattress for support.

"Maybe our oath is wrong," Daniella replied, smiling at Gale. She brushed dark hair out of her face then tied it behind her head and went back to her dresser. "I can't believe they're all monsters. Not him. And the way he works with his pack? Gale, what if we've got it wrong?"

"Shh!" Gale hissed and looked at their bedroom door. "If Mom and Dad hear you…Daniella, please, be reasonable. We've spent our entire lives training for these moments, to make sure the parahumans don't sway us to their side. You can't do this."

Daniella stopped near her bag and tilted her head at Gale. Her eyes flashed, a challenge glinting in her brown irises. "What are you going to do? Stop me?"

Gale bowed her head. "I can't beat you. But...but I should try."

"Should?"

Gale sighed and rubbed her own arm. She listened to her parents shuffle around downstairs and glanced at her sister. Thank god Hendrickson was out that night. He would have tied Daniella down himself and tried to free her mind of the corruption. "I don't want anything to happen to you. But I also want you to be happy, and you've been a lot happier since meeting those wolves."

Daniella's eyes lit up. She went to Gale's side and grasped her sister's hands between her two warm palms. "Come with me."

"Wh-what?"

"Come with me. I'll introduce you to the pack. You can see for yourself what I mean about how wonderful they are." She sat down at Gale's side and leaned her head against her sister's. "Your heart was never fully in this, Gale, we both know that. Hendrickson and I were always the better Hunters, because you hated hurting anything. God, the first time we went hunting for animals—"

Gale rolled her eyes. "I was seven, okay? I still thought ducks were cute, and I didn't want Dad to kill them."

"So you thought running into the lake flapping your arms, quaking at them, and almost drowning was the best way to save them?"

Gale pouted, shoving her sister when Daniella laughed. "Geeze, I was seven. And it worked. Mostly..."

Daniella's expression fell. She squeezed Gale's hand and held it close. "Dad never should have made you pluck that duck. Hendrickson and I were completely capable of it, but...."

"He wanted to teach me a lesson," Gale said and looked up. Across the room, a small jar of duck feathers sat on a shelf above her desk. "I couldn't be soft, because the moment I showed tenderness to an animal, I could get my throat ripped out." She looked down at their hands. She turned hers over and laced her fingers between her sister's. "But he also didn't tell us how happy parahumans could make us." She tightened her hold. "Do you really want this, Daniella? To be a werewolf? You know you'll be hunted."

"Not by you, I hope, "Daniella said with a smile that didn't quite reach her eyes. "Yes, I want this. I won't be coming back once he changes me. I can't risk Mom and Dad...caging me or finding the pack through me." Her eyes watered, and she touched Gale's cheek. "I don't want to leave you behind. Please, Gale, come with me."

Gale stared at her older sister, someone she looked up to. She never would have guessed Daniella would fall for a parahuman. But Gale couldn't deny the love in her sister's voice. Nor could she ignore the pit in her stomach at the thought of leaving home.

Gale slowly pulled her hand away. "I can't. This is my home. And...and I don't want to be a werewolf." She offered a sad smile. "But I promise I won't be the one to hunt you, and I'll try to keep them off your trail too."

Daniella fought back a sob and wrapped her arms around Gale tightly. "I love you. No matter what, nothing will change that."

Gale clung to her. They sat together for a time before Daniella glanced at their bedroom window. She kissed Gale's forehead.

"Stay safe," she whispered and grabbed her bag.

"You, too," Gale said. She followed Daniella to the window and watched her sister hop into the tree beside it. Daniella descended, landing softly in the white snow near its base. She waved up at Gale then ran toward the woods. Just before Daniella disappeared, Gale spotted a strapping young man waiting for her. He embraced Daniella and carried her away and out of sight.

Gale folded her arms on the windowsill and settled her chin on them, staring out into the cold winter night, never once suspecting that the sister she'd kissed goodbye would soon be back for blood.

***

A loud clatter startled Gale from her memories. She looked over her shoulder as a Hunter picked up a collar that had fallen off of a cart. She narrowed her eyes at him then shook her head and resumed walking. Daniella's voice and smile faded from her mind, but she heard the ghostly crash of her family's cabin door bursting open as Daniella rushed in in hysterics, partially shifted. Her parents had shouted at Gale and Hendrickson to stay in their rooms, and they'd done so, though Hendrickson had only listened to protect her. They would have died if not for their parents. But their parents had paid the ultimate price.

Gale fisted her hand against her chest and took a calming breath. That was why she hated parahumans. That wolf had corrupted her sister with the transformation. And she'd turned against her own family in her madness. She would have killed them. Worst of all, Gale had had the chance to stop it, and she hadn't. She'd watched her sister rush off into the night with that monster.

Nick's face flashed in front of her eyes.

He was a werewolf too. Would she call him a monster? In her heart, she knew she couldn't, not with the way he protected his friends and the teens just as she protected her own brother. If he had been the type of person Daniella had fallen for, then Gale could understand how she'd been charmed to run away. Was it the werewolf's fault Daniella couldn't handle the transformation?

When it came down to it, Gale felt she had only herself to blame for not stopping her sister, and not alerting their parents of Daniella's infatuation.

Maybe if she had, Daniella would still be with them. Safe. Alive.

"Gale?"

Gale jumped and jerked her head up as she nearly collided with Hendrickson. He reached out and steadied her, looking her over in concern.

"Are you all right?"

"Ye-yes. Sorry." Gale rubbed her head and took a moment to focus on her brother. At least Hendrickson was here and in her life. She looked up at him then froze when she noticed Saul and Trish over his shoulder. She frowned. "What's going on?" There was only one reason why the vampires would be around. "New mission?"

"Yep!" Hendrickson said cheerfully, looking like a boy on Christmas day. "I've been watching the fae our lovely lady wants. I think we can snag her without too much damage to our persons." He lifted a cloth bag and winked. "We have something to help us subdue her too. It shouldn't be too hard, but we get one shot. Our lady wants as many of us on this as possible. So Saul here is going to accompany us."

"And her?" Gale asked, tilting her head to Trish. She eyed the vampire warily. Ever since she'd woken up in the cave after the damn fire magus and her friend escaped, Gale hadn't trusted Trish not to have somehow had a hand in the escape.

Hendrickson smirked. "The lady's taken a liking to your pet wolf. She wants to see him."

Gale's hands and feet turned to ice, and the color drained from her face. "But why?" she asked before she could stop herself. "He belongs to us, and he's one of our best fighters. Why should we be expected to give him up? Everyone who goes there loses their mind."

"Those animals all belong to the lady," Hendrickson said and swept his arm around the pit. "And besides, if she breaks him, we've still got the demoness werewolf to fight for us. She's the reason we're up on the battle leaderboard." He clapped his hands together and rubbed them. "I can't wait until she goes against one of Slater's dogs. Would love to see his face when he loses." He snickered.

Gale set her jaw. "That still doesn't explain why she's here," she said, gesturing to Trish.

"We need to leave now. Slater's already waiting for us," Hendrickson said. He jerked a thumb toward Trish. "She'll take care of the pup. Won't you?" He smirked at Trish. "And you know what happens if little vampires betray us." He gripped his gun meaningfully.

Saul placed a hand on Trish's shoulder. "I can promise you, she's no turncoat." He looked at Gale. "She'll also be staying behind to help the Hunters here and learn more about our security system so she understands the intake process better. She's one of us now."

Trish nodded but said nothing.

Hendrickson snorted. "We'll see. Come on, Gale. Saul. We got work to do."

He clapped Gale on the shoulder and headed for the main fighting pit. Gale lingered, staring after him. They were going after the fae again? They were lucky they hadn't lost their fellow Hunters the first time!

She swallowed a lump in her throat and watched Saul pat Trish's shoulder then follow after Hendrickson. Gale ground her teeth and eyed Trish as the vampire started to leave. Gale reached out and grabbed the vampire by her shirt and jerked her close. "I know you're up to something," Gale growled in her face. "Don't do anything stupid to get my warriors killed."

Trish stared back at her and frowned. She touched the hand on her shirt and stared into Gale's eyes. There was a tiny flicker of light in her irises, a faint change of color, and Gale felt her shoulders relax. "I'm not the enemy," Trish said. "I do what I'm told, and I'm loyal. Trust Saul."

Gale's hand loosened on Trish's shirt. The vampire had done everything asked of her since arriving at the pit. She fed the prisoners without hurting them or letting them escape. She ran errands for the Hunters. And Saul would know if she was a traitor, wouldn't he?

Gale mulled it over then gave a slow nod. "Just don't be stupid," she said, though her voice held less force than before. She narrowed her eyes at Trish then turned on her heel and headed out of the hall.

They had a mission.

Chapter 15
The Fae of Dreams

Nick

Nick rested his head on Yanlei's shoulder as he tried to get some rest after the fight. He'd just barely closed his eyes when she shook him lightly. "Hm? What?"

She pointed to the door. Nick sat up as Trish approached without a cart of food. Odd. Why would she risk coming to see them unless she had something with her? She unlocked the cage and stepped inside.

Ayaan and Pavati scooted closer to Augustine who growled at Trish. The vampire ignored her and walked to Nick's side. Her face remained calm, but he could smell the trepidation sweating through her pores.

"Your presence is required," Trish said bluntly and flicked her fingers. "Get up."

Nick and Yanlei looked at one another. Yanlei started to rise along with Nick, but Trish held out her hand.

"Just him."

Nick narrowed his eyes. What the hell was this all about? Gale had just been here. If he was needed, why hadn't she come to get him herself? Unless this was part of Trish's plan to help them. He glanced at Brighton and Augustine who watched him warily, both looking ready to attack. He motioned that he was fine. "Fine. Let's go."

Trish's lips twisted like she wanted to say something, but instead she turned and walked out of the cage. Nick followed her and waited as she locked the door. She pulled something from her pocket and attached a lead to his collar. *"They'll get suspicious if a vampire is guiding a werewolf around without any guards or restraints,"* Trish explained.

Nick tugged a little and grumbled under his breath. He *hated* being treated like a dog. *"Fine,"* he grouched.

Nick kept his head down as Trish led the way, but his eyes darted back and forth, noting the path they took. They weren't headed for the fighting pit, or Gale would have brought him instead. Unless Gale was now on a mission like Hendrickson had been for the past few days.

"You're not going to like where I'm bringing you," Trish said in his head, startling him. Shit, that didn't sound good. *"Word's traveled about your fighting skills and the way you've been helping those witches. The leader of the pit wants to see you."*

Nick frowned deeply then paled. Wait, was that the same person the other parahumans had been dragged to? He glanced around, but with no one close he whispered to her, "Am I going to die?"

Trish's lack of response made his throat clench. He'd tried to stay under the radar as much as possible, but apparently it hadn't been enough. What was the last straw? Taking the teens in? Forming the coup? Did they even know about the coup?

"I don't know," Trish said after a long, terse moment. *"Not everyone comes back."*

Nick considered bolting. He could take Trish down, steal the keys, rush back to the cage and free his packmates…and then what? They'd have to fight an entire pit of Hunters. Even if they survived, they had no idea where they were being kept. They could break out and find themselves in the middle of the great white north with no civilization around. With no one to help, if any of them got injured, they might die out in the elements. Could they risk it?

He tensed, fight and flight warring in his head.

Trish jerked on his leash, causing him to stumble forward. *"Don't be stupid. If you take me out and free the others, they'll get shot down before they reach the front door. You're supposed to be the tough one, right? Then prove to this bitch that you have what it takes to survive."*

They stopped in front of a wooden door with intricate Celtic-like markings carved into its surface. A Hunter stood on either side, watching Trish and Nick warily as they approached.

"This is the one," Trish said and pushed Nick toward them. *"Survive for your pack. Hopefully, I'll be back for you soon."*

A guard grabbed his arm, and Nick glanced at Trish as she retreated down the hall. She spared one final look back at him, and he swallowed hard.

The second guard opened the door and pushed him inside, collar, leash, and all. Nick grunted as he fell to his knees, expecting to meet cold stone.

Instead, he landed on a soft, warm rug woven with purple, black, white, and silver threads. He panted and lifted his head.

The room was like stepping into a dream set in a midnight celestial plane. He couldn't make out any walls, just sparkling purple, pink, and black sky all around him. The floor was partially covered in rug, but the rest was a mix of lush green grass, rocks, and water. Steam rose from a stone pool, spiraling upwards in a soothing pattern.

A bigger pond colorful as the midnight sky rested to one side of the room, surrounded by moss. There was no moon. The sparkles, or stars, gave off plenty of light. Floating white candles pushed back the rest of the gloom.

Black willow trees with onyx and purple branches swayed in a wind he could somehow feel in a cave…or whatever this world was. And beneath one tree stood a great circular bed covered in silks and furs. He eyed it and looked at the pool, but he didn't see anyone. Slowly, he got to his feet and explored the room. He stopped near a stone table holding a bowl of fruit. He almost snorted when he realized they were pomegranates.

"Let me guess," he said. "I eat a few of these seeds and get trapped in your world."

A cold, musical chuckle echoed in the room…realm…whatever. He looked around, but the sound bounced so he couldn't place its location.

"Aren't you a clever little wolf?"

Nick flinched and turned in a circle, not wanting her to get behind him. "I've been told I have a smart mouth."

"Some do find smart tongues rather *delicious*."

A chill crawled up Nick's spine, and he glanced at the bed again. He searched for a sign of the fae, but her scent and voice surrounded him. He backed toward the door, looking over his shoulder to make sure she didn't sneak behind him.

"Are you trying to run away? My, that's quite rude."

"I wouldn't want to overstay my welcome."

"Of course not," the voice purred. "But I *love* company."

Nick turned and reached for the door handle, already knowing it was futile. But let her think him a coward. He spread his claws and aimed to shred the intricately carved wood.

Something black shot out of the shadows and wrapped around his wrist, halting it mid strike. He stared in shock, a chill kissing his skin at the base of the tendril that grasped him. It yanked him off of his feet. He hit the floor and gasped as he was dragged away from the door, streaking across the rug, grass, and stone until the onyx and violet world hid his escape from sight.

His body came to a stop and something descended upon him. He lifted his other arm to protect himself, but he felt no pain. Instead, a light, soft pressure settled on his stomach. Nick blinked a few times then lowered his arm.

He wasn't sure what he expected, but the fae before him was not it. He figured she'd be some sort of hideous monster with fangs and claws, but she looked like she wouldn't want to hurt a fly. Her skin was a pale purplish white. Long white hair flowed around her body, darkening into deep violet at the tips. Ebony feathered wings spread out behind her like some dark angel's, blocking the light from the floating candles. She smiled at him with lavender lips, her eyes sparkling with similar colored magic. Two antler-like horns protruded from her head.

Nick swallowed hard. He took in her long ebony gown that left very little to the imagination when it came to her breasts. She chuckled when she saw him staring, and she trailed a long purple nail along his cheek.

"Well, now, you're more handsome than I thought. Nicholas, isn't it?"

"N-Nick," he replied, his throat tight. He couldn't stop staring at her. He'd seen fae before, but none like her. He searched her glittering eyes and stared at her ears, pointed like some kind of elfin princess. Silver earrings dangled from them, holding black and purple stones.

"Who are you?"

"Silly boy," she laughed. "I can't give you my real name. Who knows what you would do with it?" She leaned down and folded her arms across his chest as she inspected him. "You may call me Vesp."

Vesp. Such a simple name, and yet it fit her perfectly. He swallowed, breathing in her subtle perfume. His stomach churned. This was far more similar to being seduced by a succubus than a fae. The power she held over him both intrigued and terrified him. He licked his dry lips and tried to pull his head back so she wasn't so close. "What do you want with me?" Was this the woman who had driven all those parahumans mad? She wasn't frightening in the slightest. Beautiful, yes. How could they not have been bewitched by her?

Vesp tilted her head, her white and violet hair sweeping along his cheek. "You intrigue me," she said. "Ever since you arrived, my pets have had fewer nightmares. And that just won't do."

Nick blinked. The response was so matter-of-fact, he almost missed the gravity of it. "Excuse me?"

"Nightmares," Vesp repeated and pursed her lips. "Don't you get those?"

"I...I mean, yeah, sometimes. But what do I have to do with nightmares? And why do you care?"

"Whenever you fight a parahuman, their mind is calmer. It was the same at the last pit. Each time I journeyed there you would fight, and the nightmares would flutter away, just out of my grasp." She curled her long fingers into a fist in front of his face and cocked an eyebrow. "It's rather annoying, you know."

Nick eyed the fist and shifted, but she kept him pinned, adding more force to her hold. "I don't know what I have to do with that. You'd think I'd give people nightmares when I fight them."

"You'd think," Vesp echoed. "But no, instead you do something else. You give them that which I detest most." She pricked his chin with the tip of her nail and lifted it. "Hope."

Hope? What the hell is she talking about? He stared, baffled. Did this have to do with the coup? *Shit, does she know?* Surely no one had said anything. Unless she'd dragged in one of his opponents and gotten the information out of them. "I don't know what you're talking about."

The glittery fairy-like glow in her eyes shifted to pitch-black for an instant, so quick Nick almost thought he'd imagined it. But the warm smile on her face cracked a little, her lip twitching. "Don't you?" she asked and lifted his chin higher until her nail split his skin. "You help the weak. Preserve life when you should take it. Urge your captive wolves to stay alive when others would fight for their own survival. What I don't understand is *why*. Why try so hard? You'll never escape these walls."

Nick clenched his jaw.

Vesp wrinkled her nose and made a disgusted sound. "Ugh, you reek of hope. As I heard, it was *your* friends who ruined my last pit. You really think they'll come back?"

Nick rolled his head away, intending to ignore her. She'd try to get into his head, and he didn't want to end up like one of those poor souls dragged half-mad back to their cells.

From the corner of his eye, he saw Vesp pout. "Oh dear, I thought you'd be more fun than this. I know, let's play a game." Vesp pushed herself up and flapped her wings, rising above him. She landed a short distance away on bare feet, giving him enough room to stand. "What if I gave you an opportunity to save your packmates. Would you take it?"

Nick frowned at her. Really? This was her tactic? "I doubt the Hunters would let them walk out of here."

Vesp laughed. "Sweet boy, who do you think keeps them hidden? Who keeps this pit intact?" She spread her arms and spun in a circle, looking around. "If I want someone to leave, I can help them leave. They'd never find this place again. I've made certain of that." She flapped backwards and landed on a chair beside another stone table that hadn't been there before. Glass jars filled with colorful light rested on top. The lights bounced around like living flames. They tried to escape but couldn't.

Nick grimaced, not knowing why the sight bothered him so much.

Vesp pushed the jars to one side then wiggled her fingers over the stone. Four figures took shape. Nick moved a little closer to get a better look and felt his stomach twist when he realized the figures looked like him, Yanlei, Brighton, and Augustine. "Oh, wait, you have two more little pups now, don't you?" Another jerk of her fingers, and Pavati and Ayaan joined their party. "It's precious, really, with you acting like the big alpha to your mixed group of wolves and witches." She looked at him. "How *noble*," she said, the word dripping with venom and twisting her lips into a sneer.

Nick crossed his arms. "What would I have to do to free them?"

"Oh, simple." Vesp moved her fingers over the statue of Augustine. With a pleasant smile, she flicked her finger and sent Augustine's head flying across the table. "Kill one of them."

Nick staggered like he'd been stabbed in the heart. Because he didn't just see a stone statue beheaded. He saw Augustine's actual head roll across the floor, leaving a bloody trail behind. "No!" he snarled in shock and horror. He rushed toward the head, but before he could grab Augustine, her mouth wide in shock, her face vanished, leaving the tiny stone head behind.

The fae looked genuinely surprised. "What? This is a kind gesture. If you kill one of them, you save the rest, including yourself. Isn't that what you want? None of you will leave this pit alive otherwise. One life. That's all I ask, Nick."

Nick panted and lifted his head as she magicked Augustine's skull back onto her body. An illusion. It had just been an illusion. A horrible one…but Augustine was still alive. She had to be.

Vesp plucked the statue of Ayaan up next. "Hm, maybe she was too close to your heart. What about one of your little witches? Do you value their lives as much as your packmates?" She dropped the figure toward the ground.

It took every bit of Nick's restraint not to rush forward and catch the stone statue before it shattered on the floor. This time, Ayaan's broken and bloody body lay in front of him, his limbs and neck twisted like he'd gone up against a werewolf who'd broken all his bones. Nick's heart skipped a beat, and his stomach lurched until he thought he would vomit. He fought it back and shut his eyes, blocking out the image and trying to drown the fear of having to take the life of one of his wolves or one of the witches. They were innocent, like so many other parahumans trapped in those cells.

Vesp watched him as he trembled in fear and rage. "Hm? Not even him? Interesting." Nick opened his eyes as she called the shards of stone back to her hand and reformed Ayaan. "I would have thought pack comes before outsiders."

Nick's heart pounded and skipped a beat as she played with Yanlei's statue next. Oh god, not her. He couldn't watch her die, too. "Wait," he said as she wrapped her hand around Yanlei's figure. "I can choose anyone from that table? Any statue? I can choose to take a life, and you'll free the rest?"

Vesp smiled and ran the nail of her pinky across her chest. "I swear."

Nick stared long and hard at the stone statues. He thought of his pack, the ones waiting for him in the cell and the others at home worried sick for their loved ones. Rozene and Paytah would be spending every waking moment tracking them down. They'd keep the pack together, safe, protected from any other Hunters who sought to drag them down into the pit. He thought of Tess and Iris mourning over Brighton's disappearance. And Ray, body cold and frozen, waiting for Augustine to come home and lay him to rest.

Nick walked toward the table and reached out. Vesp grinned, watching with anticipation, until he made his choice.

He picked up his own statue and held it out to her. "Then I choose me," he said and pressed his claws to his throat. "You release them, and I'll end my life."

Vesp stared at him for a moment. Suddenly, she gave a long-suffering sigh and waved her hand. All the statues vanished, including his. "How boring," she said and steepled her fingers beneath her chin. "So, you don't fear your own death. But you fear the deaths of your packmates. Hm…yes, I think I can work with this."

Nick frowned, not understanding what she was getting at or liking how her tone had shifted. He took a step away.

The purple gleam vanished from Vesp's eyes, her irises filled with a blackness so deep, it threatened to swallow him up. "Haven't you figured it out yet, boy?" she asked as her visage changed drastically. The violet faded from her skin and was replaced with ghostly white flesh. All color drained from her hair, face, and body except for black and white. "I thrive off of nightmares, and the best place to find them? Where everyone is afraid to die!"

She rushed him, black tendrils shooting out from her wings and wrapping around his limbs. Nick cried out in terror. One snapped around his throat and crawled over his face, over his mouth, his eyes. He struggled as the tendrils bound him in place and dropped him to the floor. But that was only the beginning.

As he fought to free himself, his mind was sliced open, and every horrible, dreadful fear he carried for his pack came bleeding out of the gaping wound. Paytah stood in front of him, fighting off Hunters. Suddenly, he pitched forward as a bullet went through his spine and out his chest. Rozene ran to him, clinging to him as he collapsed from a pierced heart. She cradled his head, screaming at him to hang on, but it was too late. Paytah stared back at her with dead eyes. Rozene roared her grief and outrage at the Hunters. She threw herself at the ones closest to them and lost her head to the swipe of a Hunter's sword. It rolled across the ground, landing at Kat's feet. She cowered before the Hunters and tried to run, but one by one she and the rest of the pack were killed before Nick's eyes.

He screamed as the nightmares consumed him. He fought to save his friends, but nothing he did made a difference. He was held tightly in place, silenced, forced to watch as his beloved pack was destroyed. He sobbed, thick tears rolling down his cheeks. No one was spared, not even Bianca as she tried to avenge Kat.

Suddenly, the bonds came free and he was shoved forward into a pool of blood. Nick gasped and threw his hands out to catch himself. But as he did, he saw that his hands were paws, already covered in blood. He stared at them in horror and looked around. His packmates weren't dead because of Hunters. Instead, each one had been shredded by his own claws.

"No!" Nick screamed and grabbed his head. "NO!"

He woke up lying in the middle of the rug in front of the door. Nick scrambled backward, slamming into the stone wall beside it, his eyes flying wildly around the room, searching for the bodies.

A lone figure stood out in the darkness. No more was he surrounded by beautiful purple and black clouds, trees, and a bath. The world was gone, leaving darkness and an ebony and ivory figure with her wings wrapped hauntingly around herself. She ran her thumb along her lips and licked them, her black eyes hungry. "I never thought nightmares could taste so delicious," she said in a low voice and chuckled. "You will be a nice treat, much more satisfying than humans. Their fragile minds are barely appetizers. But you, my boy, oh, you're a main course." She laughed, her voice echoing in his ears. Her tendrils struck again, driving him back into his nightmares.

Nick collapsed, tears flowing down his face as he was lost to a world of death and Yanlei's blood-curdling screams.

Chapter 16
Nightmares

Nick

"What did she do to him?"

A woman's voice broke through the haze holding Nick's mind captive. Screams and cries of pain faded, and the images dissolved. He cracked open his eyes, lids crusted shut with his tears. He stared up at the stone ceiling above him and the two Hunters looming over him. Then another face appeared, staring at him with concern.

Trish.

The vampire crouched and glared at the Hunters. "How does she expect me to get him back to his cell in this condition?"

"Drag him, I guess," one guard said with a sneer. "I thought vampires were supposed to be strong."

"Or maybe you can charm him and order him to crawl behind you like the dog he is." The other guard laughed.

Trish did not look amused. She touched Nick's head as he searched her face, trying to understand what had happened to him. He wasn't in his nightmares anymore. He knew that much. The floor beneath him was cold. Stone. He lolled his head to the side and saw the wooden door shut in front of him. He was on the other side. He'd escaped her clutches.

Tears of relief stung his eyes again, and he rolled onto his side with a grunt. The guards mumbled something else to Trish, but he ignored them as he struggled to his knees. He needed to get back to his pack and make sure they were all still alive without exposing Trish.

"Easy," she said into his head. *"You just stopped thrashing and screaming."*

Nick grimaced. His head hurt something fierce, and his stomach snarled, threatening to expel everything in his gut. He pressed his face to the blessedly cool ground and took a few calming breaths.

"Will you get him out of here? He's stinking up the hall," a guard complained.

Nick gnashed his teeth. Someone nudged him from behind, and Nick couldn't stop himself. He rounded and snarled, his eyes turning wolfish and his fangs piercing through his gums. The guard jerked back in alarm until Trish grabbed his shoulder and jerked him to his feet. But she did more than that. She provided the support he needed to get up. He staggered into her, and she gripped him underneath his armpit, holding him steady.

"Don't make me charm you," she hissed at him. "I might do worse than she did."

The guards smirked.

Nick glowered back at her then hung his head in defeat. He let her pull him away from the hall. He walked stiffly, feeling every ache and pain in his body. His throat felt raw from screaming and the squeeze of her tendril. She'd kept him wrapped up in her embrace and darkness for what felt like an eternity. He touched his head, expecting a bruise, but found nothing. "How long was I out?" he whispered hoarsely.

"You were in there for hours. She tossed you out several minutes ago, and one of the guards came to find me. You…kept screaming like she was killing you."

"Felt like it," Nick muttered. No, not killing him. Murdering every person he loved. Making *him* murder everyone. He rubbed his chest, his heart aching as if it had actually happened. "I need to see them."

"Who?"

"My pack."

Trish said nothing. She provided more support and hurried through the halls, hefting him along whenever he faltered. He held his stomach with his free arm. He was almost afraid to reach the cell in case the nightmares had come true. The fae's offer echoed in the back of his mind. Kill one of his packmates, and he could set the rest free. Did she mean it? Or was that her way of getting into his head and figuring out what frightened him? If nightmares were what nourished her, then of course she would attack his greatest fears and bring them to the front of his mind.

It was no wonder the werecat had killed himself. If Nick had to go through another episode with the fae, he wasn't sure how his mind would survive.

His packmates' scents washed over him as they neared the cell. Relief flooded through him when he saw Brighton sitting on a ledge. Augustine sat with the teens, keeping them company. Yanlei rushed to the door the moment she saw him.

Tears flooded his eyes, and Nick released a broken sob as Trish opened the cell. Wordlessly, he ran to Yanlei and pulled her into his arms. He pressed his nose into her neck, breathing in her scent, and listened to her heartbeat. He shook in her hold and felt her hug him back.

"What did you do?" Augustine growled at Trish. She hopped off the ledge and went to Nick. She came up behind him and touched his back with both of her hands, offering support without crowding him. He reached a hand back and grabbed one of hers in a vice grip.

"I didn't do anything," Trish said. "I found him like this."

Brighton came next, and Nick almost cried again when he felt the man caress his head. They stood together, surrounding him with their warmth, scents, and presence. He drank it all in, letting them chase away the chill of the nightmares and remind him that they were alive. They were safe. He hadn't lost them.

The cell door shut, and keys jangled as Trish departed.

"I'll bring you something warm to drink," she thought to him. *"I'm sorry for whatever she did to you."*

Nick released a shaky breath and lifted his head. When he met Yanlei's eyes, he leaned forward and kissed her deeply. She returned the kiss without hesitation and held him close as he drank in her love. Slowly, he released her and held her by her arms before touching Brighton and then Augustine. He looked over at the ledge where Pavati and Ayaan watched anxiously. "Come here," he said, motioning with a hand.

They got up and went over to the wolves. Nick enveloped them both as well, and the pack closed in around them. "You're safe," he said, more to convince himself. "You're all safe."

Brighton squeezed his shoulder. "Nick, what happened to you?"

"The fae," Nick replied in a guttural voice. "I met the fae. The one who governs the pits."

Yanlei's breath caught in her throat, and Augustine growled. "What'd the bitch want?"

"Language," Yanlei scolded her, nodding toward Pavati and Ayaan.

Augustine snorted, but she watched her words for the moment.

Nick sighed. "I need to sit down." He let Yanlei help him to the ground. She draped a blanket around his shoulders, and he clutched it then grasped her hand. "Stay close to me?"

She nodded and settled next to him, wrapping her arm around him. He leaned against her as the others joined them.

"She's some kind of dream or nightmare fae. She wanted to learn my worst fear. And when she did, she gave me nightmares. Made me relive it. Over. And over again. Trish said I was in there for hours." Nick swallowed. "She's not what she seems," he said. "When I walked in there, she was like this fae goddess. And then she turned into some kind of decrepit demon. I don't think I've seen anything so terrifying before in my life. And the images she sent to me?" He shivered and gripped Yanlei again. "I never want to see them again."

Brighton touched his arm. "What were they?"

Nick opened his bloodshot eyes and stared at the elder werewolf. He saw Brighton, but he also saw him getting decapitated, disemboweled, and shot in ghostly images. Nick fought back the bile in his throat and closed his eyes again. "I saw you all die. In awful, gruesome ways. And there wasn't anything I could do." He didn't mention the fact that he'd been the one to kill them in several of the dreams, nor did he bring up Vesp's offer. Would they hate him if they found out he could have saved them by taking one life? In his heart, he knew they wouldn't; to lose one packmate was to lose a part of your family, a part of yourself. But the nightmares had made him question himself.

"Nick…" Augustine said, her voice taking on a gentle tone. She pressed her hand to his cheek, and he opened his eyes. "We're not dropping dead any time soon. We're still alive, right? We still have fight in us. And we'll fight to get back to our pack and bring these assholes down."

Brighton nodded in agreement, and Yanlei squeezed his arm reassuringly. Nick tried to calm his pounding heart. He couldn't give up. Not yet. Tess and his friends and family were out there searching. They had to hold on long enough to be found.

He took a deep breath and sat up taller. "We continue with the plan," he said. "Bring more people to our side. When the time is right, we strike."

Once the others nodded, Nick slumped against Yanlei to rest.

***

Trish returned a while later carrying food and a mug. Nick opened his eyes as she unlocked the door and brought the items inside. She pulled something out of her belt and turned her hand over, showing him a small elixir. "It should help with the shock," she said and passed it to him.

Nick nodded his thanks and grasped her wrist before she could pull away. "Do you have…any plans?"

Trish swallowed. "I'm supposed to learn how to help security, which gets me close to the computers. I'll see what I can do. Just hang in there, okay? You know they're going to come."

"I know," Nick said. "I just don't want anyone else to die trying to save us."

"Yeah, I know," Trish said. She glanced over her shoulder then at him and the others. "I have to get back. I'll be taking care of you while Hendrickson and Gale are gone."

Brighton leaned forward. "Where did they go?"

"On a mission." She glanced at the witches and hesitated. "To finish what they started when they brought these two in."

Pavati and Ayaan paled. "No," Ayaan whispered. "They're going after our teachers."

Nick set his jaw. "The wind magus would be a good warrior, but I don't know what she'd do with the fae. There aren't any other fae here except for *her*."

Trish bit her lip. "There were other fae," she said quietly. "But if they didn't agree to serve Vesp, she destroyed them and trapped their souls so they couldn't go back to the Veil to be reborn."

"Trapped them?" Nick asked then blinked. The colored jars with living flames. Had those been fae? And she'd kept them on that death table like some kind of decoration or trophy! "What would happen if they did get free?" he asked.

Trish shrugged. "I assume they'd go back to the tree and be reborn. And then if any of them retained their memories, they might seek Vesp out. Or…they might not care enough. But the fact that she holds them captive makes me think she's afraid they would try to take her out."

An idea brewed in Nick's head. If he got back into the room and broke the glasses, maybe he could free the fae and right the wrong that had been done to them. If she'd treated them like she'd treated him, they deserved revenge.

But that meant delving into that demented woman's domain again, and Nick wasn't ready for that.

Trish glanced over her shoulder. "I'll let you know if I find out anything."

"Be careful," Nick said.

Trish nodded and left the room. Nick picked up the mug of tea and sipped it. The warmth spread through his chest, relieving his aches and chills. He held the mug close and stared at his pack.

No matter what, he would protect them. No matter what…he wouldn't let the fae touch them or make his nightmares real.

Chapter 17
Connections

Trish

This is wrong. Trish couldn't get the thought out of her head as she left Nick with his friends. Why were the Hunters letting someone like Vesp exist? They were supposed to protect humans from parahumans, not let the more demonic ones torture everyone! And to think Saul was working with her too; it made Trish shudder.

She rubbed her arm anxiously and headed for the security rooms. There were two designated areas that housed the security computers, one near the entrance of the pit and one in a stone room. If she was alone with the security guard, she could use charm to learn what she needed. But if Saul joined her, she wouldn't stand a chance, which was why it was so vital that she do it now while he was gone.

She stopped outside of the latter area and glanced inside. Computer screen light stung her eyes, and she blinked a few times until she could make out a man hovering over the keyboards and controls. He bobbed his head to music playing through his earbuds, the sound carrying to Trish. She looked him over, to the gun on his right hip, the taser on his left, and the remote near his thigh. She glanced to a wall of collars as well as the remotes beneath them. So this was where they kept them all. With any luck, this room also controlled them.

Trish sucked in a breath then grabbed the man's shoulder. He jumped, hand going to his gun, but Trish turned him too quickly and stared into his brown eyes. She flicked an earbud out and spoke in a low voice, her eyes burrowing into his and pushing charm onto him. "Put the gun away. I'm not going to hurt you. You're supposed to teach me about the security system."

The man slowly lowered his hand then reached up to pull a sucker out of his mouth. He tossed it in the trash and tilted his head. "Right, sorry. You just startled me."

Trish smiled. "I have a habit of doing that." She hesitated and glanced at the door. They were still alone. "Teach me how the system works. Then show me how you send out transmissions to other Hunters when there's trouble."

"Right-o," the Hunter said and motioned to a chair. "Pull one up. I'm Micah."

"Trish," she said and sat beside him.

Micah put a binder on the desk in front of her, the heavy volume slamming down and making her jump. "Huge, right? That'll give you an overview of the system, but I imagine you don't need to know quite that much." He cracked his knuckles in front of him and grinned, his eyes gleaming with her charm. "Let's get started."

Trish pulled out a notebook. She scribbled down notes as he pointed out the different systems she could use to communicate with the outside world, as well as within the cave. A huge network of speakers webbed throughout the entire pit could alert the Hunters of a breakout. That would need to be disabled if Nick stood a chance of escaping. "Do you have the schematics of where the speakers are? And security cameras?"

Micah nodded and flipped through the binder to show her a four-page spread of where the cameras and speakers were located within the maze of caves. All of the cages had cameras, but only hallways bore speakers. Trish recorded the pages the drawings were on and then outlined some of the cameras and speakers near Nick's area. "Do you have copies of this?"

Micah shook his head. "We're only supposed to have master copies. So if you need info, or if anyone needs to repair the cameras or speakers, they come in here to get the blueprints."

Trish nodded. "All right, and they're recording 24/7?"

"Yup, but we delete the feed daily so we don't use up all our data and resources."

Good to know, she thought. At least if she made a mistake the video might be deleted before anyone viewed it. Suddenly her stomach twisted, and she looked at the picture. There had to be a camera in the room they were in as well. Surely they wouldn't be concerned since she hadn't attacked him, right? She'd just told him why she was there, and he'd agreed. They wouldn't be able to see the charm, she hoped.

Trish glanced at the camera and almost sighed in relief when she realized it was facing the back of his head. No, the camera wouldn't have caught the change in his eyes. Thank goodness.

"This is great," Trish said. "Saul wants me to help where I'm needed most. Maybe I'll learn how to repair cameras and speakers. At least I'll know where to find the map." She tapped the page then nudged him with her shoulder and chuckled. "Or I could just ask you."

Micah blushed and scratched the back of his neck. "Hey, I'm always happy to help."

Trish studied him as he turned to the computer and pulled up some files. She couldn't recall having ever seen him around the fighting rings. Did he always stay back here? Did it matter? Well, it might if she required his help later on without charming him. "How long have you been with the Hunters?"

"Hm? Oh, I don't know, about ten years now. They found me right after college. Was down on my luck and had the habit of hacking into places to make a quick buck." He tugged his nose. "Not my best moment. Got arrested and then these guys got me out, asked if I wanted to help them with a project. So I've been here ever since."

"Do you go on missions?"

Micah shook his head. "Nah, they said I did better with computers than with parahumans. Said I was too soft on them." He sighed and leaned back in his chair. "I don't like to kill or hurt people. That's just not in my blood, you know? Doing this?" He gestured to the screens. "It lets me keep people safe from parahumans, and that's what I want. The Hunters pay pretty well, too. If it wasn't for them, I wouldn't be able to support my family."

Trish tilted her head, surprised. She'd charmed him to tell her about security, but she hadn't pushed him to share so much about himself. Was he always this chatty? Or did he feel comfortable with her (which was a funny thought since she was a vampire)? "Your wife is lucky to have a provider."

"Oh, heh, I'm not married," Micah said. "I take care of my siblings and their families. They work, but my brother's gotta get operations done a lot. My job helps pay for that, and nobody asks questions about where the money comes from." He looked at Trish and gave a faint smile. "Maybe it's not the most honest work, but beggars can't be choosers, right?"

"No, I guess not." It was so easy to think of Hunters as monsters, but talking to Micah…he seemed like a normal guy caught in a bad situation. He reminded her of herself. Maybe he didn't realize all the harm he was doing to innocent parahumans. He didn't seem afraid to talk to her, which was surprising. Unless he hadn't realized she was a vampire.

She shook her head. *Get your mind back in the game, Trish. You can't afford to lose this moment.* "Okay, so we've gone over cameras, speakers, general security. Now, how do you send messages to other Hunters? Which pits are active, and which ones aren't?"

He cracked a smile at her. "You are the curious one."

"I like to cover all my bases," Trish said with a shrug.

Micah chuckled and pulled up an app on the screen titled H.U.N.T. Beneath it was written, "Hunting Unnatural and Non-Normal Threats." Trish wrinkled her nose but tried to push her disgust aside as she studied the app. It seemed easy enough to use as he walked her through the different means of reaching out to different pits. The list of them, each with a unique name, made her stomach twist. There were so many!

"Are these all in the United States?"

"It's a mix. Most are US based, but we have some foreign friends as well. Sometimes we have to ship parahumans overseas to get them out of certain territories."

"There are so many numbers…how do you tell them apart?"

Micah tapped his head. "I have a good memory. But otherwise, there's a code they use to indicate state, city, and coordinates." He motioned to the numbers. Trish couldn't quite make them out until he pulled up his tablet and held it out to her. She read through it and blinked. It would be confusing without the code. But with the code in hand…. "So, where are we on this? What's our pit called?"

Micah laughed and motioned to one labeled 'Pit GG.' "Check the coordinates."

Trish compared the coordinates to the numbers listed under the pit name. Her eyes widened. "Wait, we're in Wisconsin?"

"Yes indeed. But not just anywhere in Wisconsin. The GG? Stands for 'green' and 'gold.' Can you guess why?"

She frowned before lowering the tablet. "No. You're kidding me. We're not actually under—"

"Lambeau Field, baby!" Micah laughed. "Free tickets all season! Love it. Go Packers!"

Trish almost slapped a hand to her face. They were in Green Bay! That was barely five hours away from the pack. She scribbled her notes swiftly and tucked her hair behind her ear, inspecting the list. She noticed a few of the pit names weren't highlighted in green. "What about those?"

"Those are offline," Micah said, and his smile faded. "Pits that went down. We still have them recorded, so we remember where they are and everything. It's a shame. We lost a good one some weeks ago."

Trish licked her lips. "Which one?"

He tapped Pit CSub, and a map of Chicago sprang up. "Chicago. In the subway. It was one of our bigger operations that we ran a few years ago, but it got shut down because of Legion interference. We reopened it in a new location, but unfortunately it's down again."

"Can you still connect to them?" she asked.

Micah shook his head. "When a pit goes down, you're not supposed to reach out. It's locked by a passcode only we technicians know."

Trish swallowed and glanced sideways at the camera. She put her notebook down in front of him and whispered to him, pushing her charm harder. "What's the code? Don't say it out loud. Write it down."

Micah reached for her pen and scribbled a series of numbers. Trish memorized them as best she could. Okay, if she could get in and contact the pit, maybe she could get ahold of Legion and let them know these coordinates. Or Paytah's pack. Somebody. She glanced over her shoulder again and rested her head on her hand as she looked at the screen.

"Micah, can you put the camera up there on loop for two minutes?"

Micah didn't question her; he wouldn't, not with the charm. He nodded and went to work, flying through apps and typing rapidly. Trish watched the camera out of the corner of her eye and saw the light flicker then go steady again.

"Done," he said.

"Good. Close your eyes." Once he'd done as she asked, she quickly tapped the screen and put in the passcode. She held her breath and sent out a preliminary alert to the pit with the simple message, "Parahumans in danger." While she wanted to send the coordinates of Pit GG, she feared Hunters might still be on the lookout for transmissions. And if they discovered it came from Green Bay, that risked them shutting down this pit and rushing all the parahumans to another location. She had to be sure she could trust the person on the other end first.

She waited, hoping she'd get something back. She only had two minutes. (That was all she felt she could safely risk). "Come on," she whispered. She picked up his headset and waited, listening. There was nothing but dead air on the other end. She swallowed hard and ticked down the seconds until the two minutes were about up. With a sigh, she reached to take the headset off.

A voice crackled in her ears. "I get the feeling you're not supposed to be on this line," a woman said on the other end.

Trish bit her lip. "I'm a friend to parahumans. What about you?"

"Wouldn't be answering this if I wasn't."

Trish glanced at the time and swore inwardly. She wanted to spill everything about the pit, but what if she was wrong? What if this person *wasn't* a friend? And—

Something banged in the hall followed by a few voices laughing.

Decision made. "My time's limited. I'll reach out again soon."

"I'll be listening."

Trish yanked the set off and ended the call right as the camera came back to life. She waited, expecting someone to walk into the room. Instead, two figures passed the entrance chatting and wheeling a cart. Neither batted an eye at her.

Trish sucked in a breath and rubbed her face. That had been too close. She looked at Micah who still sat with his eyes closed. "So, this has been a great training session. I'm glad to know who to herald if the pit's threatened. Can you tell me more about the collars? Do you control them from in here, or can you only control them with the remotes?"

Micah opened his eyes and looked over at the wall of devices. "We have a couple fail-safes put in place," he said and got up. He grabbed a remote and a collar and brought them over, setting them down in front of her. "Every remote is sequenced to a particular collar, but there's a universal button here." He flipped the remote over to show her. "If you hit this, it'll shock anyone within a twenty-five-foot radius. You know, if parahumans get out of control."

"Do the controllers keep the collars locked?"

Micah nodded and turned the controller to the side. "See this sequence of three buttons? You have to hit them to get the collar off. Now, if a Hunter has multiple parahumans, the remotes will work on whoever you're pointing at. And you have to push the remote to the collar you want to open. There's an insert here." He showed her the collar and pushed the remote tip inside then hit three buttons. The collar popped open. "If we have to do a mass shock or something, that's when we go here." He slid along the desk to a smaller monitor. Trish followed and watched him pull up another application. "See this? This button here activates all the collars to shock at once. And this list here indicates how many collars are active."

Trish's stomach dropped at the number of glowing lights. It was disgusting; so many innocent parahumans forced to serve these monsters. Her eyes drifted to Micah again. Well, mostly monsters. "What if there was something wrong with the collars? Say they malfunctioned, and you had to get them all off at once. Can you do a mass release?"

Micah nodded and swiped to another screen. He showed her yet another code she'd have to type in. "Yep, you'd type the code here, and that'd release the collars."

She moved the notebook close to his hand again. "Write the code," she whispered.

He did as she asked without thinking and she studied the number. So many codes they had to get through. "Goodness, that's a lot to remember. Who all knows this?"

"Select members. Those who work in security, of course, and a few other Hunters just in case security gets targeted. But we don't know who they are. That's the point…so no one else can force the codes out of us.”

Trish hesitated, wondering if he was starting to see through her charm. But the pleasant, helpful smile remained on his face the entire time. She breathed a sigh of relief. Okay, this could work. She’d *make* this work. Someone, somewhere, was listening. Now she just had to find the perfect time to reach out and get them *here* before hell broke loose.

She touched Micah’s shoulder. “You’ve been a great help,” she said. “You can close out of that stuff. I think I’ve learned enough for the day.”

“Of course! And don’t be afraid to ask me questions,” Micah said and started to shut down the apps that might draw suspicion to them both. Trish watched him closely and tucked her small notebook back into her pocket beneath her shirt. Once Micah was done, she patted his back and smiled at him.

“Have a good day, Micah.” As she spoke, she let the charm fade from his eyes. He’d still feel like he hadn’t done anything wrong, but if anyone looked at him, they wouldn’t be able to tell she’d been in his head.

“Happy to! Feel free to stop by any time. It gets lonely around here,” he added with a nervous smile.

Trish grinned back. “I might take you up on that.” With a bob of her head, she turned and left. She glanced over her shoulder after the man. She hoped no one ever found out he had helped her. She hated Hunters, but he didn’t seem quite so bad.

Trish turned and nearly ran headfirst into another Hunter. She froze, startled, but the man just gave her a look and moved around her to join Micah in the office. Trish breathed out a sigh of relief and hurried back to her quarters.

Chapter 18
The Dead Don't Talk

Kafeada

"Let's see who our next client is," Kafeada said as she approached the body on the embalming table. She checked the tag name on her ankle and then looked through her files, humming to herself. "Ah, Sarah. Well, it looks like you and I are going to be best friends for the next couple of hours." She smiled at the pale woman. From the left, she looked unscathed, but from the right, it was clear she was missing about half of her face. No wonder the documents listed her death as catastrophic.

Kafeada brushed her brown fae hand delicately across the woman's forehead. "We'll get that fixed up for you. And then I'll make you nice and beautiful for your family. I bet they'd like that. Let's get started, hon."

She popped in her air pods and turned on her "embalming" playlist which mostly consisted of gothic rock and K-pop songs. They helped put her in the right mood, though other people might have been mortified by her singing along and dancing beside a corpse. Then again, all the morticians she knew could be as kooky as her. She swayed her hips and got the embalming machine up and running.

Death, *real* death, was a very foreign thing for most fae. In the Veil, fae didn't die. The body dissolved or got dusted into light, and then was reborn from the tree of life. When she'd first arrived on Earth through a Fae Way, she'd been baffled by the idea of a funeral. And seeing her first body? Well, she'd been asked to leave after poking the body in the face several times and asking why they wouldn't wake up. Fortunately, some parahumans had been patient with her and explained the process of death, decomposition, and all the earthly rituals surrounding funerals.

Kafeada found it all fascinating. And when she learned that she could get a job taking care of bodies? She'd leapt at the opportunity. The gravity of her decision didn't really weigh on her until she had her first car crash victim while she was in training. The person had been so mangled there was little to recover. Kafeada had heard the family sobbing, begging for the mortician to do *something* so they could see their son one last time and say goodbye to him. It would have been impossible for a human to fix the body, even with the wax, clay, or plaster of Paris to help the reconstruction.

For a fae? Kafeada took a look at the picture of the young man and used her magic to more or less recreate his body. Her powers mended his wounds and straightened his limbs. She reconstructed his face using Ather and got rid of the damage until he looked like the young man in the picture.

Knowing her magic had helped the family feel just a little less grief solidified her resolve to work in the industry, especially on parahumans who died awful, mutilating deaths. She found it fortunate that the Purple Door District not only had hospital floors devoted strictly to parahumans, but funeral homes too.

Sadly for Sarah, she'd tangled with a rogue werewolf and lost.

Kafeada got out her cosmetics that were reserved only for the bodies. She set them up, considering what colors to use on Sarah. "Hmm, should we go bold and bright? Earthy?" She looked through a folder and pulled out a picture of the woman. Kafeada smiled at the purple lipstick. "Ah, a woman after my own heart," she said. "I can make this work."

She touched the woman's forehead again and pushed magic into her face. As Kafeada studied the picture and the woman's undamaged visage, she began to reconstruct her features. She could use molds and tools to naturally fix the damage, and she admired those who could make the person look lifelike again. But Kafeada's magic was her unique way to help, so she used it.

Soon, Sarah looked as whole and beautiful as she did in the picture. Kafeada patted her cheek. "There we go. Muuuuch better."

Next, Kafeada focused on cleaning and massaging her limbs. Her magic kept Sarah's eyes closed, so no need for the caps. Kafeada used the cavity injector to fill her with the embalming solution. She checked the machine and estimated that it'd take about forty minutes for the fluids to swap. She hummed behind her mask as she worked. After a thought, she opened the bag of clothing the family had sent along and made sure those colors matched the makeup.

She spun and swayed her hips, levitating in the air with her magic as another song came on.

A thump from upstairs caught her attention. Kafeada lifted an eyebrow and popped out one of her air pods, listening. The floorboards of the funeral home creaked above her, despite the fact that no one was supposed to be there. Natalia, the funeral director, might have stopped by for something, but this late in the evening? With the expensive caskets and urns in the showroom, it was a real possibility a thief could have slipped in, not realizing anyone was around.

Kafeada sighed and donned her human glamor as she removed her mask and gloves, setting them on a tray near the door. She stepped out of the room and locked it behind her, just in case. She didn't need some idiot sneaking in and disturbing Sarah. Kafeada headed upstairs and glanced around in the darkness. She'd come in the bottom entrance, so none of the lights were on.

The floor creaked near the office, and Kafeada tilted her head. "Nat?" she called, waiting to hear either the director's voice or the sudden scurry of thieving feet. The noise stopped for a moment, causing Kafeada to narrow her eyes. Something didn't feel right. She touched her wedding ring that linked her, metaphorically and magically, with Evelyn and rubbed it. Kafeada turned back around and headed for the basement.

Pain exploded in the back of her leg. Kafeada pitched forward with a cry and fell to her knees, but she didn't stay down for long. She spun on her good knee and thrust her arms forward, causing fae light to shoot through the air and illuminate the area. Three people stood in front of her, the same three Hunters who had been involved in the attack on the school

"*You,*" Kafeada growled and let the glamor drop. Vines snarled down her arms and raced toward the tall bald Black man pointing a gun at her. Really? He thought a simple human gun was going to kill her? He scattered, along with the shorter white man—Hendrickson, if she remembered correctly—while Gale fired another shot at her. Kafeada raised her arm, creating a leaf-like shield and blocking the attack. She twisted her fingers and sent vines exploding at Gale. They snagged her by the arms and slammed her against the wall where they began to wind around her body and mouth to silence her cry of surprise.

The men charged Kafeada, weapons drawn. She curled her lip and blasted Hendrickson in the chest with green Ather. It threw him into one of the show coffins, sending both of them tumbling to the ground.

Ohhh, he is going to pay for that damage, she thought scathingly and turned on the taller Hunter. She threw a blast at him next.

He raised his wrist and an amethyst stone burst with light. Her magic crashed into an invisible shield and evaporated.

"What?" Kafeada said, startled. How the hell was a Hunter able to deflect Ather? She glowered at him and struck again, hitting his amethyst shield over and over. He staggered back, but never once did her magic hit him. It wasn't possible. The only type of person who could block her magic like that was another fae or Ather user, and this man stunk of human, *not* fae.

Another blow had him staggering to his knees. She advanced on him, emerald magic snarling in her hands. He raised the shield and she reached out, snatching his wrist. The crystal squealed as her magic combated it. But in the end, the stone cracked in two and fell to the ground, sizzling.

Kafeada grabbed the man by his throat and shoved him against the glass window of the office. "Who *are* you? Where have you taken my students?"

The man struggled, his hands wrapping around her wrist. He glared into her eyes but kept silent. Kafeada raised her other hand, a vine with long, vicious thorns snaking toward him. "You've visited the right place, *Hunter*. I'll take you apart then put you back together again in time for the funeral."

The man chuckled deep in his throat. "Mine, or yours?" he asked.

She glared until a red beam reflected in the glass next to his head. Kafeada spun and threw the man to the side, calling up a shield to protect herself.

Too late.

Another shot took her in the shoulder. As she staggered into the glass, a fourth Hunter, Saul, sprang out of the darkness with a silver ring in his hands. She managed to grab one of his arms, but the other clamped the ring around her throat.

The blistering kiss of cold iron burned her flesh the moment it touched her. Kafeada shouted in pain and reached up to pull the collar off. But grabbing it with her hands made them burn just as badly. She fell to her knees, screaming, tugging, trying to blast her magic at the ring, but with the iron on, her Ather shriveled up inside of her like a frightened babe.

Saul, dreadlocks swinging around his face, stepped back and held a remote in his hand. He pressed a button, and the pain mercifully ceased. Kafeada bent forward, gasping for breath. She touched the burns with tender fingers then the collar. Her nail brushed against another amethyst stone that hummed with Ather magic. She couldn't use it, but it created a miniscule barrier between her throat and the hateful collar. Kafeada glared up at the Hunter, her gaze flaring with rage.

He smiled down at her with red, vampire eyes. "If you come along quietly, I won't hurt you further. If not . . .." He pressed the button, and the pain returned, sending Kafeada to the floor.

She twitched and struggled to breathe until he slipped his finger off the remote. Kafeada stayed down, hearing footsteps as two of the other Hunters approached her. She imagined Gale was still bound up against the wall. "You won't keep me like this," Kafeada growled at the vampire.

"Oh, I know, but I'm not the one who wants you," he said and knelt at her side. He grabbed her arms, despite the bullet in her shoulder, and twisted them behind her back. Cold shackles (but thankfully not cold *iron*) bound her wrists. She struggled and felt along her hand until she grasped her ring. She yanked it off and dropped it to the ground. The Hunter had just gotten her to her feet when a huge gust of wind exploded through the funeral home, knocking everyone to the ground.

Kafeada landed with a grunt and looked at the front door.

Evelyn, her beautiful Evelyn, stormed through the door with Rozene, Jackson, Wapasha, and Daniella flanking her. All the wolves, save Rozene, were already in their bipedal forms. While Wapasha and

Jackson had darker pelts, Daniella's was a mix of dirty white and silver, her body laced in scars. They snarled and lunged forward, seeking out the Hunters as they scrambled to reach Kafeada's side.

Jackson and Wapasha made a beeline for Hendrickson and the other human Hunter. Daniella, however, skidded as she reached Gale's bound form.

Kafeada's attention snapped toward her wife as Evelyn threw a wind barrier in front of Kafeada, blocking the vampire from grabbing her. He slammed into the magical wall and fell back, then struck again. But Evelyn's magic wasn't so easily broken.

Hendrickson shouted in rage at the magus and fired off several rounds at her. Evelyn blocked most with an Ether shield then ducked when Saul unloaded on her too. Daniella dodged a few bullets. Jackson and Wapasha both scattered out of the way, but they kept creeping forward, ducking behind one of the building's columns or using the central fireplace for cover when a bullet strayed too close.

Saul and his friend stood around Kafeada, and Hendrickson rushed the wall where Gale was held. He grabbed a knife from her belt and hacked at the vines to get her free, firing at anyone who got too close to him.

Saul glowered and pointed the remote at Kafeada. Her world ignited in pain and she thrashed on the ground, crying out in agony as the cold iron bit deeper into her flesh. It felt worse than normal, like some other magic, non Ather, was fueling it.

"Let us leave," Saul shouted, "or I'll dust her."

"Saul," Rozene shouted. "You don't have to do this! Think of your coven back home. You're one of us, not one of these *Hunters*."

He glowered at her. "These Hunters and their mistress have done more for me than your damned District. And especially your *mate*. He took *everything* from me." His eyes flashed red, and he passed the remote over to his fellow Hunter. "Let me return the favor." He trained his gun on Rozene and fired.

The werewolf threw herself to the ground and rolled out of the way. Wapasha roared in anger and charged Saul. He went in low, so when Saul turned to shoot him, he didn't move fast enough. Wapasha grabbed him around the waist and slammed him into, then through, the wall. They tumbled out of sight with a crash.

Kafeada was barely conscious of it all as she kept screaming through the pain. The bald Hunter moved closer to her and touched the wind wall. Suddenly, he pulled a stone out of his pocket and slammed it into the barrier. It crumbled apart, letting him through. He grabbed Kafeada by her hair and yanked her up, pressing his gun to her head. "Call them off!" he shouted. "I swear to God, I'll destroy her!"

"Stop!" Evelyn shouted. Kafeada wanted to scream at her wife to take the Hunters down, but she knew her dear Evelyn. She wouldn't put Kafeada's life at risk like that. She came into view, hands up. "Stop."

The Hunter glowered then glanced over his shoulder briefly when Wapasha yelped. Saul staggered back through the hole, his entire arm nearly ripped off at the shoulder. He yanked a vial from his pocket and tossed it into the air. A shot from his gun caused it to explode. Thick smoke filled the air, suffocating those closest to it. He touched Kafeada and glared at Hendrickson as he finally freed Gale from the wall, both choking on the smoke. "We're leaving. *Now.* Come over here, or be left behind."

Hendrickson jerked on Gale's arm, and they raced toward Saul together. Kafeada slumped in her captor's hold and peered through the smoke as Evelyn struggled to clear it with her magic. Ather built up around them from a talisman Saul touched on his chest. It rippled across everyone touching him. Hendrickson grabbed onto his shoulder. As Gale reached to do the same, Daniella's hulking figure burst out of the cloud of smoke and tackled her to the ground.

"Gale!" Hendrickson shouted, but too late.

Ather snarled around them and whisked them away.

Chapter 19
A Meeting of Fae

Kafeada

The world spun as Ather blipped them out of the funeral home and to their new destination. Kafeada closed her eyes to stave off the impending dizziness that sent most humans to their knees or made them vomit. When they landed, she fell to the cool, stone floor and lay there, grateful for the brief reprieve from the pain. But that meant she was very much aware she'd escaped the boiling pot and jumped into the fire. She was still bound, her magic trapped inside of her. And if she had to guess, she was in the Hunters' stronghold.

Fantastic.

Hendrickson staggered back to his feet and threw himself at Saul, grabbing him by his shirt. "We have to go back. Take us back! We can't leave Gale behind."

"She knew the risks, Hendrickson," the other human Hunter said. He got up and dusted himself off before looking Saul over. "Did the werewolf bite you, or just try to tear your arm off?"

"Both," Saul responded in a strained voice. He gripped his dangling arm, wincing as Hendrickson shook him again. "Slater's right. We can't go back. We have what we came for," he added, gesturing to Kafeada with a jerk of his head.

"I don't care!" Hendrickson roared. "We're not leaving my sister in their clutches. They'll kill her! Didn't they already kill your mate?"

Saul jerked back with a growl. *"Careful.* If you want to ask the lady to send you to rescue your sister, then that's your prerogative. I accomplished my task." He grimaced again and glanced at Slater. "Can you get her?"

Slater nodded and reached down, pulling Kafeada to her feet. She struggled against him a little, but she knew it was futile. Even with the collar on her throat, she could sense the Ather magic pressing down around her, shielding her from reaching out to her wife and friends. Better to play along and learn what she could in case she found a way to escape.

Hendrickson shook his head furiously. He grabbed Saul's good arm and yanked him closer, his hand reaching for the crystal on his chest. "Then give the transportation crystal to me. I'll rescue my sister myself."

"The crystal only had two uses, and we used them both already," Saul said, trying to shrug him off. Blood flowed out of his wound and splattered on the ground. "I can't help you."

Hendrickson's eyes burned with outrage. "So you tangle us up in your petty bid for revenge because of your mate's death, but when my sister, a *living* person, needs help, screw me, right?"

Saul narrowed his eyes dangerously, his irises glittering red. "I've heard you betrayed and left behind one sister before. What's another?"

"Son of a bitch!" Hendrickson shouted and clocked Saul under the chin. The vampire fell to the ground with a cry. Hendrickson followed, still holding one of Gale's knives in his hand. He pressed it to the vampire's throat. "I should kill you. If it wasn't for you, we wouldn't be in this mess!"

Saul stared right back. His good shoulder relaxed and he lifted his chin, never once breaking his stare. "The only person you're going to kill with that knife is you," he said in a low tone. As he spoke, eyes gleamed bright red.

Hendrickson froze. His hand started to shake around the dagger as he brought the blade toward his own throat. "S-stop. What are you doing?" he demanded, fear echoing in his voice. He tried to break eye contact with Saul, but to no avail. The metal pressed against his jugular and bit into his flesh.

"Saul," Slater said in warning.

The vampire sighed and rolled his eyes.

Hendrickson scrambled backward, dropping the knife to the ground. He grabbed his throat and felt it, as if to make sure it was still whole. "You...you were going to kill me!" he said in disbelief.

"No," Saul replied in a tired voice. "Just making a point. Don't threaten those who are stronger than you, Hendrickson. And don't think me a caged parahuman you can order around. I don't serve *you*." He pulled himself to his feet and wobbled. Slater caught his good arm before he collapsed.

"We need to get you to the lady." He glared at Hendrickson. "Either you keep your mouth shut and come with us so you can ask the lady for a crystal to save your sister, or you can bugger off."

Hendrickson glowered, but he kept his mouth shut as he sheathed the knife.

Kafeada smirked to herself. Well, well, there was unrest between the Hunters here. She could use that to her advantage. Though she'd have to bide her time, figure out how to get this collar off, and replenish her Ather.

Maybe it wasn't so simple.

They walked through the hallways, Saul guiding them with Slater just behind him and Hendrickson in the rear. Kafeada kept her head down, but she watched the path they took and listened. The distant sound of fighting reached them as they passed a larger hallway that must lead to the pit. Her nose wasn't as sensitive as a wolf's or feline's, so she couldn't scent what kind of parahumans were around, but her skin prickled with Ather and Ether magic. This entire place was enclosed in an Ather shield, and in some distant halls she caught the low hum of trapped Ether waiting for release.

She was partially dragged, partially carried to a strange wooden door. The moment her eyes fell upon the fae symbols lining it, the blood left her face. "You have no idea the abomination you're working for," she said. "You'll be lucky if any of you walk away from this alive."

"Quiet," Slater hissed at her and jerked her arm hard.

"Idiots," Kafeada snapped in return. She tensed as the door opened. Sick, twisted Ether and Ather flowed out of the room, poisoned magic that made Kafeada want to vomit. There was a reason fae didn't stay on Earth all the time. The Ether corrupted them and their Veil-born magic. And this room stank of corruption.

Slater pushed her ahead of him, and she stepped through onto a warm, woven rug. She glanced up at the smoky purple and black starlit sky above them. Water sloshed in pools, and fragrant fae flowers filled her senses. But none of it could mask the stench.

"Well," a silky voice said in the darkness. "You managed to claim my prize."

Kafeada squared her shoulders as the dream fae stepped into view. While the fae looked beautiful with her white and violet hair, her opalescent skin, and thick, luscious lips, Kafeada could see the sickly creature behind the disguise: a thin, bedraggled woman who looked like she belonged at the bottom of a well.

Slater approached the fae and bowed. "Lady Vesp, will you do us the honor of saving Saul's arm? He nearly lost it trying to catch your prey."

Kafeada's mouth fell open in shock. Though she'd suspected the culprit might be Vesp, to hear the cursed name spoken, and to see the fae standing before her, sent chills of dread racing down her spine.

Vesp tilted her horned head at Saul and curled a finger toward her. "Poor dear," she said and reached for his arm. She ran her hands delicately over his skin and around his mutilated shoulder. "Of course I'll reward you for your success." Magic glowed through her fingers as she knit muscle, sinew, and flesh back together. Saul moaned in relief as the pain was taken from him, and his arm returned to its former glory.

"Thank you," he said and flexed his arm.

"Don't thank me yet," Vesp said and cupped his cheek lovingly. She frowned and turned his head to the side. "There's sadness in you again. I thought I'd banished it."

Saul swallowed. "Evelyn and some of her friends arrived to stop us. Rozene was there...and I was reminded of what I've lost."

"Such a pity," Vesp said and stroked his face. "Let me help you." She pulled him close and pressed her lips against his.

Kafeada made a face as she watched twisted black energy leave Saul's body and flow into Vesp's. She was devouring his dark emotions, much like a succubus could. But how? Fae didn't eat emotions, and she couldn't survive off of that alone. Unless it wasn't just emotions but the energy created by his fear and grief that she was feeding on.

Saul slumped in her hold as she drained him. She held him steady once she broke the kiss and bumped her nose against his chin.

"Better?"

"Much, my lady," Saul said in a dazed voice.

Vesp smiled and ushered him toward Slater. "Very good. If that is all—"

"It's not," Hendrickson interrupted and pushed between the two other Hunters. "Gale was captured. Some werewolf snatched her right before we blipped. I have to save her."

Vesp cocked her head and frowned. "I'm afraid I can't help you."

Hendrickson's hand tightened around the blade on his hip. "What do you mean you can't help?! You gave us the tools to fight off any parahumans who came after us. You gave us a crystal to blip us there and back! Why can't you give me another to rescue my sister?"

"Because I refuse to lose another Hunter," Vesp said simply. "You all know the risks when you venture out of my care. If she's taken, she might already be tainted, bugged, marked. I won't risk the safety of this pit for one Hunter."

"But you'll risk our lives for *her*?" Hendrickson spat, gesturing to Kafeada.

Vesp glanced at her, her violet eyes sending chills down Kafeada's spine. "If you want this protective barrier to continue to exist, then yes. I'll save many, even if I must sacrifice one or two."

"That one is my sister!" Hendrickson shouted. He snatched the fae by the front of her dress. "You can't do this!"

Vesp didn't say a word or move a muscle, though Saul and Slater both drew their weapons. Suddenly, Hendrickson was thrown backward into the wall, flipped upside down, and pinned there by ebony tendrils twisting around his ankles. He grunted and thrashed to get free until two more tendrils pinned his wrists and gagged him.

Vesp walked to him and crouched down. She grabbed his hair and pulled his head close to her as he shouted fearful obscenities into his gag. "Do *not* touch me," she said in a low tone. "I have made my decision. I will not risk the safety of this pit for one Hunter, no matter who she is. If you continue to quarrel with me, I'll take your best fighter off your hands for you as well."

Hendrickson clenched his jaw, but his struggles ceased. He turned his head away from her; Kafeada thought she saw a glint of tears in his eyes. She wouldn't have expected that based on what Daniella had said about him. Curious. Very curious.

Vesp set Hendrickson back down and waved the bonds away. She waited, but he offered no resistance. Instead he rose, bowed curtly, and stormed out of the room. Both Saul and Slater watched him depart before they bowed as well.

"I'll speak with him," Slater said, holstering his gun. "He's still young and impressionable."

"See that you do. Now, off with you both. And take the night to celebrate your victory." She waved a hand. "Special gifts will be waiting for you in your quarters."

The men smiled and bowed a second time then departed. Saul shut the door behind him. The quiet click of the lock twisted Kafeada's stomach into knots.

Vesp turned haunting eyes on her. "I apologize for the wait, my sister. These Earth folk are sometimes *so* much work." She waved her hand once more.

Kafeada grunted as her wounds healed over. Bullets tinked to the ground. She glanced at them and noticed they didn't look normal. Were they made of cold iron too somehow? It would explain why she'd felt so weak after getting shot. A normal bullet wouldn't have done as much damage.

The shackles came next and fell to the floor. Kafeada flicked her wings and pulled her arms out from behind her back to rub life into her wrists. "I'd thank you, but you're the reason why I've been kidnapped."

"Not kidnapped," Vesp said, shaking her head. "No, I wanted to meet you, Sister. And I didn't think you would accept me if I visited you as I am."

Kafeada glared. "I'm not your sister. And you can drop the facade. Their minds might be simple, and they may be fooled by your glamor, but I'm not. How sick are you?"

Vesp's smile faded in an instant. She lifted her chin in defiance and magicked a chair to her side. "You've heard the stories, then, of a fae banished from the Veil?"

"Who hasn't? We tell those tales to troublesome babes and make them fear getting gobbled up by you."

Vesp's laughter startled her. She brought her hand to her lips and giggled into her pale fingers. "I've become a thing of nightmares? I suppose that's fitting. Hehe, gobble them up indeed. No, I prefer bigger prey."

Vesp vanished from sight.

Suddenly, the fae's hand wrapped around Kafeada's jaw and jerked her back against Vesp's chest. Black tendrils bound her wrists so she couldn't fight back. "Like you," Vesp purred into her ear.

Kafeada struggled, but it was no use. The moment Vesp let her face go, the tendrils jerked her down to her knees and kept her there. Vesp prowled around her and ran her fingers through Kafeada's hair, plucking a rose from her green and purple braids.

"It doesn't have to be this way," Vesp said. "I brought you here to work beside me. To help me keep this pit hidden." She pressed the rose to her chest and smiled. "And to nourish me with Ather. I may not be able to touch the Veil, but you can." She bent forward, arms wrapped around her belly. Her breasts nearly spilled out over the top of her gown, which Kafeada both admired and wanted nothing to do with. "You'd be saving many minds, you know. If you serve me, I won't have to feast on any of the parahumans here. I'm afraid I might have broken a few already. Pity."

She glanced toward her stony bath. Kafeada followed her gaze until she spotted something she'd missed earlier: bones. Bones decorated the bath. Remnants of her victims no doubt. Kafeada shook her head in disgust. "Did you really think I'd agree to serve you? Believe you?" she asked, glowering. "I know your kind, what you're capable of. The last thing I'm going to do is work with a deranged fae who eats the energy of her victims like some damn succubus. Whether I agree to serve you or not, you'll drain me regardless. So why put on this show?"

Vesp's right eye twitched, and she straightened. She glanced at the bones around the pool then to something else hidden in the shadows. There came no snide response or simpering smile. She just looked away, her expression tired, forlorn.

Kafeada blinked in realization. "You're lonely."

"Wouldn't you be if all the fae of the Earth and Veil feared you? If you couldn't ever return to the Veil, even though what you did was an accident?"

"You *killed* a fae," Kafeada protested. "Not just dusted her and sent her back to the tree. You took her life so she could *never* be reborn. That death stole life from the Veil. Don't you understand that?"

"I know!" Vesp shouted. Her glamor faded as her emotions took over. The tendrils slipped from Kafeada and quivered beneath her feathered wings. "I never meant to hurt anyone! I didn't understand my calling, my abilities as a dream fae. When it happened—" she looked down at her hands, "—I tried to restore her power. Bring her back. But it was too late."

"A fae can't survive without any Ather in their body," Kafeada said, fluttering to her feet. "You took her life force for your own. Not even Lord Oberon could breathe life into her again. That's why you were banished and why you're so feared. And then look at what you're doing here!" She gestured to the pit around them and to the odd prison she'd been brought to. "You're helping Hunters take and destroy parahumans. Why not do something good with what powers you have left instead of causing pain and suffering?"

Vesp lifted her eyes, darkness swirling behind her cold irises. She clenched her delicate hands into fists and thrust them to her sides. "Why should I when no one would give me the chance to tell *my* story? If I don't take what I need to survive, I'll be dusted and *never* return to the Veil. I'll be forced to float around this hellhole for the rest of existence. I won't let it happen. So I'll take what I need."

"Then the world will continue to hate you," Kafeada argued. She took a hesitant step forward, knowing a fae as powerful as Vesp could vanquish her and her soul if she wasn't careful. "Change sides," she urged. "*Help* us bring the parahumans and the children home. We can find another way to feed you, Sister. It doesn't have to be like this, and you don't have to be alone." She cautiously touched Vesp's cold arm and searched the fae's face, hoping there was some glimmer of sanity still in that deranged head of hers. "If you have a representative to speak on your behalf to Lord Oberon, maybe he'll hear your plea to return home."

Vesp stared at Kafeada's hand. She opened and shut her mouth, struggling with something. But then she settled her hand on Kafeada's and squeezed it. "You and I both know Lord Oberon will *never* allow me back in the Veil, and even if he did, he'd destroy me, force me to be reborn with no memories." She narrowed her eyes and tightened her hold. "And I've built too much of an empire to give it up for the chance that Oberon won't kill me."

Kafeada glowered and tried to jerk back, but Vesp kept a vice-like grip around her hand. The fae leaned closer, peering into Kafeada's very soul. "You never would have helped me anyway. Not willingly. No fae will, and I'm foolish to have thought otherwise." Black tendrils shot from Vesp's back and wrapped around Kafeada's limbs. One coiled around her head and started to push magic into her mind. She tried to shut her thoughts off to it, but it was no use. Images of her beloved Evelyn falling to a Hunter's gun flashed before her eyes. Her students burned inside of the very house she'd promised would protect them. Wapasha fell beside his mate, Daniella standing over him with bloody claws and fangs.

Unbidden, tears rolled down Kafeada's cheeks. She cried out in despair and struggled to break free of the fae's hold. As the horrible images flashed before her, and her heart wept in grief, she felt her Ather pulled out of her. The world wavered in front of her eyes. Her knees wobbled. She sank to the ground, still hearing her wife's scream as darkness took her.

Kafeada woke to find her body sprawled across something soft. She opened her crusted eyes and looked down. She lay in a comfortable violet bed with a black blanket and pillows. She sat up swiftly, but the room danced again as dizziness took her. She leaned forward, willing herself not to throw up all over the floor. How was she still alive?

She swallowed and looked up.

A barrier of black and purple magic flickered around her. She reached out a finger toward one wall and touched it. It didn't hurt, but if she tried to push out her magic, nothing happened. She rubbed her throat and found the collar was gone, thankfully. Kafeada pushed herself to her feet and moved around her little prison.

Stones sat outside of the walls, four of them etched with the fae symbols of water, fire, earth, and air. She pushed her magic out again, but still nothing. The prison kept her trapped and made it impossible to reach her wife both magically and mentally.

"You'll stay there until I need you," Vesp's voice said in the darkness. "Continue to resist me, and you'll join the rest of them in my decor."

A stone table appeared outside of the prison. Bottles containing colorful lights lined the top of it. Kafeada frowned in confusion until one of the lights moved and bounced against the glass.

"No!" she shouted in horror and banged her fists against the wall. "What have you done to them? How could you?" So many brothers and sisters who still had yet to be reborn. How long had they been here? How long had Vesp made them suffer before she stuffed their essences into those bottles?

Kafeada fell to her knees, her hand dragging down the side of the wall. "How could you?" she whispered again, but the darkness offered no reply.

Chapter 20
Reunion

Gale

The first thing Gale woke to was a pounding migraine. She moaned in pain, her head bowed against her chest. She tried to lick her dry lips, but something rough filled her mouth, stifling her. Darkness surrounded her; a cloth pressed against her eyelids, keeping them shut. Slowly, she pulled on her arms, but both wrists were bound to the arms of a chair. Her legs were similarly trapped. She sighed and rolled her head to the side, trying to remember what had happened.

They'd gone after the fae in a funeral home. Rozene and other wolves had been there, along with the wind magus. She recalled getting thrown against a wall and bound to it with thick, vicious vines. But Hendrickson had freed her, so how—

A wolf. A wolf had grabbed her, and then nothing.

Great. She was a captive. And she knew how Vesp felt about Hunters getting caught by their enemy.

She rubbed her face against her shoulder and heard movement nearby.

"Get Rozene," a soft voice said. "She's waking up."

Gale lifted her head and let it fall back to try to ease some of the pounding. It did little. Had they drugged her? Or had the werewolf decided to gift her a concussion?

A warm hand touched her head, making her jump and sending

another shock of agony through her skull from the movement. She waited for more pain, but instead someone removed the blindfold. Gale blinked a few times to chase away blurriness and an aura. When she focused, she found the wind magus standing in front of her.

Evelyn set the blindfold on a nearby table. "You're lucky to be alive," she said.

Gale gave a muffled grunt in response. She didn't consider her current situation *lucky*. She glanced around at the stone walls surrounding her. Where was she? The basement of the magus's house? Or somewhere else? There were no bars trapping her in the room, just a regular door. Yes, maybe a side room in a basement. She shifted and glanced down at the ropes and tape binding her to the chair. Her breath hitched when she noticed she'd also been stripped of her black hunter gear and left in sweats and a t-shirt. Who the hell had done that?! Her boots and socks were gone, too. Any hope of slipping a sharp object out of a hidden compartment in her clothing was out.

They were thorough.

Gale grumbled and kept still as more people filed into the room. She recognized Rozene in her human form. And she assumed the dark, hulking bipedal werewolf at her side was her beta, Jackson. She didn't quite recognize the other Native American man who joined them, but he had similar features to Rozene. Or was he the Wisconsin alpha she'd read about, Wapasha? She'd just assume it was Wapasha.

Someone else tried to walk in, but Jackson growled at the person, warning them back.

"Stay out there for now," Wapasha ordered.

Gale didn't get a good look at the figure, but the irritated grunt that answered him sounded feminine. She pressed her gagged lips together as best she could and waited.

Rozene approached her first. "We have questions for you, and you will answer us. Your life depends on it."

Gale snorted and did her best to hide her fear. It wasn't the first time she'd been captured and threatened. But unlike the last time, she felt the werewolf was very serious. Rozene pulled tape off her lips. Gale turned her head and spat a thick cloth to the floor, coughing. "If you want me to talk," she rasped, "I'll need water first."

Jackson growled, but Rozene held up her hand. She grabbed a bottle of water from the table and pressed it to Gale's lips. Gale drank it slowly, getting the awful taste of the cloth out of her mouth.

Rozene set it back down and crossed her arms. "You and your cohorts took my pack members and killed one of them. You've stolen her students," she added, nodding to Evelyn. "And now you've kidnapped her wife. Where are they?"

Gale barked out a quiet laugh that made her head hurt worse. "You really think I'd tell you? Go to hell."

Jackson swept to her side and grabbed her around her throat. His vicious claws dug deeply into her flesh, drawing blood. She choked and struggled to break free, but he held tight.

"*Jackson*," Rozene hissed.

The werewolf dropped her. Gale gasped for breath. Good god! They weren't playing around. But she also knew they couldn't kill her. They *needed* her. "I'm not afraid of you—"

"Bullshit," the voice from the shadows said. Why did it sound familiar?

Wapasha glared over his shoulder then turned his eyes on Gale. "This doesn't have to end in your death. Help us, and you can disappear. Live another life far from here, away from us and other Hunters."

Gale rolled her eyes. "Like you'd keep your word."

Rozene moved closer. "We don't make the habit of breaking promises. You have done awful things to my pack, even killed a beloved man, but I can offer you your life and freedom if you help us save the rest. Contrary to what you Hunters may think, we *are* humane."

Gale eyed her warily. The wolf sounded sincere, but she'd heard such lies before. There was something curious about the way she spoke though, a cadence that made Gale think of Nick. Her heart ached a little at the thought of him. Once Hendrickson realized she was gone, he'd take his anger out on whoever was closest to him, which would likely be Nick or one of their captives. She didn't want that. And it enraged her to realize she felt bonded to the stupid wolf.

Rozene waited, but when Gale gave no reply, the alpha sighed. "If you won't agree to freedom for yourself, then what about the freedom of your brother? What if we let you both escape and start your lives over?"

Gale blinked. How the hell did this woman know about her brother?

She narrowed her eyes. That was a low blow, dangling his freedom over her head too. "Now I know you're lying. You wouldn't let two Hunters live."

"I would," Rozene said. "If it means I'll get my pups back. Where are they?"

Gale sighed in frustration. "I won't tell you." She flinched as the big werewolf lunged toward her again, but he didn't attack her. His hot breath wafted across her face, his fangs inches from her eye. She shrank away from him, quivering in her bonds.

"Where are they?" Rozene asked.

"You can't kill me," Gale protested as Jackson gnashed his teeth in her face. "You and I both know that. I'm your only hope of finding them. All of them."

Evelyn moved closer to her. Her eyes looked tired, likely from sleepless nights. Maybe from scrying. "Why did you take my wife?"

"That's not for me to say," Gale said. Did they really think asking her nicely and making false promises and veiled threats would make her talk? Apparently they weren't used to having prisoners. She could deal with their interrogation long enough for Hendrickson to save her. If he *could* save her. There was every possibility Vesp and the rest of her minions wouldn't allow it. *I might never see him again*, she thought, and that scared her more than any pain these idiots could force her to endure.

Jackson shot a look at Rozene. The beta couldn't speak verbally in his bipedal form, but based on the glint in Rozene's eye and the shift in her posture, he was speaking mentally. She looked at him with a grimace before approaching Gale again.

Gale waited for a blow to come.

The alpha crossed her arms and stared down her nose at the Huntress. "You're right. We can't kill you. But we can change you."

Gale's heart faltered and skipped a beat. She leaned away and looked between Jackson and Rozene. He bared his fangs, saliva and werewolf venom dripping in his mouth. Gale tried to keep the fear out of her voice. "You wouldn't. It's against your oath to forcibly change someone."

"Desperate times call for desperate measures," Rozene said. "You can either tell us what we want to know, or we can force the change. All it takes is one bite." She lifted her hand and forced out a long claw.

"One scratch."

Gale sucked in a breath and struggled in her bonds, shaking her head. No, they couldn't be serious! Beat her, torture her, do anything but turn her into one of *them*! The bite had driven Daniella to madness and murder. What would it do to Gale?

The panic rose in her chest as Jackson grabbed her by her hair. He pulled her head back, bringing his fangs dangerously close to her throat. "No! Don't!"

A woman bodied Jackson into the closest wall, pinning him there with hands that had started to turn into huge paws. She snarled in his face, her back to Gale.

Wapasha swore. "Stand down!" he shouted at the woman.

"You said nothing about changing her!" the woman roared, her voice once again striking a familiar chord in Gale that she couldn't place. "I won't let you do that!"

Jackson shoved her back hard and started to shift back into his human form. "Where does your loyalty belong?" he snapped at her once he had his human voice. "With us, or with the Hunters?"

"With you, but that doesn't mean you have to change her!" the woman shouted back and got into his face. She was shorter, but her body was built.

Wapasha's hand snaked out and caught her by the shoulder. "Leave this room *now*."

"With all due respect, Alpha, *no*. There are other ways to make her talk than turning her into a werewolf. She doesn't deserve that." She turned and looked Gale directly in the eyes. "She doesn't deserve that honor."

Time stopped.

Gale stared at the ghost standing in front of her, someone she thought she'd lost years ago on a cold winter night. Back then, she'd been in her wolf form, fur tainted by the blood of their parents. Now, only the scars on her face spoke of what had transpired that night.

"Daniella?" Gale choked out, tears filling her eyes.

Daniella nodded slowly. She glanced sideways at Wapasha. "Alpha, please, let me speak with her. I brought her to you. The least you can do is allow me to talk to her. Alone."

"No," Jackson hissed. He spread his arms out to Rozene and

Wapasha. "We can't just leave them together and assume they won't conspire."

"What would I have to conspire with her about?" Daniella laughed. "She may be my sister, but she's also a Hunter. I want to know if there's any family bond left between us." She turned to the alphas. "If not alone, then how about with a guard or two outside the door, in case she manages to escape? Or if you think I'm so untrustworthy, leave Vic or Evelyn behind to take me down with their magic."

Rozene and Wapasha exchanged looks. They turned their eyes to Evelyn who scrutinized Daniella. After a long moment, she set her jaw and headed for the door. "I'll be waiting outside. And if *anyone* tries to escape, I will lay them flat."

Daniella nodded at her retreating back then arched an eyebrow at Rozene and Wapasha. Rozene grasped Jackson's shoulder and guided him through the door, but not without a last snarl directed at both Daniella and Gale. Wapasha inclined his head toward Daniella.

"Don't disappoint me," he said, then walked out and shut the door behind him and his mother.

Deafening silence remained. Daniella stood awkwardly to the side, staring at the door and leaving Gale to wonder where her sister's mind was. But it almost didn't matter. Daniella was *alive*. She was safe (even if she was with a pack of wolves). She looked fierce and beautiful and everything Gale had hoped would happen for her sister when Daniella had left to be turned, only for her transformation to turn into a nightmare for them all.

"*How?*" Gale squeaked out.

"How am I alive?" Daniella asked and waited for Gale's timid nod. She grabbed a chair and dragged it over. The legs scraped against the stone floor. She turned it around and sat down, her arms folded over the back. "After you left, Wapasha's pack found me. Took care of me; nursed me back to health."

"But...but I thought the change caused you to go mad?"

"It did. But with a strong mentor and a protective pack, I was able to finish my transformation. I'm still not entirely whole, but I can function and serve my pack. My alpha. *They* gave me a chance to live."

Gale winced.

"Something our parents and brother didn't think to offer." She rested her head on her hand. Black claws pushed through her fingers and helped brace her cheek. "What I can't figure out is why you left me there instead of taking me to a pit or killing me yourself."

"I could never kill my family," Gale said quickly then grimaced at the unintentional accusation.

"No, but I could, right?" Daniella growled.

"Th-that's not what I meant. I...I couldn't take your life. I love you."

"You have a damn funny way of showing it. What, you left me in the snow to let the elements do the deed for you?"

Gale bowed her head in guilt. It looked that way, didn't it? "I dropped you off close to the pack. I hoped they would find you. Help you."

"And you didn't take me all the way because?"

Gale laughed bitterly. "Hendrickson and I had just killed one of their wolves and caged another. I didn't think they'd appreciate seeing my face." She felt Daniella's wolf eyes burrow into her. "I was a coward."

"You were," Daniella agreed. "Fortunately for both of us, the pack found and saved me." She narrowed her eyes. "Did you even want me to survive?"

"Of course!" Gale cried. She lifted her fingers emphatically, unable to do much more due to her bonds. "You're my sister."

"And an abomination. Is that why you're so afraid of being turned? You don't want to become a monster like me?"

Gale opened and shut her mouth, but nothing came out. What could she say that wasn't a flat out lie? Parahumans weren't *normal*. They were dangerous and had caused suffering and many deaths. It was why she'd worked so hard to become a Huntress. And after what had happened to their parents, she had every reason to hate parahumans!

And yet Nick didn't hate humans after his father's death. And the very person to blame for her parents' murders was standing right in front of her, but she didn't want her sister dead. She could never want that.

"Answer me!" Daniella snapped.

"You're not a monster," Gale whispered.

Daniella chuckled and glanced over her shoulder. "Oh, but the rest of my kind is?" Her face grew somber as she looked at Gale. "Our parents are dead because of me. How do you not want me dead too?"

"They wouldn't listen," Gale said. "They didn't give you a chance to ask for help when the change didn't go well. They just tried to kill you. That's the only reason you struck them down."

Daniella's face twisted a little, her eyes growing tormented. She ran her hand along her scarred arm and sighed. "I never meant to hurt them. I wasn't in my right mind, and when I tried to ask for help, they didn't look at me like I was their daughter. I was just another target." She pressed her lips together. "It's good they wounded me. I was so out of my mind; I don't know what I would have done to you and Hendrickson." She sighed. "I'm sorry, Gale."

Gale blinked in surprise. The last thing she'd expected from Daniella was an apology! Especially not after what Gale and Hendrickson had done to Daniella and the parahuman she'd loved. "I didn't listen either. I didn't help you or argue with Hendrickson. I was so blinded by rage and pain that I took away someone important to you. And, I don't know, for a moment I wanted you to suffer too. But then I looked into your eyes, and I saw my big sister was still there. I saw something Hendrickson wouldn't allow himself to see."

"Yeah, well, he's never been good at listening to reason," Daniella said with a faint smile. She rested her chin on her arms again. "Gale, we need to know about the pit. I don't think they were kidding about changing you if you don't obey."

"That would go against everything they stand for though," Gale argued.

"They're desperate. Your people already killed one of theirs. And three are still missing. And now the magus's students and wife are gone. *Kids*, Gale. I thought you and Hendrickson would at least swear off harming them."

Gale shook her head. "It was never our intent to take the students. We only wanted Kafeada."

"*Why?*" Daniella pressed. "Why do they want Kafeada? And are the teens even still alive?"

"Yes. They're alive. They're even being protected by one of Rozene's wolves." Gale licked her lips. "I can't explain why they want Kafeada. There are…things…about the pit even I'm not privy to. And I can't give you those answers."

"Are you sure?" Daniella asked and tilted her head. "You looked pretty excited about the idea of you and Hendrickson getting to start over. Something about the Hunter life not sitting well with you anymore?"

Gale glanced away. She was that obvious, huh? Yes, starting her life over with Hendrickson away from the complications and insanity of the pit sounded perfect. The pit life had never been what she wanted in the first place. Drop her prey off? Sure. But to bid on the fights at the risk of watching the captives she had gotten to know die? This was why many Hunters didn't keep parahumans alive or with them for too long. It confused the heart and mind.

Hendrickson was another story entirely. And that was the rub. He wouldn't agree to escape, and Gale couldn't leave her brother behind. He was the whole reason she'd gone into the pits in the first place. He'd wanted to continue what their parents had started, and his taste for revenge over their parents' deaths was only satiated by watching parahumans bleed.

After losing their parents and Daniella, Hendrickson had been the only family Gale had left. How could she not follow him into the depths of the pit? She may have adjusted to it at the beginning for Hendrickson's sake, but years of screams, torture, and death wore a person down. But not Hendrickson. Never Hendrickson.

"Gale."

"I can't," Gale said at last. "I can't betray the other Hunters or Hendrickson. Not for anyone." She swallowed a lump in her throat. "Not even for you."

Daniella shook her head sadly. She glanced at a wall, her jaw set as if she was warring between walking out of the room or screaming at Gale. "I hope you change your mind, because I can't stop them if they decide to change or torture you. I want answers too." She eyed her sister. "I can probably give you until dawn to come to your senses, but after that, my hands are tied."

Gale shifted in the chair anxiously and glanced at the door, imagining the wolves lurking outside, ready to tear into her. She'd rather they kill her than force her to become a werewolf. What if she lost her mind like Daniella? Her sister might have come back from the edge of madness, but that didn't mean Gale would.

Daniella turned to leave. Gale tugged on the bonds. "Please don't let them change me."

Her sister paused and leaned her head back. "I won't make a promise I can't keep. Think hard, Gale." She knocked on the door then opened it and stepped out. She left the door ajar as she spoke to Rozene, allowing Gale to hear. "I extracted a little information from her. Ayaan and Pavati are still alive."

Evelyn's sob of relief was hard to miss. "Oh, thank god."

"What about the pit? Did she say anything about that?" Rozene asked.

"No. She won't talk to me either. I told her we'd give her until morning. After that—"

"We may not be able to wait that long," Wapasha said while Rozene sighed. "We have no idea what they're doing to Kafeada. And we have no other leads unless Tess has heard something."

"She hasn't shared anything vital with me yet," Rozene said. "I'll call her again, but Wapasha is right. We can't wait for her to play good Samaritan."

Daniella was quiet for a moment. "Call Tess, then we'll decide from there. It's possible my brother will make a mistake trying to rescue Gale."

Wapasha grunted. "Don't let your connection with your sister get in the way of *you* making the right choice either."

Daniella growled something low that sounded rather unflattering then stalked off. Someone pulled the door shut all the way, leaving Gale alone to dread her fate.

Chapter 21
Witch in Training

Tess

Tess folded her legs and sat down on the cushion opposite Arjun. A short table stood between them, covered in his wand, herbs, several colorful stones, a brand new grimoire for Arjun's notes and spells (thank you Olive), candles, and a few other items that were supposed to help him channel his inner witch. Tess had never taught anyone how to use magic before, and while there were some "witch's first starter kits" out there, it was often hard to distinguish between the real ones, typically made by parahumans, and the ones that either appropriated traditions from other cultures or just had no idea what it meant to be a witch. They were token commodities for influencers or for big corporations to steal money from small businesses.

She really needed to stop going on social media.

At least Olive had given her a starting point and a book—one cited by witchy peers—that explained the history of magic and witches.

Tess rolled her shoulders to relax.

This wasn't their first lesson together. Arjun had been eager to test out his new wand the moment they arrived back at his loft, which had been adorable. Tess had never seen a new witch at work, so she'd been surprised when he managed to turn a wilted herb back into a vibrant, beautiful plant.

Olive was right about him having natural talent.

But teaching him how to do anything big was going to take time, something they didn't have the luxury of. They were still waiting to hear back from Skye; so far, there'd been no leads. The waiting was maddening, so teaching Arjun was a nice distraction.

"We'll start the same way we did yesterday," Tess said and held out her hands. Arjun set his wand down and pressed his palms to hers. She ran her thumb along his warm skin, offering comfort. His mood fluctuated when using his magic. On the one hand, he was honoring the woman he'd killed by learning about earth powers. On the other, it brought back bitter memories. Arjun typically exuded a calm, confident energy, but now, Tess could practically taste his fear and trepidation.

She took a breath and closed her eyes. She reached deep down into her core, to the eighth chakra that connected her to the Ether and her fire. The flame woke like a sleeping beast and reared its head at her summons. It flowed through her veins, filling her body with the energy that burned deep inside of her and also drew from the Ether. It warmed her, embraced her in the way a lover might, and reminded her she wasn't ever alone. In her deepest, darkest, and loneliest moments, the magic was always present.

Was this how other magi felt about their powers? Or did a water magus call cool waves through her body? Were a wind magus's gifts wild and untamed like a herd of stampeding horses? What of an earth magus? Did their muscles hum with the vibrations of the ground?

Tess wound her magic around Arjun's hands, letting him feel the Ether as it danced on his fingers and along his skin. She opened her eyes and found him with his eyes closed. An adorable smile tugged at his lips as he felt her powers. "Every element is going to feel different, but at the core, there's warmth. A spark. That's the Ether flowing around you and through your wand. Witches don't feel it in their bodies as easily as magi do, but it's still possible to sense the power."

"I do feel warmth," Arjun said. "And it's not your fire. I know the heat of your flames," he added with a grin. He squeezed her hands to steady himself and took a deep breath. "You're staring, you know."

"I'm allowed to stare. I'm the teacher," Tess said with a smirk. She squeezed his hands back.

"So when it comes to witches, are there different kinds of practices?"

Tess considered. "Some witches focus on lighter magic while

others do darker magic. And, uh, don't tell anyone I said this, but dark magic itself isn't inherently a bad thing. Plenty of magi and witches would say otherwise, though."

"What's the difference?" Arjun asked.

"Light generally brings about creation and healing. Dark magic is more chaotic and destructive, but again, it depends on how it's used. Now, if you start dabbling in forbidden stuff like necromancy, you're going to have to find another teacher, because I don't teach senkas."

Arjun opened his eyes. "I've met a couple of senkas before. Most have been extremely unpleasant."

"Not surprising," Tess said and broke the flow of magic. She settled one hand on the table and ran her fingers over candle wicks, setting them alight. "Their magic is the most destructive, and whatever they do usually brings pain and suffering to other people or twists their victims' minds. We dealt with one a couple years ago when Bianca joined the District. And he was a magus, which is a hell of a lot scarier than a witch scnka."

"How so?"

Tess scratched her neck and laughed nervously. "Well, for one, he threw me into a ceiling and brought part of a warehouse down on me. Shattered a few bones. At least he's gone now, and Bianca's free." She shook out her hands. "But enough about that. We need to focus on *your* magic."

Arjun cocked his head. "The magic that we do, is it Wiccan? Is it like Paganism?"

Tess rocked her hand back and forth. "Yes? No? A little? I mean, Wiccans follow more strict guidelines. We're like, *modern* magic people, I guess you can say. If you're in a grove, or a ward in a magus's case, you follow the practices of your group. They share grimoires with spells and might have traditional practices. But witches and magi as a whole? We do what we feel is right to conjure our magic and use it to benefit ourselves as well as our society. Or the Districts."

Arjun folded his hands in his lap, smiling. "What about you, Tess? What practice do you follow?"

Tess snorted. "Isn't this lesson supposed to be about you?"

"Humor me."

Tess struggled to find the answer. She glanced at the grimoire she'd set out for him and ran her fingers lightly over the cover. "I've never joined a ward before. I grew up with wolves, and my closest teacher was my mother, since my birth father wanted nothing to do with me. I just...use my magic and my talisman as I need them," she said, fingering the small jar hanging from her neck. "There's no additional practice I have. I think that's the way it is for a lot of magi. We don't have to connect to the earth to use our powers. They just come. But witches use candles, stones, bones, herbs, all manner of objects to help draw on the Ether. Their wand is their biggest asset. It acts like an eighth chakra." She flushed. "Honestly, Olive would know better than me about all of this. Maybe I'm not the best one to ask." She rubbed her arm and shifted anxiously on her cushion. Why had she thought she'd be a good teacher for Arjun? She loved the idea of mentoring him, but he was a witch. And while she didn't usually have issues with witches, their abilities were very different from her own. She could only go by what she'd learned from other magic users. And none of those might even work for Arjun!

Arjun reached across the table and took her hand. He brought it to his lips and kissed it sweetly. "I can find a more experienced teacher later. Right now? I need the basics. I trust you, and your magic helps me feel the Ether. Plus, I feel safe with you. That's a start, isn't it?"

Tess lifted her eyes and forced a small smile. "Yeah, I guess you're right." She sighed and nudged the wand across the table to him. "Okay, let's continue with what we were doing yesterday. Take your wand and reach for the Ether. Draw it into the wand, and use it to grow more leaves on this plant."

She settled back, resting her hands on the floor behind her.

Arjun rubbed the wand with his fingers before he pointed it at the plant. His brow furrowed as he concentrated, reaching for the power that came so easily to Tess. It honestly wasn't fair. Witches were powerful, scary people, but break their wands, scepters, talismans, or other conduits for their magic, and they were screwed.

The wand moved in a rhythmic motion over the plant. Tess sensed magic start to coil around the stick and flow into the stem and leaves. She leaned forward, watching eagerly as the green, sparkling particles of Ether jaunted merrily around and through their host. Arjun's face scrunched with concentration, and he pushed more magic through the wand into the plant until it started to grow. First half an inch, then a full inch. Two leaves unfurled and gleamed emerald in the magic's light.

Tess tried not to bounce with excitement.

Sweat beaded Arjun's brow and trickled down his cheeks. He lifted his other hand, as if to help encase the magic as it tried to escape. But the strain became too much, and he dropped his arm with a sigh.

The plant wavered a little before growing still.

Tess smiled at him. "Look at those new leaves. That's impressive, Arjun!"

He ran his finger delicately over the plant. "It feels like it should have grown so much more with how hard I was pushing," he said.

Tess touched his hand. "I get it," she said. "Even being a magus, I wasn't exactly stellar with magic when I started. Sure, I could set my finger on fire, but I couldn't control it. I burned my favorite stuffed bear when I was little, and my mom had to fireproof my damn room so I wouldn't set the curtains ablaze during a temper tantrum. Magic babies, witch or magus, are really scary."

Arjun chuckled. "I can just imagine the look on your face as you burned the bear."

"Yeah, even the eyes melted," Tess said, fighting back a giggle. It hadn't been funny at the time, but dear god, she didn't know how her mother hadn't busted a gut at the sight of her toddler bringing in the charred remains of her favorite bear, one eye melted into its disfigured face, and the other trailing behind on a single thread.

But Arjun's smile faded, and he looked down at his wand. "It doesn't feel right."

"The wand?"

"No, the way I'm concentrating. It's like I'm trying to squeeze the magic through too small a hole."

"Well, you did look kind of constipated."

Arjun tossed a throw pillow at her, making her laugh.

"Also," Tess added. "I could say something *really* dirty about that statement right now, but I'm being nice and holding back."

"How good of you," Arjun replied with a snort. He rolled the wand between his palms and looked at the items on the table. He picked up a couple of stones and rattled them around in his hand, frowned, and set them back down. He sniffed the herbs, touched the candles, even stroked the leaf charm on his neck. But the troubled expression never left his face.

Tess sighed and got to her feet. She sat down behind him and massaged his shoulders, and he leaned back into her touch. "Okay, so let's take a different approach. Focusing on the magic itself isn't exactly your forte. How else do you loosen up and relax so you can clear your head?"

Arjun rolled his head to the side and shifted so she could rub a tight knot. "I used to meditate," he said. "Back when I was getting over my mentor's attempt to kill me and my own betrayal, I dealt with a lot of guilt and anger. A self-help group met in town that used meditation during meetings to help us better control our emotions. Simmer the fire, you might say."

He glanced at the table, reached for a small silver bell, then gave it a gentle ring. The bright chime sang around the room. "She would start by ringing a bell, then tell us to breathe in through our noses, out through our mouths. She always had candles lit, but not fragrant ones."

"Okay," Tess said and leaned forward. She snapped her fingers, snuffing out two candles and leaving a third unscented one lit. "So, why don't you try meditation and see if that helps you use your magic? Think of those lessons."

He glanced over his shoulder and smiled at her. "I'm afraid that means you'll have to stop with the backrub."

"Boo. Fine. We'll continue it later." Tess rocked back to her feet and returned to her cushion.

Arjun held the bell in one hand and the wand in another. He rang the bell again, rotating it in a circle and making the sound carry through the room. As his eyes closed, he set it down and breathed in and out. An air of peace settled over him. His shoulders relaxed. The worry lines eased on his face.

The transformation was so startling, Tess blinked a few times to make sure she'd actually seen the change.

Arjun moved the wand back and forth in front of his free hand, like a conductor with his baton. An orchestra of green magic flowed around his hand and wand and cascaded over the plant. Even the leaf necklace glowed as the stored Ether helped him fuel his power.

Tess bit her thumbnail, waiting for the plant to do something, anything.

All at once, the short plant flourished and spilled out over the pot.

The stem and leaves turned into willowing vines that coiled around the table and rushed toward Tess. She lifted her hands, trying not to disturb the magic, and watched in wonder as the vines rose faster and faster, brushing her skin and her clothing. A leaf tickled her ear, and a vine wrapped delicately around her necklace.

Unable to stop herself, she brushed her fingers over the plant and grinned when the earth magic danced over her fingers. Incredible.

Arjun's phone went off, breaking the beautiful illusion.

He grunted and opened his eyes. His mouth fell open at the sight of Tess sitting there wrapped up in his vines.

She looked over herself and flashed him a cheeky smile. "You know, if you're into bondage, all you had to do was tell me."

Arjun stifled a laugh and picked up his phone. All humor fled from his face when he saw who was calling. He swiped the screen. "You're on speaker, Skye."

"Well Firebug and Green Thumb, do I have some juicy news for you."

Tess glanced at Arjun, mouthing, "Green Thumb?"

He waved his hand. "What is it? Tell me it's something good."

"We got a break," Skye said, excited. "Get yourselves to my office. Oh, and Arjun, make sure Tess can't follow the route to my place."

Tess grumbled. "Are you seriously going to make him knock me out again?"

"No, a blindfold will do well enough this time. I need you conscious when you get here so you can verify a voice."

Arjun and Tess looked at one another as Skye hung up. Arjun blew out the remaining candle and scrambled to his feet. "Let's go."

"Um, help?" Tess said and lifted her arms, still tangled in the plants. "Unless you don't mind me burning them to a crisp."

"Don't you dare," Arjun said and pointed his wand. He breathed in and out, eyes shut. Slowly, the vines fell away from Tess, freeing her. "Let's get going."

***

Much to Tess's chagrin, Arjun did indeed blindfold her once they got into his car. She griped about it for a good portion of the drive there, but she didn't give him any reason not to trust her. She left no magic breadcrumbs, she didn't try to lift her blindfold, and she didn't ask any questions that might clue her into Skye's location. Like it or not, she had to learn to trust the pair so they could work together to get her friends and family back. She'd put the mission in jeopardy more than once already.

It was time to be more careful.

When they arrived, Arjun pulled off her blindfold. Tess blinked a few times to clear her vision and looked around. But they were in an underground carport. No view of the outside word.

Fair enough.

Tess got out of the car and followed Arjun to an elevator. She tried not to pay attention when he entered a code that let them enter. Thankfully no cheesy elevator music greeted them as they stepped inside, and Arjun hit the button for the second floor.

The doors opened to fluorescent light and the glow of many computer screens. Now this area, Tess recognized. She walked with Arjun over to Skye as the woman tapped furiously away on a keyboard. She was dressed in black pants, and she wore a button up shirt instead of her corset this time. Skye glanced at them then turned back to the computer.

"Took you long enough."

"I went the back route," Arjun said and leaned against her chair. "What do you have for us?"

"Someone made contact," Skye said with a grin.

Tess gasped in surprise and moved closer. Someone had reached out from the pit? "Who? When? What did they say?"

"Slow down, Firebug," Skye said and pulled up a file. "I'll play it back so you can hear."

Tess glared at her. "I hate when you call me that."

"That's why I do it." Skye tapped something then leaned back.

Trish's voice came through the speakers loud and clear. Tess pressed a hand to her mouth. She was alive. The vampire was still alive! She'd been terrified that leaving Trish behind was a death sentence. But here she was, reaching out to them through the comms. It wasn't a long conversation, but it was enough.

Skye glanced at her. "You recognize the voice?"

"Yes," Tess said. She brushed away a tear of relief. "That's Trish, the vampire we left in the pit. I can't believe she made it through."

Arjun didn't look as optimistic. "Are you sure she's acting on her own accord and not being used to find other people searching for the Hunters?"

Skye rubbed her chin, thinking. "I mean, it's always a possibility, but she sounded pretty rushed and anxious. I'd think if they were using her, she would have kept the conversation going to get info out of me instead of saying she'd be in touch again. Or given me a fake location to lead us into a trap. I'm impressed she managed to figure out the code." She snapped her fingers. "*Unless* she charmed someone to help her. Heh, clever girl."

Tess looked at the screen. Forced charm was frowned upon, but at that moment she didn't care. "Okay, well, how soon can you talk to her again?"

"Don't know," Skye said and leaned back, folding her hands behind her head. "It depends on when it's safe for her to reach out a second time. Could be a day. Could be a week. Who knows?"

Tess sputtered. That wasn't helpful at all! "How are we going to know if she's made contact unless we're logged in every waking moment?"

Skye turned around in her chair. She folded one leg over the other and grinned. "Hon, that's why I have some of this linked to my phone. She reaches out while I'm sleeping? I'll hear it. And I'll have a way to reach back out to her. Don't you worry." She spun toward the screen and settled her hands on her armrests. "I don't know what she's got planned. Next contact will hopefully solidify that."

"At least we have someone on the inside helping," Tess said. "Well, someone we know for certain is helping," she added, remembering Skye's excitement about the video feed of Gale dropping the SD card. She was way more willing to trust Trish over Gale. Still, this small message didn't bring them that much closer to finding the hideout. Anything could happen to Trish between now and the next time she reached out. "So we keep waiting."

"Looks like it," Skye said with a perkiness that made Tess want to punch her.

Waiting, more waiting. Was her father still alive? Were Nick and Augustine? They'd survived this long, so she had to believe they could hold on until rescue arrived. And knowing Nick, he was probably working on a plan to get them out.

Her phone vibrated in her pocket. Tess glanced down and pulled it up, seeing Rozene's name on the screen. She bit her lip. She'd been careful about her wording both in texts and calls with Rozene, per Skye's suggestions. If she said too much, she could put them in more danger, draw other Hunters' attention to them or feed the Hunters information that got her former packmates caught, just like last time. The guilt of Ray's death and her friends' capture weighed heavily on her. In the past she'd been far too rash, and she was trying to change. But this was important. She looked at Skye and Arjun. Skye's eyes darkened, and she folded her arms.

"The pack?" she asked.

"My…*their* alpha." Tess rubbed her thumb against her fingers, struggling to let it ring. But what if Rozene had information? And shouldn't she know Trish was reaching out to them?

If I want to be a real Hunter, I can't keep relying on them. But how can I not do everything I can to save my family? I can distance myself from the pack, but she's still my alpha.

Tess pressed her lips together then answered the call. "Rozene?"

"Tess…" Rozene's voice was filled with relief. "It's good to hear your voice. Are you all right? Your messages have had me a bit worried; they don't sound like you."

Tess glanced at the Hunters. Arjun offered her a comforting smile while Skye threw her hands in the air and turned around to face the computer.

"Yeah, I'm fine. I'm sorry, I…it's a long story. What's going on? Are you all okay?"

"No," Rozene replied, sending a shock of fear down Tess's spine. "Kafeada, the fae who's helping us, was attacked and taken. But we got one of their Hunters."

Tess's eyes went wide. She moved toward Skye and Arjun quickly and put the phone on speaker. "Rozene, I have Arjun on the phone, too." She thought it best not to mention Skye and give up her presence. "Which Hunter did you get?"

"The one who helped take your father and Nick in the first place. Gale."

Skye looked sharply over her shoulder, intrigued.

Tess sighed in relief. If they had Gale, then the woman could give them information on the health of their packmates. "Did she say anything about Dad, Nick, or Augustine? Are they alive?"

"We're still working on getting that out of her. She implied that at least one of them is alive. And so are the teens. She's being stubborn, which is no surprise. We're trying to get the location where the others are being held. I wanted you to know so you can be ready to join us the moment we get the coordinates."

Tess licked her lips and exchanged a look with Arjun, who nodded to signal that he would be coming, too. "Arjun and I will be ready. I have information, too."

Skye's hand snapped out and wrapped around Tess's wrist. She leaned over, tapping the mute button. "If you tell her about Trish, and Gale somehow hears it and escapes, we're all screwed."

"She won't let that happen," Tess said and jerked her arm back.

"Tess?" Rozene asked. "Are you there?"

She tapped the unmute button. "Are you in a safe location? No one else can hear you, especially Gale?"

Rozene muttered something to someone. The sound of her walking came through the phone followed by the click of a door shutting. "I am now. I even asked Jackson to stay downstairs. What's going on?"

"It's Trish," Tess said. "Trish made contact with us. She's in the pit, and she's going to reach out again, hopefully with the location."

Rozene sighed in relief. "That's some good news. Keep listening in for her, Tess. And as soon as you know anything, tell me, and I'll do the same for you. We might finally have caught a break." She was quiet for a moment. "Call your mother. She's worried sick about you."

Tess ran her hand along her neck and rested it at the base. She missed her mom. It wasn't fair that she'd been reaching out less and less, but she was still trying to learn from Arjun and now Skye about how to become a Hunter, while also training Arjun on his witchcraft. Still, her mother deserved a call. "I'll let her know I'm okay. Thanks, Rozene."

"I'm here for you whenever you need me," the werewolf added.

Tess smiled. "I know, Rozene. Thank you. Give Jackson my love. Goodbye."

"Goodbye."

Tess hung up and held her phone close. She heard Skye click her tongue. Tess rounded on her before she could say a single word. "Don't judge me," she snapped. "You have a wife and a child, and you stay involved with them. The pack is still my family. And I can't just sever my ties with them. I can be a Hunter who has family obligations. Yes, there are times I'll have to go dark. Yes, staying connected with them could, one day, put them in danger. But for now, I choose to remain a part of my pack family while also training to be a Huntress. And if you can't accept that, then I don't really give a shit."

Skye cocked her head to the side and pressed her lips together. After a long moment, she clapped her hands slowly. "So the little firebug does have a spine," she said, chuckling. "I was wondering when you were going to stand up to me."

Tess sputtered. "What?"

"Girl, I wasn't expecting you to sever *every* connection. And you were careful about what you told her. You chose what she needed to know, which is a good thing. I appreciate you not mentioning me." She sat back. "You two run along for now while I keep an ear out for Trish. Soon as she contacts me, I'll let you both know, all right?"

Tess stared incredulously at the Huntress. What the hell? She'd started out as Judgy McJudgerson, and now she was all understanding? Where did this woman get off? She huffed, but before she could put her foot in her mouth, Arjun touched her arm.

"Sounds good, Skye. Thanks. Come on, Tess. Let's make dinner at home, and then it's my turn to train you."

Tess grunted and waggled her finger at Skye, but that was it. She couldn't say anything else to that! Instead, she walked out with Arjun, mumbling about bullheaded Hunters and their riddles. Arjun's soft chuckle didn't improve her mood.

When they reached the car, Tess pulled her phone back out of her pocket and stared at it.

"What is it?" Arjun asked.

"Do you mind if I call my mom while you drive?"

He smiled at her and shook his head before slipping into the driver's seat.

Tess dialed her mother and closed her eyes. The soft blindfold settled around her face again, but she didn't mind. The moment her mom picked up, a few tears pricked her eyes. "Hey, Mom."

Chapter 22
Rogue

Daniella

Daniella sat in the dining area where the others had gathered to decide her sister's fate. She sank in her chair, arms folded defensively over her chest. None of them had gotten much sleep last night after bringing Gale in. Jackson was still guarding the door just in case her sister magically managed to break through her bonds. Danielle felt they were giving her far too much credit. They'd already stripped her of her clothing and weapons after all.

Vic and Marion brought in plates filled with eggs, bacon, toast, and fruit. Marion poured tea and coffee, stopping next to Rozene to squeeze her shoulder. The alpha had spent the early hours of the morning relaying the news to her husband. She looked about as tired as Daniella felt.

Wapasha kissed Marion lovingly on the lips and put some food on his plate. He munched away while he looked over his tablet with updates from the rest of the pack.

Daniella gathered food for herself. She glanced at the empty chairs where Evelyn and Kafeada should have been. She swallowed down a piece of fruit and asked, "Where's Evelyn?"

Rozene lifted her eyes. "Scrying for Kafeada. She hoped her connection with her wife would make it a little easier to find her. I was going to retrieve her once breakfast was ready."

"I'll get her," Daniella said and rocked to her feet. She left the others to eat and walked through the house to an office Evelyn frequented. She knocked, but there came no reply. For a moment, she considered going back to the dining room and waiting, but a sinking feeling settled in her stomach that told her something wasn't right.

Daniella grasped the knob, twisted, and pushed the door open. Magic swirled around the room in shades of blue and white. Wind gusted, pushing Daniella almost out the door. She managed to squeeze herself in and push the door shut behind her. Wind coiled around her, pulling her into the eye of the storm. "Eve?" she called.

Evelyn sat on a rug in the middle of the room, a bowl of water resting in front of her. The surface rippled as her magic swirled above it. She chanted in a language Daniella didn't understand. The werewolf wandered closer and grimaced.

Blood caked Evelyn's lips. Some flowed free and dripped on her folded legs. She kept chanting, but the more she did the faster the blood gushed, and the more her face creased with exhaustion.

Daniella knelt down in front of her and snapped her fingers in the woman's face. "Evelyn? Evelyn!" she shouted. When the magus still didn't move, the werewolf sighed and grabbed her by her shoulders. She shook the woman hard, finally breaking her out of her trance.

Evelyn blinked in surprise when she saw Daniella in front of her. Her eyes flickered with magic. Then, all at once, she collapsed into Daniella's arms. The werewolf grunted. She lowered the magus to the ground and touched her cheek.

She was cold to the touch, likely from using way too much magic. Great.

Daniella grabbed a blanket and draped it over the magus before rushing to the door. "Vic!" she called sharply. His socked feet slapped against the floorboards as he rushed to her.

"What's wrong?"

"I think our idiot friend burnt out her magic," Daniella said.

"Evelyn!" he cried in dismay. He knelt at her side and placed his hands over her face and chest. Warm magic flowed from him to her in an attempt to help restore her depleted reserves.

Daniella leaned against the wall and watched, making certain Vic wouldn't be disturbed. Honestly, magic users were so rash sometimes. What was the point of pushing your powers to the point of passing out or causing yourself physical or mental damage? It wouldn't help them find Kafeada or the others any faster, and it meant they were down another person.

Evelyn gasped in a breath and opened her eyes. She stared up at Vic and trembled in his arms. "What happened?"

"You used too much magic," Vic said gently.

Daniella snorted. "You were being an idiot," she added. "I shook you out of your trance, and you fell unconscious. What were you thinking?"

Vic shot her a glare, which Daniella ignored. Let him be pissy about it. Evelyn deserved to know the truth about the dumb move she'd made. Yes, let's completely waste all the magic with zero results.

Evelyn lifted her sleeve and rubbed it against her nose, wiping away some of the blood, but she'd need a warm cloth to do the rest. "I tried to find Kafeada. I thought I felt an inkling of her, but then it was gone. I'm sorry, Vic."

Vic shook his head. "It's all right. You did the best you could. Let me help you into the dining room so you can clean up and get some food." Vic braced himself as he hefted Evelyn to her feet. She wobbled, but Vic was right there to steady her.

Daniella shook her head. Magi. Honestly. She followed them back out to the dining room and went to retrieve a cloth for Evelyn. She heard the exclamations as people noticed the magus's bloody face. Daniella returned and passed the damp cloth off to Evelyn before taking a seat.

"Thank you," the wind magus said and dabbed at her face.

Rozene clicked her tongue as she filled a plate of food for her. "You shouldn't be pushing yourself so much. Between having Gale and the news from Tess, we might be able to figure out where they're hiding without you killing yourself."

Evelyn sipped hot coffee and held the mug between her trembling hands. "Kafeada would find a way into the underworld to drag me back just so she could scold me," she said with a tired smile. She rubbed her face. "Tess has no idea when their contact is going to reach out again?"

"No," Rozene said. "But they're keeping an ear out."

"More waiting," Wapasha muttered. Marion rubbed his arm in

sympathy.

Vic sat down beside Evelyn with his own coffee in hand. "What do we do about the Hunter? We told her we'd give her until morning. Well, it's morning, and she still hasn't said anything."

Daniella glanced at the window as pale sunlight crept through the cracks in the blinds. She frowned deeply to herself. "You aren't still thinking of changing her into a werewolf, are you?"

Vic lifted his chin. "We'll do what we must to save our friends."

Daniella dug her nails into her arms as she struggled not to snap back at him. He was a magus, born with his power. How could he understand what it was like to go through the change? To have your mind completely altered and your body feel as if it was bursting into flames, breaking, shattering with the first transformation? Maybe her experience had been different from most werewolves, but getting bitten and changed into another person could screw with anyone.

"And then what?" Daniella asked, glowering at Vic. "She's changed. Then what do we do with her?"

Vic shifted and avoided her fierce eyes. "I don't know," he admitted.

"You take a woman, force her to become a werewolf, and you don't know what to do with her after that," Daniella said with a snort. "Sounds like an excellent plan to me."

Rozene leaned forward. "We don't have to change her. The threat may be enough to get her to talk. And if not, if we change her, we'll deal with her then."

"Deal with her *how*?" Daniella pressed. "Find her a pack she might betray because she resents being changed? Force her into your pack or Wapasha's? Kill her?" She waited for a response, and when none came, she scoffed. "This is why none of you could be Hunters. You say you'll do what it takes, but then you don't. You don't want to be the bad guy. You don't want to be the one to say you'll have to kill her, even though that's what you're all thinking." She tapped the table in front of her. "We are not supposed to change people unless they ask for it. It's against our oaths as werewolves."

Vic hit the table. "Then what do you want us to do? Torture her? Make her scream to get her to tell us the truth?"

"It'd be better than changing someone against their will," Daniella replied curtly. "Not to mention she'll be less deadly if she remains human. For all you know, you could change her and she could have the same reaction I did when *I* became a werewolf and ended up offing my parents." She felt the uncomfortable silence build between them all. Let them chew on that.

She got up and headed for the stairs.

"Daniella," Wapasha called to her. "What do you think you're doing?"

"I'm going to see if I can talk some sense into her while the rest of you decide on an actual course of action." She didn't wait for Wapasha to order her to stay. She walked down to the basement.

Jackson got up from the chair and moved to block her way. Daniella cocked her head, giving him a look.

"Really? I'm giving it another go. Go complain to Rozene if you don't want me down here."

"Watch it," Jackson growled. "You might not be of my pack, but I am still a beta."

Daniella sighed. Point taken. "Apologies. May I please see the prisoner?"

Jackson eyed her, but he grabbed the door and opened it. Daniella stepped past him and walked into the room.

Gale was still awake and looked stiffer and more uncomfortable than before. Daniella could smell that she'd relieved herself. Not a big surprise given how long she'd been down there. She was probably hungry too. Daniella dropped into the chair across from her sister and rested her arms on the back.

"So," Daniella said in greeting. "Have you decided if you're going to talk or not?"

"You know why I can't," Gale replied. "It's not just the pit I'm putting at risk, it's our brother, too. They might promise my freedom if I help them, but I have no reason to trust them."

"Would you be willing to trust me?" Daniella asked. "If I swore to keep you both safe?"

Doubt flickered in Gale's eyes, which hurt Daniella more than she expected. She pressed her lips together and tilted her head back. "Gale, they mean it. If you don't tell them what they want to know, they will change you."

"And then what?" Gale asked. "They won't just let me go, will they?”

Daniella didn’t respond, because she honestly didn’t know what was going on in their heads. They were supposed to be the good guys, right? So why couldn’t any of them answer her when she asked what would happen next? “If you tell them the truth now, I’ll do everything I can to protect you and Hendrickson.”

The struggle was plain on Gale’s face as she warred with her decision. Finally, she closed her eyes in resignation. “You can’t help us, Daniella. Maybe...maybe we deserve this after what we did to you.”

Daniella frowned. “Gale.”

“Let them do as they please. I won’t betray him. I can’t.”

“But you can abandon me again?” Daniella snarled. She rose and leaned over her chair. “If you really gave a damn about what you two did to me, you’d try to make amends for it by *helping* me get the wolves back. But you’re choosing him again over me. Because I’m a werewolf, right?”

“Daniella, no, it’s just...they’ll kill him. You and I both know it. They’ll kill him, and I can’t watch him die.”

Daniella grasped Gale’s chin and lifted it, forcing her sister to look her in the eyes. “Let me ask you this. If Hendrickson was in your shoes right now, would he keep quiet because he’s loyal to you or loyal to the pit? Would he die for you as well?”

Tears pricked Gale’s eyes as she stared back at her sister. The fact that she didn’t answer right away was enough for Daniella. No, Hendrickson wouldn’t die for her. He might try to save her, but more than that? And if Gale was turned into a werewolf, she’d lose him entirely. Just like Daniella had lost her family.

She sucked in a breath and touched her sister’s cheek. “If he wouldn’t die for you, then why not save yourself, Gale?”

Gale blinked back the tears and looked away. “I can’t be responsible for his death. You can’t protect him, you know that. He’d try to kill you on sight. And after the things he’s done to the parahumans, they wouldn’t give him a chance. I can’t, Daniella. I’m sorry.”

Daniella leaned back and stared long and hard at her sister. Fear and guilt twisted in her stomach. Could she give Gale more time? Or would they off her either way? They’d find a way to torture the information out of her and then what? Imprison her? Kill her? Deep down Gale wasn't a bad person, Daniella knew it. She just needed a chance to get away from the Hunter life, just as Daniella had gotten one.

She turned away and stalked toward the door, her hands fisting and her claws poking through the skin in stress.

"Daniella," Gale called when she reached the door. "I'm sorry."

Daniella sighed. "Me too." She left and didn't give Jackson a second look as she headed up the stairs where the others were waiting. All eyes turned to her as she appeared.

"Well?" Vic asked.

Daniella shook her head. "She's cracking, but she still won't say anything. Can we give her one more day?"

Evelyn dropped her head into her hands miserably. Wapasha glanced at his mother and mate and leaned back in his chair. Vic looked ready to explode with anger.

"The longer we wait, the greater the chance we'll lose our friends. If she's not going to help us, then she's a threat."

Daniella rolled her eyes. "So then what? You kill her? Why not turn her over to Legion?"

"They'd probably kill her too, depending on her crimes," Wapasha said. "We're not trying to be cruel, Daniella, but running a fighting pit like this? It's a serious offense. Legion doesn't take kindly to those sorts of Hunters. But you're right. It would be better if we handed her over to Legion. It's in their jurisdiction, not ours, to decide her fate." He took a breath. "We can give her one more day. Right?" he asked, looking to Evelyn and his mother.

Evelyn ran her hands heavily down her face, her eyes exhausted and puffy from crying. "One more day," she repeated in a bone-weary voice.

Wapasha nodded. "Ma, we should relieve Jackson so he can rest. We need someone else to keep watch."

"I'll do it," Vic said and pushed himself out of his chair. "Maybe I can convince her to say something."

Daniella fought back a growl at his tone. He controlled the magic of fire and earth. There were plenty of awful things he could do to Gale. But she kept her mouth shut, more for Gale's sake than for her own. She sank in her chair and glanced at the window while the others ate breakfast and talked quietly to each other.

Jackson emerged and went to Rozene, looking ready to fall asleep on his feet. So much for his vicious bravado downstairs.

"Rest," Rozene told him. "In fact, I think we all should. None of us slept last night. Vic will warn us if anything is amiss."

Daniella arched an eyebrow and glanced at Wapasha and Marion as they rose. They headed off together, and Rozene followed Jackson upstairs to the guest rooms. Only Evelyn remained seated. She rested with her head in her hand, shoulders slumped with exhaustion. Daniella ran her tongue over her teeth, thinking, then got to her feet. She headed for the magus and touched her shoulder. "Evelyn, you gotta sleep. You've burned yourself out, and we'll need your magic whenever we go after the Hunters."

Evelyn sighed. She looked at her wedding ring and rolled it around her finger a little. She'd added Kafeada's ring to her finger as well. "I'm not used to my bed being empty. And not being able to feel her. What if Kafeada's dead already?"

"They wouldn't have gone to the trouble of taking her alive if they just wanted to kill her," Daniella said. "We'll get her back. But you won't be any use if you're this tired."

Evelyn eyed Daniella, but she eventually nodded and rose. She patted the wolf's arm as she passed her. "Sleep, too."

"I will," Daniella said. And she would. She needed it as much as the rest of them. She went to the downstairs guest room and settled on the bed after making sure the blinds were all shut tight. She lay on her back and stared up at the ceiling, thinking of Gale and Hendrickson. Of their parents.

I could strangle Gale for being a stubborn ass, Daniella thought to herself. *How do the Hunters have their claws embedded so deeply in her that she won't give up their location? Is it because of Hendrickson alone, or is something else keeping her silent?* Saul was working with them. What if he'd charmed her not to say anything? That was probably stretching it, but Daniella couldn't let the thought escape her mind.

She set her phone's alarm and drifted in and out for a few hours, trying to rest and ignore the building guilt in her stomach. Sleep mostly eluded her, but during her brief snatches of rest, she remembered the last night she'd been with her siblings. Hendrickson's hatred. Gale's hurt and grief. They'd had every reason to kill her, and if Hendrickson had been the one to take her to the Hunters, she firmly believed she'd be dead now.

But not Gale. As cold and malicious as being a Huntress made her, warmth and compassion still burned inside of her. Warmth that would be snuffed out if she was left to die by their little group's hands, or if she was left to rot in Legion's dungeons.

Daniella opened her eyes.

She checked her phone for the time and set her jaw.

The hell with it.

She rolled out of bed and changed into dark clothing then pulled her boots on. She laced them tight and crept through the hall. The house was quiet save for the occasional squeak of the floor shifting. She looked at the doorway that led down to her sister's prison and wrinkled her nose.

The faint scent of burnt hair and flesh wafted toward her.

Daniella went down the stairs on quick, cautious feet. She expected to find Vic guarding the door. Instead he stood in front of Gale, back to Daniella. Fire snarled in one hand while he held Gale's hair with the other.

"*Where* are they?" he snarled at her.

Gale didn't get a chance to answer.

Daniella loped in behind Vic and swung her fist into his temple. He went down like a sack of potatoes, his chin smacking the floor loudly. Daniella stood over him, panting, and looked at Gale.

Her sister lifted her head, revealing a burn on her cheek and a few on her arms. Tears rolled down her face and dampened her shirt. "What are you doing?" she asked in a hoarse voice.

Daniella grew a sharp claw and ran it along the bonds holding Gale to her chair. "Getting you out of here."

"What? Why?"

"Because if you don't do what they say, you're either going to end up in a Legion prison or dead," Daniella said and removed the tape around Gale's ankles. "You saved my life once. I'm returning the favor." She looked up at her sister. "And I hope you'll think about what I said. You can still help us. You don't have to go back to Hendrickson."

Gale frowned and didn't answer. Instead, she struggled to stand. When she wobbled, Daniella caught her and steadied her. "What about you?" Gale asked. "They'll be furious once they find out what you did."

Daniella snorted and helped Gale out of the room. She stepped over Vic's unconscious body. "I'll deal with the repercussions. Won't be the first time I've had an alpha pissed off at me."

They tiptoed up the stairs together, Daniella keeping Gale tucked close against her in case anyone tried to hurt her. The dining room was still empty. Daniella guided her to the front door and stopped near Rozene's purse resting on a table. After fishing around for a few moments, she pulled out a set of keys. They went to the car that Rozene's crew had parked in the driveway. "Get in," Daniella said. She climbed in and waited for Gale to get settled.

The engine hummed to life. Daniella pulled out and headed down the road, planning to put as much distance between themselves and the house as possible. She kept glancing in the rearview mirror, half-expecting another car to follow her any second. But the road stayed quiet aside from the usual traffic.

Daniella ran her hand through her hair. "Where can I drop you off that's safe for you?"

"I can't tell you where the pit is," Gale said.

"That's not what I asked," Daniella retorted. "*Where* can I drop you off?"

Gale rested her head against the window. "Anywhere with high traffic where I can get a clean set of clothing."

Daniella lifted an eyebrow. "I'll bring you over to the mall. You can get food too." She reached into her pocket and pulled out a thin wallet. She passed over some cash. "Use that."

"Why are you doing this?" Gale asked. "I'm supposed to be your enemy."

"Yeah, well, like I said, you saved my life. Now I'm saving yours." She turned down a side road. "And I hope you'll decide to do the right thing. Though, with or without it, we're going to take down that damn pit."

Gale chuckled quietly. "Do you really think you'll find a way in? The moment they catch a whiff of people tracking their location, they'll move, just like last time. We can't escape."

"*We?*" Daniella pressed.

Gale flushed. "They...they can't escape. And more parahumans will die."

Daniella chewed on a nail and scratched it lightly along the side of her neck. "Hope you're on the right side when it comes down to that, Gale. I'm giving you a second chance. Use it wisely."

She pulled into the mall parking lot and stopped near the doors. She looked at her sister. This could be the last time she saw Gale alive.

As her sister got out of the car, Daniella leaned over and caught her wrist. "Be careful. Don't make me regret letting you go."

Gale stared back at her. Then she turned her hand over and gripped Daniella's tightly. "Goodbye, Daniella." She let go and shut the door.

Daniella waited until her sister was inside before she headed out of the parking lot and back to whatever fate awaited her.

Chapter 23
Feast

Nick

Nick panted, blood dripping down his dark fur and onto the floor. He wiped some off his muzzle and glared at the werebird squaring off against him. She was an older avian who bore her seraph wings proudly. The feathers glistened white except for a few black speckles and a crimson splattering of blood. Feathers lined her cheeks and flowed through her hair. Her talons were the scariest part though. They stood out like vicious hooks and already had his blood painted on the tips. She watched him with bright golden eyes and flexed her wings.

Suddenly, she zipped forward with avian speed, faster than any werewolf, and raked her talons at his chest. He smacked her arm away and was bombarded by her inner owl crashing into his mind. The blow knocked him backward to the ground, and he clutched his head in pain as her inner owl tore at his mind with her talons. Blood dripped out of his nose.

He *hated* avians for that reason. Bad enough that they had vicious talons and speed, but they also had a bird that could mentally incapacitate a person. Bianca's caracara could do similar damage, though not with as much speed and grace as this woman. No, she was older and far more trained than most avians he knew.

Nick rolled back to his feet and raced toward her. She pumped her wings and rose into the air, intending to have him crash into the fence.

Nick expected it this time, crouched, and jumped as high as he could. He snagged her ankle and yanked hard. The werebird gasped and fell, slamming into the ground. He reached to pin her arms, but her powerful wing buffeted him in the face and sent stars circling in front of his vision. He staggered away shaking his head and crouched low for another attack.

The avian started to stand, only to fall to her knees with a hiss of pain. It took him a moment to realize his claws had pierced her ankle. She touched it and glowered at him. Her healing worked slowly, but she couldn't know if he'd used his venom on her or not. Werewolf claws were just as deadly as their teeth.

Fortunately for her, Nick had no intention of poisoning anyone. He rose, ignoring the shouts from the Hunters to take her down. *"Have you thought about my proposition?"*

"You really think you can get us out of here?" she asked, her bird flying through his mind. *"Many have tried and failed, myself included."*

"That's why I think you'd be invaluable," Nick replied and prowled around her. *"You've been here longer than me. You know the layout. If we disconnect the collars, there ain't much the Hunters can do to stop us."*

"Besides shoot us or electrocuting, you mean." She rolled her shoulders and stood. Her wounds were already starting to close.

"They'll do that to us whether we fight or not," Nick reminded her. *"Please. If you and all your allies help, we might stand a chance."* He leapt at her, and they exchanged several punches before her talons streaked across his arm. He caught her other wrist and twisted her arm behind her back, but once again her wing hit him and knocked him away. He was being very careful not to damage them.

"Fine," the werebird relented. *"One more fight for freedom. I hope you know what you're doing, Nick."*

"Heh, me too, Astrid."

Astrid nodded then dove at him. She slammed him into the side of the fence and struck him hard in the temple, dazing him. He dropped to the ground, and before he knew it, she twisted his arms behind him and pressed her talons against his throat.

"Yield," she growled.

Nick clenched his teeth then bowed his head in submission.

A mix of boos and cheers met them as she let him up. Nick sat heavily on the ground to catch his breath. A shock ripped across his throat, making him cry out in pain.

"What the hell was that?!" Hendrickson raged as he came around to where Nick was seated. The Hunter glared and shocked him again. "You just gave up? Do you realize how much money you lost me?"

Nick sighed and shifted back to his human form so he could speak. He leaned against the fence, grateful it wasn't electrified. "She would have ripped my throat out. I wasn't going to risk it. Sorry. I won the other two fights today."

"You should have won all three. She's a freaking bird, and you're a wolf."

Nick narrowed his eyes. "You'd think after all this time hunting, you'd realize how deadly a seraph can be even to a werewolf."

The next shock was expected and hurt worse without his fur to protect him. He pitched forward, gasping, until Hendrickson released the button. Prick.

"Get up," Hendrickson growled. "And if you give me anymore lip, I'll shock you unconscious and have someone drag your sorry ass back to the cage." He stormed off, leaving Nick a moment to recover.

He rubbed his neck and eyed Hendrickson's back. The Hunter was in a worse mood than usual these days. Ever since he'd returned from a Hunting mission, it was like a switch had been flipped, and his normal dickish nature had been upped to full-on asshole. It wouldn't have been so bad if Gale took his place now and again, like usual. But Nick hadn't seen her for days, and despite what she'd done to him and his friends, it worried him. Where had she gone? He'd tried to ask once and been met with shocks. So whatever had happened, it wasn't good.

Nick got up after several long minutes and limped to the door to be let out. Gale normally allowed him to walk at her side. Hendrickson secured a pole to his collar and dragged him along behind. Nick followed and glanced over to where Astrid was being treated. They met each other's eyes, and Astrid gave a brisk nod.

Good, at least he could count on her. Her involvement meant they'd have another five cages of parahumans to aid their coup.

He turned his head and froze.

Deep in the shadows of the room, a figure came into view. Vesp watched him with hungry violet eyes, her lips drawn up in an amused smile, revealing sinister white teeth. Black tendrils coiled around her and seemed to beckon him to come close.

Nick blinked, and she was gone. He glanced around, but there was no sign of the fae. Chills raced down his spine and he grasped his arm, feeling her touch on him, hearing her velvet voice as she offered him a way to save his packmates. Had she really been there? Or was he imagining things?

Hendrickson jerked on the pole. Nick staggered after him and looked warily where Vesp had been standing. But it was empty.

Is it all in my head? How much has she corrupted me, and after only one visit? How many more times would she bring him to her room? Would it come to the point where he yearned for the same fate as the feline?

Once they arrived at the prison cell, Hendrickson opened the door, unhooked the pole, and shoved Nick inside. The metal bars shrieked as he slammed them and left. Nick rolled his eyes and limped to Yanlei's side. She held out her hand and helped him down to a nest of pillows and blankets.

As had become a tradition, Brighton, Augustine, Pavati, and Ayaan all scooted in close to get the latest news. Even the trio in the other cage leaned in to listen. Nick nodded to Loretta who returned it. "We have Astrid on our side," he said. "The snowy owl werebird that you heard about in your last fight, Brighton."

Brighton nodded. "Lucky you two got paired up."

"Yeah," Nick said. Though it had taken several fights to get to her. He'd needed to move up on the leaderboard to be deemed worthy of fighting the werebird. "If all her people agree, that gives us five more cages."

Augustine grinned viciously. "Good. Even more parahumans to take these assholes down.

Now we just need Trish to play her part. If she's still on our side."

"She is," Nick said confidently. "She's got no reason to betray us."

"Other than that betraying the Hunters could mean her death. Or, you know, she now has Saul with her. Aren't they supposed to be buddy-buddy with one another?"

Nick nodded. "I guess, but she also said he's not acting normal." He sighed. "Look, I know you don't like her, and for good reason. But she's our only hope right now. Especially with Gale missing."

Yanlei rubbed his arm. "Have you heard anything?"

Nick shook his head. "I tried to ask Hendrickson, but you know how he is. I heard whispers about a new prize being brought in, but I don't know who it is. Maybe Trish will know when she comes to see us next."

Trish had been MIA for a few days now also, which worried him. Had Saul caught on? Had she been betrayed by someone else? If she'd been caught and spilled his secrets, he was sure Hendrickson or someone else would have come down on him already.

He settled against Yanlei and closed his eyes to rest. Three fights were a lot for a day, especially after doing four yesterday. It almost felt like Hendrickson was punishing him, but he didn't know why. Augustine, Brighton, and Yanlei had all been thrown into more rings too, and Yanlei had two fights set up for this evening, one alongside Augustine. Heh, he would pay to see the two of them fighting a pair of parahumans. Between Yanlei's speed and grace and Augustine's brute strength, he doubted anyone would stand up against them.

"Sleep," Yanlei whispered, stroking his hair. "I'll wake you when food's here."

Nick nodded and closed his eyes. He'd barely drifted off when Yanlei shook his arm. He yawned and blinked a few times, expecting to see Hendrickson with food.

Instead, Hendrickson stood outside of the cage with two other Hunters beside him. He narrowed his eyes at Nick and crooked a finger, commanding him to come forward.

Nick frowned, but he knew better than to make Hendrickson wait. He rose, brushing loving fingers along Yanlei's cheek before he limped toward the Hunter. Hendrickson eyed him then nodded to the other two Hunters. They came down on Nick, one attaching a lead to his collar and the other cuffing his wrists behind him.

"What are you doing?" Brighton snarled, storming the bars.

"None of your business, dog," Hendrickson growled back and whacked the metal by Brighton's face. "Worry about yourself. I set up a fight for you tonight."

Nick frowned. Today was supposed to be Brighton's day to rest! He'd been fighting every day this week thus far. He opened his mouth to protest, but the Hunters dragged him away from his friends before he had the chance. What did they want with him? Fear flickered inside of him as he thought of Trish betraying them. He glanced at Hendrickson, but the man kept his gaze forward, his right hand on the controller to Nick's collar.

It didn't take long for Nick to realize where they were going.

His blood ran cold. No. Oh no. They were taking him to the fae. He struggled, but a warning shock from Hendrickson stilled him. All he could do was follow along. His heart pounded in his chest. Dread filled his mind. What more was the fae going to do to him? Would she make the same offer? Would she torture him? The anticipation of what could happen was almost worse than the actual punishment.

They reached Vesp's door and the Hunters undid the cuffs and the pole. Hendrickson opened the door and pushed Nick inside.

"Enjoy," he sneered.

Nick fell to his knees on top of the plush rug again. He glanced at the door as it slammed shut behind him. Black smoke curled around the frame, and it vanished into a night sky bejeweled with stars. Nick slowly turned around.

The room looked much the same as last time. Water gurgled merrily in the bath to his right. The bed was more visible this time, and in the distance, he thought he saw a box decorated in a spiderweb pattern of crackling black and purple light. Someone sat behind it, but he couldn't make out who.

"My, you're in a state," Vesp said as she materialized on the edge of her bed in all her regal glory. She'd reclaimed her beautiful facade, her hair flowing down her back and shoulders. She looked him over and clicked her tongue. "If they wish for you to continue fighting, they must learn to take better care of you." She swept to her feet and crossed the floor in three quick strides. She crouched and touched his cheek; he knew better than to flinch away. "Let me help you."

Cool magic flowed through his skin, chasing away the heat of his wounds. He felt the marks on his face close as he watched the ones on his arm mend. It was so strange seeing his body heal in an instant rather than over a few hours or days. The magic lent him strength and chased away the exhaustion. He slumped in relief. He couldn't help but admire her magic, even if it was cold and corrupt. "Thank you," he said before he could stop himself.

Vesp smiled. "I'm glad I can make you happy in some way," she replied. She patted his cheek then grasped his arm. "You must be hungry."

Nick rose with her help. One of her wings wrapped around him as she brought him over to her stone table. He tensed, expecting to see the twisted stone pawns from before or the jars of trapped light. Instead, the table was covered in delicious food: a full chicken, mashed potatoes, buns, green beans, and was that wine? He salivated at the sight of it all and took in an appreciative sniff.

"I asked the cooks what sorts of food humans like the most. I didn't think you'd want to eat anything I conjured up." She gestured to the chair. "Sit. Eat."

Nick eyed the banquet. "What's the catch?"

"I provide food, and you have a conversation with me," Vesp said. "I want to talk. That's all."

Nick gave her a look, but the food called to him like a siren's song. He hadn't eaten this well in months. Against his better judgment, he pulled the chair back and joined her. He filled his plate with food and started to devour it before she changed her mind. His stomach unleashed a happy growl.

Vesp smiled. She twisted her fingers and created a glass of bluish wine in her hand. "I'm glad you like it. I saw your match today. The one between you and the werebird? You held your ground well."

Nick paused with a piece of chicken halfway to his mouth. He lowered it. "So...that was you in the corner?"

"Maybe," Vesp said. "Or maybe you were just hoping I was there."

Nick fought back a snort. Hardly. He'd had enough nightmares about her; he didn't want her visiting him in person. And yet, here they were. He resumed his meal, eyes darting to and from the web-like cage and back to Vesp. The way she sat, staring at him like a viper waiting to strike, made his skin crawl. He took a drink of wine to calm his nerves. "Why did you want me to come here? It wasn't just to feed me, right?"

"I was wondering if you'd considered my offer any further," she asked.

Nick curled his lip. He set the silverware down and leaned back, arms crossed. "I told you then, and I'll say it again. If you make me choose, I'll die to free the others."

"Hmm, yes, you are quite the martyr, aren't you?" Vesp asked and folded her hands beneath her chin. "Do *they* know about the bargain? What if one of them chose to sacrifice themselves instead?"

Nick arched an eyebrow. "I thought this was between you and me."

Vesp chuckled. "True." She tapped her chin with her long nail. "What if I changed the deal? Offered you and your pack your freedom if you pick another parahuman to die. Would you do it?"

Nick narrowed his eyes at her. He hated this game. Was this just another way for her to get into his head, to see the cogs moving in his mind?

His appetite vanished.

He pushed the plate toward her. "I don't make deals with fae, especially when those deals involve taking lives."

Vesp held out her hand. Ghostly images of a few parahumans appeared before him. And to Nick's horror, he realized two of them were parahumans who had agreed to help him. Astrid stood in her winged glory, eyes glittering gold. Loretta appeared on her left with a simpering smile on her face. "What about them?" Vesp asked. "The avian beat you in the ring and caused your Hunter to hurt you. Or her?" She gestured to Loretta. "I hear she troubled the children you wanted to protect. Why not end her for her atrocities? Or her?" She pointed to the fire witch who had taken the sight in one of Yanlei's eyes and almost killed him. "If you don't want to end her for yourself, then why not to avenge your lovely wolf friend?"

Nick's hand twitched under the table as he stared at the witch. She stood with her hair down, her eyes hateful and angry, ready to turn the next person who came near her to ash. It was the same expression she'd worn while trying to protect the water magus.

It was like looking in a mirror. Hadn't he worn a similar expression when protecting his pack from the Hunters? How could he even think they were different when they were fighting for the same thing: survival?

"Well?" Vesp pressed.

"No," Nick replied. "We're all here against our will. They've hurt me, yeah, but I've hurt them all too. I can't hate them." He pressed his lips together. "Why do you keep playing this game, Vesp? What do you get out of it?"

"It helps me understand my prey better," Vesp said, but there was an odd glint in her eye.

She wasn't telling the whole truth.

Nick leaned forward. "Do you do this with all of your prey? Invite them for meals, talk with them, then feast on them? Or am I different?"

For the first time, Vesp grew quiet. Her eyes flicked toward the cage behind him then back to the table. She seemed to struggle with what to say, which came as a surprise. She usually spouted witty or cruel remarks without issue.

Nick studied her then tilted his head toward the cage. "Who's in there?" he asked. He was almost afraid to find out in case she'd caught Rozene or someone else in his pack.

Vesp looked behind him. "Someone I had hoped would help me," she said in a low voice. "But I'm starting to realize trusting others is a foolish endeavor. You don't get what you want out of it."

"And what's that?"

Vesp chuckled. "Aren't I the one who should be asking the questions?"

Nick shrugged his shoulders. "Humor me. You wanna know more about me. Shouldn't I get to know about you too?" It felt weird to say, to care about the fae. She was the reason they were all captive. Yet maybe breaking down her walls would let him get the answers he needed or help him unravel the mystery of this fae and why she did the things she did.

Vesp sucked in a breath and climbed to her feet. "Don't pretend you care."

Nick barked out a laugh. "Like you care about me? Woman, you had your goons drag me in here, and then you played a mind game with me to figure out which person I wanted to kill off, and when I didn't give you the answer you wanted, you twisted my mind. Now you're offering me food but still asking me to target people so you can understand your prey? Come off it, Vesp. What do you want out of me? Because I've seen what's happened to your victims. Did you know one of them killed himself in front of me?" Nick gestured to her. "If you want to talk, then talk. If this is you buttering me up before you devour my mind, then get it over with, because I ain't playing this game."

Vesp grunted, frustrated. Her wings flared like she was going to explode with rage, but she took a deep breath and calmed herself much to Nick's amazement. "What if I was to tell you I want to find another way to feed so I don't make my prey...." She struggled with the words. "I don't make my acquaintances go mad?"

"I'd have a hard time believing that, but go on," Nick said.

Vesp stretched out a wing and pulled it close, playing with a few feathers. She plucked a loose one off and tossed it into the air. "It's tiring, going through one person after another. I've enjoyed watching you and having our conversations. I've enjoyed others too, but they all end the same. They go mad or something happens to them in the ring, either because their wounds were too grave to survive or because they were beaten down by their Hunters. Perhaps if I had someone I could feast from more regularly, it wouldn't be as troublesome."

Nick looked her over, thinking. "Or as lonely either, I imagine." She liked to talk. And maybe she wasn't exactly lying about wanting to get to know someone. It seemed strange coming from her, but then again, she was alone in this room all the time except for her screaming meals. And the only other fae around were trapped in bottles.

Vesp paused her preening and curled her fingers back to her chest. "Yes, lonely." She tapped her finger on the table. "So let me offer you another proposition."

Nick frowned at her. Now who would he have to kill?

"You come live in my chambers with me. Be the one I take from, and I'll speak with your Hunters about letting your friends go."

Nick stared at her like she'd grown another head. She wanted him to become her meal ticket, more or less, and in turn, she'd let the others go? No, no, not let them go. *Talk* with his Hunters about letting them go. Just how desperate and lonely was she? He thought of Yanlei, Brighton, Augustine, and the teens. They needed him. And so did the parahumans they'd promised to help. He couldn't just abandon them. What had she said the last time he was here? That he imbued hope? Could he trust that she only desired company and not that she wanted to snatch hope away from everyone else?

"You can't promise they'll be freed?" he asked.

"I'm the mistress of this pit. They'll have to obey," Vesp said confidently.

Nick bit his lip. "But they'll turn against you, won't they? If you take away all of their investments?"

Vesp waved her hand deftly. "I'll pay them. The mortals of this world favor currency more than life anyway. I'm sure a large enough investment will appease them."

Nick swallowed a lump in his throat. If he agreed, that meant a world of pain and suffering for him. He could do it for the sake of his packmates. But something felt wrong. She was hiding something, and he did not want to be her means to an end. If she feasted off of him only, would it make her stronger? Could she stretch her tendrils out further, create a larger pit, and torment more people?

He glanced at the table, at the good meal she'd had prepared for him. "How do I know you'll keep your word? How do I know you won't free them only to have them killed outside of the pit?" He tilted his head at her. "You and I both know they can't survive, otherwise they'll risk blowing the secret of this place."

Vesp stared back at him and shifted, growing more frustrated. "I can wipe their memories of the pit so they can't bring anyone else here. Why are you being so stubborn? I'm giving you a way to free them that means keeping them all alive. I'm not even asking you to take a life!"

"Because I think you're holding out on me. There's something you're not telling me, and that's going to matter." He waited for her outburst. When it didn't come, he got up and walked toward the cage. "Who is in here?" he asked again and reached out to touch the wall.

"Get away from that!" Vesp snapped.

But Nick ignored her and pressed his hand against the barrier. Through the flickering black and purple energy, he saw movement. And then a hand touched the wall opposite of him. The webbing cleared briefly, and another fae stared back at him. Her hair was done up in green and purple braids and roses, her skin even darker than his. She stared at him then looked over his shoulder. Her eyes widened as she mouthed the word, "Run."

Nick spun in time for two thick tendrils to wrap around him and hurl him away from the cage.

"I said to stay away!" Vesp shouted.

Nick rolled and ended up in a heap near the rocky pool. He sat back up as she advanced on him, anger in her eyes. "You're keeping one of your own hostage? What the hell's wrong with you? Why should I trust you when you enslave your own kind? Why would anyone give a shit about you if all you do is betray them? Are you going to add her to your bottle collection next?" he snarled. "You backstabbing—"

"Silence!" Vesp roared and wrapped her tendrils around him, twisting his arms behind his back and tethering his legs together. He flopped over and bared werewolf teeth as she advanced on him. "Foolish boy. I gave you a chance to save them, and you squandered it! You want me to get it over with? Fine, I'll get it over with."

A tendril rose and slammed into Nick's head. Before he could do anything, he heard the voices of his packmates scream out in agony. Images of them dying flashed before his eyes. All he could do was scream and writhe on the ground while the fae feasted on his nightmares.

Chapter 24
Countdown

Nick

"Nick? Nick!" a voice shouted through the haze.

Nick sputtered like he was drowning. He flailed his arms to push back the terrible nightmares and sat up. The world spun around him. He slumped, but warm hands caught him. Tremors ran through his body as his packmates' lingering screams echoed in his ears. "Brighton...Yanlei...Augustine," he whispered. His hands groped to find them.

"We have you," Yanlei said and pressed his head against her warm chest. Her scent filled his nose and helped clear his clouded mind. He wrapped his arms tightly around her and held her close while someone else stroked his hair.

"You're safe," Brighton added, patting his back.

Nick shuddered and peered out from Yanlei's embrace. His pack surrounded him, watching anxiously as he pulled himself together. He didn't realize he was crying until tears pattered on his leg. Nick dried his eyes and tucked his head under Yanlei's chin for comfort and safety. She touched his cheek with her warm hand. "You're all safe," he said, more to reassure himself than because he didn't believe what he was seeing.

Augustine nodded. "They dragged you back to us kicking and screaming. We thought you'd lost your mind."

"Felt like it," Nick said.

Yanlei lifted his chin and pressed their foreheads together. "What happened?" she whispered.

"It was the fae again," Nick murmured, shutting his eyes. "She wanted to talk. I made her angry. And then she made me relive you all dying so she could eat my nightmares."

Brighton sighed in frustration near his shoulder. "Why does she keep going after you?"

"I don't know," Nick lied, because he didn't want to tell them the truth. About the propositions she'd made. That she thought he was the one who could bring them home. What if they hated him? Or, as Vesp had said, what if one of the others said they'd die for the pack? He couldn't lose any of them.

He glanced behind Augustine where Pavati and Ayaan watched him. His expression softened, and he held out his arm. "Hey, come here. It's okay. It's me."

They scooted closer, and he draped an arm around them. He needed the comfort more than he cared to admit. He breathed out heavily, slumping against Yanlei. "I'm sorry," he said.

"What do you have to be sorry for?" Yanlei asked. "She's the one torturing you."

"I should be stronger."

Augustine snorted. "Bullshit. Nick, she's a fae and she's screwing with your head. What do you expect to happen? Any one of us could be laid flat because of her. It's not your fault any more than it would be if she took Brighton, or Yanlei, or me."

Nick clenched his teeth. "I'm terrified of losing you all. That's how she keeps me under control."

"Fear of losing someone you love isn't a weakness," Yanlei said and rubbed his cheek with her thumb. "It shows your heart, your spirit. She's weak for having to prey off those feelings to get her meals." She shook her head. "I wish it wasn't you."

"I wouldn't want it to be anyone else," Nick said honestly. No, he would not wish Vesp on anyone. He bowed his head. "I just want to sleep."

Yanlei pulled him down beside her to the pillows and blankets on the ground. She held him close and he snuggled against her, feeling her warmth, her strength, and her love. Nick laced their fingers together while Brighton and Augustine both settle nearby to watch over them. Nick stayed awake only a few minutes before sleep claimed him again.

***

He woke to the jingle of keys in the door. Nick opened his eyes and glanced up. To his surprise and relief, Trish walked in with a tray of food and water. He searched the area behind her, but there was no sign of Hendrickson. He also realized Brighton was no longer in the room.

Yanlei squeezed his shoulder. "Hendrickson fetched him about half an hour ago," she whispered into his ear. "You should have some time to talk to her."

Nick nodded. He motioned to Augustine and the teens to come close as Trish brought the food to them. She handed Nick a plate first.

"*I made contact with someone outside of the pit,*" she said in greeting.

Nick gaped at her. Had he heard that right? "Who? When? How?" At Yanlei's and Augustine's confused expressions, he sighed. "She made contact. Trish, talk out loud."

The vampire nodded and crouched, handing food to Yanlei, Augustine, and the siblings while she spoke. "I charmed one of the security guards to teach me how to use the system. I took a chance a few days ago and reached out to the Chicago pit. Someone responded, and she said she'd be waiting for me to contact her again."

Nick narrowed his eyes. "Did you recognize her voice?"

"No. I'm not sure who she is."

Augustine growled. "Then how do you know we can trust her? What if it's someone on the inside who's testing you?"

Trish snorted. "Do you think I'd be walking free or bringing food around if they thought I was a traitor?" She shook her head. "Micah said the pit was shut down. No one should have answered. So, whoever did, didn't want to be found either." She glanced at the wolves. "How far along are you with finding parahumans for your coup?"

"Far," Nick said. "We just enlisted the help of a werebird named

Astrid who led a coup once before but was found out." He squeezed Yanlei's hand. "Do you know how to get the collars off?"

Trish nodded. "I think so. Micah showed me the controls to use. I wanted to wait until help was on the way before I did it. Plus, you know, I had to make sure you had the forces to fight back."

Nick bit his lip. "The fae said the Hunters would make this place vanish fast if they realize you've asked for help. We might just have to rely on ourselves."

Trish glanced over her shoulder then back at Nick. "Even if I can get the collars turned off, it won't be long before the Hunters realize something is up. Someone will come in and take me down to get the collars active again."

"Hopefully we'll have them off by then," Nick said. "And there are plenty of parahumans to cause a distraction to prevent the Hunters from reactivating the collars."

"You have no idea," Trish murmured. "The number of parahumans here is awful, Nick. I've never heard of a pit this big before. And we thought the one in Chicago was huge." She ran her hands across her face. "I think they've put better security into place too because of their new guest."

"New guest?" Yanlei asked.

Nick narrowed his eyes. "The fae. There's a new fae here, is that who you mean?"

"Yes," Trish whispered. "Her name is Kafeada."

"No!" Pavati cried. Ayaan clapped a hand over her mouth to silence her.

"Shh! We can't let them hear us," he said, though tears of anger burned in his eyes. He gripped her arm and held her to his chest. "She's our teacher," Ayaan said. "If she was kidnapped, what chance do we have?"

Nick touched his arm comfortingly. "How did they get her?"

"Saul, Slater, Hendrickson, and Gale all ambushed her. A werewolf almost took off Saul's arm, but the fae healed him." Trish frowned. "Gale didn't come back."

Nick's stomach flipped in a way he didn't expect. Gale was gone? Captured? Or gone gone? He looked at Yanlei who wore the same worried expression. "Is she dead?"

Trish shook her head. "We don't know. Vesp won't let Hendrickson go after her, and we've heard nothing from Gale. Since she was captured, the Hunters consider her dead to them. I think if she tries to get back in here, she'll be shot on sight. They don't want to risk this place being exposed."

"Damn," Nick murmured. For a moment, he felt sympathy for the Hunter despite all she'd done. She'd helped him, too. Talked to him. Unlike Hendrickson who would probably work them to death. At least his missing sister explained his foul mood. "Okay, so we might have a contact on the outside. Did you figure out where we are?"

Trish chuckled. "Oh yeah. We're in the cheddar state, just below Lambeau Field."

"You're shitting me," Augustine said until Yanlei whapped her on her tattooed arm for swearing. The wolf growled in frustration. "Oh come on, they're teenagers. They've heard it before." She curled her lip. "We're in Wisconsin...geeze. The pack's probably got no idea."

Pavati tugged at her sleeve. "But that means we're close to our teacher's home. She could find us. She could bring help."

Augustine sighed. She opened her mouth as if to say something negative, thought about it, then patted Pavati's back. "You're probably right."

Trish glanced at the door again. "I need to get back before Saul gets suspicious. I'm supposed to meet with him. So what's the plan?"

Nick looked at his friends then back to Trish. He nodded firmly. "Get in contact with this person. Tell them they need to come *now*. Get the collars off. Then we'll take care of the rest."

Trish nodded and stood up. "I'll do what I can to keep them from turning the collars back on."

Nick hesitated, not liking her tone of voice. "Trish, don't do anything rash."

"It's me," Trish said with a little smirk. "When have you known me *not* to do something rash?" Before he could argue, she pulled the tray out of the room and locked the door behind her.

Nick took a deep breath and glanced at his wolves. "When you go to your fights, tell the others to be prepared." He glared at the walls of the prison. "We're taking back the pit."

Chapter 25
Fractures

Kafeada

Kafeada chewed on a nail as she watched Vesp rage from behind her prison wall. The black and violet light had faded after Nick's departure, leaving it easier for her to see Vesp in all her fury. The fae's beauty had vanished, leaving behind a sickly, decrepit figure with hateful eyes that wept black tears. Tainted Ether and Ather flitted through the room and made Kafeada's stomach twist in disgust.

A small part of her felt sorry for the corrupted fae. But most of her sneered at the thought of pitying the creature. She'd brought this upon herself by killing fae and feasting off of Earth's mortals. She was paying her price, but so was everyone else.

Vesp threw another stone stool to the ground and stomped to her warm pool. She stepped in and sank into the waters, dunking her face under. Smoke roiled above the pool. When the fae emerged, some of her beauty had returned. She brushed her hair back and folded her wings around herself in a protective embrace.

Kafeada walked to the closest wall. "That was a bit dramatic, wouldn't you say?"

"Quiet," Vesp growled.

"This isn't the first time you've brought that boy here," Kafeada went on, ignoring her aggression. "Did you honestly want him to be your consort?"

"What does it matter to you what I want?" Vesp said and shot a look in her direction. "He's a means to an end."

"Is he?" Kafeada leaned against the prison. "Because I saw something else. You *care* about that boy, don't you?" When Vesp didn't respond, Kafeada smiled to herself for having guessed it. "Why? He's a werewolf, not another fae."

"Because he has something I haven't had in a long time," Vesp said.

Kafeada gestured for her to go on.

"Hope," Vesp said. "And bravery. The rest have fallen at my feet, begged me not to hurt them. They're unworthy of my affections. But not him."

"He wouldn't survive you, you know that," Kafeada said, not caring how harsh it sounded. It was the truth. "You would drain him dry until he was a husk of himself. A mind can survive only so long if it's constantly plagued with nightmares."

"Then why am I still alive?" Vesp asked. She lifted her hands out of the water and stared at them. "Living here is an eternal nightmare. Yet I still breathe and suffer, because that's what our *Lord* desires."

Kafeada caught herself before she could say something nasty about the insult to Lord Oberon. "And you think a consort would help," she said.

Vesp sank lower in the bath and rested her head on one of her wings. "Perhaps. As you so astutely said, I'm lonely. A consort would alleviate that for a time."

Kafeada leaned her head against the wall and touched her collar. The cold iron didn't burn her, not with Vesp's spell on it. "Why stay here?" she asked. "You say it's because you need to feed, but if you're so lonely, why not try to make a better life for yourself? You could leave this place. Free those fae you hold captive. Prove to Lord Oberon you're not the same fae you were in the Veil."

Vesp ran her hand along the stone. "And where would I go? Who would even accept someone like me?"

"Come to my school," Kafeada offered. "My wife and I can provide a place for you, help you the best we can."

Vesp chuckled, the sound eerie in the quiet room. "Are you really going to try this sorry attempt again to get me to change sides? I told you. Oberon will *never* accept me back. And if I've done nothing else with my life, at least I've built an empire."

"An empire of pain and suffering. Of tortured souls. Of imprisoned brethren!" Kafeada cried, gesturing to the glowing bottles. "Vesp, *please*. End this. Maybe that boy will reconsider your offer if you free him and his friends. If you show that a fae, even one twisted by Ether, can do the right thing. You wanted my help *here*. I can't offer that. But I can offer you help beyond these walls."

Vesp rolled her head toward Kafeada and stared at her with cold, tired eyes. She snaked one of her tendrils across the floor to Kafeada's cage and tapped it. "And how can I trust you not to eliminate me once I free you? You could hand me over to Legion where they'd do everything in their power to dust me. You'd free the other fae and become a hero." Her eyes flashed and she turned in the pool, glowering at Kafeada. "That's it, isn't it? That's what you want? To bring the evil, wicked fae to justice so you can be the hero and seek Oberon's favor."

"What? No!" Kafeada shook her head and pressed her hands against the barrier. "I want to help. That's the whole point of the school; we help those who struggle with their magic. 'I've watched you these past days, Vesp. You're in pain. You're withering away no matter how many beings you give nightmares and devour. There has to be a better way *away* from here."

Vesp laughed, the sound wheezy and icy. She rose from the pool, her magic drying her off in an instant. Her beauty faded again, revealing her bedraggled visage as she approached the prison. She pressed sharp nails against it and glared at Kafeada. "I won't let you betray me. Another fae tried that." She flicked her finger, and a bright golden bottle rushed to her hand. Vesp held it and stared at the dancing light inside. "He tried to convince me he'd help me and save my soul. I believed him. And the moment I freed him, he stabbed me in the back. But he didn't realize how powerful I was." She brought the jar to her face. "Did you?" she hissed.

The orb of light darted away from her and quaked at one end of the bottle. She shook it roughly and glared at Kafeada. "I'll not be made a fool a second time. Keep your false promises of salvation to yourself, or I'll remove your voice permanently."

"Vesp—" Before she could finish, the tendril shot through her prison and wrapped around her throat. Kafeada gurgled in surprise and clawed at it. Without her magic, she couldn't stop it from strangling her.

Vesp bared her teeth as she tightened her hold, forcing Kafeada to her knees. Only when Kafeada's vision began to darken did Vesp yank her tendril back. Kafeada fell forward, gasping for breath. She heard the bottle clink as Vesp returned it to the table within Kafeada's sightline, a taunting reminder of what might happen to her.

She rubbed her throat and stared at the nightmare fae as Vesp strode past her prison. "Cross me again, and I'll bring one of your students in here next." With a snarl of magic, Vesp vanished from sight, leaving a plume of smoke behind.

Kafeada sat down on the ground and stroked her sore throat. She glanced at the bottles on the table as the lights moved inside and struggled to break free. It was torture watching them, knowing at that moment there was nothing she could do to help.

But that didn't make her entirely helpless.

She waited a few minutes to make certain Vesp wasn't going to pop back into the room. Then she pressed her hands against her collar and started to push deep down inside, reaching for her magic to try to break through. Vesp was flawed and fractured, and so was her magic. She was spreading herself too thin by hiding the entire pit, keeping Kafeada captive, and using her powers when she was already running on empty. Something had to give.

So Kafeada worked and whittled away at her collar, beating against it with the magic inside of her. If she broke free, she could reach out to Evelyn. Her wife would be scrying for her and for the kids. And once Kafeada was free of this nightmare, she'd release the captured fae and make Vesp pay.

"Hold on a little longer," she said quietly to the bottles. "I'll get you home."

Chapter 26
Guilt

Trish

Trish hurried through the halls with the cart squeaking in front of her. She kept her head down and tucked a little into Gavin's jacket, ignoring the Hunters around her as she headed back to the kitchen. The sight of Nick kept flashing before her eyes. She hadn't brought him to and from the fae this time, but she still remembered the way he'd looked when she'd helped him back to his cage the first time. The haunted, terrified, almost maddened glint in his eyes. The way he shook and mumbled the names of his packmates. He'd had some of that same madness in his irises when she'd spoken to him moments ago. How long would the fae torment him before he broke?

She set the cart in the kitchen and departed. The sounds of the fights made her grimace inwardly; she couldn't show her disgust on the outside for fear of someone noticing she wasn't enticed by the bloodshed and destruction. She'd noticed Brighton was missing and decided to make a slight detour from Saul to make sure the man was still alive. The smells of blood and disinfectant were almost overwhelming to her senses as she entered the main fighting arena. She hated it. For some reason, it made her think of a morgue. But that was kind of what the pit was, wasn't it? A place that held bodies waiting to be sent to their final resting places. She'd seen some of the death totals; it was nauseating. And it was also why she made it a point not to venture in and watch the midnight death fights.

Trish rubbed her face and plucked a small bottle of lotion out of her jacket pocket. She smeared it beneath her nose and breathed it in to help deaden the smell. Maybe that was why Gale always smelled like lilacs. The lotion, perfume, whatever it was masked the smell of blood, torture, and corpses.

Several fights were on display, though no one was in the big ring. Trish slunk around the Hunters, glancing in the cages until she came upon the one with Brighton. He snarled in his bipedal form, saliva dripping from his vicious teeth. He faced off against a snowy owl werebird, likely the same one Nick had mentioned. She must have won another fight to get to Brighton. The pair circled around each other and fought with talons and claws. Brighton landed two blows, but the owl tripped him up and slashed his back with her talons. He roared in agony.

Trish grimaced. Since Astrid was on their side, she probably wouldn't cause irreparable damage. Or so Trish hoped. She folded her arms and studied the Hunters watching the match. The pair had gained quite a crowd, but they were split down the middle, half cheering for Brighton, the other half cheering for Astrid. Had she not known they were working together, she would have put her money on Brighton. But he was also a softie and didn't like hurting people.

She heard a familiar voice curse as Brighton went down again. Hendrickson stood near the cage and pounded his fist against it.

"Come on! Get back on your feet!" he screamed, spittle flying from his mouth. Without Gale there to temper his rage, he was a ticking time bomb waiting to explode. He hit the fence again then suddenly paused. Hendrickson reached into his pocket and pulled out his phone, a confused expression on his face. He answered, and while Trish couldn't hear his words, she saw his eyes widen. He grabbed the nearest Hunter and pointed at Brighton, passing off an order before he bolted from the room.

Trish narrowed her eyes. She glanced around to make sure no one else had seen then followed Hendrickson. She kept close to the wall, not wanting him to spot her listening in. He would not forgive her for that.

"Where are you?" Hendrickson snapped.

Trish doubled back and glanced down an empty corridor.

Hendrickson paced as he held the phone to his ear. She leaned against the wall and closed her eyes, listening with her sensitive vampire ears. If she strained just hard enough, she could hear a familiar voice on the other end.

"I'm hiding out near a local mall. I escaped," Gale said.

Hendrickson grunted in surprise. "How? I saw them grab you, Gale. Are you sure they aren't tracking you?"

"Yes. I...Hendrickson, listen. It was Daniella."

He took a sharp intake of breath. "Daniella's dead, Gale. What are you talking about?"

"Daniella is with them. She's the one who grabbed me and stopped me from going back with you. Her friends questioned me. I didn't tell them anything. But then they threatened to change me into a werewolf if I didn't give up the pit. She let me go."

"Just like that?" Hendrickson said doubtfully. "You have to be seeing things or they're doing something to your head, Gale. Daniella's dead. And even if she wasn't, she's insane! She wouldn't save you."

"I know it's hard to believe. But it was her. The pack helped her recover. She's...she's sane."

Hendrickson scoffed in disbelief. He struck the wall lightly with his fist, but hard enough that Trish heard it. "Don't tell me you believe in that bullshit of packs saving deranged wolves. Why the hell would you believe she wants to help you? She killed our parents."

"They tried to kill her first. She wasn't in her right mind."

"And you think she is now? She kidnapped you! You said they burned you for information."

"One of them did, yes. But that's when Daniella freed me. She knocked him out. She risked her life to save me."

"It sounds all too convenient," Hendrickson said with a growl. "Are you working with them?"

"What? No! How could you ask that?"

Hendrickson snorted loudly into the phone. "They don't just let Hunters go. They torture us. Kill us. You shouldn't be alive right now."

There was silence for a moment before Gale spoke again. "You almost sound disappointed that I'm alive."

"That's not what I meant," Hendrickson said. "Gale, look, I'm just saying it's possible she could be using you as bait. That magus might have screwed with your head. Or...or you could be bugged."

"What are you saying?"

Hendrickson swallowed hard and pressed his hand against the wall. He bowed his head, sighing. "I'm saying I can't come get you."

"Why? Hendi, I'm free! I'm safe. You can bring something with you to inspect my body to make sure I'm not bugged."

"I can't, Gale. The fae...she won't let me. She forbade me from saving you from those assholes. If I try to leave, she'll kill me. I know it."

Gale's voice quivered on the other end. "Then what do you expect me to do?"

"Stay out of sight," Hendrickson said. "Don't call attention to yourself. Maybe I can convince Vesp to change her mind and let me bring you back. But Gale, we can't risk this place. We already lost the other pit, and they blame us because it was *our* wolves Legion was after. Our wolves were the ones that caught their attention. What do you think will happen to us if I bring you back, we get betrayed, and Vesp finds out? I don't want either of us to die."

Trish bit her lip. Hendrickson's steps carried him a few paces forward, but he stopped before coming around the corner. Gale's voice came through louder now.

"So that's it? You're just going to leave me? You're my brother."

"Yeah, I know, but I'm trying to keep us both safe."

"How am I safe when they want to force a transformation or kill me!" Gale shouted. "They're going to hunt me down. I want to come home to you."

Hendrickson sighed and pressed his head against the wall. He struck the stone with his fist again. "I can't, Gale. I'm sorry."

"Hendi! Hendi, don't—"

Trish grimaced as the call ended. Damn, that was cold. On the one hand, she did understand some of his concerns, but why not run away with his sister and leave this place behind? He didn't even give that as an option! She pressed a hand to her lips and quickly moved away before he spotted her. She didn't want to feel sorry for Gale, but wow. That was like the ultimate betrayal. A sister who kidnapped her and a brother who refused to help her. Just what—

A hand twisted in her hair and slammed her into a wall, cutting her face open on the stone. Stars burst in front of her eyes as she reached back, trying to grab the hand holding her. She was whipped around before she had the chance and met Hendrickson's angry eyes.

"Did you enjoy listening in, you bitch?" he snarled at her.

Trish narrowed her eyes at him. "I don't know what you're—"

"Don't play dumb," he growled and shook her roughly. "I smelled your vampire stench the moment I went around the corner. You were listening." He reached for a knife on his hip. "I knew you were trouble."

Trish snatched his chin and stared into his eyes. "Stop," she ordered, her irises pulsing as she pushed charm into him. He froze, hand still on the blade. "I didn't hear anything. I was just walking down the hall."

Hendrickson slowly removed his hand from his blade. His fingers loosened in her hair and then fell away. "What are you doing here?" he asked in a calmer tone.

Trish wiped the blood from her face. "I was returning a cart and looking for Saul. You were watching Brighton fight. You should get back to the ring."

Hendrickson stared at her with a sleepy expression as her charm worked on his brain, redirecting his thoughts away from her and the fact she'd heard him. With a slow nod, he turned and returned to the fights.

The moment he was gone, Trish slumped down and held her aching face. That had been too close. She needed to be more careful or she'd end up in a cage next.

Using her sleeve to wipe away the residual blood, she walked to Saul's room. She bypassed the fighting ring this time, just in case Hendrickson saw her and had second thoughts, but her charm was strong. She didn't think it would wear off that easily.

Once she arrived, she'd just touched the door when Saul opened it and smiled at her.

"There you are. I was—what happened to your face?" he asked in concern and pulled her inside.

Trish shook her head. "Just a little dispute with a Hunter. It's nothing serious, Saul."

Saul frowned gravely. He sat her in a chair and grabbed a piece of gauze and ointment. This time, blessedly, there wasn't a woman tied up in the room. He did, however, pick up a bottle filled with blood flakes. "Take a couple of these. They'll help with healing."

Trish didn't argue. She popped a few in her mouth and sucked on them while he put salve on her face and treated the wound. She eyed his arm; she'd seen the damage when he'd been brought back. "How are you feeling?"

"Perfectly fine," he said and pulled another chair over. He sat across from her, stretching his arm out in front of her. "Lady Vesp worked wonders, as always."

Trish forced a smile. Yes, Lady Vesp was just a peach, wasn't she? "You seem calmer now."

"I also have Vesp to thank for that." He leaned back in the chair and smiled. "She took away the pain in my mind and heart."

Trish lifted an eyebrow. "How?"

"With a kiss," Saul said. "It's some of the wonderful magic she has. She can remove nightmares and bad emotions. She's done it since I arrived here to serve her. It's how I've been able to survive without…" He hesitated and rubbed his chest. "It's how I'm surviving."

Trish narrowed her eyes. "Saul, say her name."

Saul glanced sideways at her and cleared his throat. "I'd rather not. I'm in a better place now, and I'd like to stay there."

"Are you just having her wipe your memories of Fraula? Is that why you're working with her?"

Saul grimaced. "Trish, please. Let it be."

She wanted to say more. She wanted to demand to know how he could let this fae take away his emotions, his memories of his mate. How could he betray his coven because of the pain Fraula's death had caused him, and yet ask for her to be erased from his mind? Didn't he think Trish mourned Gavin's death? They might not have been mates, but they could have been! And he'd just chosen to forget!

"Would you forget about me, little bat, if you had the option?" Gavin's voice came as a whisper to her. She glanced over Saul's shoulder and saw the ghostly figure of her friend look at her from a dark corner. *"Would you?"*

"No." She gripped the cuff of his jacket tightly. *"No matter the pain I feel from your loss, I would never want to forget you.*

Because you made me grow. Helped me become the person I am."

"You give me too much credit, love." Gavin chuckled. *"But I'll take it. Tread carefully. A wounded heart can make someone do foolish things."*

"Heh, no kidding. The Nightmother knows I've made enough of my own mistakes," Trish said.

She took a breath and touched Saul's cheek. "I'm sorry. I won't bring her up again." She reached down for his hand and rubbed it with her thumb. Saul relaxed and squeezed her hand back. "You said you wanted to see me?"

Saul nodded. "Micah reported you did a fine job working with him. I'm glad you took the initiative to start learning the systems here."

Trish grinned and shrugged. "It's pretty fascinating. I'm glad he had good things to say." And nothing else. Her charm must have worked if he didn't remember anything Trish had forced him to do. "I took notes," she added, chuckling. "I was hoping to take some more lessons from him soon."

"Good," Saul said with an approving nod. "He works himself very hard for the pit, and he could use the help." He tilted his head. "And I think it would be better for you to work behind the scenes than go on missions. I talked with Slater, and he feels the same."

Trish blinked in surprise. She hadn't expected that. "Really?"

"I saw the way you reacted to those teens coming in," Saul said. "You were uncomfortable. Hunting...is not for everyone. And we have other uses for your skills. Help with security, and you'll more than earn your keep."

Relief flooded through her. It was a comfort to know that if she got stuck here longer because their mission failed and if she survived, she wouldn't be forced to hunt. Slater, Saul, and Hendrickson might have the stomach for it, but she didn't. At least, not this sort of hunt. Going after someone for blood? Sure. But not stealing people from their homes. "Thank you, Saul."

Saul cupped her cheek with his hand and smiled at her. "I want you to be happy. I know you weren't with the coven, especially after Gavin passed. I hope you can feel at peace here knowing you're making a difference."

Am I? She wondered to herself. *Am I really making a difference? Or am I another chess piece on the board, being moved around by those in power?*

"*Careful, little bat,*" Gavin said. "*I'm rubbing off on you.*"

Trish took a breath and leaned her head into Saul's hand. "I am happier here. Even if I have the occasional run in with idiots," she added, motioning to her cut face. She met his eyes briefly then lowered them. "I'll do my best to make you proud, Saul."

"I know you will, Trish. I trust you."

It felt like a punch to the gut. He trusted her. Here she was, plotting behind his back, and yet he still trusted her. Nightmother, was this her lot in life? To keep betraying people for the greater good? She was tired of being the turncoat, making everyone hate her as she struggled to do the right thing. Except Saul. Saul never seemed able to hate her.

He will when this is all done, she thought. Provided she was still alive to feel his hate.

"Trish?" Saul asked softly. "Is something wrong?"

She blinked a few times and shook her head. "No, sorry. Lost in thought. Just remembering the old days. And Gavin."

Saul pulled her into a hug. He held her head to his shoulder, hand brushing her hair. His scent filled her nose comfortingly as he squeezed her. "I could ask Lady Vesp to take away your pain too, Trish. I don't think it would be too much for her."

Trish released a shaky breath. She stared at the dark image of Gavin watching her, his head cocked a little to the side as if he were still alive. It almost felt like she could reach out and touch him. Was she going mad? Was he some sort of ghost? Or did she grieve for him so deeply that she wasn't ready to let him go? This fae's magic could help, but she didn't want to forget the things they'd shared. Or how their relationship had shaped her.

"No," she said after a long moment. "I want the memories. They remind me of what more I could lose if I'm not careful."

Saul nodded against her head and kept her in his arms. Trish closed her eyes and relaxed in his warm embrace, wishing for all the world that they were on the same side. One day she would betray him. And she dreaded the look in his eyes when he realized she'd been against him the whole time.

Chapter 27
Contact

Trish

"Hey! There's my lady of the night," Micah exclaimed cheerfully.

Trish chuckled as he swiveled to greet her. "Hey, Micah. Good to see you, too." She pulled up a chair and settled down beside him.

It had been days since her conversation with Saul, and this was the third time she'd worked beside Micah. Each session she charmed him for a short while just to make sure no one was watching. She hadn't attempted to reach out to her contact yet for fear someone would notice. But after two times of no one running in, screaming that she was using charm, she figured it would be safe to try again. Especially since things were getting worse in the pit.

Brighton had survived his encounter with Astrid, but he'd lost the fight, which had set Hendrickson off. Trish didn't know if Brighton was in more pain because of Astrid's talons or the shocks from Hendrickson's remote. He'd been unconscious for nearly twenty-four hours, and he now sported a burn on his throat. Trish had treated him herself that morning, and it had helped her decide that tonight would be the night she reached out and set the plan in motion. She'd waited for the midnight shift when the Hunters who were awake would be busy watching the death matches, which left Micah alone with her, or so she hoped.

"Just us tonight?" she asked and leaned over to check the fighting screens.

Micah nodded. "Yep. I'll get relieved at about 3:00 a.m., so we have until then to go over things. The guy who replaces me . . . well, he's not quite as friendly toward parahumans, so I'd suggest you stick with me." He winked at her and slid the binder to her. "So, what are you interested in tonight?"

Trish picked a random topic for the time being, letting the camera record their conversation so she didn't raise suspicion. Besides, she was trying to figure out the schematics of the pit. There were several different entrances, and most of them looked heavily guarded. She wasn't even sure how people came and went, which was the downside to not going on missions. She'd made notes in her book about drop off points, but how she was going to explain them to her contact?

If she could even trust the woman on the other end.

She glanced at Micah out of the corner of her eye as he clicked through a few screens and took notes. He'd been incredibly helpful teaching her, and the more she talked with him, the more she realized he wasn't a bad guy. Were his ideas about parahumans twisted? Yeah. But he saw the captives as people who had done terrible things. They weren't bad because they were parahuman, necessarily. They were bad because he'd been lied to about their transgressions.

"Something on your mind?" Micah asked.

"Hm?"

"You were staring," he said, a bright smile on his face. "Something else you want to learn?"

"Oh, no. Sorry, I was just thinking." Trish licked her lips. Now was as good a time as any to reach out, right? She drummed her fingers on the desk then leaned her head on her hand and looked at him. "There is something you can help me with," she said softly. When Micah looked at her, she let her eyes glimmer, pushing charm onto him in an instant. "Can you loop the cameras? Set it for about fifteen minutes?"

"No problem," he said with the same joviality she'd started to expect from him. He changed the parameters on the computer and she waited until she could tell from the screen that their camera in the security office was on loop.

"Good," Trish said and reached for two sets of headphones, one that would cancel out sound and one that would let her hear the person she'd be contacting. She handed him the first. "Put these on and close your eyes. Relax for a minute."

"That sounds good," Micah said and did as she asked.

Trish clicked the keys to connect her with the Chicago pit, just like before. "Is anyone there?"

Static greeted her and she pulled lightly at her fingers, waiting, hoping her contact would whisper to her again.

"The prodigal mole returns," a familiar voice said on the other end.

Trish sighed in relief. It was the same woman. "I have about thirteen minutes to talk before I cut the feed."

"Plenty of time. What do you got for me?"

Trish hesitated. This could be a trap. But so far no one had come down on her about reaching out to other pits. "First, how do I know I can trust you?"

"Well, sweetheart, you really don't know. But I will say this. I know Arjun and Tess, and they both heard your voice and identified you as Trish."

Trish blinked in surprise. Well, that was a plus at least. And she didn't think any of the other Hunters here personally knew who Tess and Arjun were or that she knew them. "What's your name?"

"Not part of the deal. You give me the info, and we'll go from there."

Trish took a breath. "All right. I have parahumans here planning a coup. I can give you the numbers of parahumans versus Hunters. I can also shut their collars off, but that'll only last for so long before someone else gets in here and turns them back on."

"That won't be a problem," the woman said. "I'm accessing your database as we speak. I can turn the collars off and keep them off. The Hunters will have a hard time overriding the bug I put in there. Where are you located?"

"Green Bay, Wisconsin. Underneath Lambeau Field."

"Go Packers," the woman said with a chuckle. "Hiding them in plain sight. Interesting. How soon can your crew be ready to fight?"

Trish glanced at the clock. Nick wanted them out as soon as possible, as did she. "Depends on when your forces can amass. How does twenty-four hours sound?"

"Hm, I can make that happen. Per Tess, the Chicago packs are on standby, waiting to go in an instant. Why so soon, though? Don't you want more time to plan?"

Trish shook her head. "No. There's a fae leading this pit who's kidnapped another fae. The more she drains her captive, the stronger she gets. Also, a Hunter was captured, and even though she escaped, it's already put the other Hunters and the fae on edge. They could decide to move at any time, and we can't miss this window of opportunity. Do you think Legion will help?"

The woman snorted. "Legion does what Legion wants. They didn't get there fast enough last time. We'll tell them, but they can do their own thing while we take care of the rescue *our* way." The sound of fingers tapping on keys came through the headset. "Are these schematics up to date?"

Trish looked on the screen and was startled to find a map of the place pulled up. She stared at it then frowned. "That's not what matches my manual. Some of the entrances look the same, but one of them must have been updated and the other hasn't been. I'm not sure which entrance would be the best for them to come through. They'll all be guarded by magic."

The woman grunted. "We might have to get creative," she said. "So at midnight tomorrow night, I'll turn off the collars and bug their systems. You get the parahumans out. Our crew should come in at that time and draw attention to them and away from the captives. What about the doors? Let's see if they're automated."

"I've had to use keys," Trish said. "I imagine they wouldn't want to make it possible for everyone to get out at once."

"Unless they had to do a mass exodus," the woman murmured. "Ah, here. Okay, the cells do have an emergency button to both unlock and lock the doors all at once. I'll make sure that gets triggered too so your parahumans don't have to bash through metal."

"Good," Trish said. She watched the screen change as whoever was on the other end went through more of the infrastructure of the pit.

"What's going to be our biggest obstacle?" the woman asked.

"The fae, Vesp," Trish said. "Hunters are one thing, but she's conniving and vicious. I've seen what she does to parahumans. And like I said, she's been getting more powerful since she kidnapped another fae."

"How many fae captives are there?"

"Still in one piece? Just one. The others are, uh, dusted and trapped in bottles."

"Splendid," the woman said sarcastically. "Well, we'll add them to the list of folks we need to rescue. A few more questions for you."

"Okay, but we're running short on time," Trish said. She sat and flipped through the manual, answering a few more logistical questions as the woman rattled them off. She slid one earpiece back, listening to make sure no one was listening in. A loud noise in the hall startled her. She looked over her shoulder, but no one appeared. She breathed out in relief.

"You're on edge," the woman noted.

"Wouldn't you be? I'm betraying a pit of Hunters, and I'm still waiting for one of them to pop their head in here."

"Is there anyone in there with you?"

"Yeah, an IT guy named Micah." She glanced at the man as he sat with his eyes closed, head tilted back. "Hey, uh, is there a way to guarantee his safety? He's been very helpful."

The woman laughed quietly in her ear. "Willingly helpful or helpful under charm?"

"Well...."

"Hon, there are a couple hundred parahumans who need rescuing. My last concern is for a random Hunter who may or may not shoot us in the back. If you want him protected, you deal with him yourself. My job is to make sure the others get in and out without getting shot."

Trish grimaced. "Fair," she muttered. She checked the time. "Cameras are going live in sixty seconds. You might want to cut your feed."

"Already done. We'll be there in twenty-four hours, 12:00 a.m. on the dot. It'd be a great help if you could get into the room and take out any techs working on the system so I won't have anyone competing with me."

"I can do that," Trish said, though she hoped it wasn't poor Micah. "Thank you."

"Heh, don't thank me yet. Let's hope ya'll make it out of this alive. Good luck."

"You too." Trish heard a click then static filled her ears. She took the headphones off and removed Micah's as well, setting them where they'd been before the cameras looped.

Micah opened his eyes and looked at her. "You all right? You look worried."

"Just fine," Trish lied and smiled, her eyes glimmering with charm. "Make sure the cameras are running normally now."

Micah nodded and resumed tapping on the keyboard while Trish watched him. What would his fellow Hunters do to him once they realized he'd failed to protect the sanctity of the pit? If the parahumans didn't kill him, the Hunters might, which wasn't fair. He was just doing a job to support his family. She was the one screwing with everything.

He finished up on the cameras then sat back with a satisfied grunt. "There we go. All good." He tilted his head as he studied her face. "Hey, I know this might be a shot in the dark, but . . . would you want to grab a drink after my shift ends tonight?" He waved his hands. "Purely as friends, of course."

Trish blinked in surprise. "Won't the other Hunters give you shit if you're seen with a vampire?"

"Even if they do, they can piss off," Micah said with a grin. "It's my decision what company I keep, and you seem like pretty good company."

Trish blushed and cleared her throat. Oh, if only he knew. "I—" she started but then paused. He wanted to get a drink with her. Be alone with her. "I'm actually planning to meet Saul after I'm done here," she said and watched his expression deflate. "What about tomorrow though? Say, 11:30 p.m.? Are you working?"

The smile returned in earnest. "My shift ends earlier, but I don't mind sticking around. Sure, 11:30 p.m. sounds great. Meet outside of here?"

Trish shook her head. "Why don't we meet at your quarters? If that's okay."

His grin widened. He reached for her notebook and pulled it over, adding the number and location of his bunk. "There you go. I'll see you then, Trish."

She took the book back and smiled warmly, trying to hide the guilt gnawing at her stomach. "Thanks, looking forward to it. Now, can we talk a bit more about the security around the entrances?" she asked and turned back to the computer.

Chapter 28
Preparations

Tess pressed her arms together, blocking a blow from Arjun's fist. She panted, sweat dripping down her face and into her clothing as they moved around the sparring ring. They'd been going at it for a couple hours after taking a break from Arjun's magic lessons. And despite everything Arjun had taught her, he was still kicking her ass more times than she cared to count.

She dropped low and swiped at his ankle. But he shifted his balance to his other foot and dove for her, knocking her off balance and onto her back. He pinned her down like he'd done many times before and gave her that smarmy smirk of his. A knife appeared in his hand, and he pressed it to her throat.

"Dead," he said cheerfully.

"Damn you," Tess complained and flopped her head onto the floor, exhausted. He was too good. Even when Skye had stopped by the previous day to check on their progress with fighting and magic, Tess hadn't been able to take him down more than once. And boy had she crowed when she knocked him off his feet. He'd silenced her in the next match, and Skye had stood over them laughing.

Tess both hated and liked the woman.

Arjun rocked back and held out his hand, helping her up.

Tess dusted dirt off her legs. She tilted her head, her dark hair falling to one side of her face. A thought occurred to her. "Why don't we try *with* magic this time? You've gotten better with your witchy powers."

Arjun frowned. "Tess, you're far more experienced with your fire magic than I am with my earth."

Tess held out her hands. "So? You're way more experienced with fighting. Come on, let's try it and see what you can do with the vines. Besides, we have the tools right here." She gestured to the table with his plants, stones, bell, and candle. "You have to learn to use your magic on the fly anyway."

Arjun eyed the items and then Tess. When he still resisted, Tess walked up to him. She placed her hand over the leaf necklace and pushed a bit of Ether into it. "Trust me," she said. "I'm not going to hurt you."

He stared down into her eyes. Slowly, he relaxed his shoulders and gave her a warm kiss on her forehead. "I know you won't. It's just...difficult for me, mentally, to use magic."

"Even more reason to practice." Tess walked over to the table and gestured to his wand. She wouldn't touch it; only the witch who used it should touch it. "Show me what you've got."

Arjun arched an eyebrow, an emerald light sparking in his beautiful eyes. "Is that a challenge?" he teased as his lips pulled into a smile. He picked up the wand, but he didn't grab the plant, which surprised her. This early in training, she'd have thought he'd want to work with something that was already partially grown. "Challenge accepted."

"Oh, did I strike a nerve?" Tess said, chuckling. She stepped away from him and moved her hand through the air. Ether sparked around them, creating a barrier to prevent loose fireballs from setting something ablaze. She'd learned the hard way with her pack not to underestimate her abilities.

They faced off against one another, fire flowing through Tess's fingers. She'd taught him the basic techniques of creating a shield to block enemy magic. Now was her chance to test if he'd learned her lessons.

Tess struck first, sending two balls of fire snarling at him. Arjun ducked the first, but for the second he raised his wand and touched his necklace. "Shield!" he barked.

The fire exploded against a green barrier at the tip of his wand.

Tess grinned at the sight of it. It wasn't a very big shield, but it was enough to disperse her magic. "Good, let's try a few more." She sent three more fire balls at him, and each one he deflected with his wand. For the third, he stopped touching his necklace and instead used the Ether he pulled through his wand. The barrier wasn't quite as big, but it served its purpose.

He wove his wand through the air. The wooden boards rumbled beneath Tess's feet, causing her to lose her balance. He moved his hand and sent tiny items scattering across the ground.

"What—?" she started to say before she realized what they were. Seeds.

Arjun sent magic into the seeds. Green sprouts poked through and struggled to rise.

Tess chuckled and backed out of the circle. She flicked fire at a few of them, killing the sprouts. "Cute, but you have to act faster than that, Arjun."

"I'm trying," he said as sweat dotted his brow. He twisted his wand to the side and moved out of the way as Tess tossed another fireball at him. As he deflected the attack, she burned more of the seeds then sent a spiral of fire toward him. Arjun struggled to maintain his shield as the fire coiled around his body, a hair's breadth away from burning him. He pushed against her heat with his shield, gritting his teeth in his effort, but he couldn't break her magic.

She walked to him and brought her hand up, placing the tip of her finger to his forehead. Fire flickered around his face without touching his skin. "Dead," she said. She spread her hands, breaking the magic. Even if it had touched him, it would have only left a hot mark; she'd learned to use cooler flames in sparring matches.

Arjun bent over at the waist, resting his arms on his legs while he panted. "You're too strong for me. I need more practice."

"You did well," Tess said. "Especially with your shields." She glanced at the circle of seeds. The ones she'd burned gave off small puffs of smoke. "I think you had the right idea with the seeds. But you put too much attention into growing too many at once. Focus on one or two. You burn yourself out too fast otherwise."

Arjun nodded in understanding and ran his hand along his face. He smoothed his hair back and rolled his shoulders. "All right, let's go again."

Tess smiled. "That's the spirit." She backed up to the edge of their fighting ring. She decided to leave the seeds where they were in case he chose to use them again.

The fight started out similarly with Tess tossing fire orbs and Arjun blocking them. He moved in closer, surprising her, and used his shields to buffet her away from her spot and to another section of the ring. It was an interesting tactic, though she wasn't sure if he was trying to wear her down or what exactly he was hoping to accomplish.

She dodged the seeds and shot fire at his arm and his leg. He sidestepped one burst and blocked the other. Then he reached into a pocket once more and tossed seeds at her feet. Tess burned several, figuring she could help him focus on a smaller amount. The seeds sprouted like before, but they would still fall victim to her flames.

What is he doing? He already tried this once, and it didn't work.

In fact, he looked like he was using even more energy than before. The seeds barely grew, but his hand shook as he strained his magic. Tess frowned in confusion. The last thing she wanted him to do was to burn himself out. She lifted her hand to bind him up in her fire again.

Vines snapped around her wrist and jerked her backward.

Tess cried out in surprise as she was lifted off the floor and yanked against a pillar. Her head and back struck it, jarring her senses, as more vines wrapped around her. Tess looked down, mouth falling open in shock. He'd maneuvered her toward the table where his plant sat. While she'd been distracted by the seedlings, he'd grown a great monster out of his plant which now bound her limbs to the pole.

Tess laughed in surprise and struggled to break free, but they were inexorable. More twisted around her throat, and one even had the audacity to cover her mouth. Tess called fire to her hands, fully intending to set the plant aflame.

Thorns pricked her throat, scraping her flesh. A bead of blood trickled down her skin.

Arjun approached her as more thorns prodded her skin, bringing pain if she moved too much. His eyes flashed with green magic, as did the tip of his wand. "Dead," he declared, the thorns digging in just enough to still her movement.

Tess gaped. Well...that was *not* something she had expected, but she was delighted he'd taken her advice to heart. Gagged and pinned, all she could do was grin a little around the vine parting her lips.

Arjun flicked his wand, removing the thorns but leaving the vines binding her. He grinned mischievously. "You know, I kind of like you like this."

Tess grunted in protest and wiggled her body.

With a chuckle, Arjun removed the vine from her mouth but left the rest. "Hm, you really look beautiful."

Tess snorted. "Jerk. Now, free me—mph." The protest died on her lips as he kissed her. Tess melted into it. She closed her eyes, her body tingling as he twisted his fingers into her hair and pressed their lips together harder. All thoughts of protest and breaking free of the vines vanished. Okay...yeah, this felt good. Like, really good.

Arjun broke the kiss first and pressed his forehead against hers. "You're so beautiful."

She smirked and nipped at his nose. "What are you going to do to me now that I'm at your mercy?"

Arjun ran his hand through her hair, along her neck, and down to her chest. "Oh, I can think of a few things." His eyes sparked, and then he wobbled.

"Arjun!" Tess cried as he fell to a knee, shaking his head. She touched the vines with her magic and burned her way free before crouching beside him. "Arjun, what's wrong?"

"Sorry, I...feel weak," he said.

Tess lifted his chin and looked in his eyes. She touched his skin and felt the chill in his cheeks. "You used too much magic," she said. "You pushed yourself too far. Don't worry, I know how to fix that." She helped him up and draped his arm over her shoulders. "I'll grab you some food, and then I'll get you warmed up in bed."

Arjun cracked a weary smile. "Heh, I like the sound of that second part."

"Quiet you," Tess said with a laugh.

***

Tess got Arjun to eat some warm food then join her for a shower to help him relax. If she could teach him anything about magic, it was how to take care of himself after he used too much. Witches didn't often burn out since they used a conduit to draw the Ether to themselves. But new witches didn't know how to distinguish using the conduit, the wand, from using their own energy to fuel the magic. Arjun would learn that in time and likely from a better teacher. But for now, she couldn't believe how well he was doing learning from *her*.

They settled in for the night in his bed, both of them warm and naked under the covers. She snuggled against his chest while he held her protectively to him. Tess wasn't out long when she felt Arjun shift. She woke to the sound of his phone ringing obnoxiously.

Arjun rolled over and snatched it off the end table. "Skye, what is it?" he asked.

Tess pulled herself to him and touched his arm, trying to hear.

Arjun put the phone on speaker. "We can both hear you now."

"Trish reached out tonight. The plan is to go in twenty-four hours—well, twenty-three-and-a-half hours now—and rescue your friends. So get your asses up and dressed and contact your old pack."

Tess's mouth fell open, and she exchanged a look with Arjun. "You know where they are?"

"Yep. Lambeau Field, underneath the stadium."

"You're shitting me," Tess said in shock.

"Heh, I thought the same thing, but I got into their system and everything checks out. Things are going downhill pretty fast there, so we gotta get them out ASAP. Can you get the pack ready and up to Wisconsin in time?"

"Yeah," Tess said and rolled out of bed. "I'll call Rozene. We'll move out as soon as possible. Do they have a plan?"

"Not the most foolproof one, but it'll work."

Tess listened as Skye rattled off the plan. She pulled on black pants and a black shirt and jacket that matched Arjun's, the attire of a Hunter. She braided her hair and pinned it to her head so it couldn't be easily grabbed.

Skye finally took a breath. "You got all that?"

Arjun had crawled out of bed to get dressed as well. "Yes, Skye. We'll let you know as soon as we have a plan of action. You'll stay in their system and keep it bugged the whole time?"

"Of course. That's why I won't be joining you on this merry jaunt. Now remember, don't use my name, all right? I'm just your friendly neighborhood hacker."

Arjun chuckled. "Of course. We'll keep your identity safe, Skye. Thank you."

"Thank me by coming home alive, got it? I'm shooting the info to your phone. Good luck, love birds."

Tess sputtered as Skye hung up. She rolled her eyes and grabbed her phone. "You drive to Paytah's place while I call Rozene."

Arjun snatched up his keys, and together they bolted out the door.

Chapter 29
Gatekeeper

Rozene

Rozene lay on her back in bed, staring up at the ceiling, thinking. A few days had passed since Daniella's betrayal. Poor Vic had a welt the size of a tea cup on the side of his head from her blow. He'd found Gale and Daniella missing first and had sounded the alarm, breaking them all out of their peaceful slumbers. They'd pulled together to go after Daniella and stop her and Gale when the wolf in question had walked through the door, minus the damn Hunter.

Wapasha had been *furious*, and rightfully so. He'd taken Daniella in at her worst and turned her into the sane—and what they'd thought was upstanding—werewolf she'd become. But this betrayal struck them all deep. Had Evelyn not spent the entire day scrying for her wife, she might have blasted Daniella through a window with her magic. Instead, her wail and power had just upended all the chairs and knocked them into the walls.

Daniella offered no fight or apology. Instead, she allowed Wapasha to bring her downstairs to the prison and be chained so she couldn't escape on them again. Marion had begged him not to do it, citing that Daniella must have had a good reason to free her sister. But Daniella's response was sorely lacking.

"I can't let you change or kill her. She's my sister. I believe she'll come around and help us in the end."

Several days later, and there was still no evidence of that. Gale was likely back with the Hunters, telling them all about their small group of rebels. And now they were down another wolf as Daniella languished in the prison.

Rozene sighed in frustration and rolled over, fluffing her pillow, but it was no use. She couldn't sleep. Tess had no news. Paytah kept letting them know as more people went missing. They were no closer to finding the Hunters now that Gale was gone. And Evelyn still hadn't had any luck reaching her wife. They'd come to a standstill, and it was maddening. Rozene hated inaction. She could sit still and be patient when she knew something was going to come of it, like getting answers out of Gale. But with no more leads, what hope did they have?

Rozene pushed herself out of bed and slid her feet into her slippers. She wrapped a robe around herself and pulled her long hair free, letting it cascade down her back. She stepped out of her room and took the stairs quietly, heading for the kitchen. Light in the dining room made her pause.

She slipped inside and found Wapasha sitting with a beer and Vic who held a glass of whiskey. The swelling had gone down on magus's head. They looked up at her when she walked in.

"Ma," Wapasha said, raising his beer to her in greeting.

Rozene went to him and ran her hand along his hair. "Can't sleep either?"

They both shook their heads.

"I went out and searched for Gale," Wapasha said and rested his chin on his hand. "No luck. Daniella still won't tell us where she dropped her off." He exhaled sharply through his nose. "I still can't believe I was foolish enough to let her be alone with that woman even once. I want to believe the Hunter toyed with her mind, but I know that's not true. Daniella did this of her own free will."

"Yes," Rozene agreed and sat down next to him. "Maybe she honestly thinks Gale will provide some service to us."

Vic snorted. "Do you actually believe that shit? What I don't get is why the hell she'd help that Hunter after what Gale did to her. With all the anger she harbors toward her family, why save one of them?"

Rozene shrugged. "Sometimes we do drastic things for family, don't we?" she said and glanced at Wapasha. "Including moving to another state to avoid fighting with an alpha father and ending up leading a pack of one's own."

He rolled his eyes and reached out to squeeze his mother's hand. "That was to keep the peace. Daniella doesn't even know her sister anymore. I don't get how she could trust someone who did her so much harm."

"I don't know, son." Rozene rubbed her face and glanced at the clock. "Do you know when Daniella was last fed?"

Both men shook their heads. "Jackson's been watching her," Wapasha said. "He might know."

Rozene kissed her son's cheek as she rose. "Both of you should try to get some sleep. You won't be any good to us if you're exhausted. Did Evelyn finally go to bed?"

"I saw her head off a couple hours ago," Wapasha said. He chuckled. "I think she took your reprimand to heart when she burnt herself out."

"Well, good. That won't help us either." Rozene walked into the kitchen and pulled out some leftover chicken from dinner. She heated it up along with rice and added a bun. She snagged a bottle of water and silverware and headed downstairs.

Jackson sat on a chair next to the door, arms crossed and head down as if he was sleeping. She knew better though. The moment the scent of the food reached his nose, he opened his eyes and stared at her. "What are you doing up so late?" he asked in concern.

"Couldn't sleep," Rozene said. She nodded to the door. "Has she eaten?"

"Not since lunch. She wasn't interested in dinner."

Rozene nodded. "Open the door."

"Alpha—"

"I said, open the door." Rozene said patiently.

Jackson sighed and stood up. He unlocked the door and opened it for her.

Rozene walked in. A light had been left on inside. They'd placed a cot in the room for Daniella to sleep on, but the chains didn't allow her to move very far from the bed. She lay on her back, arm over her eyes to block out the light.

Rozene put the food on a tray in the room and pushed it toward the wolf.

"Wasn't expecting a meeting from you, Alpha," Daniella said. She pulled her arm down and looked over at Rozene. When she saw the food, she sat up.

"Is there a reason you ignored dinner?"

"Vic brought it. Let's say I wasn't sure if it was safe." She took the tray and bit into the chicken. "Any word from Gale?"

Rozene tried not to bristle. She pulled a chair over and sat down, facing Daniella while she feasted. "None. And none from anyone else."

Daniella nodded. "And has Wapasha decided what to do with me now that I've, according to him, turned tail and betrayed him?"

"You seem very unconcerned about your potential fate," Rozene noted.

Daniella put her fork down and chuckled. She stared at Rozene with her scarred face and held out her wrists to show off the shackles. "I've been through worse. I'll survive another punishment."

"That *worst* was by the hands of your own sister, the one *you* set free."

Daniella lowered her hands with a sigh. "It's to be a lecture, I see," she muttered. She flopped back onto her cot. "Forgive me, Alpha, but I've heard enough from Evelyn, Vic, and Wapasha. I know none of you understand *why* I did it. But let me say it again anyway. I have hope that Gale will make the right decision and come back to us. Once she realizes there's nothing left for her at the pit, she'll return."

"What about your brother?" Rozene asked.

Daniella swallowed. She licked her lips and tilted her head back. "He's the only hitch in my plan. He's still alive. Gale loves and trusts him. And if he saves her, well, I don't know. But if he doesn't, then we might have another ally."

Rozene rubbed her arms. "There are far more uncertainties in your plan than I care to count. We could have gotten information out of her."

"Are you so sure?" Daniella arched an eyebrow at Rozene. "How far were you willing to go? Would you have dared to step into the shoes of a Hunter and torture her?"

Rozene narrowed her eyes. "You have no idea the things I have done to keep my pack safe. I will do whatever is necessary to bring them home."

"Then why didn't you?"

The question caught her off guard. "What do you mean?"

"She was here a couple days. You could have done something to break her. Why didn't you?"

Rozene took a deep breath. "Just because it's something I *can* do doesn't mean I delight in it, Daniella. I wanted to give her a chance to come clean."

"That's what I'm doing too," Daniella said. "Our plans aren't that different."

"Except for the fact that you freed her, so we've lost our bargaining chip ," Rozene retorted, baffled at how Daniella didn't get that. Was she as sane as Wapasha claimed her to be, or was there still some insanity lurking behind those eyes of hers? She shook her head. "Daniella—"

Her phone went off in her robe pocket. Rozene recognized the ring instantly and picked it up. "Tess?"

"Rozene, I have news for you."

Rozene met Daniella's eyes and headed out the door. "Lock the door and join us upstairs," she said to Jackson. "It's Tess."

Jackson didn't argue. Rozene hurried up the steps and snapped her fingers to get Wapasha's attention. "Fetch Marion and Evelyn."

Once everyone save Daniella was assembled, Rozene put the phone down and hit speaker. She folded her hands beneath her chin and listened with everyone as Tess filled them in on the information they'd gotten from their *friend*. Rozene still wasn't so sure if they could trust this person, but Tess and Arjun seemed pretty certain of her credentials.

Evelyn covered her face and ground her teeth. "Green Bay. They've been in Green Bay the whole time? Why couldn't I sense them?"

"Probably because of the fae guarding the place," Tess said. The sound of a car rumbling through the streets of Chicago filtered through the call. "I'll send you a text of the possible entrances, but we don't know which ones are best, unfortunately. So you might get delayed."

"I can cloak us in my magic when we head there," Evelyn said. "If there are guards outside, they won't be able to tell how many cars are coming."

Rozene nodded and typed notes into her tablet. "You're heading to

Paytah now to get the pack together?"

"Yeah. The sooner we get out there the better if we have less than twenty-four hours."

Wapasha grimaced. "Things must be bad if they've given us such a short timeline."

"That's what it sounds like," Tess agreed. "And Trish could be caught at any second. We can't risk them all vanishing on us again. We gotta hit hard and fast."

Vic drummed his fingers on the table. "We should . . . well, Paytah should notify Legion. See if we can get their help."

"Legion might take too long to organize," Arjun said on the other end. "Plus, we're trusting the word of a vampire who's known to be a turncoat. They might not want to risk their people."

"So we risk ours?" Vic said. "We do realize who this is we're talking about, right? How do we know Trish isn't working for them, and this isn't all a huge trap?"

"She's not," Tess said firmly. "Look, I don't like her much more than the rest of you, but she saved our lives. She's a bitch, but I think she knows what side she's on."

Vic snorted. "I'm hearing a lot of 'I thinks' in this conversation. I don't like going in without certainty."

"Well, this is the best we've got," Tess said. "Unless Gale has come through with anything."

Rozene exchanged looks with the others. "That was a dead end. She escaped."

"What?! How?"

Rozene waved her hand and sighed. "It doesn't matter now. She's gone, so all we have is the information you're giving us. I'll send an emergency message to the pack once we're done talking. It'll get them to Paytah faster so you won't have to wait as long for them to mobilize."

"Thanks, Rozene," Tess said. "We'll get there as soon as we can."

"Be safe," Rozene said. She picked up her phone and ended the call. While the others digested the information, she sent a group message out to all of their packmates. She heard Jackson's phone buzz beside her. "I wish we had more time, but I understand why we can't wait."

Evelyn rubbed her neck. "There's still the problem of getting in. If we choose the wrong entrance where more of their forces are gathered, we might be taken down before we do much good."

Marion chuckled. "I think the Hunters will have more on their hands to worry about when our contact releases all the trapped parahumans at once. That chaos will be to our advantage."

Rozene nodded in agreement. Marion had a point there.

Rozene stared at her phone for a long moment, pondering. Vic was right too. There was a lot of uncertainty in their plans, a lot of relying on unknown faces and former enemies. It could all be a trap, and then what? Would more of her pack fall victim to the Hunters?

"Someone's at the door," Evelyn said suddenly and stood up. She narrowed her eyes and walked toward it swiftly, Rozene on her heels. Who would be coming at this late hour? Tess was still in Chicago! Evelyn grabbed the door and wrenched it open before sucking in a breath of surprise.

Rozene looked over her shoulder and froze.

Gale stood on the step before them, looking tired and bedraggled. But it was her. The Huntress glanced up at them and rubbed her arm. "I'm sure you didn't expect to see me back. I thought about what you said and your offer to help me and my brother escape the pit. I want to take you up on it."

Evelyn stared at the Huntress while Rozene just wondered at their dumb luck. They finally had a lead with Tess, and *now* Gale wanted to help?

Evelyn crooked her hand. Wind wrapped tightly around Gale and jerked her inside. Evelyn kept her pinned and shut the door behind her before dragging Gale toward the dining room. Rozene heard the collective gasps as they saw the Hunter again.

"What the hell is she doing here?" Vic spat.

Gale flinched away as fire danced in his eyes. It was in the light of the dining room that Rozene noticed a few burns on Gale's skin. Had Vic done that?

Evelyn forced Gale down in a chair and left her magic swirling around her, keeping her restrained.

"Talk," Wapasha said.

Gale took an anxious breath. "I know where the pit is."

"So do we," Vic sneered. "You see, we have our own resources, so I don't think we need you anymore."

Rozene expected Gale to look horrified, but the Huntress merely glared back at him. "Fine, you know where it is, but do you know how to get in? Do you know the right passcode? Or if you need a badge?"

Vic shut his mouth while the others exchanged looks.

Rozene sat down near Gale. "You can get us in?"

Gale nodded. "I know the entrance where you'll be least detected. Without the code, you won't be able to get in easily."

Vic leaned forward. "Then give us the code."

"That's probably the only thing keeping me alive," Gale replied. "I'm not just going to give that up. You take me with you, and I'll get you in."

Jackson growled quietly beside Rozene. "How do we know you won't just betray us?"

"You have my sister," Gale said. "And I know they'll kill her if they see her. I don't want that to happen. Think of it as me swearing on my sister's life that I won't betray you." She looked at Rozene and sighed wearily. "I've gotten to know Nick. I hate what they're doing to him, and I want him to survive. His whole pack. I've never seen wolves so devoted to one another and interested in helping others." She turned her eyes to Evelyn. "Your students?

Augustine is acting like a big mother wolf to them. She won't let anyone go near them."

Rozene's throat tightened as emotion washed over her. Oh, blessed Augustine. She was still alive. "And Brighton?"

"Also alive, but he's taken a lot of hits," Gale said. "He, Nick, and Augustine have stuck close, along with the kids and Yanlei."

Rozene blinked in surprise. "She's still alive? Kat thought she'd been killed."

"She almost was, but she survived. They're all together. I can get you to their cage and make sure they're freed."

The room fell silent for a moment as everyone looked at one another. It was good news. Honestly, better news than what Rozene had expected. Her packmates were alive, but for how much longer, they didn't know. Something about Gale's comments struck her though. "You said you hate what's happening to Nick. What's being done to him?"

"A dream fae named Vesp leads the pit. She started taking him to feed on his nightmares. It's left him a mental mess. I'm afraid if she keeps doing it, he's not going to survive."

Evelyn swallowed hard. "What does she want with my wife?"

"I assume to have someone to feed off of," Gale said. "I was kidnapped before I saw what was done with her. Vesp is strong. You're going to need your wife to fight her. Or a lot of magic."

"Iris," Rozene murmured, thinking of her poor friend. She looked at Vic. "Can you get your Ward to join us?"

Vic nodded. "I'll send out a call and tell them to meet us here as soon as possible."

Gale looked over at Wapasha. "I know you probably want to blame Daniella for my escape, but please don't do anything to her. Do what you want with me, but leave her alone."

Wapasha lifted his chin. "Punishment can be decided later. For now, we need all the help we can get. Will you fight beside us?" He ignored Vic's baffled expression.

"Yes," Gale said. "I'll fight to protect my sister, to help Nick, and to hopefully save my brother."

Rozene pressed her hands on the table and stood. "We have our plan. Vic, reach out to your magi, and I'll talk with Paytah before Tess arrives. This will be our only shot to get in there and rescue our people." She looked at Gale. "We'll do anything to save them, no matter the cost."

The Huntress stared back and gave a slow nod of understanding.

Chapter 30
The District Unites

Tess

Paytah's house was already surrounded with cars by the time Tess and Arjun arrived. Though Paytah had been staying at Gladus's old place, it wasn't big enough for the entire pack to come together as well as the other council leaders, if they'd agreed to fight alongside the werewolves. She got out of the car and watched Pedro walk into the house without Quince at his side. Likely Quince was stuck at the hospital or home with the girls. Good. At least one of them wouldn't be going to fight. She didn't want to risk Phoebe and Eliza losing both of their fathers.

Tess stepped inside to a cacophony of voices. Warmth spread through her chest at the familiarity of it all. She'd missed the pack. While she loved training with Arjun and learning how to become a Hunter, the pack remained at the core of her heart. She squeezed Arjun's hand and guided him through the hall and to the main room where the others were gathering.

She didn't even have a chance to step inside before someone grabbed her and yanked her into a hug. Tears filled Tess's eyes. "Mom."

"I've been worried sick about you," her mother said and held her tightly against her chest. She ran her hand through Tess's hair and pressed Tess's head to her shoulder. "You've been so quiet, I thought something horrible had happened."

Tess kissed her cheek. "I'm sorry, Mom. I promise to be better about reaching out." She pulled back and touched her mom's face. Her stomach dropped as she saw the dark circles under her mother's eyes and the gauntness of her cheeks as if she hadn't been sleeping or eating. "Mom, are you okay?"

Iris shook her head and grasped Tess's hands. "I want you and your father *home*."

Tess squeezed her mother's hands back. "We're getting him back, Mom. I promise. But you need to sleep and take care of yourself."

"No," she said with a growl, her eyes flashing with magic. "I'm not staying behind. This is my fight too."

Fear twisted Tess's stomach. She didn't want to lose her mother because she wasn't at full strength. But she also knew how stubborn her mom could be. If she wanted to fight, there was little Tess could do to stop her. She sighed and pulled her mom into another hug. "Promise me you'll be careful."

"I'll try. And you better be safe too, Tess."

Tess nodded. She looked over to Arjun and motioned for him to come closer. "Arjun and I make a great team. We'll watch out for each other."

Her mother glanced up and gave him a slight withering look before sighing. "I hope you do."

Tess rubbed her back and guided Arjun and her mother into the meeting area. To her surprise, Carlos sat on the edge of a couch next to Kat and Bianca. Kat looked much better than the last time Tess had seen her. The werewolf squeezed Bianca's hand and spoke to Carlos who frowned at her. He shook his head, but Kat gave him a stubborn look until he sighed and tossed up his hands. Bianca just giggled.

Tess crossed over to them with her mom and Arjun in tow. "Hey, how are you feeling, Kat?"

"Tess!" Kat cried. She sprang to her feet and wrapped her arms around the magus. "It feels like forever since we've seen you. I'm doing better. So's Carmen, but she's still working on walking properly. Paytah told her she needed to stay in bed, but you know how she is." She nodded to the aforementioned werewolf as she reclined in a nearby chair.

Tess chuckled. "Totally not surprised." She looked between Kat, Carlos, and Bianca. "So, what was the whole bickering thing I just saw about?"

Carlos snorted. "Kat insists on joining the fight. I told her she still needs to rest, but she isn't listening. Played the whole 'you're not my alpha' card on me. And now, of course, Bianca wants to go too."

Bianca lifted an eyebrow. "I was going regardless," she said. "You need help, and if everyone could risk their lives for me, then I can do the same for them."

Tess smiled at the pair, watching as Kat snuggled up against Bianca and stole a kiss from her. Tess couldn't help but to slip her hand into Arjun's and squeeze it. He rubbed her hand comfortingly with his thumb. "You know how serious this is, right? This isn't going to be an easy rescue mission."

Bianca glanced at her, her expression stern. "We know. Kat nearly died in the pit, and if you recall, I was kidnapped by Hunters. I know what they can do. That's why we have to go. They need our help, Tess. All of the parahumans do."

Kat nodded in agreement.

Tess sighed, but she didn't argue. If Carlos was going along with it, then she'd hold her tongue, though he looked about as pleased as she felt. She bent down and hugged both women.

"Tess," Paytah called.

She looked over her shoulder to her former alpha. He stood at the front of the room, Tamara at his side. With Jackson off with Rozene, Tamara was the acting beta in Chicago. Tess waved at her friends and walked over to Paytah, Arjun on her heels.

"How are you feeling?" she asked him.

Paytah grunted. "I'm alive and functional," he said. "We'll get the meeting started in a moment. Is there anything else you need to share with me? Rozene gave us a rundown of what you told her."

Tess shook her head. "The only thing we have to remember is that we're on a tight timeline. And we need as many people as possible. Is the council going to help?"

As if in answer, Mia stepped out of the kitchen with a drink in hand. The queen walked toward them and grinned at Tess, her eyes slitted. "The prodigal daughter returns," she purred.

Paytah nodded. "Yes. Mia, Carlos, and Akeno are already here. We're waiting on Joseph and Selene to join us, along with a few more wolves. The council and I have been talking. They're going to send their best warriors with us." He glanced at Mia. "This needs to end *now*. And we can't risk the pit vanishing again. Vic's calling on his magi for support, especially with this fae involved."

Mia set her drink down and went over to a computer connected to a TV in the room. "Which is why we're having a nice little Zoom conference so we can all agree on the plan. Not everyone could make it here tonight, and I don't think the house would hold everyone anyway."

She sat down and got the computer running. Tess watched the Zoom conference window pop up and breathed a sigh of relief. At least more than just the werewolves were traveling to Wisconsin with them. "Thanks, Paytah."

"Thank you for your hard work," Paytah said and glanced at Arjun. "And yours."

Arjun bobbed his head politely. "You're welcome."

While Mia got the conference going, more wolves and a few other parahumans arrived. Joseph and Selene walked in followed by Mikayla, who already looked like she was ready to jump into a fight. Mikayla perked up at the sight of Tess and pounced on her.

"Firebug!" she shouted.

Tess gasped for breath. "Breathe! Can't breathe!"

Mikayla dropped her and laughed. She looked Tess over and fussed with her face and hair. "I can't believe you're in that Hunter get-up. It looks good on you though. Sexy." She shot Arjun a predatory glare. "You taking good care of her?"

"Of course," Arjun said and smiled at Tess. "And she's also taking good care of me."

"I'm teaching him how to be a witch," Tess explained.

"No shit?" Mikayla said in surprise. "When did you go from the student to the teacher?"

Tess chuckled anxiously and shrugged her shoulders. "A lot of it has been on the fly, believe me. But Arjun's picking it up fast."

Mikayla eyed the Hunter and the wand attached to a loop on his belt. "Uh huh. Well, hopefully you'll put those skills to good use. I can't believe we're *finally* going in." She turned more serious and touched Tess's arm. "We're gonna get them home. No matter what happens."

"I know," Tess said and clasped Mikayla's arm. "I'm glad you're going with us."

"Wouldn't miss it." Her eyes flickered gold, revealing the hungry wolf deep inside. "I'll kill those bastards for what they did to Ray. Augustine deserves revenge."

Tess couldn't agree more. She squeezed Mikayla's bicep in comfort. It would be good to lay Ray to rest when this was all said and done.

They talked together for a short while before Becky joined them, still with her waitress apron on. She looked tired but alert. Tess greeted her with a hug. "Where's Heidi?"

"I brought her over to stay with Quince. He's watching over the kids while we're gone." Becky reached up and bound her hair into a bun. "I hate leaving her like this."

Tess tilted her head and frowned. "Are you sure you don't want to stay behind and help Quince? There's no shame in not going, Becky."

Becky's eyes flashed. "No. Our pack needs us. Besides, Paytah's been giving me fighting lessons. I can help."

Tess held up her hand and nodded. It was starting to feel more real now, seeing all the familiar and beloved faces about to throw themselves into battle. Would they all come back? Would they bury more packmates before the week was out?

Arjun draped his arm around her shoulders as they started to tremble. "I have you," he whispered into her ear.

Tess leaned into his comforting embrace.

They waited another half hour before Paytah called for silence. He stood at the front with Akeno, Carlos, Joseph, Selene, and Mia. The TV screen filled with more and more names as the parahumans of the community joined in for the conversation. Paytah gestured for Tess and Arjun to join him.

They walked to the front together and stood beside Paytah as he addressed the crowd.

"Your leaders may have already filled you in, but for those who still haven't heard the news, we've discovered the location of the pit." He waited for the murmuring to die down before he continued. "They're hidden in Wisconsin below Lambeau Field. Tess and Arjun have made contact with someone working in the pit to help coordinate a rescue mission."

"Who?" a magus asked.

Tess exchanged a look with Paytah then spoke. "Trish."

This time the murmur was a lot louder, and she saw the disgruntled expressions on people's faces. Trish still had a very poor reputation within the community. Tess bit her lip and glanced over at Bianca. The avian rose and walked toward Tess.

"Permission to speak?" she asked, looking at both Paytah and Carlos. The pair nodded.

"Please," Bianca said and held up her hands. "I know how hard it is to trust her. She was the reason I was kidnapped a few years ago. But she's changed. She's part of the reason we were able to find the first pit here in Chicago. And now she's helped us find this one. She's putting her life at risk to save our friends. If you don't want to trust her, then at least trust Alpha Paytah."

Carlos squeezed Bianca's shoulder, a look of pride for his adopted daughter spreading across his face. "I second this," he said. "She could have betrayed Arjun and Tess in the pit, but she didn't. And all she's done is feed us information. In the past, she would have been the last person I trusted, but now? She may be our only way in."

The muttering eased, and while many didn't look happy about this turn of events, they didn't protest.

Paytah resumed, glancing between those in the room and on the screen. "Tomorrow at midnight the collars will be shut off, and the security protecting the pit will go down. That's when we strike. We have someone else who can help us get to the right entrance, and a magus who will cloak us to keep us hidden from the Hunters' eyes. Vic said he may need more magi to help her though," he added, looking at the screen.

Vic's voice came through. "Evelyn's powerful, but it's better to share the load so she doesn't burn out."

Mikayla lifted a hand. "And what about the fae in Chicago's Fae Way? Are they going to help us?"

"No," Vic said wearily. "I spoke to them a few days ago. They're afraid of losing more of their kind, so they're protecting their own."

"Cowards," Mikayla growled under her breath.

A few people echoed similar sentiments.

Paytah held up his hand, urging silence. "We won't be fighting the Hunters alone. We've learned there's an uprising happening within the pit. Once the doors are opened and the collars unlocked, the parahumans there will also join in the fight. My hope is that we'll be able to pin the Hunters between us and take them down."

"What of the fae leading the pit?" a magus asked on the conference call. "There's only so much Ether magic can do against a fae."

A white-haired woman appeared on the screen, her cheeks plump and her eyes kind. "My wife Kafeada, also a fae, was captured by Vesp, who's overseeing the pit. If we can free her, then she'll be able to take on Vesp."

Akeno looked up from his tablet. "And if we can't?" he asked. "We have to consider the possibility that the dream fae will keep her trapped. My witches won't be able to stop a fae, and even the magi will struggle. What's to stop this Vesp from blipping them all away?"

Tess bit her lip, but it was Evelyn who provided the answer.

"Our hope is, as powerful as the fae is, this entire pit is far too big for her to just blip. She's an Ether eater primarily, so she won't be as strong as other fae we've encountered."

Unless she keeps feasting off Kafeada's Ather, Tess thought, but she kept the comment to herself.

Evelyn went on. "We should have a line of strong magi to keep her at bay while the rest of the parahumans worry about the Hunters."

"Agreed," Vic said. "My ward is prepared for battle. I reached out to Olive, and she provided talismans to help protect us against fae magic."

Tess sighed in relief. At least they'd have something to help them. She glanced around the room and stared at her mother for a moment as she sat with Kat. Once more, she wished her mother and Kat would stay behind. She didn't want to lose either of them.

Paytah filled everyone in on the rest of the information Tess had gathered from Skye and Rozene. Her heart started to pound faster as she thought about all lives that might be lost. Hopefully most of them would be Hunters. At the thought, she reached for Arjun's hand and held it tightly.

Okay, maybe she didn't want *all* Hunters to die.

Paytah folded his strong arms as he finished up the plan. "Each group will work with their designated council leader to decide who goes and who stays. Once you've made that decision, travel to Wisconsin. We will send you the coordinates of where to meet Evelyn, Vic, Rozene, and the Wisconsin pack led by my son, Wapasha." He set his jaw. "I know I'm asking all of you to put your lives on the line, but this isn't just about my wolves. This is about Hunters stealing our people, *all* our people and putting them into cages. Killing them. We will not stand by and let this happen. Not any longer. So I ask you to join me and rescue them."

Tess looked around at the uncertain faces. She could understand their doubt and fear. They had to weigh the threat against the best possible outcome. Was it worth it?

In the end, she saw only nods and resolved expressions.

Their Purple Door District was going to war.

Chapter 31
Joining Forces

Tess

Tess sat in the passenger's seat as Arjun drove, following the caravan to Wisconsin. Her mother, Bianca, and Kat had all chosen to ride with her. The rest of the cars were filled to capacity with parahumans. Leaving as late as they had meant no issues with rush hour and a much smoother drive than they would have otherwise experienced. But not everyone was leaving right at that moment. Some parahumans had to take care of their jobs, families, and final affairs should the unthinkable happen.

They talked for most of the trip, catching up on how Tess and Arjun were doing with their lessons and how the pack was fairing. The consensus seemed to be that everyone was dealing with some form of depression, which also explained her mother's haggard appearance. Tess glanced in the review mirror at her mother periodically as she rested; she'd fallen asleep not long after they'd started out.

"She needs the sleep," Kat commented quietly. "Iris has spent so much time watching over the rest of us that she's barely taken time for herself."

Tess twisted around in the seat and looked at them. "Me not calling enough didn't help with that."

Bianca and Kat grimaced. "No," Kat agreed. "But she also understood you were busy training and tracking the pit. She misses your father a lot, and she was worried about you."

"Yeah, she's where I get my anxiety from." Tess sighed and leaned her head against the seat as she stared at her friends. "You sure you're up for this? After what the Hunters have done to you?"

Bianca laced her fingers between Kat's and held her hand close. "We've talked it over. We can fight. And maybe we both want some closure after our own Hunter experiences." She cracked a smile. "Just try not to get thrown into the ceiling again, all right, Tess?"

Tess snorted. "You're never going to let me live that down, are you?"

Kat and Bianca laughed. It hadn't been funny at the time, but Tess could chuckle about it now. She'd been even more hot-headed then. At least now she was taking the time to listen before she acted. Arjun's calm nature was rubbing off on her in a good way.

She turned forward and stared ahead while her friends joined her mother in sleep. She drummed her fingers on her leg, thinking, until Arjun took her hand. Tess blinked and looked at him.

"It's going to be okay," he said, still watching the road. "I know you're anxious, and you want to see your father again. Getting worked up won't help you. Rest and conserve your energy."

Tess sighed and leaned her head against the window. "You sound so sure. How do you know we'll win? What if something goes wrong? I...I don't want to be the reason people get hurt again."

"You have Skye in your ear, don't you?" Arjun asked. When Tess didn't respond, he shook his head. "She made a good point about you rushing into things. But your intentions were good. And this time? You're waiting. You're being patient...or as patient as Tess Montgomery can be," he added, chuckling.

Tess punched his shoulder lightly. "I'm trying," she said. "I hate feeling useless."

"Which is why our training was so important," Arjun reminded her. "It kept both of our hands and minds busy."

Tess nodded in agreement. They hadn't had much time to mope or wonder what was taking Skye so long. And she'd enjoyed their sparring and magical lessons. Those would come in handy, especially since they'd be underground. He'd have a lot of earth to work with.

She ran her thumb along his hand and took a shaky breath. "I'm scared."

"I am too."

Tess lifted an eyebrow. "Really? You never seem scared of anything."

"I do a good job of not showing it," Arjun said. "We're up against a fae and a lot of Hunters. And many lives are on the line. Frankly, you'd be an idiot not to be afraid."

She didn't know why, but that brought her comfort. Maybe because it made her feel a little less alone. She placed his hand on her cheek and leaned into it. "I don't want to lose you."

Arjun glanced at her. "I don't want to lose you either. We stay close, and we protect each other."

"I hope it's enough," Tess whispered.

He brought his hand back down to her leg and massaged her thigh. "Get some rest, Tess. I'll wake you once we're close."

Tess didn't want to, but Arjun's gentle massaging and the rumble of the road beneath their tires lulled her to sleep. She slept deeply until the first rays of the morning sun warmed her brow. She opened her eyes and glanced at the other cars around them, some that belonged to pack. She yawned and looked back at her mother and friends, but they were still out.

"We're almost there," Arjun said. He smiled at her. "You still snore."

"Oh, shut up." Tess laughed and shoved his arm. "Nice way to greet me."

He reached down and picked up a cup, handing it to her. It warmed her palms as the pleasant smell of hazelnut coffee wafted to her nose. "I had to make a pit stop and thought you'd like this."

"Yumm," Tess said happily and sipped the blessed coffee. "Fine, you're forgiven."

She nursed the drink for the last half hour of the trip. Arjun pulled off the expressway and traveled through the local streets. Tess recognized some of the area, but she was more familiar with Chicago than Wisconsin. She blinked through the sunlight and studied the signs and houses that passed. It looked like such a nice little town, hardly one that would be a cesspool of Hunters.

Arjun slowed the car in front of a large house, and at least a dozen cars parked nearby. He parked and Tess climbed out, stretching her arms over her head. She passed him the coffee and ducked her head back inside to shake her mother.

"Hey Mom, we're here."

Her mom woke with a start and blinked owlishly at Tess. "Tess...you really are here."

Tess stared and smiled. "Yeah. I'm not going anywhere." She helped her mother out of the vehicle while Bianca shook Kat awake. Tess stepped around to the front, watching a few more parahumans head into the house.

The wind magus, Evelyn, greeted them at the door. "We're meeting in the back garden where there's more room. We've prepared food."

Tess nodded. She didn't know what she expected to find in the backyard, but a huge stone wall, tables, and a giant tree filled with witch orbs was definitely not it. Her mouth dropped open at the sight of it all, as well as the many parahumans gathered around a table filled with eggs, meat, toast, and juices. Someone must have made a late-night grocery run.

She looked around until she spotted Rozene next to Wapasha. Tess sighed in relief and hurried toward her. "Rozene."

The alpha turned to her and pulled Tess into a warm embrace. "There she is," she said and kissed her hair. She patted Tess and held her arms out to Arjun next. "Come here," she said.

Arjun chuckled as he gave her a hug as well.

Rozene patted his back and searched the crowd. Her eyes grew soft as Paytah stepped through the growing numbers with Tamara. She moved past Tess and to her mate. The moment he saw her, he grabbed her and wrapped his strong arms around her. Wapasha quickly followed, reuniting the family.

Tess bit her lip. Paytah and Rozene normally weren't away from each other for such an extended period of time. Paytah pulled Wapasha into a hug, then Marion when his daughter-in-law approached. Tess named them off to Arjun and felt her mother touch her shoulders with her warm hands. "I'm surprised Paytah came with us," Tess said and looked back at her mother. "He's still healing."

"He's an alpha. He won't be left out of a battle."

"He's also Violet Marshall," Tess commented. Or at least he had been until he passed the title temporarily to Joseph and Selene while he was gone. She leaned back into her mother's gentle touch as more people poured in.

Vic carried over another bowl of eggs and transferred them onto the tray. Tess waved to him, and he smiled. Jackson walked up behind him with a tray of meat. He did more than just smile. He barreled over and pulled Tess into a big wolf hug.

"Tess! I missed you," he said and ruffled her hair. "You look so...official," he added, looking her up and down in her Hunter attire. "Not sure I like it."

Tess chuckled. "You don't have to like it." She patted his chest. "It's good to see you too, Jackson. I take it you've been taking really good care of Rozene?"

"Always," he said with pride. He looked around and whistled. "I didn't expect to see so many people. But that's good. We need—" He paused as his gaze fell upon Tamara. She froze as well and stared at him, a big smile spreading across her face.

Tess pushed on his back. "Go on before you start drooling."

He didn't need any more urging than that. He rushed to his mate and gathered her into his arms, spinning her once before kissing her deeply on the lips, not caring who saw.

Tess smiled after them and tugged on Arjun's sleeve and took her mother's hand. "Let's get some breakfast."

They gathered food and took a seat at a table with Kat and Bianca. Other members of the pack joined them, including Jackson, Tamara, and Pedro. Becky and Mikayla were in the same car and running behind. Tess nibbled on her eggs, admiring the backyard. "This place is amazing."

"It is," Jackson agreed. "Evelyn and her wife teach students magic here, you know, when Hunters aren't trying to ransack the house and kidnap children or fae." He gave Arjun a disgruntled look, but Arjun didn't rise to the bait. Jackson huffed out a breath. "It's been a good stronghold. We're just hoping all the cars don't call attention to it."

Arjun frowned. "Do you think someone is watching the house?"

Jackson shook his head. "Hard to say. But one of our new *helpers* found it, and we're still worried she could've been followed."

Tess frowned. "Helpers?"

"Oh, Rozene didn't tell you." Jackson snorted. "We captured a Hunter, but Daniella released her. We thought she was long gone, but she came back and offered to help us get into the pit. We have her downstairs and guarded for the time being."

Tess narrowed her eyes. "Wait, are you talking about Gale?"

The fork clattered out of Kat's hand. She stiffened and stared at Jackson, her face going pale. "Gale? Gale's here? There's no way she'd offer to help."

Jackson shrugged. "We thought the same thing, but she came back and gave us information that corresponds with what you sent us, Tess. We promised her safety if she helps."

Tess glanced at Kat as the golden-haired woman pressed her hands to her face and swallowed. "Kat?"

"She was our captor. Well, Gale and her brother Hendrickson. I just never thought she'd switch sides. Are you sure we can trust her?"

Jackson curled his lips. "I'm not, but Rozene is. She's hoping the sisterhood between Gale and Daniella will prevent Gale from betraying us."

Kat poked at her sausage while Bianca rubbed her back comfortingly. "Or she'll put a bullet in one of our heads," the wolf murmured.

"Which is precisely why we're not giving her a weapon," Jackson said. He reached over and patted her hand. "Hey, I'm in the same boat as you. I don't think we can trust her as far as we can throw her, but we've run out of options. She knows the way in, and we're using that to our advantage. We have less than twenty-four hours. No time to change our minds, right?"

Kat nodded and fisted her hand. "Just keep her away from me."

Bianca kissed her cheek. "I've got you," she said.

Tess frowned to herself. Gale. Kat had talked a lot about her. Part of her didn't want to believe the Huntress had had a change of heart, but then again, Tess was in love with another Hunter. It wasn't like they were all bad.

She grasped Arjun's hand under the table.

It took a few more hours for the rest of their party to show up. But more than just people from Chicago were joining them. Evelyn greeted unfamiliar men and women who came through her door and offered them hugs. She introduced them as magi from the ward she belonged to. They were acquiring quite a group of magic users.

Once everyone arrived, they took seats in the garden while the leaders sat up front. Joseph, Selene, and Akeno had all stayed behind to keep an eye on the District in case anything went south while they were gone. Akeno had decided his witches might not be up to a battle against a fae, but a few had still tagged along to heal wounded parahumans.

All of Paytah's pack members had joined in except for Quince. And most of Mia's pride had also shown up. The queen sat beside Paytah, holding a mug of coffee and looking as calm and cool as always. Carlos had brought many members of the cloister. And while Joseph and Selene hadn't made the trip, their vampires had. Saul was their primary target, from what Tess had heard. And that was fine by her. They needed that vampire out of their hair as soon as possible.

Tess folded her hands beneath her chin as, once again, their leaders laid out the plan before them. Just before midnight, they'd all gather and drive over to Green Bay. Evelyn and other magi would shield them from sight, and then Gale would get them inside. At the confused expressions on the parahumans' faces, Jackson retreated downstairs and retrieved the Huntress, as well as her werewolf sister.

Kat almost bent a fork in half when Gale walked into view. Her hands were cuffed in front of her. Daniella wasn't shackled, but Wapasha and Marion kept her closely guarded.

Tess's stomach twisted with anxiety. There were a lot of variables: Skye hacking the computers, Gale not betraying them, Trish also not betraying them, Nick breaking free. One wrong move could upend the entire operation, and then what? Would Vesp destroy them? Steal their loved ones again? She was the biggest threat.

"I'll join the magi who intend to free Kafeada and keep the fae busy," Evelyn said, breaking Tess away from her thoughts. "We need the strongest magi with us. Gale has agreed to guide us to Vesp's room."

Tess wrinkled her nose. "Feels like they're being led to a buffet for the fae," she murmured to Arjun. He cracked a tiny smile.

Upon the meeting's conclusion, all they could do was wait until it was time to move out.

Tess and Arjun wandered away from her pack to check in with

Skye and make sure everything was set on her end.

"You worry too much," Skye said. "So long as Trish doesn't screw us over, I'll get us in, take down the collars, get those doors open. You two focus on not getting killed."

Arjun snorted. "Thanks for the vote of confidence."

"Hey, it's hard to find fellow Hunters to trust. And who else is going to make omelets with avocado smiles for me?"

"You can always make your own."

"Nah, there's no fun in that." Skye turned uncharacteristically somber. "But seriously, you two. Come home. Don't take any unnecessary risks, or I'll talk to a witch about resurrecting you so I can beat your asses."

Tess laughed. "Noted. Thanks, Skye."

"Good luck."

"You too," Arjun said fondly. Once they hung up, he looked at Tess and touched her cheek. His eyes softened, the corners misting. "I love you."

Tess pressed herself against his warm chest and tucked her head under his chin. "I love you too."

***

The hours ticked by, drawing closer to the night of reckoning. Tess spent most of the time with Arjun and her pack, trying not to fret. But it was hard. So many things could go wrong. Vic alerted Legion to their plan, and of course they told Vic and his team to stand down. They would take care of it.

"Like you took care of the first pit?" he'd said. "We're not waiting that long this time."

Maybe it wasn't the best idea to get the parahuman police pissed off at them, but Vic had a point. Tess wished she could have talked to their Legion contact, Jay, and gotten her advice, but they were committed now. No turning back. And no surrender.

Near midnight, they gathered into cars and drove to Green Bay. This time Kat, Bianca, Arjun, Tess, and her mother were all somber as they made the trip. Her mother and Arjun were the only ones armed with physical weapons. Tess's dad had taught them both how to shoot, and he always reminded them that sometimes bullets worked better than magic or fangs.

Tess fingered her Ether necklace and glanced back at her mother. They exchanged a private look, and her mother reached for her hand. Tess squeezed it. "Be careful," she whispered.

Her mother nodded and patted the gun on her hip. Her magic would help too, but she wasn't opposed to firearms.

As they got closer to the stadium, a strange feeling settled over Tess's skin. She shivered and saw the others flinch as well. "Magic," she remarked. "They must be cloaking us now."

The cars pulled up, stopping near an area that looked like a loading dock. Gale got out of the car she was in and walked toward it. She tapped an area on the wall that looked like plain brick to Tess. But then the concrete beside her opened up, leading to an underground path that shouldn't have existed.

"Magic," Arjun muttered.

"Fun stuff, isn't it?" Tess said.

She checked her phone. It was about ten to midnight. She hurried with the others toward Gale, and they went down the hidden ramp. Tess frowned and whispered to Arjun. "Isn't someone going to see us going in?"

"No," her mother said. "Only Gale. The magic isn't protecting her. She's our ticket in."

Tess grimace. Hopefully that didn't mean Gale would end up with a bullet in her head before she got inside. They walked together, the sound of their feet slapping stone echoing off the tunnel walls. She heard an odd groan as the ground closed up behind them. And for a moment, she felt trapped and claustrophobic. She had to keep reminding herself that Skye would get them out.

She checked her phone again.

No bars.

She grabbed Arjun's arm and showed him. When he checked his phone, he winced and showed it to her. Also no bars. There was no way for Skye to contact them if things went wrong.

They were on their own.

Gale stopped near another loading dock. She tapped a number into an actual number pad this time. The metal door squeaked open. It was halfway up when another Hunter ducked underneath and pointed a gun at Gale.

"What are you doing?" he asked in a curt voice. "There are no parahuman orders coming in tonight."

Gale held up her hands. "I went for an evening hunt. No luck. Just decided to come back this way."

The man narrowed his eyes at her. He looked her up and down and glanced toward the group, but Evelyn's magic kept them hidden. With a shake of his head, he held out his hand to help her up. "Well, come on in then."

Gale took it and climbed up onto the dock.

Suddenly, the man shoved her face first into the wall and pressed a gun to the base of her neck. "Do you think I'm stupid, Gale?" he growled at her. "Everyone knows you've gone missing. Did you really think you'd be welcomed back?"

Gale grunted and struggled. "I just want to see my brother."

The man chuckled darkly and cocked the weapon. "Yeah, that's not going to happen."

A figure darted forward and tackled the man to the ground. The dirty white and black werewolf smacked his gun away and silenced him with a single blow to the head. Gale had fallen to her knees, and she looked up as the werewolf reached out a furry hand to help her up.

Evelyn's voice swept through their minds. *"If you need to shift, then shift. This is it. We're going in."*

Chapter 32
The Broken Collar

Nick

The next twenty-four hours were the longest in Nick's life. With every passing second, he expected something to go wrong. Maybe Trish would get caught, or one of the parahumans in their coup would turn on them. Maybe Vesp would drag Nick away so he wouldn't be available to help his pack when the time came. It made sleeping difficult, though part of that was due to his worry for Brighton.

The wolf returned from yet another fight looking beaten and worn. He'd won this battle at least, but Hendrickson's torture had left burns on his neck that were starting to smell infected. If Gale had been there, she would have treated Brighton with a fae tonic. Instead, he was left to heal on his own. His werewolf healing did a lot, but it couldn't chase out infection.

Nick went over to the werewolf, bringing a bowl of water with him. He sat down and nudged Brighton awake. "Hey, let me clean your neck."

Brighton yawned and sat up without complaint. He tilted his head forward and closed his eyes as Nick shifted his collar and cleaned the wound as best he could. "Is it sad that I'm beginning to miss Gale?"

"Nah," Nick said with a faint chuckle. "I miss her, too. She might have been a bitch, but at least she tried to keep us alive." He dabbed the burn mark and used a torn piece of blanket to wipe away some puss. "It'll be over soon. And then we can all get the help we need."

Brighton cracked a smile. "Yeah, I hope you're right. Still waiting for something to explode in our faces."

"I thought you were supposed to be the optimist," Nick joked.

"Being here has made me start singing a different tune." Brighton rolled his sore shoulders. "God, I miss my wife and daughter. What I wouldn't give for all of us to snuggle in a big wolf pile."

Nick warmed at the thought. "Yeah, I miss that." He glanced over at his companions. Yanlei slept under a blanket (how she could rest, he didn't know). Augustine snuggled in the corner of the cage in wolf form with the teens while they snoozed against her. She looked at Nick, sensing his eyes on her. She tilted her head at him in question, but he waved his hand. "Knowing Jackson, he'll pounce us into a wolf pile once we're home."

"Home," Brighton said dreamily. "I can't wait."

Nick couldn't either.

He wished he knew what time it was. They'd had dinner a few hours ago, so it had to be getting close to midnight. He touched his collar but could still feel the steady hum that told him it was active. And the cells were closed. If this didn't work, he didn't think he'd have enough strength to survive another encounter with Vesp.

He squeezed Brighton's shoulder once he was done and returned to Yanlei. She cracked open an eye as he crouched down next to her. "Did I wake you up?"

"Hm, no, I was just dozing. I wanted to be at full strength before the fight."

Nick nodded in agreement. He grasped her hand, rubbing it. "Stick close to me once we move," he said. "I don't want you to get lost in the fray. Any of you," he added, looking at his other pack members. Augustine gave him a bob of her head. He knew she'd keep the siblings safe. He sat down beside Yanlei and stroked her hair. She snuggled closer, settling her head on his lap. They'd all taken turns during their fights to let the other parahumans know that midnight was their hour to act. He hoped word had spread. Astrid had been glad to hear it, and Loretta was craving freedom. He looked at the other cages near them and watched parahumans pace or prep themselves. They were awake, alert, but they also looked afraid, as they should. No matter their numbers, they were going up against a lot of Hunters. And

Vesp.

"Nick?" Yanlei asked.

He sighed. "I'm scared," he admitted to her.

She smiled and kissed his hand. "I'd be worried if you weren't," she said. "Fear will help you be more cautious." She met his eyes. "No matter what happens, you did everything you could to save us. And you should be proud of that."

"I'll be proud once we're all home." He bent down and kissed her.

The collar vibrated on his throat, although not painfully. He froze, and Yanlei's eyes widened as hers did the same. And then the hum stopped all together. When Nick turned her collar, the light was off. He pushed out his wolf claws and grabbed his collar. Any attempt at removing it would normally send shocks through him. This time, as he dug his nails into the metal, the collar broke away. With a grunt, he snapped it in half and dropped it to the ground.

He wasted no time grabbing Yanlei's and breaking her free of her collar. Augustine took care of her own and the teens' while Brighton rendered his useless. By the time they had the collars off, Nick heard the door click. He hurried to it and pushed lightly on the bars.

The door opened.

"Come on," he called to the others and shoved the door wide.

Loretta left her cage and shifted into her big bipedal puma form. She gnashed her teeth and spoke mentally to him. *"Fight hard, Nick. Hope to see you on the other side."*

Nick nodded and shifted as well.

Brighton slipped out the door in his human form and yanked other cells open. "Come on," he called to those within. "The collars are broken. We need to get out of here."

While a few parahumans looked afraid to leave the comfort of the painful world they knew, others rushed out and shifted or bolted down the hall in their human forms. Nick waited until Yanlei helped the siblings onto Augustine's back.

"We need our wands," Ayaan said.

"If I run into Hendrickson, I'll get them for you," Nick promised.

Yanlei shifted into her smaller four-footed werewolf form, favoring speed over strength.

Brighton changed forms as the sound of gunfire rattled down the hall.

Nick grimaced and took the lead. *"Let's go."*

The others fell into step behind him and rushed down the hall. Nick was thankful for all the times he'd been brought to the main fighting ring. He'd memorized the pathways of the pit. That still didn't tell him where their rescuers were going to be coming in, but if they could hold off the Hunters long enough for their friends to arrive, it didn't matter.

They bolted down a corridor the Hunters were already starting to fill, guns drawn. Someone tried to point a remote at him to shock him, only to gape when he realized Nick was no longer wearing a collar. Nick snarled and rushed the man. He ducked a bullet and slammed into the Hunter, bringing him down with the weight of his body. He banged the man's head on concrete, knocking him unconscious.

Brighton took down another Hunter beside him then pounced Nick and pushed him low as several bullets rang out over their heads. The parahumans behind them pressed themselves against a wall, but they still heard cries as two were hit. Nick searched frantically to make sure Yanlei, Augustine, and the teens were safe. Fortunately, they all got back to their feet and charged the Hunters.

It was chaos. From every direction Nick heard fighting, screaming, gunshots, snarls, screeches, yowls, and every other bestial sound he could think of. A red-tailed hawk flew over his head and circled before dive-bombing a Hunter and gouging her eyes out. Nick finished the job and bodied two men with shields, sending them tumbling backwards. One lifted his gun and fired.

The bullet grazed the top of Nick's furry shoulder, splitting flesh but flying through the other side. He snarled in pain, but it didn't slow him down. He charged forward with Brighton and entered the main fighting room.

Lights blazed down on parahumans battling Hunters. Smoke bombs went off to one side, causing parahumans to stagger and cough. Nick squinted through the smoke and saw electric sparks as Hunters brought tasers or shock sticks down on their victims. He ground his teeth and looked sharply at Brighton. *"Keep them together. I'll be right back."*

Brighton nodded gruffly then snarled and swiped out a paw, knocking a smoke bomb out of midair and sending it skittering toward a group of Hunters.

Nick fell upon the Hunters attacking parahumans trapped in the smoke. The screams of anguish as parahumans were shocked made his rage rise. He saw red as he broke through and slammed into a woman lifting a shock stick in the air. He bit down on her arm, forcing her to release it. She screamed in pain and raised a knife in her other hand. Nick barely pulled back in time. Instead of going into his temple, the blade sliced across his cheek. He yelped in pain and smacked her wrist hard, breaking it. The knife flew off in another direction. He brought his paw down on her face, snuffing her life out before he moved on to the next attacker.

Something caught his foot and made him trip and fall. He looked back and found a lifeless werecat staring at him, her mouth open and frothing blood. He panicked for a moment, thinking it was Loretta. But her pelt was too dark. He grimaced and moved on, going from one Hunter to the next while trying to ignore his wounds.

Another smoke bomb exploded nearby, but the screams that followed were different. Wolf howls turned to frightened human shouts. He frowned in confusion until some of the smoke cleared. At the edge of the fray, Brighton staggered, suddenly a human rather than a wolf. Nick didn't see Augustine or Yanlei. Where were they? Why had Brighton switched back?

Something whistled through the air toward him, and he looked up.

At the same time, a body crashed into him and knocked him out of the way. He raised his paw to lash out, until he realized Yanlei was pinning him down in her wolf form.

"Stay away from the green canisters! They have wolfsbane in them. They're starting to fire things to make us transform back."

Nick's stomach dropped. Shit! He knew the Hunters had guns with bullets that could suppress their shifting abilities, but he hadn't thought of canisters of those poisonous herbs! He bumped her with his nose and got back to his feet before following her through the crowd to where Augustine stood defensively in front of the teens and other parahumans, mostly witches and a few younger lycans. Her teeth and maw were drenched in blood. She looked sharply at Nick and Yanlei.

"They're starting to block off the exits to trap us in here. They hit us with enough wolfsbane, henbane, mistletoe, or whatever else and we'll be forced back into our human forms. The magi and witches will be useless."

Nick ground his teeth and looked around for a higher vantage point. It would put him in more danger, but he had to get a better feel for what was happening. He loped toward an outcropping and pulled himself up onto it, just above the heavy smoke. Sure enough, Hunters with shields were starting to block the halls leading into the main fighting room. That meant other parahumans who wanted to help them were trapped by their cages.

He licked his muzzle and searched for an exit that wasn't closed off.

A wave of darkness swept through the room, snuffing out the lights and leaving everyone in pitch black. Nick gasped in shock and fright. Had the lights gone out? How the hell were they supposed to fight like this? The vampires and werecats would have a better chance with their night vision. He squinted and searched for the source of the darkness.

With a hiss, the lights came back on, and a new horror greeted them.

Nick staggered as Vesp appeared in the center of the room. She flapped her powerful wings, her black tendrils arching in the air then shooting out toward parahumans. No, not just toward them. Some of the tendrils went *through* the parahumans. Four fell dead, skewered with her magic.

"Enough, *children*," Vesp snarled at them and swept a long black tendril across the room, sending parahumans scattering but leaving the Hunters unharmed. Brighton and Yanlei were both slammed into a wall and covered by falling bodies.

"*Yanlei*! *Brighton*!" Nick shouted, but neither replied (not that Brighton could in his human form). He snarled and glared at Vesp as she attacked more parahumans.

Astrid, in her seraph form, her great snowy owl wings carrying her through the cave, flew toward Vesp with a shock stick in her hand while the fae's attention was diverted. Astrid lifted the stick and brought it down on Vesp's back.

Black tendrils shot out behind Vesp and snagged Astrid out of midair. She turned and hurled the avian toward a wall with deadly force. Astrid smacked it, her wings crunching beneath her body. The avian screamed in agony. The stick fell from her limp hand as she clawed desperately with her other one to break free.

Vesp just laughed and started to squeeze her.

Nick shook his head. He couldn't let this happen. *"VESP!"* he shouted mentally at her.

Vesp paused and looked around until she spotted him on his stone perch. Her eyes flashed, and she loosened her hold on Astrid, but only a bit. "You're behind this, aren't you? From the beginning, you planned this!" She lifted her hand, magic snarling in her palm.

Nick crouched, waiting to dodge.

Before Vesp could attack, she screeched in pain and whirled toward Astrid. Somehow, the avian had managed to get her arms moving again and brought full talons down across Vesp's tendrils. The attack freed her, and Astrid dropped to the ground. Just as Astrid landed, Vesp grabbed her by her throat with another tendril. With one jerk, Astrid's head snapped to the side. Her lifeless body slumped in Vesp's hold.

"NO!" Nick shouted in horror. He stared at Astrid's broken body then heard more bird screams. A flock of raptors shot into the air and went after Vesp, likely members of Astrid's cloister. Vesp swatted them away, but it distracted her from another enemy.

The fire witch Nick and Yanlei had fought broke through the crowd and lifted her wand. She brought a snarling whip of fire down across Vesp's back. The fae shouted and whirled on the witch. But the witch didn't back down. She lashed out again and again with her magic, tears of rage streaming down her cheeks.

Nick leapt off his alcove and bolted toward the witch as Vesp dove toward her. He panted, slamming through bodies, knocking people off their feet. Out of the corner of his eye, he saw a black tendril race for the witch. He leapt forward, wrapping his furry arms around the woman and jerking her out of the way. He heard the tendril smack the floor behind him as he and the witch rolled into another group of parahumans.

"Let me go!" she screeched and shoved him off of her. She panted and narrowed her eyes once she got a good look at him. "Wait...*you.*"

Nick held up a paw. *"I only want to help. I'm sorry for what happened to your friend. We never meant to hurt him."*

"It doesn't matter now," the witch said and glared at Vesp. "I just want her to know my pain."

Nick shook his head firmly. *"You can do more by helping the others get out of here. Please. It's easy to die for revenge. It's harder to live and help others. We need you."*

The witch glowered at him then up at Vesp who was being buffeted by magic as well as birds. With a growl, she gripped her wand harder. "I'm going to make them all pay."

"Do that, but save the others in the process."

Reluctantly, she nodded and parted ways, going after Hunters terrorizing a group of vampires.

Nick dashed toward Yanlei and Brighton. The parahumans had started to clear out, and he spotted the pair together. Yanlei stood on four paws, stiffening her body to help support Brighton who had his arm around his waist. Nick knocked a Hunter away and looked them over.

"Are you hurt?"

"Just my ribs. And my pride," Brighton said with a pained smile. He looked around. "Where did Augustine go?"

Nick pointed over his shoulder as the great wolf took down a Hunter. She had a growing pile of bodies in front of her, not that he could blame her. She'd been waiting for this moment since the second she was captured.

He glanced at Brighton. *"Can you shift back?"*

Brighton shook his head. "Breathed in too much wolfsbane. I need time to recover. Not sure how much use I'm going to be to you two."

Nick swore. *"Yanlei, can you keep him safe while I make a clear path?"*

"Yes, but where?" she asked and looked around.

Nick swallowed and grimaced as he heard more gunshots followed by tortured screams. He was going to be hearing and seeing this in his nightmares for the rest of his life. He searched for a way out when a familiar figure caught his eye. *"Trish!"*

The vampire had joined the fray, but she was keeping to the bordering walls. She looked up at his shout and searched until she found him. With the speed of her kind, she zipped over to his side and grasped his bleeding shoulder unintentionally. She quickly pulled her hand back when he winced. "Sorry. Thank the Nightmother, I didn't know if I'd find you!"

"We need a way out," Nick said.

Trish pointed toward a wall of Hunters. "There. I know there are a lot in the way, but if you can make it through, that'll take you to the docking area. That area usually isn't as protected. It's your best bet to get out of here."

Nick nodded, but the number of Hunters was a huge concern. They had their shields and weapons drawn and a pile of parahuman bodies in front of them to create an extra barrier.

Suddenly, several of the Hunters appeared to be lifted and slammed into one another. Their bodies got tossed aside like ragdolls. A huge gust of wind flew into the room, spiraling around the smoke and raising it toward the ceiling so they could see better. Nick narrowed his eyes until new parahumans poured into the room. A few birds flew to the sky, screeching and diving at Hunters. The moment a familiar caracara flew inside, Nick's heart swelled.

"*Bianca*!" he shouted.

The caracara paused and circled around, searching. When her eyes fell upon him, she laughed in his head. *"Oh my god, you're alive! Hang on, Nick! We'll be there soon! We're just—"*

Black tendrils swung out and knocked Bianca and the other birds out of the sky.

"*Bianca*!" Nick screamed in terror.

The caracara spiraled toward the ground. Inches from hitting stone, a golden wolf leapt into the air and caught Bianca in her mouth, bringing her to safety.

Nick gasped. Kat? Was that Kat? He almost sobbed in both fear and relief. His pack was here. They were coming to save him!

"Nick!" Trish shouted, grabbing his arm. She pointed as Vesp slammed tendrils into the wall above their escape route. Rocks and boulders started raining down, trapping Hunters and parahumans alike. A group of magi collectively burst through with their magic, sending Hunters scattering. They put their attention to Vesp, some driving her back while others tried to keep the wall from caving in.

Nick bared his teeth and glanced back at Brighton and Yanlei. *"We gotta go now, before the exit is cut off."* He looked around. *"Augustine!"*

Trish pushed him toward the exit. "I'll get her. And I'll check on Bianca and Kat. Go, Nick."

Nick met her eyes and tipped his head. *"Thank you, Trish."*

She flashed a fangy smile and bolted toward Augustine.

Nick guarded Yanlei and Brighton as he pushed through the Hunters. Shots rang out, and he had to shove his friends to the side to protect them from bullets and darts. At one point, Yanlei pushed Brighton toward him and zipped forward, breaking through three Hunters in their way with her speed and snapping jaws.

Brighton marveled at her. "She's incredible."

"*I know,*" Nick said proudly.

Brighton grabbed his arm and pointed. "Nick...Nick look."

Nick followed the path of his finger, and the breath hitched in his throat. Amidst the group coming in, he saw Tess send a wave of fire snarling over the Hunters. She created a barrier, blocking them from attacking the other parahumans coming through the weakened exit.

Nick grinned and looked at Brighton as tears of joy streamed down the man's cheeks. "*Let's get you to your daughter.*"

Chapter 33
The Dying Flame

Tess

Tess spread her hands, creating a fiery barrier between herself and the nearest Hunters. She'd expected things to go to hell, but not this fast!

After they'd made it through the docks, Gale had brought them to a fighting ring. The room was in complete chaos, filled with parahumans and Hunters. Bodies littered the ground, and the smells of smoke, blood, sweat, and death filled the air. It made her stomach twist, especially thinking her father might be one of the dead parahumans.

"Stay focused," Arjun said at her side and shot a Hunter through the throat. The man gurgled and collapsed.

Another group of magi was already trying to keep Vesp at bay. And what a terrible sight she was. Tess glanced up as the fae flew over them, attacking magi with her vicious tendrils, her wings flapping through the air, dark and foreboding. She was like a thing of nightmares, a demon that had crawled from the depths of a haunted well.

Tess shuddered and glanced over her shoulder as her mother's fire crackled and snarled in the form of whips, slicing through shields and melting guns. She floored two Hunters and blocked an avian from getting shot. Tess grinned to herself, impressed by her mother's powers. And people wondered where Tess had learned it from.

Their group moved in further, the magi creating a perimeter of protective shields to block gunfire as well as attacks from the fae. One of the black tendrils slammed down on them and Tess raised her hands, sending a flaming shield shooting into the air. It knocked the tendril away, but another followed, this one nearly smashing Tess's shield. She fell to her knees with a grunt.

"God, she's strong," she groaned as Arjun helped her back to her feet. She shook her head and looked around, searching for Nick, her father, really anyone she knew. Jackson had headed out in front of them and was steadily working his way to the wounded parahumans, Tamara at his side. Rozene and Paytah hung back to cover the rear in case they were attacked from behind.

Tess caught a glimpse of gold and saw Kat in the crowd with Bianca dangling in her mouth. She swore. *"You both all right?"*

"Yeah, Bianca got the wind knocked out of her. I'll get back to you in a minute. I saw your dad and Nick!"

Tess gasped and looked frantically for him. *"Where? Where are they?!"*

"I don't know! I lost them in the crowd."

Great. Tess tugged sharply on Arjun's arm. "Kat saw my father."

Arjun nodded and pulled out his wand with one hand while he fired his gun with the other. "Let's find him. Iris!" he called to her mother. "Brighton was spotted."

"I'm coming with you."

Arjun and Tess nodded and broke away from the group with her mother. They waited until someone filled their place before they worked together to create a path through the Hunters. Tess saw Kat run off in a different direction but didn't pay her much mind as she tried to find her father.

Above them, Vesp roared in anger and brought her magic down upon the crowd of magi. Shields broke, and people screamed in fright and pain. Tess skidded to a stop and looked back, seeing the damage the fae's attack had wrought. About half of the group had been knocked off its feet and was trying to recover. As Vesp attacked again, Evelyn burst through and created a wind shield that combated the magical tendrils. They bounced off, and the fae hissed at her.

Tess blew out a breath of relief. She shoved aside two more Hunters as their guns fired. Several bullets ricocheted off her magical shield or were devoured by her flames. One scraped her leg and caused her to stumble, exposing Arjun's side. He fired back, hitting a Hunter in the chest while another ducked down to avoid being made a target.

Tess glowered at them and forced herself onward until she spotted Nick in his werewolf form supporting her father. He was human, which sent a jolt of terror through her. What had happened? Why wasn't he changing into his wolf form for added protection? "There!" she shouted to her mother and Arjun.

Nick held onto her father while a smaller four-footed wolf snapped at and tackled the Hunters in their way. The space between them closed painstakingly slowly, but at last the barrier broke. Tess lowered her flames and rushed to her father ahead of her mother who got held back while saving a werewolf from a Hunter.

"Dad!" she shouted and wrapped her arms around him.

"Firebug," he whispered, holding her close. He breathed into her hair and held her head. Water dripped onto her shoulder, and when she pulled back, he was crying. "I never thought I'd see you again."

She laughed, fighting back her own tears. She could hear Nick, Arjun, and the other wolf defending them as she reunited with her father. "I'm so sorry. I tried to get to you sooner."

He touched her cheek and kissed her forehead. "It's okay, Tess. It's not your fault." He cupped her face in his hand. "I'm so proud of you."

Warmth and pride swelled in her heart, and she hugged her father again.

"Brighton!" her mother cried. Suddenly, they were both enveloped in her mother's firm hug. "Brighton, oh my god," her mother sobbed.

For just that moment, the war around them faded, and Tess basked in the comfort of her parents' embrace. She sniffled and kissed them both. Her father looked smaller and weaker, but he was alive. And that was all that mattered to her.

Tess squeezed his hand before looking at Nick. "We need to get you guys out of here. Come on. We're working on a pathway to the docks where others are waiting to protect you."

Nick nodded and pushed a small wolf toward Tess. It took her a moment to realize this must be Yanlei. She smiled and looked around. "Augustine?" she asked.

"*Trish went to grab her*," Nick said. He patted Tess's shoulder then froze. "*Gale?*"

Tess looked behind her.

Gale and Daniella had both managed to follow Tess's group to Nick's. They'd given the Huntress a gun back, and she was using it to their advantage, taking out other Hunters who got too close. Daniella kept a close eye on her (though Tess wondered why they were trusting Daniella again, but she could worry about that later).

Gale offered Nick a sheepish shrug. "Well, you hoped I would switch sides one of these days, right?" She gestured to the big werewolf with her. "This is Daniella, the sister I told you about. She's alive."

He gave Gale a wolfish smile then grimaced as magic rippled across the room, sending those sensitive to it to their knees. Tess went down along with her mother, while her father and Arjun stood over them protectively.

"Ugn," Tess moaned. "We need Kafeada to take down this monster."

Nick exchanged a look with Gale. "*I can take you to where she is. She's trapped behind a barrier of magic. Do you think you can break it?*"

Tess grimaced. "Probably not alone, especially if we don't know what kind of barrier it is."

Her father helped her and her mother back to their feet. "Tell me what I can do to help."

Tess shook her head. "No, you need to leave," she added, looking at her mother. "Nick can lead the rest of us to the fae."

"I'll help," Gale promised. "I might be able to—"

A bullet whizzed past her face and knocked her backward into Daniella. The werewolf snarled and shoved Gale down, standing over her with her hulking form.

Tess called up her shields and searched for the shooter, but there were so many bodies around them, and the smoke was starting to descend again. More shots went off, some landing painfully close to their group.

Daniella rose up on her hind legs to get a better look. Suddenly she roared, her side and leg peppered in red. She fell back to all fours, keeping Gale down.

This time, Tess saw the sandy-haired man pointing a pair of guns at them, his eyes filled with rage.

Hendrickson.

Two more Hunters flanked him, bearing down on the group with their weapons drawn. Another shot rang out, and Tess was too slow to stop a dart from striking her mother. Her mother gasped in pain and ripped the dart out, but it was too late. Her fire magic faded, breaking down one of their protective walls. Tess struggled to wrap her shield around her whole group while Arjun returned fire.

The Hunters had managed to grab physical shields and blocked the bullets. They drew closer and closer, peppering Tess's magical barriers with more bullets and darts. She gasped and looked at Arjun. "Get my mother and father out of here!" she shouted at him. "Nick! Get behind me!" She shifted on her feet, extending her shield in front of Daniella and Gale as well. Nick, of course, didn't listen and snarled at her side, placing himself in front of Yanlei in the process.

"Let me go after them. Keep the bullets off me until I take the Hunters down."

"I can't split my magic that much," Tess said. "Not without risking you." She grimaced as another bullet hit. She saw Arjun trying to pull her mother and her father away to safety. Good. At least they wouldn't get hurt. She gritted her teeth and drew from the Ether in her necklace, further fueling her magic.

An object hit the ground beside her. Light exploded out of it, blinding her and making her cry out in pain. She covered her face, still trying to keep the fire up, but the flash bomb had dazed her. Through her buzzing ears, she heard Nick roar and felt him shove her down as she struggled to recover. She opened her eyes, her vision splotchy from the light.

Hendrickson and his men came down on them with weapons raised. His face twisted into a sick smile as he and his men pointed guns at her, Nick, and Yanlei.

Tess stretched out her hand, creating a flickering shield to protect them, but at such close range, she didn't think she'd be able to hold them off. "I'm sorry," she managed to say to Nick before they fired.

Something dove in front of them.

Tess blinked frantically and tried to see what had happened. The moment she did, she screamed.

Her father wavered in front of her, blood pouring down his bare chest. He staggered and fell to his knees then to the ground.

"Dad!" Tess shrieked. She scrambled forward and rolled him onto his back, placing his head gently into her lap. "Dad, Dad, hang on. Just hang on," she said and touched his face.

He coughed, blood splattering his lips. "Tess...get back," he ordered weakly.

Tess held him close and lifted burning eyes to Hendrickson. "You son of a bitch!" she bellowed at him.

Hendrickson sneered and cocked his gun again. "At least I got to take one of you dogs down."

He pointed the gun...which never fired.

Like a bloody avenging angel, Augustine loomed behind him and brought her massive jaws down around his head and throat. With a single crunch, his body fell to the ground in a bloody pool. His cohorts cried out in terror. She shredded one with her claws while Nick took out the other.

Tess panted and looked down at her father. She ran her hand through his hair and touched his cheek. His skin was already taking on a grayish hue as his blood pooled around her knees. "Dad. Daddy, come on. Stay with me." She looked around frantically for her mother, but Arjun had managed to pull her far away enough, and closer to safety, that a few groups of fighting Hunters and parahumans stood between them.

Tess cursed and blinked back more tears. "Please, hang on."

Her father forced a weak smile. "Not...this...time...Firebug," he wheezed. Tess knew enough from listening to her father and Quince talk about bullet wounds that one of his lungs was gone. But...but he could still survive!

She fought the tears as she held him close. "You can't die. Mom needs you. I need you. Just hold on a little bit longer. We...we have healer magi!" Yes! A healer could help! She reached out mentally toward the magi. "*I need a healer magus! Please! Please! I need help!*"

But there came no reply. They had their hands busy with the fae.

Her father touched her cheek and turned her head toward him.

"Hey," he said softly. "It's gonna...be okay." He coughed and gasped for a breath.

Tess shook her head and bowed it over his. Tears flowed down her cheeks and onto his face and chest. "I love you, Daddy. I love you so much."

"I love...you...too."

She sobbed brokenly and held him as his breathing grew weaker and more labored. It wasn't fair. It wasn't fair! They'd just found him and now...she couldn't just let him go, but her magic wouldn't be enough to save him. She didn't have healing powers like the others. She'd never felt so helpless. "Don't go," she whimpered.

She lifted her head enough to see him smile at her. His gazed into hers, and he moved his mouth, trying to say something else, but nothing came out. So instead he placed a hand on her cheek and held it there for as long as he could.

His chest rose and fell slower and slower. His fingers slid down her face, leaving behind a bloody trail before his hand fell back over his waist. A deep breath left him and he sank into her arms, his eyes still staring up at her until they grew unfocused.

A sound she'd never made before tore through her throat as she screamed her grief.

He was dead.

Her dad was dead.

And there was nothing she could do to change it. She shook him and patted his cheek. "Come back, Dad. Come back!" she sobbed and pressed her forehead to his. She rocked him in her arms, not caring about the chaos around her.

Her father was dead.

Nothing else mattered.

Chapter 34
Father and Daughter

Trish

Trish crouched over a Hunter as she ripped her fangs out of his throat. Blood flowed through her body, bringing strength in her weakness and fear. She stayed low and searched for Augustine, Bianca, and Kat. Too many Hunters had gotten in her way while she was going after the big werewolf. She rose and zipped between the battling crowds. Gunshot pops followed by a vicious wolf snarl made her turn in time to see Augustine end Hendrickson. Her eyes went wide, and she couldn't stop herself from fist pumping the air. If anyone needed his head taken off, it was Hendrickson.

But her smile faded as two more parahumans fell to Hunters near where Kat had caught Bianca. She took a deep breath and raced toward them, nails and fangs extended to their full lengths. She pounced on the back of one Hunter and snapped his neck then whirled to find a gun in her face. Trish looked over the top and held out her hand. "Stop!" she shouted at the Huntress, her eyes glimmering.

The Huntress's eyes dilated as the charm washed over her, and she lowered the weapon. Trish took it from her hands and clocked her in the temple with the butt of the gun. She looked around and spotted a witch, crouched and panting. Trish pressed her fingers in her mouth and whistled, catching the witch's attention. When he looked up, she tossed the gun to him.

And then she took off after the next Hunter, her long jacket fluttering behind her.

It felt *strange* to be fighting with such a purpose. Two years ago, she was sauntering through the District acting like she owned the place, then shrinking under her coven's admonishments. Shame, guilt, and despair had followed her like shadows during her house arrest and then her attempt to redeem herself. Back and forth she'd flitted from one group to the next, yearning to find her place, trying to understand the right thing to do.

She never would have thought her ultimate decision would lead her to helping overthrow a fighting pit, battle Hunters, and save parahumans she didn't even know. And it felt *good*. So good. And to top it off, she'd saved Micah from this destruction and carnage. She'd met him by his room like she'd said and charmed him to stay hidden, no matter what he heard outside.

"Everything will be okay," she'd promised him. "I'll find you when it's all over."

And after seeing reinforcements arrive, she knew she had to get him out after she made sure Bianca and Kat were okay.

She shoved through another group of Hunters and found the werewolf still in her wolf form. Bianca had shifted back to human for the moment, but her talons were out and bloody. Trish smiled in amusement. They'd come far, hadn't they? They'd both been terrified women who didn't know their place, and now they were fighting together on the same side. She didn't think she'd ever want to face off against Bianca again.

"Bianca, Kat!" Trish called as she skidded to them. "You good?"

Kat gave herself a shake and licked her muzzle. Bianca brushed her furry head and nodded. "Yeah. The fae just knocked me down pretty hard." She looked up, and Trish followed her gaze.

Vesp terrorized the magi attacking her, beating them back with her magic with one hand and healing some of the wounded Hunters with her other.

Trish grimaced. "We've got to end her. If she keeps healing the wounded, we'll have too many Hunters to take on." She searched for Nick and spotted him standing next to Gale. She reached out to him mentally. *"Nick, Vesp is healing the Hunters. You need to get Kafeada or send someone to help her."*

"I know," he said, but something felt wrong with his mental voice. It was laced with a pain so deep it made Trish tremble. *"We're trying. We just...I...."*

"Nick, what happened? Are you hurt?"

"It's Brighton. Hendrickson...Hendrickson killed him."

Trish froze, her mouth falling open in shock. Brighton? Brighton was dead? But they'd come so far! They were almost out! But Hendrickson, of course, had to deliver one final blow before he was killed. That son of a bitch. Tears of rage stung her eyes. In her short time in the pit, she'd gotten to know Brighton, Nick, Yanlei, and Augustine better. Brighton hadn't deserved to die. *"I'm so sorry."*

"Augustine avenged him. Hendrickson won't hurt anyone else."

It was a small comfort at least. *"Bianca and Kat are okay. I can try to lead some of the magi to the room—"*

"No," Nick interrupted. He looked through the crowd until he saw her. *"I'll bring them. If Vesp comes after us, I might be able to stall her. Get out of here, Trish. You've done your part."*

Trish opened and shut her mouth. It didn't feel right leaving. The parahumans still needed help, and she had Micah to rescue too.

"Trish?" Bianca asked.

Trish broke her gaze from Nick and looked at the pair. She brushed tears out of her eyes. It was better they not know about Brighton; it might distract them from escaping. "Nick is going to lead magi to free Kafeada, the other fae. I need to help someone else. Can you get back to your group?"

The avian nodded. "Yeah, but what about you? Do you need help?"

Trish managed a playful snort, hiding the pain in her heart. "I've gotten out of stickier situations than this. Be careful!"

Before they could argue, she headed for a hallway that led to both the cages and the Hunters' barracks. She'd make sure no other parahumans had gotten stuck behind enemy lines.

Three Hunters with shields and guns blocked her path. She readied herself then bolted forward. She slammed into one of the shields and drove the Hunter back. Swiftly, she grabbed his chin and stared into his eyes. "Get rid of the other two," she ordered and pointed at the two Hunters. She leapt away as he turned his gun on his companions and fired. One dropped, but the other swung up her shield, trying to deflect his bullets.

Trish left them to their battle and ran. More shouts and gunfire echoed to her right. She poked her head into the hall in time to watch a werecat take down a Hunter. Two parahuman bodies lay strewn on the ground while another feline limped away from her kill. Another Hunter trained his gun on her, but Trish flew at his back and grabbed him. She threw him hard into the wall. He crumbled to the ground with a gasp and went still.

Trish panted and looked at the still living felines. "You can go out that way," she said, pointing to the entrance she'd cleared.

They nodded and hurried in that direction.

Satisfied, Trish continued to the barracks where Micah was tucked safely away. Hopefully he wouldn't hate her for the part she'd played in protecting him. She reached for the door to his room and opened it.

She froze at the sight that met her eyes.

Micah dangled in Saul's arms. One of the vampire's hands was wrapped around the Hunter's throat, the other twisted in his hair. Micah looked over at her, his eyes free of her glimmer and filled with someone else's.

"Saul…" Trish said slowly. "What are you doing?"

Saul snapped his head toward her, his irises burning red. "You. It was you all along."

Trish swallowed hard and held up her hands. "I don't know what you're talking about. I just came—"

"Stop lying!" Saul shouted and dug his nails deeper into Micah's throat, causing blood to drip. "I broke your pitiful charm on this fool and forced him to tell me the truth. The truth you denied me!" His face crumpled as he lowered Micah an inch. "How could you, Trish? I took you in. Gave you a home. A new family. And this is how you repay me?"

Trish shrank under his burning eyes and disapproval. Despite what Saul had done, she still felt a bond between them. A connection that had been there since she was first brought to the coven, a scared, broken, little bitten-born vampire. "I'm sorry. I couldn't let them die, Saul." She looked at Micah and saw the terror in his eyes. "Please, let him go. He only did what I ordered him to do."

"He was weak," Saul said in a cold voice. "And your puppet. He has no more use."

Trish lunged forward. "Don't!"

Saul slashed his nails across Micah's throat and dropped his writhing body to the ground. He caught Trish mid-leap and threw her out of the room. She flew backward and smacked into the wall, her head cracking painfully against stone. As she fell, Saul snatched her up and threw her down the hall.

She hit the ground and rolled several times before landing in a heap. Her head pounded from the vicious strike to her skull. She groaned and slowly got to her knees, rubbing her face against her jacket to clean off the blood.

"I took you under my wing. Trained you. Defended you against Joseph. Against the Hunters!" Saul shouted as he advanced on her.

Trish scrambled backward to avoid him. He streaked forward, grabbing her around her throat, and shoved her up against the wall. She gurgled in surprise and grappled with his wrist. "Saul…please," she begged.

He stared into her eyes, his entire body trembling. His irises grew redder, but there was also a strange black flicker in them she couldn't identify. "You were the last person I cared about after Fraula died. I found a new home here. And peace with Lady Vesp. She helped heal my shattered heart." He touched his chest with one hand while keeping her pinned with the other. "How could you take that away? Are you so broken that you'd betray the very person who's always been a father to you?"

Trish coughed and pulled on his fingers. He finally dropped her. She fell against the stone, touching her neck. "You are like a father," she said. "I've always looked up to you, but this is wrong, Saul. You and I both know it." She looked up at him. "You were so heartbroken over Fraula that you let your grief blind you. You turned against your coven. Betrayed your Duke. Tried to assassinate the Violet Marshall."

"He killed her!" Saul roared in her face, spittle flying. "Paytah killed her, and he deserved the same fate."

Trish shook her head. "It wasn't his fault. Blood magic forced him, you *know* that."

"She's still dead," Saul growled. He grabbed her by the arms, restraining her. "He's still guilty. And if I couldn't kill him, then I'd make him pay by destroying his pack."

"And our coven!" Trish shouted back at him. She shoved against his chest, breaking free of his hold. "You corrupted Joseph! You turned him against the coven and me. You broke the person you swore you would always protect."

"Because he did nothing to avenge my mate! He wasn't fit to be Duke."

"Who made you judge, jury, and executioner?" Trish spat. She panted and held out her hands imploringly to Saul. "Saul, this has to stop. I won't follow down the path you're on. I know where I belong." Her eyes burned with unshed tears as the realization dawned on him. She would no longer be at his side. No matter what he said or did or how he pleaded, she would not follow him. Not anymore. "I belong with the Purple Door District."

Saul took a step away from her like she'd slapped him. He looked her up and down and bared his fangs. "I should have known you'd be nothing more than a turncoat, mewling at the feet of the people you think are going to win. You only serve yourself. You're a coward."

"You're right," Trish said, raising her chin. "I am a coward. But at least I'm a coward who's finally fighting for what's right."

Saul narrowed his eyes at her. They turned a darker shade of red, almost bordering on black, and he took a step toward her. Bat wings exploded from his back, looming above her dangerously. His hand snaked out and caught her by the chin. He peered into her eyes, his own glimmering. "You're just confused. I'll make you see the truth, and then you'll *always* stay with me."

Trish gasped as his charm chipped away at her mental defenses. "Saul, no!" she shouted, striking him in the chest and then kicking his leg. He staggered back but yanked her with him, hand still on her chin. "No!"

Saul bared his fangs.

A big black figure smashed into his head and knocked him to the side. He lost his hold on Trish. She fell to her knees and looked up.

Kat stood at the other end of the hall snarling, fur bristling. The dark figure shot back toward her, and Trish realized it was a caracara.

Saul roared in outrage and flew past Trish, fangs and nails flashing in the light. His eyes had completely blackened over, sending chills down Trish's spine. Unnatural ebony streaks webbed through his veins.

"Run!" Trish shouted and bolted after Saul. She leapt forward, tackling him to the ground. He rolled and struck, catching her in the face. She clawed him across his cheek and kicked him off of her. Trish scrambled to her feet and tried to throw her charm at Kat as she met the wolf's eyes. "Run!"

Saul grabbed Trish by the arms and threw her into a wall, but she didn't relent. She raced after him and plowed into his side, sending him into one of the prisons where they'd kept the parahumans. Trish punched him in the face and kicked him in the stomach. He stumbled backward, tripping over broken collars and chains.

Trish grabbed the door and slammed it shut just as Bianca and Kat made it to her.

"What are you doing?!" Bianca shouted.

Trish grasped the metal and pressed it hard together, twisting it so that they wouldn't be able to get in easily, and Saul wouldn't be able to get out without going through her. "Get out of here before he kills you. Please, let me do this—ah!"

She cried out as Saul's hand twisted into her red hair and threw her. She collapsed to the floor and watched him stick his hand through the bars, clawing at Kat and Bianca. They dodged in time. Snarling, Saul attacked the door like a madman.

Trish wobbled to her feet and grabbed him from behind again. This time, his wings threw her off of him. She rolled twice, but she didn't stay down. She leapt and wrapped her arms around his throat. Just as he started to work the metal on the door loose, Trish hissed and dug her fangs into his neck.

Saul screamed in pain as her fangs dug deeper than they ever had on a person before. She clung to him as he shook his body and tried to shove her off. With a roar, he jumped backward and smashed her between his back and a wall. She grunted in pain, but she kept her fangs in his neck and dragged them downward, creating a thick gash that bled profusely. She hooked her legs around his waist to give her more purchase and clawed at him like a wild animal. She had to keep him away from Kat and Bianca. She had to stop him!

Saul smacked her up against the wall again and again. A rib broke. Her shoulder dislocated. His hands went down to her legs and snapped one. She screamed in pain into his neck. But still she held on.

In a last-ditch attempt, he reached back and grabbed her shirt and neck. Snarling, he jerked forward at the same time as he pulled on her and sent her flying through the air. The ground smacked against Trish's body as she landed and rolled. Air whooshed out of her lungs. Rocks cut into her arms and body. She ended up in a crumpled heap against the wall, gasping for breath.

As her vision pulsed and blurred, she watched Saul rush toward her. She reached for the closest thing to her hand: a broken chain. He grabbed her by her jacket collar and jerked her up. Trish coughed up a little blood and glanced over his shoulder as Bianca and Kat managed to yank the door Saul had weakened open.

Then, barely hearing his snarls, she brought the chain wrapped around her hand up and smashed it across his face. He screeched in pain. With one hand pinning her, he lifted his other and shoved it into her stomach.

There was a moment of blinding pain, and then Trish barely felt anything at all. She looked down. His hand, wrist, and part of his forearm were buried deep into her body. She blinked and stared at him, her mouth twitching, but no sound came out.

For a moment, his black eyes cleared, and he looked down at what he'd done then back at Trish. Grief flooded his face. "Trish...."

Trish stared back at him and brought her hand to his cheek. He leaned his head into it, but looked away with a hiss as Kat rushed him. Trish closed her eyes then opened them. She spread her claws, and as he started to let her go, she raked them across his throat. Saul staggered away from her, his hand leaving her body. She crumpled to the ground and lay on her back, listening to Kat snarl and Saul shout before his voice was silenced forever.

Trish blinked slowly. It was so strange. She could feel and see her heartbeat in the corners of her eyes. She placed a hand over the gaping wound, but she didn't feel any pain. No, she just felt cold, despite her jacket. It figured that she'd die alone, too.

Warm hands lifted her head and planted it on a soft lap. Trish blinked a few more times, looking past the tears. She stared up at Bianca as the avian touched her face.

"Trish, hang on," Bianca said, sniffing. "We've got you. We'll...we'll—"

"Stop," Trish whispered. "You...know it's too late." She cracked a weak, bloody smile. "Why are you crying anyway? Thought you didn't like me."

Bianca brushed her face against her sleeve to dry a few tears. "You know that's not true, at least not anymore. I'm so sorry. Why didn't you let us help?"

"He would have killed you," Trish said. She coughed and tried to ignore the taste of blood on her lips. "Couldn't have your deaths on my hands, too. My damn death list is too long as it is."

Kat padded over and whimpered. She settled down at Trish's side. Her warm, furry body helped chase away some of the awful chill. Trish ran her fingers gently through the wolf's fur and patted her.

"You keep an eye on this one," she told Kat and nodded toward Bianca. "She's as much of a troublemaker as I am."

Kat whined and licked her hand. *I will. I promise.*

Trish smiled. At least they were safe. At least she'd done something good with the remaining hours of her life. She rocked her head in Bianca's lap and stared up at the darkening ceiling.

"Is there anything we can do for you?" Bianca said between her tears and sniffles.

"Just...stay. I don't want to be alone." Trish closed her eyes. It was getting harder to breathe, and she felt so *tired*. All she had to do was fall asleep, and then things would be okay. She'd...she'd be okay.

She took a deep breath then let it out, and the world around her faded.

Trish lay there, waiting, but she didn't know for what. The chill vanished. So did the warmth. It was like there was nothing at all.

And then, something soft touched her hand. Trish slowly opened her eyes and looked up into the familiar face of the one she'd missed for so long. Gavin smiled cheekily at her and pulled her sweetly into his arms.

"Hey, little bat."

Chapter 35
Dust

Nick stared, unable to comprehend what had just happened. One moment Brighton was alive, fighting for his life, and now he lay lifeless in Tess's arms. Brighton, a man who had supported Nick his entire life in the pack. Who had comforted him after he lost his father to senseless violence. Who had taught him to fight alongside Paytah. He was gone. Dead. Like Ray.

Augustine whined in anguish as she stepped over Hendrickson's beheaded body. She bumped her nose lightly against Brighton's head and Tess's arm, as if to try to rouse him. But nothing, neither magic nor science, would save him.

Gale fell to her knees, but Nick didn't know if it was because of Hendrickson's death or Brighton's. Maybe a little of both. He glanced at her then behind Augustine as Ayaan and Pavati came into view. Pavati clapped her hands over her mouth, her eyes filling with tears. Ayaan pulled her to his chest to spare her.

Nick bowed his head. A warm face brushed his cheek, and he looked at Yanlei as she nuzzled him.

"Nick, I'm so sorry," she said, her voice laced with emotion. She'd grown close to Brighton as well.

He nuzzled her back and took a shaky breath. He wanted to howl his grief alongside her and Augustine, but a battle still raged around them. And if they didn't do *something,* they wouldn't make it out alive, and Brighton's death would be for nothing.

He pressed his head against Yanlei then touched Tess's arm. *"Tess...I'm so sorry. I...we can't—"*

"I know," she said between a break in her sobs. Her arms trembled as she lowered her father to the ground. She placed a hand over his eyes and bowed her head. "I know," she repeated. Fire sparked around her hands and glimmered at the corner of her eyes. The heat rushed over her body, driving Nick back. With a sudden roar of grief, she spun on her knee and shot out her hands, sending waves of fire slicing through the crowd. Humans and parahumans were thrown back by the force of her heat, but it created a path back the way they'd come. Iris stood at the end of it beside Arjun, looking back at Tess in confusion. Tess wrapped magic around her father and lifted him into the air, sending him along the path and depositing him gently on the ground next to her mother. The moment Arjun saw who it was, he dashed for Tess. Iris's mournful screams shook Nick to his very core.

"She'll protect him," Tess said in a raspy voice and staggered to her feet. Arjun reached her side and steadied her. She squeezed his arm then looked at Nick with burning eyes. "Let's get this done."

Nick nodded and padded over to Hendrickson's body. He nosed along the man's pockets.

"What are you doing?" Gale cried and scrambled to stop him.

"He has Ayaan's and Pavati's wands. They need them to protect themselves."

Gale swallowed hard. "Let me."

Nick backed off as she reached into her brother's belt. Tears ran down her face which she tried to hide from Tess, who looked ready to burst into flames at the first wrong word. One wand came back whole, but the second was snapped, either by Hendrickson's own hand or his collapse. She held them out to the pair of witches.

Pavati sniffled as she picked up the whole wand. Ayaan's shoulders fell as he collected the broken one. His sister looked at it then squeezed his hand. "I'll protect you," she promised and waved her wand in the air. Water sprang to life before Nick's eyes.

Nick didn't want to bring them, but he knew they didn't have time to get the teens out. The path Tess had created had already been swallowed up by fighting bodies, and he didn't think she could send out another blast like that. He looked toward the hall that would bring them to the fae's room and flicked his tail. *"All right. Stay close. I don't know if Vesp will follow, so keep your eyes open."*

"I'll reach out to Evelyn," Tess said. "She said she could help free Kafeada."

Nick nodded and left that task to Tess as he faced the fighting Hunters and parahumans. *"Augustine, help me create a path. Gale, Daniella, Tess, and Arjun protect Ayaan and Pavati. Yanlei—"*

"I'll protect your sides," she said.

Nick nodded. He waited for Augustine to join him, then together they barreled toward the forbidden hall. He snapped and clawed his way through. Augustine's big form frightened both warring sides, especially her blood-coated fur. She knocked a Hunter onto his back and picked up another and threw him into one of his companions. There was no sympathy, no forgiveness in her actions. She was done being a pawn to these people. Anyone who she or Nick missed, Yanlei took care of. She raced between Hunters' legs and tripped them up, sending them tumbling into each other.

Nick smacked another Hunter away and spotted four more blocking the hall. Before he could snarl at them, Augustine barreled ahead. They tried to hold their ground, but the werewolf smashed through them and slashed anyone who opposed her with her claws. Nick would have whistled if he could have. He glanced over his shoulder at Vesp, but she was still distracted by the magi.

One of the four Hunters managed to avoid Augustine's jaws of justice and lifted his gun. Wind wrapped around his body and chucked him out of the way. Nick swore he heard the Wilhelm scream accompany his flight.

He glanced to the side as a wind magus, likely Evelyn, joined them. With a nod to her, he guided them down the hallway to the intricate wooden door. There were no Hunters in front of it this time. Why would there be when they were all fighting in the pit? Nick broke through the door, sending it swinging inward. The world they entered was just as he remembered. He traversed it quickly, taking everyone to the box prison with the crackling magic.

"Kafeada," Evelyn said and rushed forward. She pressed her hands against the box. Inside, the fae pressed hers to the wall as well. "How do we free you?"

Kafeada glanced around. "I'm still bound by cold iron, but I was able to make a small crack. I think she bound me with Ether stones."

Nick frowned and looked at the magi for explanation.

Tess searched the foot of the prison, assessing the thick rocks on the ground. "She's right. Vesp must have put elemental magic into the stones to make a kind of four-way lock. Each stone is powered by an element."

"Can you just...pick them up and get rid of them?" Nick asked.

"No," Evelyn answered. "They're tethered to the box. But each stone can be destroyed by its own magic. We just need to have enough magi." She looked at Tess. "You're fire. I'm wind. We need water and earth."

Pavati bit her lip and held up her wand. "I...I can use water magic. My brother can do earth."

"No, I can't," Ayaan said, showing them the broken wand.

Nick swore. Damn Hendrickson. Even in death he was screwing them over.

Evelyn swore too and hit the cage with her fist. "We have earth magi, but we have to get one here." She pushed off and started for the door. "I'll—"

"Wait," Tess said, grabbing the wind magus's arm. She shook her head and looked at Arjun. "Arjun, your wand."

Nick furrowed his brow. What was she talking about? What wand? Wasn't Arjun just a Hunter?

Arjun pulled it out of his belt strap and then reached into his shirt. He plucked a necklace with a metal leaf on the end free. He glanced at Tess. "Do you think I'm strong enough?"

Evelyn waved her hands frantically. "It doesn't matter how strong you are. If you're an earth magic user, that's all that matters. Each of you, find the stone that matches your power. You'll sense your magic humming with it."

They broke apart, each finding the large stones that coincided with their abilities. Evelyn held out her hand over the wind stone. "On three, blast the stone with as much magic as you have. One, two, three!"

Earth, fire, wind, and water rained down on the stones. Nick swore he heard the rocks screech as the magic hit them. But then he realized it wasn't the stones screeching. It was Vesp. He gasped and bolted to the door as dark tendrils snaked through the hall toward them. He slammed the door shut, shoving his body against it. *"Hurry! She's coming!"*

The witches and magi worked together to break the lock. Augustine and Yanlei ran to Nick's side to help keep the door closed, followed by Gale and Daniella. Something pounded against the wood, causing them to stagger, but they held their ground. The banging turned to clawing, and a tendril punched through right next to Nick's stomach. He shoved Gale back so she didn't get hit and clawed the tendril. He heard a shout as it coiled in retreat. Another tendril punched through, smacking Augustine in the head and hurling her to the ground. She bounced and rolled, dazed.

Nick swore. *"The door's going to give. Be ready to fight."* He glanced back at the box, which had started to glow so brightly it chased away the shadows in the room. The stone table with the glittering orbs appeared. He licked his muzzle and looked at Daniella, Gale, and Yanlei. *"Hold the door as long as you can,"* he told them.

They nodded.

Nick bolted over to the table. The lights danced and shook inside of the bottles, creating a tinkling noise. He scooped them up in his paws and looked at the box. Taking a deep breath, he lifted the jars over his head. *"Be free,"* he said and threw them to the ground. The glass shattered into pieces. Multi-colored lights shot into the air and danced around him at the same time as the box broke into millions of twinkling lights.

Evelyn threw herself into Kafeada's arms and cried in joy.

It was short-lived.

Daniella was sent flying, along with the door, across the room. Yanlei and Gale tumbled after her, landing in a heap.

Vesp zoomed in, wings spread, tendrils looming above them with deadly points. She took one look at the shattered box and screamed. The fae flew at Kafeada and Evelyn, but Nick moved too. He threw himself at Vesp and wrapped his furry arms around her, dragging her down before she could attack the pair. Evelyn worked frantically to get a single silver collar off Kafeada's throat.

Vesp twisted and struck Nick across the face with sharp nails. "Let me go!" she screamed at him. "You've ruined it! You've ruined it all!"

"No, I freed your captives. This was how it was always going to

end, Vesp," Nick said. He brought his teeth down on her arm. She screamed in pain.

Tess and Arjun turned on the fae and struck her with fire and earth, trying not to hit Nick in the onslaught. He held on as long as he could until her arm seemed to blip out of his mouth and reappear above his head. She brought her elbow down on his skull with crushing force, knocking him to the ground. Nick groaned in pain and held his head while Tess and Arjun tried to drive Vesp back. Even Pavati launched waterballs at the fae while forcing her brother behind her.

Tess swung her hands again and again, throwing fire orbs the size of her head at the fae. Sweat flowed down her body and mingled with her father's blood on her shirt. She gritted her teeth fiercely and screamed at Vesp. Fire snarled through her hair as she drained every ounce of magic from her body.

"*Tess, you're going to kill yourself. Stop!*" Nick shouted at her.

But Tess didn't stop. She took a step forward, battling the tendrils threatening to consume them. Nick grimaced and looked at Kafeada and Evelyn who were having no luck with the collar. He twisted around until he found Augustine just getting to her feet. She shook her head roughly and growled under her breath.

Nick struggled to stand when a black tendril came crashing down on him. Suddenly, Yanlei was there, snapping her teeth through the offending magic and driving it back. She snarled after Vesp. With a snort, she pressed her body against his and lent him the strength to rise. He got up and touched her furry face with his paw. "*Have I mentioned I love you?*"

"*Just took a battle of life and death for you to say it,*" she teased.

Nick smiled at her then reached out to Augustine. "*Get the collar off Kafeada!*"

Augustine gnashed her fangs and rushed toward the fae.

Tess shouted in pain.

Nick spun around and saw her hit the ground with a tendril wrapped around her waist. It squeezed her as it jerked her into the air. Arjun shouted, sending vines after the tendril. Nick circled around the fae and launched himself at the offending tendril. He snapped down on it until it released her. Tess plummeted from the ceiling. Nick tried to catch her, but Arjun got there first. He caught her in his arms and ducked low to the ground to avoid another of Vesp's sweep attacks. Nick threw himself in front of the pair and faced off against Vesp, teeth bared.

Vesp panted and lifted a clawed hand into the air. She didn't offer any taunts or final words. Instead, her eyes gleamed with the intent to kill. Nick squared himself, prepared to take the blow to protect his friends. Out of the corner of his eye, he saw Yanlei rush toward him.

"Nick, don't!" she shouted.

He offered her a loving smile then glared defiantly up at Vesp.

A green blast of magic struck Vesp in the side, throwing her into the wall. The fae screeched in pain, but she wasn't left alone for long. Kafeada flew after her. Her wings glimmered emerald and had grown to twice their usual size. Her hair broke loose of its rose-bound bun and coiled around her face like Medusa's snakes. She shouted and brought her hand down on Vesp, blasting her with Ather magic that caused the room to shake.

A clatter jerked Nick's attention toward Augustine. She stood beside the broken collar and nodded at him. Nick almost sank to the ground in relief, but the battle wasn't won yet.

Yanlei reached his side and nipped at his cheek reproachfully.

"You and I are going to have words later," she said.

"I'll take every scolding you have to give me, just help me protect them first." He and the others stayed close to Tess and Arjun as the two fae threw magic at each other, Kafeada attacking with vines and Ather and Vesp lashing out with black tendrils and tainted Ether. They clashed again and again, leaving burns and marks on each other's bodies. But Kafeada did not let up. She fought with everything she had.

Vesp struck the ground hard and panted, glowering up at Kafeada. She looked over at Nick and his friends. With one hand, she sent a blast at Kafeada, and with the other she shot magic at Nick.

He barely had a chance to brace himself before Evelyn stepped in the way. She spun her hands, creating a wind shield that combated the magic but couldn't disperse it. Her hair and clothing whipped around her as she fought, the force of Vesp's blow driving her back step by step.

Tess leaned forward and pointed at Evelyn's shield. Her fire magic snarled weakly to life but joined in protecting them. Arjun's vines came next, then Pavati's water. They stood together, battling against the magic trying to destroy them while Kafeada fought the power preventing her from saving them.

Nick saw his friends waver. *She's too strong*, he realized in horror. *She's too strong! She'll kill us all.* He spread his claws and took a step forward, preparing to launch himself at Vesp to distract her and give Kafeada and his friends a chance.

Yanlei bumped his side with hers. *"Together,"* she told him and crouched low.

Before they could act, a pair of beautiful lights, one purple and one gold, flashed by Nick's face. The souls of the once captive fae danced before his eyes, stopping him in his tracks. They twisted around each other then flew at Vesp with the rest of the beautiful lights. Together, they launched themselves into Vesp's body.

The fae cried out more in shock than in pain. The distraction was enough; her attack broke as she looked down at the lights flowing out of her.

Evelyn, Tess, Arjun, and Pavati threw their magic at Vesp at the same time as Kafeada. The power crashed into the dream fae. Vesp unleashed a tortured scream as a blinding light filled the room. Nick threw his arm up over his face protectively.

When the light faded, Evelyn fell to her knees in front of him, spent. Pavati collapsed into her brother's arms, and Tess and Arjun slumped to the ground. Nick moved in front of them again, but it didn't matter.

Vesp lay on the ground in a crumbled mess, gasping for breath. The lights bobbed around her as Kafeada landed on her bare feet beside the broken fae. Kafeada shook her head sadly.

"This is not how I wanted this to end, my sister," Kafeada murmured.

Vesp blinked back tears as she stared at Kafeada. "Just...do it. Destroy me."

Kafeada bowed her head. "I wish you could be reborn. I truly do."

Vesp laughed weakly. "At least...Lord Oberon...finally has his revenge."

Kafeada stretched out her hand. The ground beneath them shook as thick vines emerged and twisted together to form a beautiful staff. At the very tip, a stone spearhead formed. Kafeada lifted the staff in her hands over her head. "I'm sorry," she said and drove the spear through Vesp's heart.

Nick tucked his head against Yanlei as the fae's life was extinguished. He'd seen enough death to last him a lifetime. When he looked back, Vesp's body had already faded, leaving behind a pale white mist that hung in the air. The other lights flew around it with far less merriment than when they'd been freed.

Kafeada held out her hand to the lights. "I'll keep her essence safe." She cradled Vesp's dusted light against her chest and smiled at the other souls. "Go, be reborn."

With a whispered tinkle, the lights flew through the air and vanished from sight, returning to the Veil through the nearest Tear and to the tree of life.

Nick sank to the ground with Yanlei, exhausted. He didn't know how much strength he had left to fight their way back out to the docking area. It seemed impossible to get there, especially with the many weary bodies around him.

Tess huddled in Arjun's arms, either resting or unconscious, he couldn't tell. Ayaan held Pavati while Augustine crouched beside them, keeping them warm with her large body. Gale sat beside Daniella, cradling the werewolf's head where she'd fallen. The wolf groaned and rubbed her face. Kafeada fluttered to Evelyn's side and knelt down beside her wife. She pulled her close, Vesp's light glowing inside of Kafeada's right hand.

Nick huffed out a tired sigh. No, there was no way they were in any shape to get out of there. Maybe they'd get lucky and the Hunters would flee with Vesp gone, or their friends would find them. He glanced around the room and gaped. The magic that had turned it into a star-lit paradise faded from sight, leaving them in a very dismal, empty cave.

Suddenly, he heard pounding in the hall. Nick clenched his teeth in frustration and glowered at the door. Now what? How many more people were they going to have to fight?

Yanlei rose and planted herself above him, ready to fling herself at the first enemy that appeared. Nick tried to rise too, but exhaustion dropped him back to the floor. Flashlights nearly blinded him as a group of people rushed into the room. He managed a weak growl before they lowered the lights and revealed themselves.

Nick's mouth dropped at the sight of Legion uniforms. Was it possible? Was Legion actually here? He searched the faces until his eyes settled on a member he recognized from years ago, someone who had helped Bianca.

"*Jay?*" Nick asked.

Jay took off her helmet, letting a blonde braid fall down her shoulder. She squinted then blinked in surprise. "Nick? Tess?" she said, seeing the magus on the ground.

Tess managed to lift her fingers in a victory sign before dropping her hand again.

Jay shook her head and tucked her helmet on her hip. "Don't worry. You're all safe now. We have control of the pit and are taking the Hunters into custody."

The relief that flooded Nick's body was beyond anything he could describe. But with it came pure, utter exhaustion. He sighed and flopped his head to the ground, finally allowing his body and mind to rest. Yanlei settled on top of him and pressed her face to his.

"*We're safe,*" she said, her mental voice hitching with emotion.

Nick closed his eyes.

Safe.

Chapter 36
The Parting Glass

Nick

Nick woke what felt like years later to the steady beep of a heart monitor. He cracked open his eyes and grimaced against the bright glare of an overhead fluorescent light. He raised his hand to block it out. A tube dangled from an IV stuck in his arm. He stared at it, his brain struggling to understand where he was.

"Nick?"

He blinked and rolled his head to the side.

Rozene rose out of her chair, shaking Paytah to wake him. The moment he saw Nick, he was up on his feet.

"Nick," he whispered, drawing close. "How are you feeling?"

"Where...am I?" he asked, his mouth moving slowly. It almost felt like he was drugged. Based on the IV in his arm, that was a possibility.

Rozene sat on the edge of his bed and ran her hand over his head. "You're at a Legion hospital along with the rest of the rescued parahumans."

Nick sucked in a breath. Hospital. They were in a hospital, not the pit. Was it true? Was this real, or was this another one of Vesp's twisted games? "Augustine...Yanlei?"

Paytah shifted so Nick could see to his left. "They're both here and safe."

Augustine lay sprawled in her bed, wrapped in blankets and with an IV in her arm as well. Back in her human form and asleep, she looked so small and frail. The pit had done more to her, to them, than he'd actually realized. His eyes darted across the room to where Yanlei slept under a mound of blankets.

They were both here. They were alive. Someone else was taking care of them and him. He didn't have to be the strong one anymore.

Nick could only stare as his two parental figures wrapped their arms around him. And then, like a dam, his eyes flooded with tears, and he sobbed into their embrace. He clung to them desperately. The emotions overwhelmed him as he thought of Ray and Brighton, both of their deaths still fresh in his mind. How many more had died?

"The rest of the pack?" he said with a sniff. "Is...are they—?"

"They're safe," Rozene said, squeezing his hand. She hesitated. "Everyone except Brighton. Tess said you were there when it happened."

Nick sniffed again and rubbed his eyes against his shoulder. "Yeah. I...I saw it." And he was never going to get that image out of his head either. "Pavati and Ayaan? And what about Gale and Daniella?"

"All safe," Paytah replied. "Gale is in Legion custody answering questions. She's been very cooperative, which has surprised us all, but we're thankful for it."

Nick released a choked laugh. "I can't believe Gale helped us. If she had from the beginning, Trish wouldn't have had to spend so much time tricking everyone into believing her and learning the security systems."

Paytah's and Rozene's expressions turned grim.

Nick's stomach knotted. "What?" he asked. "What is it?"

Rozene sighed and bowed her head. "Nick, Trish didn't make it."

A cold hand gripped his heart in a vice. Nick gasped and stared at Rozene in shock. "What do you mean?" He had to have heard her wrong, right? Trish...she'd saved them. All of them.

Rozene took his hand in hers and rubbed it. "Bianca and Kat went looking for her and found her and Saul fighting each other. He tried to go after them, but Trish trapped him in another room. By the time they made it in, Trish was too gravely wounded. She died, Nick."

Nick slumped back against the pillows. Trish was dead. Months ago he might have thought she'd gotten what she deserved after what she'd helped Hunters do to Bianca, but now? She'd stayed behind to help them, protect them. She'd fed them and healed them, been a friend to all of them despite Augustine's snarls. And now there was no way to thank her for any of it.

He fisted his hand and dropped his head back on the pillows. "I was supposed to protect her. She went to help Augustine. I thought...I should have gone with her."

"No," Paytah said, shaking his head. "Don't you dare blame yourself for what those Hunters and Saul did. They're the ones responsible for all your suffering and for the deaths." He touched Nick's face gently. "Augustine told us how you kept everyone going. We're so proud of you, son."

The tears came again, and Nick hugged Paytah. The elder wolf pulled him close and stroked his head lovingly.

"Get some rest. We'll be here when you wake up."

Nick didn't think he could sleep any longer. But the warm arms around him and the familiar scent of his pack, his family, sent him under again.

***

Except for that brief moment of consciousness, Nick didn't wake again until two days later, only to find Paytah and Rozene plus Mikayla, Jackson, Tamara, Kat, and Bianca in the room. The nice thing about Legion hospitals was that they understood the importance of cloisters, packs, prides, and covens, so some of their recovery rooms were quite a bit bigger to accommodate more people.

His pack and friends pounced on him, giving him hugs and some kisses. He laughed and cried, the realization that he was free and safe filling him with an odd mix of joy and sadness.

Freedom meant he could finally go home. But it also meant he had to deal with the reality that not all of his packmates and friends had survived.

The doctors came and went, checking on him, Augustine, and Yanlei. Augustine was the worst off, suffering from a few cracked ribs, a dislocated jaw, and malnourishment. Her werewolf healing was working slower than they liked, mostly due to the latter issue. Nick and Yanlei, likewise, were malnourished and healing from their own wounds. The doctor inspected Yanlei's eye and determined that there were a couple of surgeries that could possibly repair or lessen the damage. But they would have to wait until she fully recovered.

On the day of discharge, Nick perched on the edge of his bed tying his shoe. Bianca and Kat sat in nearby chairs. None of the pack was ever very far, and they'd taken turns watching over Nick, Augustine, and Yanlei. Kat and Bianca had decided to take this shift.

He sat back up and sighed. "It's going to be weird to go back home," he said. "We've been gone so long."

Kat smiled at him. "I promise you that home hasn't really changed."

Other than the fact that Brighton and Ray are dead, Nick thought to himself, but he didn't say it out loud. He didn't want to ruin anyone's good mood. They were all excited to be going home, though they planned to make a quick stop at Evelyn and Kafeada's. Nick wanted to thank them and also check in on Pavati and Ayaan.

Someone knocked lightly at the door.

Nick looked up and smiled a bit as Jay stepped in. She was dressed in civilian clothing rather than Legion garb, though the Legion uroboros badge sat proudly on her chest. "Off duty?" he asked.

"More or less. The hospital isn't technically my area. I'm just checking in." She looked between him and Bianca. "You know, I wish I could see you all when I'm not helping to save you."

Bianca managed a playful snort. "You mostly come in for cleanup, don't you? We have to do all the dirty work first."

"Well, that's true," Jay said. "But maybe if you'd all told us you were storming a pit sooner, we might have been there with more reinforcements." She chuckled. "You should have seen the faces of our Wisconsin team. Two of them were monitoring for magical flareups. One moment the boards were dead, and the next, they were lit up like a fireworks show gone wrong on the 4th of July. I don't think they'd ever seen that much activity. But at least it guided us directly to where you were hidden."

Nick smirked. "I guess fae battles will do that." He rolled his sore shoulder and thought of Vesp. "The fae who ran the pit, what's being done with her?"

Jay held up her hands. "Outside my paygrade."

Nick rolled his eyes. Figured. Well, maybe Evelyn and Kafeada would be privy to that information. He climbed to his feet and went to Jay's side, clapping her on the shoulder. "Thank you."

"You did most of the grunt work," she said. She sighed. "I'm sorry for everything you went through. All of you. I can promise you that the Wisconsin pit is shut down for good, and we're working on tracing their network to find other pits we can upend. We plan to put a stop to fighting rings and trafficking of parahumans."

"Good luck," Nick replied. "You're gonna need it."

Kat and Bianca joined him as he headed out of the room and down to the first floor where the pack was waiting for them, including Augustine. It was good to see them all together. The moment they caught sight of him, they crowded around him, providing the love and comfort he had so desperately missed. They'd even accepted Yanlei as an honorary member of the pack—though she'd gotten a protective stink eye from Mikayla, their resident matchmaker.

Yanlei had called her parents to let them know she was alive and insisted they wait for her until she could come home. They hadn't listened of course (what parent would have?) and had shown up anyway to check on their daughter. Once she was free to go home, they'd taken her back to their pack with them but with the promise that they would all talk together once Nick was home safe.

She'd only been gone a day, and he missed her terribly.

Augustine broke through the crowd and drew him into a hug. He returned it and sighed. "We're going home."

"Yes…" There was a sadness to her tone that Nick's heart echoed. He touched her arms and met her eyes.

"Whatever you need, ask me, okay? And if it's just to be around the pack, I'm sure Paytah and Rozene will be happy to have you stay at the house with us."

Augustine chuckled and squeezed his shoulder. "Hey, aren't I supposed to be the one comforting you? When did you grow up so fast?"

"Pits will do that to you," Nick said with a somber shrug. He patted her back and moved to join the others. Mikayla glomped him and shook his shoulders.

"Ohh, boy, don't you ever pull a disappearing act like that again."

Nick held up his hands, laughing. "Not like I had much of a choice." He hugged her back. "I missed you guys."

"Same," Mikayla said and ushered Tamara in who held him in her motherly arms. Tears filled his eyes, but he fought them back. There would be plenty of time to cry later. Right now? He was just happy to be with his pack.

They piled into the cars, Nick with Paytah, Rozene, and Augustine, and headed to Evelyn's home. He stared out the window, watching Wisconsin pass him by. Daylight felt foreign to him after spending so much time in the pits. He rolled down the window and breathed in the fresh air, letting it wash over his face and chill his ears.

"Are you going to stick your tongue out the window, too?" Augustine teased.

Nick glanced at her in time to see her stick her own head out the window to enjoy the cool breeze. He smiled to himself and sat back with a contented sigh.

When they reached Evelyn's house, the number of cars filling the driveway and the surrounding streets suggested a block party. A spot had been left for the alphas, so Paytah and Rozene parked in the driveway. Nick got out and followed the other werewolves into a gorgeous house. It was filled with boisterous laughter and people genuinely having a good time. Snacks were put out on tables in the dining room, but as he walked through, sliding doors opened onto a huge backyard.

Tiki torches glowed in the afternoon light, chasing away bugs and giving a very peaceful ambiance to the garden outside. Tables had been set up, and wolves from his pack and Wapasha's stood together, catching up and sharing stories. He recognized some of the council members and other District members as well. Mia looked up at him and tipped her head in a sign of respect. He returned it out of habit, not quite understanding why she seemed proud of him.

He glanced at the food and filled a plate with fresh fruits, vegetables, and a little bit of meat. Honestly, anything other than steak, potatoes, and bread was welcome on his plate. He made to select a cupcake but thought better of it as his stomach rumbled in protest. Okay, maybe he wasn't ready for those kinds of foods yet.

He walked outside and looked at the many faces who had come to rescue them. It took him a moment to realize that there were also some familiar faces from the pit. He hurried over to a woman chatting with a werecat.

"Loretta?" he asked, surprised.

The feline looked at him and cracked a smile. "Well, well. I didn't know you were from the Chicago Purple Door District."

Nick blinked. "Wait, you too?"

Loretta nodded. "Guess we don't know everyone in all of our groups, eh? Glad to see you made it out in one piece."

"You, too. Is there anyone else here from the pit?"

Loretta gestured to where Evelyn stood next to the fire witch who had fought against him and Yanlei. His mouth dropped in shock, and he slowly made his way over. The witch turned her eyes to him and stiffened. He quickly held up a hand.

"Hey, we didn't really get the chance to introduce ourselves. My name is Nick."

"I know who you are," the witch said in a low voice. She looked around him. "Where's your friend? The dhole?"

"Yanlei is with her family, recovering."

The witch wrinkled her nose. "Well, at least *she* made it out."

Nick sighed and set the plate of food on a nearby table. "I'm sorry about what happened in the pit. She never meant to hurt—"

"*Kill,*" the witch corrected him.

"Kill…your friend. We were fighting for our lives. I'm sorry. Really, I am. And Yanlei would say the same if she was with me right now." He held out his hand. "I hope there's a way that we can mend our differences."

The witch stared coldly at his hand. With a sneer, she shoved it away. "*Mend* our differences? You and your friend are still alive. Mine's not. You can't *mend* the dead." She rolled her shoulders. "Good luck to you, but I'd rather not see either of you again."

Before Nick could say anything, the witch stormed into the house. He sighed and wrapped his hand around the back of his neck. Well, he couldn't blame her. He just hoped she didn't end up following the same path of revenge as Saul. The last thing his pack needed was a fire witch with a vendetta coming after them.

"Nick?" Evelyn said, catching his attention. "Are you all right?"

He hesitated and looked at the wind magus. She'd visited him in the hospital to give him her thanks for protecting Pavati and Ayaan. "Yes...no. I mean." He gestured after the fire witch. "She and I fought in the ring. And, uh, her friend was killed by mistake."

Evelyn stared after her. With a heavy sigh, she turned and squeezed his shoulder. "No one can blame you for what happened in that pit. You were all trying to survive. I'll watch over her. She can hold a grudge for a while, but in the end, she's usually the forgiving type. Don't worry, Nick. She'll find love and safety back with the ward."

Nick nodded in thanks and looked around the garden. "It's beautiful here. Pavati and Ayaan said they loved learning lessons with you and Kafeada. How are they?"

Evelyn smiled. "Resilient and alive, thanks to you and Augustine. They're back with their parents. Oh, they told me to give you this." She reached into her pocket and handed him a letter. "They wanted to thank you and hope you'll stay in touch with them."

Nick opened the note and smiled as he saw the sweet message they left behind. They'd included their phone numbers as well as e-mail addresses. He held it close and nodded at Evelyn. "Thank you."

She inclined her head. "I have you to thank as well. You helped save my wife."

As if summoned, the fae in question appeared at Evelyn's side holding a green and purple fruity drink that fizzled and popped. It reminded him of the drinks at one of the clubs in the Fae Way. She held it out to Evelyn. "Here, have a sip. I think I added enough kick to it this time." She looked at Nick and brightened. "Well, now, it's good to see you escaped the hospital! How are you feeling?"

"Better," Nick said. "Still a little exhausted, but I'm getting stronger each day." He licked his lips and glanced around. "I, uh, wanted to ask you something about Vesp."

Kafeada's expression went from jovial to somber in a split second. "Yes?"

"What happened to her...light? I tried to ask one of the Legion agents, but she said it was above her paygrade."

Kafeada exchanged a look with Evelyn and sighed. "We have her in a sealed box for the time being. She's dusted, but she can't return to the Veil to be reborn. So we'll keep her essence safe in case one day Lord Oberon changes his mind."

"And the others?" Nick asked. "The other lights, er, fae that were in the jars?"

Kafeada smiled gently. "Because you freed them, they went to the tree to be reborn. I popped in myself to see and found a couple of them. They have no memory of what happened in the pit, and I can assure you they're living their lives the best they can. Thank you for freeing them."

"It seemed wrong to keep them in the jars," Nick said. "I had to do something."

Kafeada tilted her head to the side and admired him. "I will say this, Nick, you've found favor with the fae." She reached up and plucked a rose petal from her hair. With a flick of magic, the petal hardened. She passed it over to him. "If you ever need help, hold this close and speak my name twice. I'll come to you." She wagged her finger at him. "But only call me for serious things. I'm not helping you with school or with a hot date or something." She smirked. "Although I wouldn't mind the juicy details."

"Kafeada." Evelyn laughed and nudged her wife in the side.

Nick chuckled as well and stared at the rose petal. To receive a gift from a fae was a huge deal. They did not offer gifts like this lightly. He held it close and smiled up at her. "Thank you. I'll cherish this."

Kafeada took a drink from the cup. "See that you do." She turned to Evelyn then paused and held up a finger to Nick. "Actually, there's one other thing I wanted to offer you and your pack."

Nick blinked in surprise. What more could she do? "Yes?"

She passed the drink to Evelyn. "I know you lost people you loved during the fight. I work as a mortuary cosmetologist at the local funeral home. I'd be happy to make your pack members presentable for a memorial. I already offered for Ray."

Nick's breath caught in his throat at the offer. Thinking about having a funeral for Brighton, Ray, and Trish felt like too much right now. But getting the chance to say goodbye like that warmed his heart. "I. . . I don't know what to say."

"Say yes," Evelyn said. "Her magic works wonders, Nick. They'll look as you remember them."

Nick reached up and brushed stubborn tears from his eyes. "Uh, yeah, that...that would be great. You'll have to talk with Paytah about preparations. And Joseph and Selene, too, for Trish. But I think they'd like that."

"Good," Kafeada said. "It's the least I can do. You helped bring me home to my wife, to my family." She pulled Evelyn close and kissed her lovingly on the lips. "I'm forever grateful. When the time comes, contact me with the petal." She laughed. "Oh, and if you need help decorating once you and that pretty wolf of yours get hitched, you can definitely call out to me."

Nick blushed brightly, causing both fae and magus to chuckle. "I'll keep that in mind." Waving, he scurried back to his plate and retrieved it. Marriage, honestly. He and Yanlei had only known each other for a couple of months. And she was back with her family anyway. He didn't even know if they'd still be able to see one another.

He swallowed down a lump at the thought and tried to chase away the dryness in his throat with a piece of melon. He worked his way around the garden, checking in with some packmates, getting hugs from Wapasha and Marion. Everyone seemed so relaxed and at ease now that the pit was gone and their loved ones were free. But for Nick, there were still questions left unanswered and an empty pit in his stomach without Yanlei and Brighton.

He sat down at a table away from the others, letting his emotions settle. He chewed on a strawberry and stared at the petal in his hand. Too bad he hadn't met Kafeada before all this had gone down. Having a gift from a fae would have solved a lot of their issues.

Someone plopped onto the tabletop beside him, jerking his attention away from the petal. He put it in his pocket and looked up at the dark-haired woman. He had to do a double take at first, because at first glance she looked like Gale.

"You're Daniella, right?"

"Good guess. My sister tell you about me?"

Nick nodded and scratched his neck. "Though when she talked about you, she thought you were dead."

Daniella smirked. "Yeah, I'm full of surprises." She folded her arms over her lap and leaned forward. "Wanted to tell you you're part of the reason why my sister turned against the Hunters. I gave her a chance to help us, and she decided it was worth the risk to save you and your friends."

Nick's throat tightened with emotion. So their long talks *had* helped. A blessing in and of itself. He glanced around but didn't see

Gale anywhere. "She still with Legion?"

Daniella sighed. "They're questioning her. Like it or not, she was involved with the pit and a lot of kidnappings for a long time. She's giving them as much information as she can and trying to cut a deal with them. She's not the first Hunter who's switched sides. Legion sometimes enlists people like her to become Hunters for *them* after extensive training. But this time they're actually tracking the bad guys. I think she's hoping for that to atone for all the bad shit she did."

Nick found comfort in that. Gale might have a chance for a better life and to make up for her mistakes. It also meant he could see her again. He glanced at Daniella and thought about Hendrickson. "I'm...sorry about your brother."

Daniella barked out a laugh. "Oh please, kid, you don't have to be. I know the awful shit he did to people." She tapped a scar on her face. "He got what he deserved. I might sound heartless saying that, but you know, you can't choose your blood family." She glanced over at Wapasha and Marion. "But you can definitely choose your friends and pack. The brother I knew? He died a long time ago. Gale hung on too long, hoping for him to come back." She shrugged. "I'm sorry for your loss. Gale spoke highly of Brighton."

Nick forced a smile. "She probably thought he was a pain in the ass."

"Hm, that too, but a noble pain in the ass."

He chuckled. Yeah, that was a good way to describe Brighton. Noble and stubborn as a mule, just like his daughter. The thought of Tess caused him to look up again, but he didn't see her anywhere. He swallowed and pushed himself to his feet. "It was nice to meet you, Daniella. Thank you for all your help."

"Glad I could do some good. I'm sure I'll see you again."

Nick nodded to her and stepped away from the table. He searched the crowd fervently for Tess, but with no luck. Instead he found Augustine sitting at a table near Jackson and Tamara, talking quietly. He stopped over by them and sat down. "Hey, have any of you seen Tess or Iris?"

Jackson lifted an eyebrow. "They headed back to Chicago a couple days ago. They wanted to get Brighton home."

Nick's shoulders slumped. "How are they?"

Tamara shook her head sadly. "Not well. We tried to insist they stay with us until you and Augustine were ready to travel, but they didn't want to wait. Becky traveled with them and is going to check in on them. And Pedro, too. He returned home to be with his family."

Nick rested his head on his hand. "I wish there was something we could do for them. I mean, Tess saw it happen right in front of her." He paused, realizing Augustine had seen Ray die as well. "I'm sorry. I didn't . . . I shouldn't have—"

"Nick, shush," Augustine said and flicked his ear lightly. "I've spent weeks dealing with Ray's death. I won't have closure until we put him to rest, but I'm okay. You can ask for advice." She took a breath. "Be there when she needs you. Step back when she wants space. That's all we can do. And remind her, and Iris, that they are both loved. They still have a home and family with us."

Nick reached for Augustine's hand and squeezed it gently. He looked up at the werewolf and met her eyes. "You're loved too, Augustine. I hope you know that."

She leaned toward him and pressed her head against his. They sat together, feeling the presence of Jackson and Tamara as they reached out to touch their hands as well. In that quiet moment, Nick's aching heart eased a little. No matter what, he still had his pack and his family.

Chapter 37
Home Again

Nick

They left Evelyn and Kafeada's home in the late afternoon. Nick nestled in Paytah and Rozene's car with Augustine and fell asleep not long after the drive started. He dreamed of the pit, of his friends surrounding him and offering him comfort while Vesp and Hunters lurked just out of sight. Then a clawed hand wrapped around Brighton and jerked him away. Nick tried to go after him, but Yanlei and Augustine held him back.

He woke himself thrashing, gasping for breath.

Augustine touched his arm. "Nick, easy, you're okay," she said.

He blinked and looked at her in surprise. Streetlamps spilled light into the car, casting part of her face in shadow. Nick swallowed a lump in his throat, still trembling from the terrible dream. He held his arms, trying to calm himself down.

Augustine pulled him close, letting him rest against her chest. "Hey, I've got you."

Nick nodded and snuggled up against the werewolf, basking in her warmth and smell. He drifted again and stayed asleep until they arrived home.

Nick went up to his room and stood in it for a few minutes, staring at all of his things. Posters, desk, clothes, bed...familiar yet foreign at the same time. He ran his hand along the picture of the whole pack standing together during a picnic last year. Ray winked as he planted a kiss on Augustine's temple. Brighton stood with a hand on Tess's shoulder and his arm around Iris.

Nick sniffed and sank down into his bed, holding the picture frame in his hand.

Someone knocked gently on the door.

"Come in," he said.

Rozene walked in with a tray in her hands. He smelled spiced tea (one of her remedies when people didn't feel well), and saw a plate lined with toast covered in homemade preserves. "I thought you might be hungry, but I didn't want to upset your stomach too much."

Nick set the picture back on his night table. "Thanks, Rozene."

She placed the tray near him then sat down on his bed beside him. When he didn't say anything, she ran her hand down his back. "I'm sorry."

"For what?"

"For taking so long to rescue you. For not being able to protect you all from this tragedy." She kissed his head. "I wish we could have done more."

"You did everything you could," Nick said and patted her leg. "The Hunters were conniving, and having a fae protecting them definitely didn't help." He tilted his head up to look at her. "We're home. That's what matters now." He glanced over at the picture and sighed. "I just wish we were all here."

"Me too."

He licked his lips, thinking. "Have you talked to Tess at all?"

"I left a couple voicemails for her, but she hasn't returned them. I'm sure she and Iris are trying to make plans for the funeral."

Nick stared at his hands. He was home, but he didn't feel ready to settle in yet. Too much needed to be done, and there were packmates who required looking after. And then there was Yanlei. What would happen with her? Would her parents let her stay with him? Would she want to?

He set his jaw, resolved to do *something*. "Can I borrow the car?"

Rozene looked surprised. "Nick, you just got home."

"I know, but...there are some things I need to do. I want to see Tess. And Yanlei. And—"

"How about this?" Rozene said and turned to him. "I'll drive you to see them both."

Nick stared at her then smiled. "I'd appreciate that." He got up and took a bite of toast and a drink of tea. The warm, familiar flavors eased some of his anxiety. Rozene always did make the best preserves. He licked his thumb and walked with her downstairs where he tied on his shoes.

Paytah approached them, a look of concern on his face. "What's going on?"

Rozene grabbed her coat. "Nick wants to run a couple of errands. I offered to take him."

Paytah glanced over his shoulder to where Augustine rested on the couch. After a moment, he scooped up his keys. "Why don't you stay with Augustine and the others? I'll take Nick."

Rozene hesitated, but at a kiss from her mate, she smiled and nodded. "Call me if you need anything," she said. She put her coat back on the peg and brushed Nick's arm.

He didn't care who took him just so long as he got to see the other people he cared about. He walked out with Paytah and got into the alpha's truck.

"Where to first?" Paytah asked.

"To see Tess."

Paytah nodded and pulled out of the driveway. They rode together in silence for a while. Nick stared out the window and mulled over what he wanted to say or do once he saw Tess. Nothing felt quite right. Maybe being present would be enough. And Yanlei? Hopefully her parents wouldn't be too cross with him for visiting this late. But he couldn't sit still, not with things left undone.

"I'm proud of you," Paytah said, jarring Nick out of his wandering thoughts. He looked at Paytah as the werewolf went on. "Augustine told me how you took those kids under your paw to protect them. And worked closely with Trish and Brighton to create the coup. You found a way to bring all those different people together to fight for freedom. If you hadn't done that, I don't think as many people would have made it out of the pit. You kept the fae distracted long enough for Legion to come in." He looked at Nick. "I've said it before, and I'll say it again. You have the makings of a great alpha. And I'm proud to call you my son."

The praise brought a blush to his cheeks and dampened his eyes, but he didn't cry. He'd always wanted to please Paytah. Even when he was young and bullheaded, he'd still sought his alpha's favor. But he hadn't done all this for Paytah. He'd done it to save the people he loved. But Paytah knew that. How couldn't he? "I wish I'd done more."

"Don't we all?" Paytah said. "All of us wish we could have prevented this, or saved you sooner. But lingering on the what ifs won't help us move forward. Reflect. Remember. But continue to look to the next sunrise." He reached over and squeezed Nick's shoulder. "The best way to honor the people who fell is by living your life."

Nick reached up and touched his alpha's hand. "So their deaths won't be in vain."

Paytah nodded. He let his arm slip away and gripped the wheel again. "Brighton would have been proud of you, too."

This time, tears trickled down his cheeks. Brighton dying in front of his eyes. Tess's anguished scream. Iris wailing. He *never* wanted something like that to happen again. He remembered how he'd felt when he'd watched his dad die. No one really ever understood what it was like to lose a parent until it happened to them. It was like having a part of you die with them and being left floundering, wondering if you'd ever be able to breathe through the pain.

He touched his heart with his hand, memories of his birth father flowing through his mind. Tess would have to go through that now. And if there was anything he could do, it was provide proof that she could survive this tragedy.

They pulled up to Iris's apartment; Tess's was still under repairs thanks to the Hunter attack. Nick got out and walked with Paytah up to the door. He buzzed them and waited.

"Hello?" Tess's tired voice said over the intercom.

"Hey, it's Nick and Paytah. Can we come up?"

In response, the door buzzed loudly. Nick pulled it open and walked with Paytah over to the elevator. They took it up to the third floor and went to Iris's door. Tess was there to greet them. Dark circles hung below her eyes. Her normally well-kept hair was tied up in a bun on top of her head. She forced a smile. "Hey, wasn't expecting to see anyone. Everything okay?"

Nick nodded. "Yeah, just wanted to come see you."

Tess held out her arm and walked into her apartment. Nick stepped in and looked around. The dining room light illuminated a table covered in poster boards and pictures of Brighton. A couple of beer bottles rested next to them. Arjun sat in one of the chairs and nodded to Nick.

Paytah shut the door behind him. "Where's your mother?"

"In bed," Tess said. "She's probably still awake. She hasn't been sleeping at all, and it's all Arjun and I can do to get her to eat."

Paytah grunted. "Do you mind if I go and see her?"

Tess shook her head and gestured to the hall. Paytah walked to the room and shut the door quietly behind him. Tess stared after him then looked at Nick. With a sigh, she walked to him and pulled him into a tight hug. "I'm glad you're okay."

He held her close. "I'm so sorry, Tess. I tried to keep him safe."

Tess pressed her head against his shoulder. "I know. Augustine told us everything. I just...it was my fault. He died protecting me."

"*Us*," Nick said and lifted her chin. "He died protecting you, me, and Yanlei. You can't put this blame on yourself, Tess. It'll kill you."

Tears filled her eyes, and she fisted her hands. "Why shouldn't I? He was the one taken that night, not me. I failed to bring help in time before you all were moved to another pit. And then I couldn't protect him when he needed me most. Why shouldn't I blame myself!" She pushed off him and went to grab the beer bottle. She sucked a few gulps down then set it roughly on the table.

Arjun reached for her hand and squeezed it. "Tess—"

"Don't," she said, jerking it back. "Just...don't. Nothing you say is going to help. He's still dead."

"Yeah," Nick said. "He is."

Arjun looked at him sharply as Tess's shoulders slumped. Nick ignored the Hunter and went to his packsister. He grabbed her arm and turned her around to face him.

"He is dead. Nothing will change that, you're right. But you can decide what to do next. Are you going to spend the rest of your life blaming yourself for something that wasn't your fault? Or are you going to live your life to the fullest like your father wanted you to?"

Tess struggled a little in his hands. "Nick, stop—"

"No," he said and tightened his hold. "Bianca and Kat told me about your mom withering with you and Brighton both gone. Paytah can take care of her, but I'm not going to let you do that to yourself, Tess. It's going to hurt like hell that he's gone. It's going to feel like waves are crashing down on you over and over again, and you can't break your head through the surface and breathe."

Tess started to tremble. "Nick, please. I...I can't."

"You can," Nick said and pulled her into his arms. He held her tightly and placed his hand on the back of her head. "Some days you'll wake up and feel like you can't get out of bed. That life isn't worth living without him in it. You'll ask yourself why it was him, why it wasn't you instead. And you'll have to learn to fight those demons and remind yourself that he'd be asking the same questions if your positions were reversed. He shouldn't have died. What happened to him was wrong. But it's not your *fault*." He closed his eyes as she sobbed into his shoulder. He stroked her back and kissed her head.

"But then there will be a day when you'll wake up and you'll hear the birds sing. You'll smell coffee and want to drink it. You'll feel the breeze, and it'll be the first time you've noticed it in months. The pain will be a little less, and you'll wade in the water instead of drowning. Grief doesn't know the meaning of time. There's no right or wrong way to grieve, and you'll mourn him for as long as you need to. But through it all, you need to keep living. To grow around your grief." He brushed tears off her face with his sleeve when she looked up at him. He searched her eyes and smiled tenderly. "And remember you're not alone. You've got me. You've got the pack. You've got Arjun." He glanced at the Hunter. "Who I'm also gonna have words with while he's dating my packsister."

Arjun held up his hands and smiled. "Of course."

Nick turned his attention back to Tess. "I get what you're going through. You've joined a club that I hate being a part of. But it means you have people who get it. Who know what this feels like."

Tess nodded and pressed her head against Nick's shoulder. "Arjun's part of the club, too. But I guess I wasn't ready to listen to him yet."

"He's your packbrother," Arjun said and got to his feet. He nodded his head respectfully to Nick then came up behind Tess and rubbed her back. "You have a bond with him you don't have with me. And you've told me how stubborn he can be. I can see how he'd make you listen."

Nick chuckled. "My reputation precedes me, I see."

Tess managed a quiet laugh. "Don't worry, I'm about as stubborn as you are. We both learned it from Paytah. Just don't tell him that."

Nick snorted. "Oh hell, he already knows." He kissed her forehead again. "Promise me you'll tell me what you need. I hate feeling useless, so don't even question if you're burdening me or something. I need things to do."

Tess nodded slowly and hugged him tighter. "Thanks, Nick. I don't know what I'd do if I'd lost you, too."

"Well, fortunately, you don't have to find out." He held her a while longer then passed her off into Arjun's arms. He eyed the Hunter, his irises flashing with his wolf in warning. Tess might like him, but Nick was watching him. He wasn't going to let anyone hurt his packsister. Especially not while she was so vulnerable.

Paytah returned a short time later. "I helped her get to sleep," he told Tess. "Alpha abilities sometimes have their perks." He gestured for her to come to him, and he enveloped her in his arms. "I love you, pup. Let me know if you need anything."

Tess nodded as she basked in the warmth of his hug. When he released her, she went to Arjun and squeezed his hand. "Let's go get some sleep. I think it's better if we do this in the morning," she said, nodding to the table.

"I couldn't agree with you more. Go on. I'll follow you to the bedroom in a minute."

Tess gave Nick and Paytah final hugs and headed off. Arjun watched her go then looked at the pair.

"I promise I'll watch over them both. I'll cook for them and make sure to contact you if I'm not enough support."

Paytah nodded. "Thank you, Arjun." He held out his hand. The Hunter blinked in surprise then shook it. "You can consider yourself an honorary member of the pack."

Arjun stared in shock, but Paytah headed out the door before he could respond. Nick smiled to himself. Well, if Paytah was willing to grant him that sort of favor, then Arjun must not be too bad.

He eyed the Hunter. "I'll tell you the same thing I told Bianca. You break her heart, and you'll have me to deal with. Until then, welcome to the pack, brother."

Nick smiled to himself as he headed out of the apartment. Let

Arjun chew on that.

He joined Paytah at the elevator and crossed his arms, feeling a little more content now that he'd seen Tess.

"Where to next?" Paytah asked.

"To see Yanlei."

***

The lights in the house were still on when they pulled into the driveway. Nick sat in the passenger's seat with his phone out, staring at it and trying to get up the nerve to message Yanlei that he'd dropped by for a visit. Now that they'd arrived, his bravado had faltered, mostly because he was afraid Yanlei had changed her mind about wanting to see him again, or her parents wouldn't approve of him, or Paytah wouldn't approve of Yanlei. Though he really wasn't that afraid of the latter part. Paytah had said the conversation between him and Yanlei's parents had gone well. But still, he was worried.

"Are you sure you want to do this now? You can wait until tomorrow or after you've had a few days to rest," Paytah said.

Nick blew out a breath and shook his head. "No, I'm not sure about this, but yes, I want to do it now." He texted Yanlei then looked up at the door. He didn't want to ring the bell and disturb them if anyone was asleep.

His phone beeped a minute later.

I'll be downstairs in a minute. Meet me at the door.

Nick smiled and got out of the truck. Paytah followed him up to the door. Nick shifted anxiously and waited. The porchlight turned on and the door opened, only it wasn't Yanlei who greeted them but a slightly older man with a sprinkling of gray in his dark hair. He looked at the pair with a small smile.

"My daughter said you might be stopping by," he said. "Come in, please. Leave your shoes in the rack by the door. We have slippers here for you."

Nick stepped inside and put his sneakers on a rack lined with shoes, Paytah following suit. As he slid his feet into a pair of soft slippers, he looked around the neat house, the walls decorated with many pictures of Yanlei and her family. His heart warmed at seeing her smiling face in so many photos.

Yanlei hopped down the steps and beamed at the sight of them.

Her father glanced at her. "LeiLei, go get your mother."

"Yes, Baba."

He watched her go to the kitchen then gestured to the couch. "Please, sit." He sat down on a sofa while Nick and Paytah took the other couch.

Yanlei and her mother appeared shortly. Her mother was closer to Yanlei's height with darker hair. Her beautiful features were mirrored in her daughter's face. Yanlei got her hair color from her father, though.

Her mother carried a bowl full of fresh apple, melon, and pear slices. "Welcome, welcome," she said, sounding almost flustered that she hadn't been the one to greet them. She set the bowl down as well as a container of toothpicks. "A treat for you. Would you like juice or soda?"

Nick blushed at being fussed over.

Paytah smiled and bobbed his head graciously. "The fruit is plenty enough. Thank you for your hospitality."

Once sure her guests were content, Yanlei's mother sat down beside her father while Yanlei took another chair, hands folded in her lap. Her eye was still marred by scars, but that didn't detract from her beauty in Nick's opinion.

Yanlei gestured to Nick and Paytah. "Mama, Baba, this is Nick and Paytah."

Her mother nodded in greeting. "I'm Mary, and this is my husband, Charlie. LeiLei has told us all about you."

Nick bowed his head. "It's an honor to meet you."

Mary smiled warmly at him. "She says you were the one who helped lead the rebellion in the pit, yes?"

"Well, we worked together to do that," Nick said and glanced at Yanlei. "I couldn't have done it without her and the other members of my pack."

Yanlei chuckled. "He's being modest. But yes, we did work together. It took all of us."

Nick smiled at her and blushed a little. It was so hard not to reach out and take her in his arms. "While we were in the pit, Yanlei and I grew close. And I was hoping I could continue seeing her. With your blessing, of course," he said, looking at her parents. "And only if Yanlei wants to, that is," he added nervously.

Charlie and Mary glanced at one another before Mary turned her attention to Paytah. She sat up straighter, her posture of one about to discuss a business transaction. "We appreciate your offer to join your pack, but we have a good, long-standing relationship with our pack, an important bond that LeiLei also shares. I hope you understand. Leaving would mean we are not…happy with our pack leader, or that others are offering something better, and we don't feel that is true."

"I understand," Paytah said. "Being from different packs doesn't mean Nick and Yanlei can't see each other if they so desire, does it?"

Mary shook her head. "No, but it also can't interfere with the duties our daughter has to her pack."

"I wouldn't let it interfere, Mama," Yanlei said. "I am dedicated to my pack." She looked at Nick and smiled. "But I also care about Nick and would like to continue seeing him."

Nick brightened and had to refrain from launching himself at Yanlei and pulling her into his arms. She wanted to be with him! And having her choose to stay with her pack made no difference to him. He could respect that. Later down the road they could decide which pack they wanted to be part of. For now, he was just happy to have her in his life. "I do, too."

Mary placed her hand on Charlie's and rubbed it affectionately. Paytah just smiled at the pair.

They spent some time talking about their families and packs, Mary asking most of the questions. Nick munched on the delicious fruit and couldn't stop smiling at Yanlei as she watched him. He wished they could have a moment alone, but Yanlei stayed beside her parents, poised and at ease.

Mary looked to a nearby clock and pressed her hands together. "It's getting late. It was nice to meet you both. LeiLei, get your friends anything they need, then see them to the door." She nodded to Nick and Paytah. "Have a safe trip home."

"Goodnight," Charlie added politely.

"Goodnight," Paytah said.

Nick watched Charlie and Mary head upstairs together, leaving them alone with Yanlei. She waited a moment then chuckled. "Do you need anything for the road?"

Paytah shook his head as he rose. "No, but thank you. We should get back to the pack."

"I'll see you out." Yanlei guided them to the door.

Nick slid the slippers off his feet and pulled on his sneakers before he and Paytah walked outside. He opened his mouth to ask for a moment with Yanlei, but Paytah beat him to it.

"I need to make a call in the truck. Come when you're ready." Paytah patted his shoulder and wandered off, leaving them alone at last.

Yanlei waited until Paytah was gone before she pulled Nick beneath the patio awning into a deep kiss. Nick melted into it and held her against him.

"I missed you," he said and pressed his forehead to hers.

"I missed you, too. I've been so happy to see my family and pack again, but it felt wrong not to have you by my side." She touched his cheek. "Thank you for understanding that I want to stay with my pack."

Nick turned his head, kissing her palm sweetly. "Yanlei, I want what makes you happy. I wouldn't dream of taking you away from the people you love. I'm thankful you have room in your life for me too." He grinned widely and took her hands in his. "So, can I officially ask you on a date, say, next Friday at seven? I'll take you out for a nice dinner."

Yanlei squeezed his hands back. "I would love that," she said and leaned in for another deep kiss.

Epilogue
Closure

Tess

It felt like déjà vu hosting a celebration of life for her father, Ray, and Trish at the same place where they'd said goodbye to Violet Marshall Gladus over two years ago. Tess hoped this wasn't going to become a regular thing. She'd gone to enough memorials recently to last her a lifetime.

They'd hosted a private funeral for her father and Ray days prior, and then a larger one for her father that lived up to the custom of laying a police officer to rest. The number of people who joined them for *that* memorial had shocked her, and it helped ease the grief to hear stories about her father's good deeds on the force. The hardest part was listening to them perform the last call for her father and for him not to answer back.

His badge number PO1961 would stay with her forever.

After the funerals, the District wanted to come together for a celebration of life for all those who had lost their lives in the pit. Tess would have rather spent the day in bed, mourning her father. But then she thought about what Nick had told her and figured that being together with the pack and hosting a celebration might actually lift her spirits. At least she'd hear more stories about her father.

She fussed with one of the picture boards from her father's funeral, specifically one filled with images of the two of them. She'd brought along the signed record from her wall to show off as well, a nice memento to him and their time together. Tess brushed her hand along the pictures then looked at the table. It was covered in flowers, pictures, her father's police hat and badge, and a box Paytah had put out to collect donations for her family. Though the police department had offered her and her mother more than enough.

Her eyes drifted to other poster boards of Ray and Augustine together. She walked over, her heels clicking quietly on the floor. She stared at their happy smiles and goofy expressions. Ray dressed in his chef outfit, looking proud and proper. Augustine giving him a tattoo on his arm while he looked ready to faint, and then his big smile afterward. Baby pictures of Ray pretending to be a cook and serving up food to a table of stuffed animals.

She chuckled to herself and glanced at his chef's jacket and hat on another table. Her gaze lingered on the big picture of the whole pack together, one they all had been given and that hung on the wall in her mother's apartment. She brushed her fingers along her father's face and took a shaky breath.

Arjun stepped up to her and ran his hands up and down her arms. "Hey," he said. "Are you okay?"

"No," Tess said honestly then turned and hugged him. "But I will be." She took his hand and walked over to another memorial. Trish smiled one of her simpering smiles in a large picture frame, her eyes alight with life and mischief. Her urn rested in a nest of black and red roses, which seemed fitting for her. Her coven had put together pictures, though there weren't quite as many of them since Trish had come to them only a few years ago. Still, they'd taken enough, and she looked happy in most of them.

The one that really caught Tess's eye was a picture of Trish and Gavin. Gavin smirked at the camera while dipping Trish. Trish had her head thrown back in a boisterous laugh. His urn sat close by as well, bringing the two vampires back together once again. She brushed her hand along Trish's ebony urn etched in thick roses. "Thanks, Trish," she whispered. "For everything you did."

"She surprised us, didn't she?" Bianca said as she and Kat joined them at the table. They both laid roses next to the urn. Kat wrapped her arms around Bianca's waist and held her close as the avian shook her head. "I hated her when we first met, after the whole Hunter incident. I never thought she'd risk her life like she did to save people."

"Me either," Tess agreed. She chuckled, trailing her finger down one of the vines. "She kinda made it easy to dislike her. But in the end, I think she just wanted to figure out where she belonged. Find a home."

Bianca nodded in agreement. "She saved me and Kat. I don't think either of us would have survived Saul's attacks without her. Maybe the three of us together? But Trish seemed so determined to take him on herself."

"They were close," Tess said and looked at Bianca. "Almost like father and daughter. I can only imagine what his betrayal did to her. And what her's did to him."

Bianca licked her lips. "Is that why that's there? Because of their connection?" She gestured to a small wooden box close to Trish's urn with Saul's name written across it.

Tess nodded. "I think so. He betrayed the coven, but he was still part of them for a long time. He did a lot of good. He just never healed after losing Fraula. I don't think Joseph wanted to have a private ceremony for him because of the mixed feelings of the District and the coven. So, at least the Saul they knew gets some respect by being here with Trish and Gavin."

She leaned back into Arjun and reached up to take his hand. "It's too many," she said in a whisper.

"I know," Bianca replied. She looked over at Tess and Arjun. "At least the pit is closed and the others are getting shut down, that we know of anyway."

"Yeah, but what's to stop more from forming?" Tess asked. "Hunters, the bad ones, still exist and want to hurt us. Their ideology won't change. If anything, seeing their numbers decimated in the pit might bring more crazies forward."

Kat buried her face in Bianca's dark hair. "Well, I guess that just means we'll have to be more diligent about protecting our District," she said. "And we have to learn to work together better. That'll keep us all safer, so something like this doesn't happen again."

Tess closed her eyes and tilted her head back. No, she didn't think any of them could handle another loss as great as this.

Bianca reached out and tugged on her hand. "Let's go grab some food. Carlos brought a bunch of goodies from the Guacamole Grill, and Kat's manager donated sweets and teas from the Lavender Lyre. We'd better get our pastries before Jackson eats them all."

Tess chuckled and pulled Arjun along, bringing him over to the tables overflowing with delicious food. Carlos and his wife Haley dished the delicious Mexican food out to eager guests. Meanwhile, their children Madison and Henry ran around with Phoebe, Eliza, and Becky's daughter Heidi, chasing one another and rushing to the games the District had supplied for the kids to play with while the adults talked.

Bianca snuck away and snagged Henry in her arms mid-run. The boy laughed loudly and held onto her as she swung him around then set him down and pushed him after his sister.

Tess smiled to herself and picked up a plate. She went over to where the scones and tea from the Lavender Lyre were laid out. Arjun grabbed a few things, and they wandered over to a table and sat down together. Kat, Bianca, Nick, and Yanlei joined them a few minutes later. Nick pulled out Yanlei's seat and sat down beside her, looking better than he had in days. Rest and healing had done him a lot of good, and the same could be said for Yanlei. He kissed her sweetly on the cheek and laced his fingers between hers.

Tess smiled. "So are you two officially a thing, then?"

Yanlei grinned over at Tess and nodded. "I would say so. Nick and I had a lovely date on Friday. And we have another planned next week."

Tess nudged Arjun playfully. "Hey, aren't you ever going to take me out on dates that don't include one of us trying to knock the other on their ass?"

Arjun lifted her hand and kissed her fingers. "If my lady wishes."

Tess blushed while Kat and Bianca "awwwwwwed" obnoxiously. She waved her hand at them. "Quiet, you. You're not much better."

Kat brushed her hand along Bianca's cheek. "Can you blame me? I have an amazing girlfriend."

"So do I," Bianca said and stole a kiss from Kat that made the werewolf melt.

Tess rolled her eyes playfully and dipped her scone into her tea. She relaxed being around her friends. At least there was some normality after all of the sorrow and heartbreak. She glanced up at Arjun as he leaned over and kissed her temple.

"I mean it. I'd be happy to take you out on dates, once things are quieter."

"I'd like that," Tess said and rested her head on his shoulder.

They ate and chatted together for a while as members of the District filtered through and admired the pictures and left cards. Joseph and Selene stopped beside Trish's urn and spoke quietly together over it, both vampires touching the urn lightly with their hands. Joseph even picked up Saul's box and shed a few tears. Before the betrayal, they had been close friends. She couldn't imagine losing a dear friend like that to both hatred and death.

Tess watched a few more folks walk through then lifted her head when Olive stepped in with a small bag in her hands. The magus wore a beautiful long dark blue dress and flat black shoes on her feet. A hairband with tiny wire flowers and gems held her frosted blonde hair out of her face. She placed a flower and a crystal at each of the little memorials.

Tess squeezed Arjun's shoulder and went to join the magus. "Olive?"

The woman turned and spread her arms. "Oh Tess, honey. I'm so sorry."

Tess went into her arms and sighed as Olive hugged her tightly. The scents of herbs, incense, and flowers filled her nose. She relaxed a little. "Thank you. And thanks for your help with Arjun's wand and everything else."

Olive touched her cheek. "I wish I had a potion to chase away grief, but I'm not that powerful." She reached into her bag and pulled out a small glass witch orb streaked through with purple and red. "I wanted to give this to you. Your mother said that you both have had trouble sleeping because of nightmares. Hang this in your window; it should help. I already gave her a bag of tea and tonics that'll help her sleep and relax."

Tess looked over at her mother who stood surrounded by pack members. Rozene held her mother with one arm. The dark circles still hung beneath her mother's eyes, but not as badly as a week ago. She stared at the bag in her mother's hand with the Crystal Corvid Apothecary's logo on it. "Thank you, Olive. It means a lot." She turned to the magus and took her hands. "You know, would you be interested in having tea together sometime? My mom said you have a lot of fun stories about my dad."

Olive's eyes lit up. "I would love to. And yes, working at the apothecary as long as I have has let me gather many fun stories about the District." She giggled. "Remind me to tell you about his school days when he asked if I had a love potion that could help him woo his crush."

"Nooo," Tess said, laughing. "Really? Mom never told me about that."

Olive winked. "Because I promised never to tell her. But I think you'd enjoy the story." She shook Tess's hands. "Call me anytime, and we'll set up a tea date together. I'll even have scones and those little snack sandwiches delivered."

Tess beamed at the magus. "I'd like that, Olive." She waved as the woman went to join a few other members of the community. Shaking her head, she made to return to the table and nearly ran face-first into Skye. Tess jumped back in surprise. "Whoa...Skye? What are you doing here?"

"What? I can't pay my respects, too?" the Huntress asked. She stood there dressed in a gorgeous black business suit with a blue camisole underneath, very different from the attire Tess was used to.

Tess shook the shock off. "Oh, of course you can. I just didn't expect you to come out into the open like this."

Skye shrugged. "Believe it or not, I'm not a recluse. I do enjoy human interaction. Besides, I doubt anyone here is going to remember my face with all the folks coming and going." She held out her hand. "I'm sorry about your dad. We all did our best; I just wish we could have done more."

Tess shook her hand back. "Thanks, Skye. If it wasn't for you, none of them would have made it out. I don't know how to repay you."

"Eh, I'll send you a bill," Skye said casually. When Tess stared at her, she laughed and waved her hand. "Kidding, kidding. Bad joke." She pitched her voice a little lower. "I can tell you that as of today, another seven pits have gone down. I'll continue feeding intel to Legion. Thanks for the contact."

"Yeah, Jay's a good person to feed info through," Tess replied. She tugged on Skye's hand. "Why don't you grab some food and join me and Arjun at the table? I can introduce you to some of my packmates."

"Eh, as nice as that sounds, I'd rather not call attention to myself.

But I wanted to pass something off to you." She held out a piece of paper to Tess. "Whenever you and Arjun feel like getting back into the Hunter game, I have a few jobs you can help me with."

Tess took the paper and looked at it. It included a date and location. "What's this?"

"A time and a place to meet me if you feel up to it." She winked. "I think the three of us are going to work well together. At least you'll keep me on my toes."

"Heh, and you'll keep me on mine." She tucked the paper away in her dress pocket. "Thanks for coming by, Skye."

The Huntress nodded politely and made her way up to the memorial tables. Tess returned to Arjun and sat down with him. He took her hand, and she leaned against him and listened to Kat, Bianca, Nick, and Yanlei trade stories.

Despite her grief, Tess found herself smiling. Her father might be gone, but his spirit would live on in the memories of the pack and District. She might have lost him, but she'd gained new friends and a fresh determination to do *everything* in her ability to keep her loved ones safe. Even with the pits gone, the District would need protecting, and Tess was more than ready to take up that challenge, especially with Arjun and her pack at her side.

The Purple Door District and its mission to protect parahumans would live on no matter what.

About the Author
Erin Casey

Erin Casey graduated from Cornell College in 2009 with degrees in English and Secondary Education.

She attended the Denver Publishing Institute in 2009 and has been a recruiter ever since. She is a founder of The Writers' Rooms, a non-profit corporation that focuses on creating a free, safe environment for writers no matter their experience, gender, background, and income. Just like in her book, community is very important to her.

An advocate for mental health, Erin's written and published several articles on the Mighty, and created characters in novels and short stories representing those with anxiety, depression, and eating disorders.

She's also a devoted bird mom.

When not volunteering and working, she's querying her LGBT YA Fantasy dragon book, writing short stories with LGBTQIA+ representation, and trying not to doze off to the glow of the computer screen while her bird sleeps on her.

Learn more about The Writers' Rooms: www.thewritersrooms.org

* * *

Follow Erin

Website
www.erincasey.org
Amazon
amazon.com/author/erincaseyauthor
Goodreads
goodreads.com/erincaseyauthor
Instagram
@erincaseyauthor
Facebook
@erincaseyauthor
Twitter
@erincasey09
TikTok
@authorerincasey
Wordpress
erincaseyauthor.wordpress.com
Patreon
patreon.com/erincasey
AllAuthor
Allauthor.com/author/erincasey
BookBub
Bookbub.com/profile/erin-casey